MOTHER IS A VERB

MOTHER IS A VERB

a novel

KIM HOOPER

LAKE UNION
PUBLISHING

Published by Lake Union Publishing, Seattle
www.apub.com

EU product safety contact:
Amazon Media EU S. à r.l.
38, avenue John F. Kennedy, L-1855 Luxembourg
amazonpublishing-gpsr@amazon.com

ISBN-13: 9781662526404 (paperback)
ISBN-13: 9781662526411 (digital)

Cover design by Lucy Kim
Cover image: © Rachel Campbell / Bridgeman Images

Printed in the United States of America

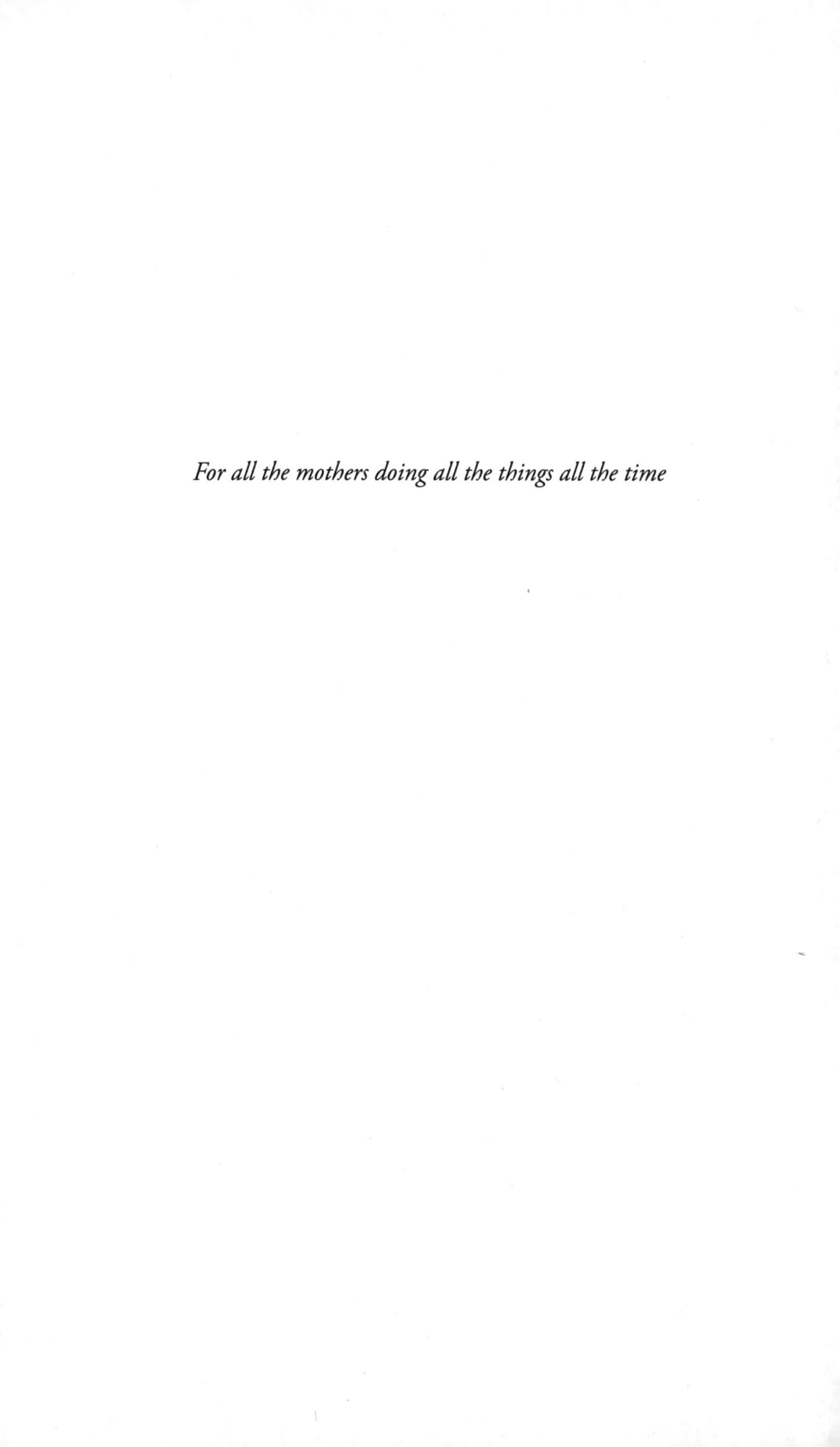

For all the mothers doing all the things all the time

Prologue

Gwen

Now

Gwen Fisher has never been inside a police station before. She assumes many people her age (thirty-five) have been in a police station for one reason or another. A class field trip in elementary school, at the very least. Not Gwen, though.

The Bainbridge Island Police Department is in a sleek, modern building that looks nothing like a police station. A sign out front refers to it as the **Ted Spearman Justice Center**, and Gwen wonders if that's the new, more politically correct way to refer to a police station. *Justice center.*

A fleet of black Ford police SUVs occupies the parking lot, more patrol vehicles than she expects for a relatively small town. How many calls do they get in a day? She assumes today's events are significant by Bainbridge Island standards. The shooting will be all over the news.

The shooting. Gwen has been involved—loosely, but still—in a *shooting.*

She parks in a spot near the front of the building and gets June from the back seat. When Detective Steele asked her to come in for questioning, Gwen hesitated, said, "But I have my baby with me."

The detective said coolly, "I don't mind if your child is present." She didn't seem to consider that Gwen might mind. Sure, June is only three months old and has no idea what's going on, but Gwen still doesn't like her being party to a conversation about a potential attempted murder.

Gwen approaches the building, lugging the car seat with sleeping June inside it. She's nervous. She doesn't want to talk to Detective Steele. What she has to say will make her sound like a lunatic.

How did I get here? What was I thinking? The questions torment her. It's like she was hypnotized, wandering through a dream, and that gunshot broke the spell.

~

The lobby is warm, in sharp contrast to the damp, cool air outside. It's August in the Pacific Northwest, but it feels nothing like summer today. June stirs in her car seat as Gwen sits in one of the lobby chairs. She frees June, places her in the baby wrap against her chest. Two female officers come to look at June, cooing—*Isn't she just darling?* When Detective Steele comes out, she does not coo. She just says, "Ms. Fisher?"

Detective Steele looks to be in her early thirties, though she has the disposition of a curmudgeonly old man. Her hair is pulled back and seemingly shellacked into a bun that's as tight as her smile. She is very short, even with the solid inch from the shiny black police boots. The uniform looks like a costume on her. It would be hard to take her seriously except that she has the deep voice of a burly man.

She leads Gwen to a small room with a table and four chairs and closes the door behind her.

"Thank you again for coming in, Ms. Fisher," she says.

"No problem. And you can call me Gwen."

Detective Steele looks at her like *No, I fucking cannot call you Gwen* and extends an arm toward one of the chairs, indicating that Gwen should sit. She does, then removes June from the wrap and places her in her lap. Detective Steele remains standing. She must appreciate any opportunity to be taller than a suspect.

Not that Gwen is a suspect.

Is she?

"Is my husband still here?" Gwen asks.

They called Jeff in too. She can only imagine what he is telling them. Whatever it is will confirm her lunacy. Gwen doesn't know if they can survive this—her and Jeff. If she were him, she would consider calling a divorce attorney, stat.

"Yes, they should be finishing up soon."

Detective Steele walks in a little circle around the table, hands clasped behind her back. June's eyes follow the detective's movements. She breaks into an adorable gummy smile. Unlike Gwen, June finds the detective amusing.

"Your family . . . you don't live here on the island, correct?"

"Correct," Gwen says. "We live in Seattle."

Bainbridge Island is about a half-hour ferry ride from Seattle. All these years it's been so close, and yet she's never visited until now. She can't imagine they'll make another family visit anytime soon, not after this.

"And what brought you over here?"

There is no way to answer this that makes Gwen look good.

"I wanted to visit the . . . compound," Gwen says, immediately regretting her word choice. *Compound*? Is that the right word? It sounds very David Koresh.

"The *compound*?"

"Where Angeni Luna lives . . . with her . . . people."

"Her family?"

"And the others. It's like a . . . group."

"Right. There are multiple dwellings on the land. Is it your understanding that this is some kind of *cult*?"

Gwen flinches at the word, thinking of every horrifying Netflix documentary on the topic. She does not want Detective Steele to think she is someone who would pursue a cult.

"No, not a cult, per se."

Gwen bounces June in her lap, and she squeals happily, oblivious to her mother's angst. Pools of sweat gather in Gwen's armpits; beads of it dot her forehead.

"A commune?" Gwen ventures. "Maybe that's more like what it is."

Commune doesn't sound great either, but it conjures more images of hippies than of serial killers.

"A commune. Okay. And you had never met Ms. Luna before?"

Ms. Luna. It sounds absurd. That can't be her real last name.

"No," Gwen says, staring at the back of June's head, the whorl of her hair. "I just, um, followed her on social media."

Followed. Like a stalker.

Detective Steele lets out a deep breath that tells Gwen she might be here longer than she thinks. The detective pulls out the chair across from Gwen, the feet of it screeching against the linoleum floor for what seems like a purposefully long time, and sits.

"Ms. Fisher," she says. Not Gwen, never Gwen. "Why don't you start from the beginning?"

Gwen hands June a teething ring, hoping it entertains her long enough for Gwen to attempt to explain.

Chapter 1

Gwen

Gwen doesn't remember the exact day she started following Angeni Luna. It was during her pregnancy with June, though the real obsession didn't take hold until June was born, when Gwen turned to her phone for companionship during the lonely nighttime breastfeeding sessions.

The sessions were long in those early days—up to forty-five minutes. Gwen had tried reading novels, a favorite pastime in her pre-baby life, but could not focus enough to follow the simplest plot. So she went on social media to wade through a deluge of advice and advertisements preying upon her new motherhood. Each night felt a hundred years long, and she felt so alone, though another human was quite literally attached to her. She should have told Jeff about those hours of despair, but she didn't want to deviate from The Plan.

When she was pregnant, she and Jeff had had a weekly "State of the Union"—meaning their marital union. Gwen had gotten the idea from an Instagram account called @conscious.co.official. The ".co" was supposed to stand for *couples*, but over time, it began to seem like it should stand for *company*. They sold all kinds of workbooks and webinars to "elevate your relationship." A previous version of Gwen would have found this eye-roll-inducing, but pregnant Gwen was tapping the little heart icon on several of their posts each week. She wanted her and Jeff to thrive as parents as much as they'd thrived as a romantic pair. The Conscious Couples people made it seem like this would take a significant amount of work, since "adding a child to the bond is essentially creating a love triangle."

During their State of the Union meetings, she and Jeff discussed how they would divide household tasks during the early days, when Gwen would be physically exhausted and recovering, all while establishing a feeding rhythm with their daughter. They decided that Jeff would act as a support to Gwen and manage anything that did not involve the baby—the laundry, the dishes, the cooking, the cleaning. Gwen would sleep with the baby in the guest room so that Jeff could get a good night's sleep and be rested enough to tend to his duties during the day, when Gwen would attempt to take the entire world's advice and "sleep when the baby sleeps."

Gwen thought this arrangement made logical sense, and "logical sense" was her religion. She and Jeff had met in law school. When she'd gotten pregnant, they'd both been on partner tracks at their respective firms. They prided themselves on being logic-based people. The thing is, nothing about a newborn is logical. The best-laid plans, et cetera.

At some point during her pregnancy, the Instagram algorithm realized she was pregnant, because she was suddenly following a bunch of accounts about motherhood, and suggested she check out @mother.nurture.official. Like a good social media citizen, she tapped right on over, scrolled through a few posts, determined that they resonated with the kind of mother she wanted to be, and became a follower. Soon after, she discovered that the Mother Nurture account was a sister account of Conscious Couples. Members of these communities would call this *alignment*, and she was all about it.

The basic gist of @mother.nurture.official was that motherhood is the most important role a woman can ever have. As a mother, a woman is birthing and raising the future of humanity, and if we want a kind, loving collective, we must give as much love and kindness to our children as we can. This involves a steadfast connection that is best fostered with an attachment parenting style. Co-sleeping, long-term breastfeeding, and skin-to-skin bonding are good; separation, authoritarian discipline, sleep training, and formula are bad. A good mother is one who is tuned in to her child's every emotion and bowel movement. A good mother is one who is willing to set herself aside to tend to her child's every emotion and bowel movement.

Gwen wanted so badly to be a good mother.

~

Gwen chose the name June for their baby the week after they found out they were having a girl. They were not the whimsical types who wanted to wait to know the sex; they were planners. June was Gwen's grandmother's name, and she liked the idea of infusing some family legacy into their child's identity. Plus, the baby was due in June—right in the middle, June 15. So if she was born a couple of weeks early or a couple of weeks late, the name would fit. It felt fated, perfect. As the baby grew in her belly, Gwen called her June Bug. *I can't wait to meet you, June Bug.* She was smitten.

Then her water broke on May 20.

She had just come back from a three-mile run. She'd been running a few times a week throughout her pregnancy. Her obstetrician, Dr. Blake, an exceedingly relaxed man who had been a "baby catcher" (his words) for thirty years, said, "Pregnancy is not a medical ailment. If exercise feels good, do it." When she asked him if he was sure, he looked at her over the top of his glasses and said, "You are very type A, aren't you?"

Gwen had been a track star in high school and then a Division I runner at the University of Washington. Everyone has their thing, and running was hers. When it became physically uncomfortable—not painful, just weird feeling, as she told her OB—she got one of those belts to wear around her middle to help support the weight of her belly.

She slowed her pace, reduced her mileage, and felt grateful every day she got out the door.

She wanted to be one of those women who go for a run on the day they deliver their baby. She thought it would be particularly spectacular if her water broke *while* she was on a run. She imagined posting an Instagram story: Gotta cut this run short. Water broke! She'd already thought up captions to accompany the expected photo of her holding June against her chest in the delivery bed—*The greatest finish line of my life* or *I've run many marathons, but nothing quite like this* or *Labor is the ultimate endurance event, and my daughter is the ultimate prize.* The Instagram comments would roll in, many of them with that flexed-bicep emoji. She would relish all of it.

But none of that happened.

~

The now-infamous three-mile run felt normal. There was no niggling pain, no tightening in her abdomen, nothing to suggest that the harmonious birth she'd planned for was about to go horribly awry. When she returned from her run, Jeff had already left for work. Gwen normally went into the office but had arranged to work from home a few days a week during her pregnancy.

She stripped off her damp clothes and admired her belly in the mirror. From behind, she did not look pregnant at all. It was only from the side or front that it was obvious. She was one of those pregnant women who look like they just have a basketball under their shirt. In other words, she was one of those pregnant women that other women hate. She chalked it up to doing all the things she was supposed to do. She took her vitamins and ate super-clean food. She exercised. She'd started meditating to practice bringing her body to a calm state. She was the epitome of a healthy mother-to-be, could envision herself as the smiling cover model on a pregnancy magazine.

When she reached into the shower to turn on the hot water, she felt a sudden twinge of pain. Her first thought was Braxton Hicks, those contractions the uterus does leading up to delivery. It seemed too soon for those types of contractions, but if anyone's body was going to start practicing early, it would be hers. She took deep breaths, inhaling and exhaling like she'd seen Lamaze teachers instruct in YouTube videos. But the pain continued. Then she felt liquid running down her leg. Some of it was clear and some of it was red, and all her meditation learnings went out the proverbial window.

She called Jeff and Jeff called her doula, because of course she had a doula. The doula's name was Essence, because of course her name was Essence. Jeff had her on speaker, and she said, in a singsong voice, "Oh, my dear, this sounds like quite the emergency. You need to go to the hospital." She then informed them that she would be unable to attend "the arrival" because she was at the Esalen Institute in Big Sur.

Jeff called the OB's office, and they said Gwen's doctor was on vacation but another doctor would meet them at the hospital. Gwen cried and cried because none of this was right. Jeff ushered her to the car, and she briefly grieved her lack of a hospital bag, complete with a plush robe and her favorite organic snacks. By fixating on this detail, she could be in complete denial of the possibility that she and her baby might die.

When she'd hired Essence and Essence had asked about her ideal birth plan, Gwen had tried to sound easygoing because she didn't want to be one of those controlling women who demand Enya and twinkly lights and an inflatable tub. In reality, though, that was exactly the kind of woman she was. She had a playlist on her phone that she'd been secretly curating, and it did include a couple of Enya songs. She'd purchased a special chromotherapy lamp that was supposed to emit green light to relax her during labor. She had chosen her OB because he was the director of a birthing center that had tubs available.

Water births were very much recommended by @mother.nurture.official and the vast number of commenters on their page, many of whom had delivered their babies at home, away from medical equipment and liability-obsessed doctors, "as nature intended." Gwen had suggested to Jeff that she birth at home, and he'd said, "Hell no" before reminding her of this time in law school when he sliced his finger while chopping vegetables and promptly passed out at the sight of blood.

Truthfully, Gwen was relieved by his refusal. As much as @mother.nurture.official encouraged her to "trust the magic" of her body, she was terrified to give birth without professional assistance. The twenty-thousand-square-foot birth center at Virginia Mason Hospital, which included a staff of midwives, seemed like the next-best option. She even commented on a Mother Nurture post about home birth:

> This is such a beautiful thing. I am so sad that my husband insists on me birthing in a center, but am grateful to live in an area that has a center with such a progressive, mama-empowering mindset.

She tagged the birthing center in the post. Her comment got many likes and many replies applauding this respectful compromise she'd made—both supporting her husband and his "male prerogative" while also honoring most of her wishes. Even the Mother Nurture account itself replied:

> Love your flexibility and openness. This will serve you well in motherhood! Best wishes with your delivery.

Gwen was adamant with Essence that she did not want an epidural or any medications. These were very much frowned upon by @mother.nurture.official and the like. There were complications that could arise, potential negative effects for the baby. Besides, women's bodies had been birthing babies without interventions for centuries. Jeff had asked if Gwen was sure about this. She was, after all, someone who had no qualms about popping a couple of ibuprofen at the hint of a headache. She told him she was sure, told him that even if she begged for something to relieve her pain, he was to refuse. Essence assured them that she would also help Gwen stay true to her wishes, even when "primal sensations" attempted to lead her astray.

Gwen was also adamant with Essence that she wanted to avoid a C-section at all costs. Essence waved a hand in the air, like *duh*, and said, "Honey, that goes without saying." They were both in agreement that C-sections were terrible, that they were violent interruptions of the natural birthing experience that women's bodies were made for. Gwen had done the research. She knew women were four times as likely to die with a surgical birth. She knew that babies born via C-section were more likely to have respiratory distress and low Apgar scores. They were often lethargic from the anesthesia given to their mothers. Without traveling through the vaginal canal and absorbing all its healthy bacteria, they were more likely to have asthma, child-onset diabetes, and allergies. The Mother Nurture account had a whole post series about the rise of C-sections:

1 out of 3 deliveries is via
C-section. Women's bodies
must be trusted instead of
brutalized. Enough is enough.

A C-section sounded like a personal failure and a betrayal of all womankind. In the private confines of her mind, Gwen judged other women who had them. Were they not educated enough to raise objections with their doctors? Did they not know all the different labor positions to try? Had they grown impatient or panicked during the arduous process of laboring? What, exactly, had they done *wrong*? Gwen didn't know, but she was quite sure she was doing everything right.

~

When they arrived at the hospital, she was taken upstairs immediately. She heard the words *placental abruption* and knew that was not good, but she felt somehow detached from the scene. She was losing blood as fast as she was losing her grip on reality. People were bustling about. A doctor she didn't know said they were going to have to do an emergency C-section, and before she could remember that this was the thing she was supposed to avoid at all costs, they were wheeling her into a too-bright operating room and erecting a blue curtain that prevented her from seeing the lower half of her body and all the frantic efforts underway to save her and her baby.

Her arms were stretched away from her body, in a T, like those of Jesus on the cross. She shouldn't have gone for that stupid run. She was dying for her own sins, that was it. Faster than she would have thought possible, she could not feel anything below her boobs. There was the smell of something burning—her flesh, she understood later. She felt pressure, jostling, tugging. Jeff was next to her, stroking her sweaty hair with his palm, telling her, "It's going to be okay." He looked terrified and pale, and Gwen would find out later that he lost consciousness shortly after she did.

~

There were all kinds of things Gwen would find out later. The doctor would explain to her that when the placenta detaches from the uterus, as hers had, this creates an internal wound that bleeds. The internal bleeding triggers a reaction of proteins in the blood, and they become abnormally reactive. This is the first stage of something called disseminated intravascular coagulation, or DIC. At this point, blood clots were traveling throughout Gwen's body.

After delivery, the uterus usually contracts like a fist, which closes off the blood vessels that ruptured during the birth and stanches the bleeding—the female body is an amazing thing. But Gwen's uterus did not contract fully, and the bleeding continued. This led to the second stage of DIC. The proteins that naturally cause clotting had all been used up during the first phase. With no coagulants left in her system, she experienced what they call catastrophic hemorrhaging. At that point, the only chance of saving her life was to remove the uterus and stop those particular vessels from bleeding. It was a Hail Mary.

~

Gwen spent eight days in the hospital, five of those in the ICU. Baby June was whisked away to the NICU due to being preterm, but was quickly transferred to the regular nursery when they determined she was completely healthy, albeit small.

Gwen lost her blood volume, twice. They had to give her ten units of blood. Even then, it was touch and go. There was nothing to do but wait and see if her body could recover and produce the coagulants needed to stop the deep internal bleeding.

For the first three days in the ICU, Gwen was not fully conscious. They'd hooked her up to a ventilator, a ribbed white hose arching out of her mouth and connecting to a machine that was breathing for her. Jeff would tell her that he couldn't even see her face because of the white straps crisscrossing it. She was completely still, her skin chalk white, her lips colorless. Her body still looked pregnant. She was covered in tubes, her hands cuffed to the side rails of the bed, her legs wrapped in thick pneumatic pads that inflated and deflated to circulate her blood while she lay there. A bank of monitors showed jagged lines going up and down, various cursors blinking. The hospital staff let Jeff stay the night, which wasn't something they usually allowed in the ICU. It was that dire.

On days two and three in the ICU, she was critical but stable. Jeff held her swollen hands, rubbed her swollen feet. They kept telling him there was nothing to do but wait. The risk was organ failure, but they were hopeful her body would start to recover before that became a reality necessitating further discussion.

On day four, she made the turn they'd all been hoping for. They took her off the ventilator, removing the hose from her mouth and the white straps from her face. It was then she opened her eyes and said to Jeff, in a raspy voice, "Hi."

Jeff lost it then, burying his face in his hands and crying—not gentle, soft crying, but full-on blubbering. Jeff was usually so composed. This reaction, the massive bags under his eyes, told Gwen that whatever had happened was serious.

"Oh my god, I'm so glad you're okay," he said, his head hanging low against his heaving chest.

Had she ever seen him cry in the fourteen years they'd been together? She didn't think so. Her usually stoic sweetheart, destroyed.

"What happened?" she asked, not sure she wanted to know. Maybe this amnesia, this obliviousness, was for the best.

"Where's June?" she asked.

June, born in May.

"She's okay. She's okay," he said, his eyes big and wild and frantic. "She's in the NICU and they say she's doing very well, considering she's preterm. She'll be able to go home no problem."

The words rushed out of him. He seemed like someone on a massive number of uppers.

"She has your nose. She's so small. Four pounds and . . . Shit, I can't remember how many ounces. But she's good, okay? She's good."

It sounded like there was a "but" coming.

"Am *I* okay?" Gwen asked.

He started sobbing again.

"I thought you were going to die," he said. "They couldn't stop the bleeding. They had transfusions going from all these ports."

Gwen just stared at him. It was like he was talking about someone else, an acquaintance of theirs. Janice, their neighbor. Carmen, their house cleaner. She was still so out of it.

"I'm okay," she told him.

And he lost it again.

~

On day five, color started to return to Gwen's skin. They took her off the Dilaudid, an opioid pain medication that had made everything feel like a dream. One by one, they disconnected machines. They removed the pneumatic pads from her legs, pulled the electrodes off her chest. Jeff helped her get out of bed, repeating "Nice and easy" as she set her feet on the floor. She wasn't strong enough to walk, but she shuffled, wincing in pain.

"I feel like I got cut in half," she said. Then, glancing down toward the vertical incision in her belly: "I guess I did."

On day six, they transferred Gwen to the maternity ward, and that was when they said she could see June. Jeff sat by her bedside as they waited for the nurses to bring in their girl.

"Honey, there's something I have to tell you," Jeff said. "The doctors and I thought we would wait because we didn't want to upset you."

Gwen felt her heart free-fall in her chest. The baby was dead. That was what he was going to say. They had been lying to her all this time about how well the baby was doing, waiting for her to recover enough strength to absorb the tragedy.

"No," she said. Then: "No, no, no, no."

He looked at her with a quizzical expression.

"Is it June?" she asked, her voice high pitched and panicked.

He put his hands on hers. "Oh god, no. June is fine. She's coming. God, I'm an idiot. It's not that. It's . . . they had to take it out."

Take it out? The baby? Of course they did. She had no idea what he was talking about.

"June?"

He looked apologetic, like *I'm sorry I have to be this messenger.*

"Your uterus, sweetie," he said. "A hysterectomy. To help stop the bleeding."

His face was pinched. He knew this would devastate her.

"My uterus?"

He nodded.

"They had to. To save your life," he said. "But the most important thing is that you're going to be okay. June is okay. Right? That's the most important thing, right?"

His "*right?*" was so desperate that she felt she had no choice but to say, "Yeah."

"I need to see her," she said.

Before they brought June, a doctor came in and reiterated what Jeff had said. Hemorrhaging. Hysterectomy. He wanted Gwen to feel lucky that she was alive and that her baby was alive. He wanted her to fixate on this bright side and not think about the fact that her womb had been removed, the future of her family completely rewritten. She'd always thought they'd have two kids, maybe three. She and Jeff had both known the strange loneliness of being only children. They'd grown up desperately wanting siblings.

"When can I go home?" Gwen asked.

She wanted out of this place that had taken so much from her.

"A couple days. We want to make sure everything is stabilized," he said. "You had us pretty worried."

She didn't like this phrasing, as if she was at fault for burdening them, for keeping them up at night.

"I don't anticipate any setbacks with the healing process. Definitely tap into family for help during the recovery, but I think all will go smoothly," the doctor said.

"Thank you, Doctor," Jeff said to him, speaking with a kind of hero worship that made Gwen think he was going to kiss the man's feet. All Gwen wanted to do was spit in the smug doctor's face.

~

Gwen was expecting June to be hooked up to tubes and machines like she had been, but no. She was perfect, just small—"petite," the pediatrician on staff said, as if all babies weren't "petite." They had put the typical blue-and-pink-striped hat on her little head. Gwen held her against her chest, and it was like holding a guinea pig, a little ball of mammal, warm and scared and eager for affection. Gwen was overcome by a surge of heart-exploding love and warmth, but with cold terror on its heels. It was the simultaneous immense joy of having and fear of losing. This, she would realize, was motherhood.

It wasn't supposed to be like this, Gwen meeting her baby all this time after she had arrived in the world. They had missed their skin-to-skin "golden hour," the magical time of postdelivery bonding that was said to set up mother and baby for years of healthy connection. The research said it also helped the baby's temperature regulation and blood sugar stabilization. And it was supposed to trigger hormones in Gwen for producing milk, as well as decrease her stress and anxiety. Babies who do not have the "golden hour" time with their mothers tend to have worse sleep quality and more issues with growth. It was proven.

Gwen had already failed so miserably.

"Oh, honey, it's okay," Jeff said, wiping tears from her cheeks before she realized she was crying. Her body had become foreign to her, doing things without her awareness, making decisions without consulting her.

"She's doing remarkably well," the pediatrician said, as if trying to perk her up.

Gwen stroked June's back, marveling at how it was the length of her hand, from the tip of her middle finger to the bottom of her palm.

"She's breathing just fine. No issues there, which is great," the doctor went on. "And she's taking formula without any problems."

Gwen took her eyes off June and looked at the pediatrician, dead in her eyes.

"Formula?" she asked.

The pediatrician must have seen Gwen's horror, because she said, "It's very common for preemies to need a boost to get started. You can breastfeed her if you so choose."

If you so choose? What else would a good mother choose? Was this woman aware of @mother.nurture.official and the "breast is best" mantra Gwen had been chanting to herself for months?

As if in response to her thoughts, Gwen's breasts started to leak, little circles of wet blooming on her pale-blue hospital gown. She saw the pediatrician notice before she noticed herself.

"Well," the doctor said with a smile, "looks like your milk is coming in. That's great! Good timing—the lactation consultant is scheduled to pop in any minute."

Jeff helped Gwen untie the front of her gown, and she positioned June's body across her chest, the baby's tiny mouth next to her nipple. She did not want to wait for the lactation consultant. She did not want to need this stranger's tips and tricks. She wanted to do *something* naturally, *something* by instinct.

"Look at her," Jeff marveled as June's mouth started to move, her nose likely picking up on the scent of the colostrum nearby.

"That's a good girl," Gwen murmured, shifting the baby slightly. She kept repeating it—*That's a good girl*—until, abruptly, June clamped down. The pain was so immediate and excruciating that Gwen lost her breath.

"Is she doing it?" Jeff said, his eyes searching Gwen's face, trying to figure out if she was shocked in a good way or a bad way.

"I think so," Gwen said.

The pain, though. The pain.

Gwen pulled her off gently, and there was blood all around June's mouth, smeared onto her cheeks. It was like something out of a demented horror film.

"Oh my god," Jeff said.

That was when the lactation consultant walked in and said, "Oh my."

~

To this day, Gwen is convinced June was punishing her in her newborn-infant way, lashing out at Gwen because she'd been cut out of her belly in a too-bright operating room full of terrifying people wearing masks over their faces, then abandoned for days and fed a chemical-rich powder mixed with water by hands that did not belong to her mother. Her daughter hated her, right from the start. How could Gwen blame her? Gwen hated herself too.

This all relates back to Angeni Luna. Because sometime in the middle of a night Gwen can't pinpoint now, she went down an Instagram rabbit hole, looking for things to make her feel like she could redeem herself as a mother, and discovered that Angeni Luna was the woman behind both the Conscious Couples account and the Mother Nurture account. There was a smattering of photos from her personal life intermixed with the regular posts on each account. Those personal-life photos were like a behind-the-scenes view of the wisdom that had guided Gwen in her relationship with Jeff, and now her relationship with June. Angeni Luna's husband was Erik, and he was ridiculously handsome and seemingly tender and ideal in every way. They had a daughter, born just a few months before June. Her name was Freya Odina, "paying homage to her father's Norse roots and the Indigenous cultures that are the bedrock of this country," according to the birth announcement post. In the comments, people revealed that they had googled the name origins—Freya was the Norse goddess of fertility, love, and beauty; Odina was an Algonquian name meaning "mountain," which the googlers/commenters said was perfect because Indigenous people see mountains as connective points between earthly life and the divine.

Gwen didn't care much about Angeni Luna's baby's name, though it did make Gwen feel silly for the name she'd chosen for her baby. June, born in May. She hadn't even given June a middle name. She was still so shell shocked and doped up on pain medication when they brought the birth certificate. She'd burst into tears of indecision about the middle name, unsure which to choose from the list they'd made—Eloise, Amelia, Lenora. "I just don't know, I just don't know," she'd cried. Jeff said, "We can always choose one later, hon."

There were about a dozen photos of Angeni Luna's baby, this tiny Norse goddess existing between earthly life and the divine. In most of the photos, she was suckling at her mother's teats, which were round and full and glorious, with no visible wounds, no evidence of her daughter's hatred of her. The latch looked so perfect. It was like Angeni Luna angled the photos so every mother could see that latch.

Gwen could not get enough.

Angeni Luna became her inspiration.

Angeni Luna became her North Star.

Angeni Luna became her nightmare.

Chapter 2

ANGENI LUNA

All that I am, or hope to be, I
owe to becoming a mother.

While she was busily entering the requisite hashtags in the comments section—#motherhoodjourney #motherhood #consciousmotherhood #motherisaverb #connectedparenting—Angeni watched people's comments roll in.

> Such true words, yet again. You are a beautiful soul 🙏
>
> OMG. This. Who was I even before having my child? I don't even know
>
> It is the most wonderful journey, isn't it?
>
> I can't believe I ever doubted having children. It has changed me in the best ways

She had long ago stopped "liking" each of the replies. She couldn't keep up, and she didn't want people to wonder why she "liked" someone else's comment and not theirs. Each post got thousands of replies. People had to understand that she simply could not engage with each one. She had a baby to care for, dinners to make, a house to tend to, new posts to write.

Occasionally, though, she had to respond.

> You seem to think that a woman's life is not complete if she doesn't have a child. It's kind of #tradwife and 😫

These were the kinds of comments that just had to be dealt with.

> I do not believe every woman needs to become a mother, but I do believe in the sacred beauty of motherhood. It is a true gift. I have grown in ways I never could have before. I will continue to speak about this sacred beauty because there is too much in our cultural narrative about the difficulties of motherhood. I am sharing my view of its wonders.

The person, this @betty-bo-betty, wrote back immediately.

> Easy for you to be detached from the difficulties. You live in a fucking commune with people who tend to your family and fawn over you like you're the messiah

She swiped left on that comment, then tapped the little red trash can icon. Delete.

Then she promptly blocked @betty-bo-betty. Buh-bye. The world did not need exposure to this kind of vitriol.

For the record, she *did* think a woman's life wasn't complete if she didn't have a child. That was why the womb was there—to harbor a life. Not utilizing it was like refusing to ever put weight on your right foot. She couldn't say that, though, not outright. There were all these feminist types, these @betty-bo-bettys, who spammed her with hate when she tiptoed near suggesting that motherhood was imperative. But it was. It was, quite literally, the crux of humanity.

Also for the record: She *was* a feminist, if *feminist* meant being pro-female. That was her whole point—a woman's body was incredible. It could create. It could give so much. Every woman deserved to see the full potential of her body and soul.

All these Gloria Steinem enthusiasts had steered things so wrong.

~

Erik walked into the kitchen, shirtless and sweaty from chopping wood in the backyard—eleven acres of misty forest land they'd purchased with the profits from their first years of offering their Conscious Couples Communicating (CCC) webinars. The webinars had been lucrative beyond Angeni's wildest dreams. So many people were in need of guidance on how to create real, meaningful connection within themselves and with their partners. Angeni and Erik served as an example of that connection. They had done so much work together, exploring their pasts, their traumas, their attachment styles, their relational needs. She was proud of their marriage, proud that they had spent years building the foundation of their togetherness before calling Freya into her womb. People said her life seemed idyllic and, well, it was.

"I think we've got enough wood for the year at this point," Erik said.

In their life before Freya, a life that felt light-years away, in another galaxy, Angeni would have been aroused by this sight of her handsome man, aroused even by his body odor. Now, though, her eyes were trained on Freya, looking for slight shifts in facial expressions that would suggest she had gas—Angeni had eaten broccoli the night before, and she knew that cruciferous vegetables had compounds that would make their way to her breast milk and, perhaps, cause her baby to have some gastrointestinal distress. Her current nose found Erik's smell off putting, but her daughter's poops mildly sweet and pleasant.

Still, though, Erik's eyes locked with his wife's, as if he was checking to see if the old Angeni had returned yet. Poor Erik—he hadn't realized that she was never coming back.

"You guys have been working hard out there," Angeni said.

He wiped the sweat from his brow with the back of his hand and said, "We sure have."

Someone had made a comment recently about how her household seemed divided along traditional gender lines, with the women (Angeni; her soul sister, Aurora; and their newest addition, Sitka) canning tomatoes and caring for Freya while the men (Erik and his soul brothers, Jer and Matt) tended The Land. This had been her dream—to create a loving community where members could contribute their individual strengths for the greater good. While she was the matriarch, everyone had their cherished part. She felt so supported in an era when she knew so many new mothers lacked support. Freya would grow up knowing her auntie Aurora and uncles Matt and Jer. There was so much affection, so much warmth. Angeni loved to share Instagram posts and reels of the life they'd created. They were living proof of a different way to do modern life. Angeni was convinced that if more people lived like them, they would be happier, less stressed. We are made to live in tribes she'd posted recently, along with a photo of her tribe. The responses had varied—several people commented with #lifegoals, while others posted eye roll emojis with no further explanation. Erik said people were envious of the life they'd built, and, well, who could blame them.

> Our division of labor is according to the interests and skill sets of the people involved. I expect other people divide labor according to what works in their unique family situation ❤

The person wrote back:

> And why do you think you're interested in baking cookies and sewing booties while the men are getting a workout building a yurt? #gendersocialization

She didn't respond to that one. There was no winning.

What people didn't seem to understand was that she had the typically male role of breadwinner for their family. The Instagram accounts, the webinars, the workbooks—they were all her creations, and they all generated enough income for their family to live on. Erik participated in the couples-based work, yes, but there wouldn't be couples-based work without Angeni's initiative and ambition. Of course, calling attention to these facts would be detrimental to Angeni's relationship with Erik. She understood his childhood wounding, his sensitivity to feeling unimportant and overlooked.

Freya fussed in her baby wrap, waking from the nap she'd taken while Angeni was making pasta from scratch. Angeni wiped her hands on a dish towel and lifted Freya from the wrap.

"She heard Daddy's voice and wanted to say hi," she said, holding the baby out to Erik.

Erik took Freya in his arms, his biceps flexing as he held their baby against his bare chest. People seemed to think skin-to-skin contact was only relevant for the newest of newborns, but Angeni was hoping to shift the cultural narrative about this by posting photos of Freya continuing to love skin-to-skin contact with her parents. Angeni was usually topless beneath the baby wrap, allowing Freya to nuzzle her breasts and feed whenever she needed. Angeni didn't share this fact with the outside world, as she knew there were prudes that would be horrified that her boobs were on display daily in an environment shared with men besides her husband. People already thought it was strange that she lived in community with men besides her husband: anyone think she's boning those two beefcakes? Sex was such a ridiculous fixation of modern society. Their community rose above all that. They didn't believe in mind-numbing substances or escaping through screen time. They didn't condone meaningless sex outside the bounds of a loving relationship. Matt had a girlfriend, Annika, who lived on Point White, at the southern end of the island. They had all met her, but she never stayed overnight on The Land. Matt stayed at her place a few nights a week. Angeni had made it clear that the community was to be kept small, intentional. She wanted everyone to feel completely safe. Jer was shy, private. If he dated, he kept it to himself, never advertising if he was spending the night elsewhere. Aurora hadn't shown interest in romance, said she was more than fulfilled by the platonic love she felt on a daily basis. They all lived in peace, free of the drama that so many people seemed addicted to online.

"Morning," Sitka said, stumbling into the kitchen, rubbing the sleep from her eyes.

She'd been up most of the night with Freya so Angeni could get some much-needed rest. Angeni couldn't deny that Sitka had been a wonderful, if unexpected, addition to their little community.

She'd arrived a month ago, showing up quite literally on Angeni's doorstep, peddling turquoise the way Girl Scouts peddle cookies. She had all these pieces of jewelry in a little cart on wheels, the kind teachers use for classroom art supplies. She looked to be in the first half of her twenties, thin as a reed, gold hoop in her septum. When she introduced herself as Sitka, Angeni gasped.

"Sitka? Like the spruce tree?"

See, Angeni had a special relationship with trees, communed with them when feeling the need for grounding, planting her bare feet in their soil. The Sitka spruce was one of her favorites. There were a few of them on The Land. She could see the tallest one from the picture window over the kitchen sink. Majestic, she'd called it in one post.

"Yes, like the spruce tree. Not many people know that," Sitka said with a nervous laugh, as if she were embarrassed by her namesake.

Angeni was convinced that this was not a chance encounter.

She invited Sitka in for tea and watched Sitka and Freya connect instantly with each other. Angeni believed that soul bonds were not just of the romantic variety, but could exist between any two human beings, regardless of age, gender, or sexuality. Love at first sight was a more far-reaching phenomenon than people realized.

As they drank their tea, their conversation strayed from small talk to something deeper. They discovered that both Sitka and Freya were water signs—Sitka a Scorpio, Freya a Pisces. Sitka and Freya also had the same 6–3 Human Design profile, each carrying a potent mix of innocent curiosity and wisdom. *Uncanny* was the word Angeni used to describe the whole thing. *Fated* was the word she felt in her heart.

Angeni decided, rather impulsively, to invite Sitka to live on The Land. Their community did not have a formal handbook of rules, but Angeni had once stated that any new members would be welcomed by group consensus. Inviting Sitka without discussing it with anyone, especially Erik, was unusual, but she was the matriarch, and, well, she'd felt so drawn to Sitka. That was how she explained it, first to Erik, then to the others. They were noticeably skeptical. Especially Aurora. Angeni and Aurora had been friends since childhood, growing up in a poor neighborhood in Chelan County before making their way together to Seattle. Angeni had a feeling Aurora's apprehension was less about Sitka being a stranger and more about Sitka being a potential threat to Angeni and Aurora's bond.

"I don't know what it is—I just feel this is right," Angeni told the group when making her case for Sitka.

"Past-life type thing, maybe?" Erik ventured.

"Maybe. It's the oddest thing. I feel like Spirit brought her to us."

They didn't like the word *god* for all its connections to traditional religions and their power structures. Instead, they spoke of Spirit. Spirit had brought Angeni and Aurora together as girls. Spirit had brought Angeni and Erik together as partners. Spirit had brought Freya into Angeni's womb. Spirit had brought Sitka to their doorstep.

"Your intuition is so powerful, Ang," Jer chimed in. He was usually so quiet, to himself. When he spoke up, it was especially meaningful.

"Surrender to the universe," Matt said, lifting his arms to the sky in his usual demonstrative fashion.

Aurora's arms were crossed over her chest, her mouth a straight line.

"Trust the mysteries," Erik said.

It was something they preached in their webinars—surrender to the universe, trust the mysteries. When Angeni looked to Aurora for her approval, Aurora gave the slightest nod. The nod said she would accept the addition of Sitka, but she didn't have to like it.

~

From day one, Sitka had offered to help with Freya during the nighttime hours. They fell into a natural rhythm together. Angeni took care not to mention the arrangement on social media. She continued posting photos of Freya resting on her chest in the early-morning hours, letting people think the baby had been there with her all night. She continued to mention her exhaustion—because even with help from Sitka and the others, she *was* exhausted—and then reminded herself and her followers that this was all just a phase in this precious season of life. #blessed #grateful

She wasn't ashamed that she had overnight help. She was living in accordance with how human beings were meant to live. New mothers were supposed to be surrounded by other adults who could offer care. It wasn't her fault that so many people had distanced themselves from age-old traditions to pursue the modern version of success—a massive home in the suburbs, big enough for six people but housing only two, significant distance from family and friends. Whenever people were critical of her circumstances—must be nice they wrote—she chalked it up to envy.

She did include Sitka in some social media posts, introducing her as a new member of the community. Angeni appreciated that Sitka was Black. Or half Black. Or some percentage of Black—Angeni knew it wasn't appropriate to ask for a specific racial breakdown. In any case,

Sitka's presence was the perfect solution to the hordes of people who had begun criticizing Angeni for, as one person wrote, promoting an all-white cis community with zero interest in representation of BIPOC or queer people.

As if Angeni could control the demographics of her social media platforms. She happened to be a white woman with a white husband and a white baby. Sue her.

Angeni hoped that Sitka would want to stay on The Land long-term, but they hadn't discussed this yet. Aurora, Matt, and Jer each lived in their own four-hundred-square-foot A-frame cabin made of logs from pine trees felled on The Land, while Angeni, Erik, and Freya lived in the main house. Their master bedroom was a family bedroom. They'd taken the king-size mattress off its frame and put it on the floor—it was safer for Freya that way. When Sitka arrived, they gave her the guest room down the hall. If she stayed, they could build her an A-frame cabin too. They weren't paying her, after all. Instead, they were giving her a home, a community, a priceless sense of belonging.

~

"How was last night?" Erik asked Sitka.

Sitka stretched upward, exposing her perfectly taut midriff, and yawned dramatically. Angeni wished Sitka would try a little harder to conceal how fatigued she was. It made Angeni feel guilty, and guilt was one of the most toxic emotions for her nervous system. She had spent years becoming a person who did not feel guilt for having her own needs, for prioritizing her own rest and rejuvenation.

"She did not want to settle last night," Sitka said.

Erik lifted a coffee mug to Sitka, an offering, and she nodded. He poured her a cup, set it in front of her as she sat at their giant island. The island was made of cedar from The Land, and Sitka liked to run her hands over it, tracing the grain lines with her fingertips.

"I'm wondering if it's a growth spurt," Angeni said. "It felt like you brought her to me to breastfeed a dozen times!"

Angeni had to remind all of them that she was still doing the work in this situation—creating milk in her body to feed this child. It took an enormous amount of energy, physically and mentally.

"I'm sure it'll be better tonight," Sitka said. "I bet she naps really well today too."

"She already took her first one," Angeni said.

Freya reached her chubby baby arms out toward Sitka, a big toothless grin on her face. She adored Sitka so much. Angeni had to continue to remind herself that this was a good thing.

"I can hold her," Sitka said to Erik, and Erik put Freya in her lap. She was bouncy and giggly, and Sitka's coffee kept almost spilling out of her cup as she got Freya settled.

"Careful with the coffee," Angeni said. She couldn't help herself.

The side door opened, and Aurora came in, wearing her paint-covered sweatshirt and jeans. She'd recently returned to her past love of painting, covering huge canvases in splotches, Jackson Pollock–style. She wanted Freya to participate, to dip her little hands in the paint and press them to the canvases, but Angeni was too concerned about the chemicals in the paint leaching into her daughter's skin.

"Morning, all," Aurora said, going straight to Freya and nuzzling her face. "Is she extra cute today or what?"

Angeni beamed. "She is, isn't she?"

"I *loved* your post this morning, Ang," Aurora said.

"I haven't seen it yet," Erik said, taking his phone from his back pocket. He read aloud: "'All that I am, or hope to be, I owe to becoming a mother.'"

"Aww," Aurora said, hand to heart.

"Beautiful, honey," Erik said.

"Isn't that an Abraham Lincoln quote?" Sitka said, still bouncing Freya—and the coffee—in her lap.

Angeni's response came out like a screech: "*Abraham Lincoln?*"

Sitka's eyes remained fixed on Freya as she said, "Yeah."

Erik tapped at his phone, then lifted his head and said, "She's right. I mean, it's sort of a paraphrase, but—"

"But Abraham Lincoln wasn't a *mother*," Aurora said.

"Right. He said, 'All that I am, or hope to be, I owe to my angel mother.' Looks like his mother died when he was nine," Erik said.

"Aww," Aurora said again.

Angeni didn't know what to say. She was not aware of these Abraham Lincoln words, at least not consciously. Had they been sitting there in the depths of her subconscious, waiting to be put to use?

"I mean, your post is fine," Sitka said. "Maybe just add a line to credit Abraham Lincoln?"

"I'm not sure that crediting an old white man is very on brand," Aurora said, putting "on brand" in air quotes.

Angeni said, "I'm not a brand" at the same time Sitka said, "But he did say that."

"Have any of the followers even noticed this weird . . . coincidence?" Erik asked.

Reconsulting his phone, he scrolled and scrolled and scrolled, then said, "I don't see any comments about this."

"I'm not surprised. It's kind of an obscure reference," Aurora said.

"Well, I knew it," Sitka said with a shrug. Angeni wished she would shut up. She was making Angeni doubt herself, and Angeni hated doubting herself.

"Are you a big Abraham Lincoln fan?" Aurora asked. "He was so important to ending slavery, right?"

Aurora looked so serious, so earnest. Angeni was horrified. There was a dreadful silence in the kitchen as they all stood there, waiting to see how Sitka would respond.

Angeni could feel all of them holding their breath before Sitka erupted in laughter.

"Oh my god, Aurora," she said.

And then they were all laughing, and Angeni felt the tension slowly leave her body. That was all they needed—a laugh—for harmony to be restored.

"I'm sorry—I was just wondering," Aurora said.

She was so clueless sometimes. Her naivete was both her best and her worst quality.

"Can you imagine if I really was an Abraham Lincoln superfan? Like, I had a fan page for him on Instagram?" Sitka said.

She was still laughing, so they all followed her lead. Freya was enjoying it most of all.

When her laughter died down, Sitka said, "On second thought, just leave the quote. You guys are right—nobody's gonna notice or care. Or they'll just think you made a slight tweak to a famous quote."

"Is it really a famous quote?" Angeni asked.

Sitka just shrugged. "Guess not."

"Erik, can you keep a close eye on the comments section today?" Angeni asked him.

Erik nodded, a grave expression on his face. He took his role as online bodyguard, patrolling Angeni's social media feeds, very seriously. There had recently been a Reddit thread with strangers taking bets on when he and Angeni would "consciously uncouple" (most guessing before Freya turned two), and Erik could not get it removed, despite repeated engagements with the Reddit help center. He left comments on the thread, things like *I don't know, guys, they seem solid to me* and *sounds like most of you just wish you had what they have*. That just generated more wrath, and Angeni told him to just leave it, so Erik backed off. Eventually, people lost interest, and after a grand total of ninety-one comments, the thread was archived. It was still there for all the world to peruse, but people couldn't add new comments. Erik assured Angeni that he checked every day for a new Reddit thread to patrol, but there was nothing.

"I'm thinking it's time to release the birth story," Angeni said, sitting on a stool across from Sitka at the island.

She had been waiting for the perfect time to share The Birth Story. Her community was clamoring for it, and she had repeatedly told them that she would share it if and when it felt right in her heart. It was so precious, she'd said. She wanted to possess it for herself and her loved ones, she'd said. Now, though, with engagement on her Mother Nurture posts slightly down—Erik checked the metrics weekly—it felt like the right time.

"I love this idea," Erik said, as if it was his first time hearing it, though they had just discussed it the night before.

"The world *needs* to see this. It's *so* beautiful," Aurora said, her eyes welling up.

Aurora had been there, at Freya's birth. Angeni labored for hours in a giant birthing tub, with Aurora and Erik taking turns massaging her lower back and shoulders while whispering affirmations. Erik filmed the whole thing, which Jer, their resident video production expert, had spent weeks editing. What nobody but their community knew was that Angeni had actually delivered Freya at the hospital after the midwife, an elderly woman named Pearl who Angeni trusted implicitly, was concerned about the baby's heart rate dropping. This would create issues with the Birth Story video, of course, as Angeni had no plans of telling her followers that she'd abandoned her home birth. She instructed Jer to show the laboring process, and then they would cut to Freya in her arms later, footage they got once Angeni and Freya came home from the hospital. If people complained about not seeing the actual delivery, Angeni had a planned response: Some moments of this life are sacred, meant to be held close to the hearts of those present. This was one of those moments.

"Are you thinking a written post, or are there photos or a video or what?" Sitka asked.

Angeni appreciated Sitka's input. She was a decade younger than Angeni, hipper and more savvy about social media. This didn't bother Angeni. She didn't aspire to be savvy with a technology made to disconnect people from the natural world. For her, social media was a necessary evil, something to help spread the messages she was born to spread—her Human Design profile indicated that this was her calling, to guide people toward their inner truths and help them find meaning and healing.

"We have the video, edited down to a couple minutes, so I was thinking of posting that with accompanying words," she said.

"You had her at home, right?" Sitka said.

Angeni hated to lie, and Erik knew this about her. She was grateful when he jumped in:

"She was in this huge tub. It was so special," he said.

Which was true.

"We wanted a water birth for our water-sign baby," Aurora added, for good measure.

This was also true. They *had* wanted that. Angeni had done so much inner work in order to accept that the birth had not gone exactly to plan.

"Maybe just mention in the post that home birth isn't right for everyone," Sitka said. "You know, to promote women having options and—"

"Home birth *is* for everyone, though," Angeni said. "It's the medical establishment that says otherwise. It makes women question their abilities and lose faith in their bodies. This is one of the things I want to focus on with Mother Nurture."

Her own birth experience hadn't changed her fervor. Yes, she'd needed to go to the hospital, as a last resort. But for most women, the hospital was their first and only consideration. That was what had to change. Modern medicine should be the exception, not the rule. If she shared that she'd delivered in the hospital, people would see her as the rule, not the exception. She shuddered at how much harm that could do.

Angeni watched Sitka's jaw muscles tighten and clench, as if she was having to physically restrain herself from saying something. She didn't agree, clearly, but what right did she have to such a passionate opinion?

"Maybe just a disclaimer to cover yourself in case of liability, then," she said finally, with a tight smile.

"That's not a bad idea," Erik said.

He was so agreeable, always—a blessing and a curse.

"Birth doesn't need a disclaimer," Angeni said, her eyes locked on Sitka's.

Sitka stood from her seat, holding Freya against her chest.

"Don't listen to me," she said with a smile that Angeni couldn't read. "I've never had a kid."

Freya squealed, and Sitka kissed her cheek.

"I'm going to take her for a little nature walk," Sitka said.

Angeni nodded her consent and told Sitka she'd have buckwheat pancakes ready when they returned—"for the adults, I mean." They were just starting Freya on solids, but Angeni was determined to stay away from sugary offerings that would ingrain a preference for sweet foods for decades to come. Salmon roe, lamb meat stock, bone broth—these would be her daughter's first experiences with nourishment beyond her mother's breasts.

After Sitka and Freya had left, Aurora said, "Sitka seems off today."

"I can't imagine she got much sleep," Erik said.

"Let's not talk about her when she's not here," Angeni said.

It was one of their community rules, in place to keep the harmony and encourage healthy communication. It made Angeni feel good to remind them of this. This was what the haters didn't understand—she always had the purest intentions.

"Sorry," Aurora said. "I didn't mean it in a gossipy way. I just . . . I hope she's okay. Sleep deprivation is, like, a torture device in the military."

"She's not sleep deprived," Angeni said. "She's fine."

She could hear the edge in her voice despite her best attempts to curb it. Erik came up behind her, pressed his thumbs into the knotted muscles of her shoulders.

"You're my queen," he told her.

She closed her eyes, let herself luxuriate in his devotion, and said, "I know."

Chapter 3

Britt

Twenty-five years earlier

Britt Taylor had just turned seven years old when she got up in front of her first-grade class to announce what she wanted to be when she grew up. Every kid was taking their turn, saying all the usual things—doctor, astronaut, gymnast, veterinarian, scientist. Britt didn't aspire to any of those usual things. She wanted something decidedly unusual, something that would be a grand departure from a dull childhood spent hovering just above the poverty line in Chelan County, Washington.

"Britt's doing the potty dance," the asshole kid, Mikey, said.

Britt was doing the thing she always did when she was nervous in front of an audience—shifting her weight from one foot to the other. As everyone laughed, she stopped, willed herself to be still.

"Mikey, stop it," their teacher said.

Ms. Wallace was the teacher, and she was friends with Britt's mom. Or maybe *friends* wasn't the right term. They liked to go to the bar and drink together sometimes. Britt's mom referred to Ms. Wallace as Amy, but Britt was never allowed to refer to her as Amy.

"Britt, go ahead," Ms. Wallace said.

The class quieted, and Britt cleared her throat.

"I want to be . . . famous," she said.

There was more laughter. Britt was an easy kid to laugh at. She wore the same burgundy corduroy pants every day, paired with one of three favorite T-shirts, all of which were threadbare. Her mom would bring home clothes from the Salvation Army every now and then, but nothing was ever the right size. She seemed to think Britt was either a toddler or a teenager, could never seem to see Britt for who she actually was.

"Famous? Okay," Ms. Wallace said. "Famous for what?"

Britt didn't know. She had a vague idea of being some kind of performer, though she had no talent for singing or dancing. All she knew was that fame offered everything she didn't have—a sense of belonging, adoration, an escape.

"I don't know yet," Britt said.

More laughter.

"Okay, well, how about you spend some time thinking about that," Ms. Wallace said, before calling up the next student.

~

That school day was memorable for another reason: because it was Becky Reynolds's first day of school, and Becky Reynolds would become Britt's lifelong best friend.

They met in the lunch line when Britt said, "I've never seen you before."

"It's my first day," Becky said.

"Oh," Britt said. "That's weird."

It was March, just a few months from the end of the school year, not a usual time for a new student to appear.

"We just moved here, me and my mom," Becky said.

"You don't have a dad?" Britt asked.

Britt was always on the hunt for other kids who didn't have dads.

Becky shook her head.

"Not anymore," she said.

"Did he die?" Britt asked.

Becky shook her head again. "He just left."

"Oh," Britt said. "Mine did too."

That was all Britt's mom had told her about him—that he left. She did not know the color of his eyes or how tall he was or the sound of his laugh. She only knew that he was someone who had left.

"Do you want to sit with me?" Britt asked.

Becky nodded, and that was that—a friendship was born.

~

Britt assumed that Becky's single mom was like her own single mom, but that was not the case. Becky's single mom seemed like she'd just stumbled out of Woodstock. She was always smiling and wearing a flowy dress. She didn't walk; she swayed, as if she always had a song in her head. She let her armpit hair grow wild and free. She made most of what they ate from scratch. Their apartment always smelled like sugar cookies and incense.

When Becky invited Britt over for the first time, Britt called her mother Ms. Reynolds, and she laughed and said, "You can call me Rainbow, sweetie." Britt wasn't sure if that was her name, or just something she wanted to be called, but she did as she was told. She would have called her anything she wanted, because Rainbow hugged her and kissed her cheeks and made her feel loved in ways her own mom never did.

~

After meeting Rainbow, Britt began going home with Becky every day after school. It took three weeks of this routine before Britt's mom registered her absence in the afternoons and inquired about her whereabouts.

"Where you been going every day after school?"

Britt hadn't already volunteered the information because she'd learned it was best to say as little as possible to her mom. She never knew what would spark an outburst, what would piss her off.

"I have a new friend," Britt said. "I go to her house. It's close, by the park."

She held her breath while awaiting her mom's response. Either her mom wouldn't give a single shit about Britt's new friend, or she would have a huge, irrational fit about Britt's new friend. In this moment, it was the former. Britt's mom just shrugged. She didn't ask the friend's name, what she was like. It would take years for Britt to understand that her mother's disinterest wasn't malicious; she had tunnel vision, focused each day on just surviving until the next.

Her mother referred to the problem as The Darkness. It descended upon her without warning and lingered for days, weeks sometimes. Britt noticed a pattern over time, saw that The Darkness was often preceded by a phase of unrestrained joy and frantic activity—what she would later learn was called mania. Her mom loved those phases, the vitality of them. Britt did, too, before she knew better. They were the only times she danced around the apartment with her, the only times she threw her head back and laughed, the only times she took Britt's face in her hands and kissed her cheeks. The older Britt got, the less able she was to enjoy those upswings. She knew what was coming. She was always bracing herself.

Britt's mom had worked as a morning-shift grocery clerk for the past year, which was the longest she'd held a job since Britt had been born. Britt was old enough now to call the store when The Darkness came and tell the manager that her mom was sick and wouldn't be able to come to work. They weren't pleased with the number of days she missed, but they didn't fire her. Her previous jobs had fired her because she couldn't even manage to call and inform them of her absence; she just lay in bed for days.

"Bill's coming for dinner tonight," her mom said.

Bill was her mom's sometimes-boyfriend. Their relationship was as unstable as Britt's mom's moods—they were madly in love one day, close to murder-suicide the next. When Bill drank, which was often, he became overly affectionate with Britt, pulling her onto his lap and wrapping his fat arms around her tiny body. Her mom seemed to think it was cute, said things to Britt like "Isn't Bill like a giant teddy bear?" The teddy bear turned into an angry grizzly after a few drinks, and that was when the yelling started and Britt went to her room and tried to ignore it. It was impossible to ignore, though. It was so loud that the neighbors had called the police on two separate occasions.

"Oh, Becky's mom invited me for dinner there, actually," Britt said.

It was a lie. Becky's mom hadn't invited her, but Britt didn't want to have dinner with her mom and Bill. She knew if she showed up at Becky's house, she'd be welcomed inside, no questions asked.

"Well then, I'll tell Bill he should take me out to dinner," her mom said.

It was a well-known fact that Bill refused to take both Britt and her mom out to dinner: "I don't need to pay for two ladies in my life," he'd said once. Britt's mom always cooked elaborate meals for him, consulting hardcover cookbooks from the 1970s that she got at thrift stores. For Britt, she never, ever cooked anything besides grilled-cheese sandwiches. Britt had been making herself frozen entrées since she was tall enough to reach the microwave on their kitchen counter.

"That sounds nice," Britt said, though she doubted Bill would take her mom out to dinner. It was more likely Britt would come home from Becky's house to the sound of her mom and Bill slur-shouting at each other.

~

As predicted, Rainbow welcomed Britt inside and set a place for her at their small kitchen table. They didn't have much; they were clearly just as poor as Britt and her mom, but Rainbow and Becky's home felt abundant in other ways. Rainbow had potted plants occupying every inch of wall space, succulents and pothos with their tendrils of leaves dancing across the windowsills. Strands of twinkly lights were thumbtacked to the walls, traversing from one corner of the living room to the other. Records were always spinning, candles or incense always burning.

"It's actually a wonderful night for you to join us," Rainbow said. "We are doing my friend's name ceremony tonight."

Rainbow explained that a name ceremony was when someone decided to choose a spiritual life and wanted a new name to reflect that journey. Rainbow was all about a spiritual life. She liked to read tarot cards. For work, she did a special kind of massage that involved working with someone's energy without even touching them. It sounded magical to Britt. Rainbow was magical to Britt.

"Name ceremonies are cool," Becky said. "I'm going to have one when I'm older."

"If you want to, sweetie. There's never any pressure from me," Rainbow said.

"Did you have a name ceremony?" Britt asked Rainbow.

"Duh," Becky said. "She wasn't born *Rainbow*."

"What was your name before?" Britt asked.

Britt was intrigued by this idea of becoming a completely new person.

"I prefer not to revisit—" Rainbow started to say.

"It was *Maura*," Becky said.

Rainbow looked peeved for about a half second before returning to her usual Zen appearance. Years spent with a mother whose moods turned on a dime had made Britt adept at clocking half seconds of irritation.

"Why did you pick Rainbow?" Britt asked.

"I didn't pick it. Spirit bestowed it upon me."

Spirit. Rainbow used this term often. Britt didn't want to ask what it meant. Rainbow spoke of it with such reverence that Britt thought she'd seem stupid for not already knowing.

"I think the name captures the different shades of me," Rainbow went on. "I am not monochromatic. I am a color wheel."

Britt had no idea what she was talking about, but she was still intrigued. What name would she choose if she could choose anything?

Rainbow served them homemade macaroni and cheese, rich and creamy, nearly overflowing from a casserole dish that Rainbow had pulled from the oven. Rainbow poured herself a glass of wine and tall glasses of grape juice for the girls. She lit a candle in the middle of the table. They took a moment to thank Spirit for the meal before them. Britt was always starving because her mom didn't keep enough food in their house, but she told herself to eat slowly. She matched Becky's pace, let herself get accustomed to the laid-back rhythm of their mealtime. Britt and her mom only ate at the table if Bill was over. Every other time, they ate in front of the TV, and often Britt's mom didn't eat at all. Britt had suggested once that they eat at the table together, "like a normal family," and her mom had laughed at her as if she'd just told the funniest joke, and said, "Britt, you are too much." It was true—anything Britt wanted was too much for her mother. Britt's basic existence was too much for her mother.

As they finished dinner, Rainbow's friends arrived—two men and two women who also looked like they'd stumbled out of Woodstock. They all had wavy hair, greasy at the roots, and they were all wearing Birkenstocks. Rainbow asked them if they minded if Becky and Britt witnessed the proceedings, and they said they didn't, that they thought it was beautiful for "young souls" to participate.

The two men were named Wilder and Zephyr. The women were Indigo and Julie.

"Julie is the one who's changing her name," Becky told Britt, as if that needed to be clarified.

"What's she changing her name to?" Britt asked.

Becky shrugged. "They say they don't know and then the name comes to them during the ceremony."

Spirit.

The ceremony involved all of them, Britt and Becky included, sitting in a circle in the living room, holding hands, eyes closed. They'd turned out the lights, their faces lit by a collection of candles in the center of the circle. Rainbow started humming a tune, and they all joined in like it was a ritual they performed on a daily basis.

"Julie, we are so honored that you are choosing a spiritual path with us. Please share with us the name that is coming to you in this moment."

Britt opened one eye to peek at what Julie was doing. Her head was titled toward the ceiling, eyes still closed. She took several deep breaths, inhaling and exhaling dramatically. Her eyelids fluttered.

"The name that is coming to me is . . . Angeni," she said.

"Angeni," Rainbow said.

"Angeni," they all repeated.

"Welcome, Angeni," Rainbow said.

They resumed their humming for several minutes, during which Britt repeated the name to herself in her head—Angeni, Angeni, Angeni. She'd never heard the name before. It was as pretty as it was unusual.

Angeni.

Chapter 4

SASHA

Sasha Robinson knew the exact moment she'd first heard the name Angeni Luna. She was having dinner with her sister, Daphne, and Daphne's husband, Jay, at their little rundown rental house in Ballard. Occasionally, Daphne invited their mom to join, but this night wasn't one of those nights. It was just the three of them.

Daphne was seven months pregnant with her first baby, a fact that astounded Sasha. Daphne, six years older than Sasha, had been like a mother to her little sister, so it shouldn't have been hard for Sasha to believe that Daphne was going to become an actual mother. But it was hard to believe. Or maybe Sasha was just in denial because she didn't want to share Daphne. It was inevitable that her sister would have less time for her once the baby came. Sasha was doing her best to pull away more, to train herself away from needing Daphne so much. She'd thrown herself into studies—at twenty-five, she was the youngest student in the University of Washington's feminist studies doctoral program. Daphne was onto her, said, "I see what you're doing, sis. Pushing me away. But you better not miss family dinner."

The moment Sasha walked into the house that night, she smelled her sister's chili. It was her specialty, something she'd made every week when they were growing up—starting when Daphne was eleven and

Sasha was five. Daphne took it upon herself to become the chef of the house when they were young, mostly because she got sick of Chef Boyardee and the other cheap boxed and frozen stuff their mom kept stocked for them. Daphne had a magenta three-ring binder with recipes scribbled down on notebook paper. The chili recipe was titled "Bowl of warmth and love." Sasha had so many fond memories of that chili. Or maybe they were fond memories of her sister taking care of her. They rarely saw their mother during the week. She came home from her day job at the hospital—she'd started in the janitorial department before moving over to administration—just to change her clothes and go to a night shift at the pharmacy. It was Daphne who fed Sasha and helped her with homework and cuddled with her until she fell asleep. It was Daphne who picked out her school outfits and laid them out before bedtime. It was Daphne who packed her school lunches, always including a piece of Halloween candy from the bucket they kept in their closet throughout the year.

"Wow, that bump is bumpin'," Sasha said as she walked into the tiny galley kitchen and saw her sister standing at the stove. Daphne flinched—she hadn't heard Sasha come in.

"You trying to give me a heart attack?" she said, putting her hand to her chest.

"Sorry," Sasha said. She went to her, wrapped her arms around Daphne in a tight hug, pulling her sister as close to her as the bump would allow.

"I fear something's come between us," Sasha said with mock seriousness.

They both started to laugh. They had the same high-pitched laugh, the same wide-mouthed smile. They both had their mother's facial features—her nose, her eyes. Daphne's skin was darker because her father had been Black; Sasha's father had been white. Daphne used to joke, "I'm the seventy-two percent dark chocolate, and you're the yummier milk chocolate."

Jay came into the kitchen and said, "All this giggling must mean little sis is in the house."

Sasha loved Jay. He and Daphne had been high school sweethearts—a modern rarity. When they'd started dating, Sasha was only ten. She'd grown up with Jay. He was like a brother to her.

"So what's sis been up to? Still trying for the highest IQ in the world?" he teased.

She play-hit him in the arm.

"Oh, silly me. You already have the highest IQ in the world. Apologies."

She play-hit him again.

Sasha's intelligence had never not been a part of her identity. She started kindergarten at age four and was reading chapter books intended for eight-year-olds by the time she turned five. She skipped first grade and went right to second, and she probably could have skipped another grade somewhere along the way, but her mother had wanted to be sure she could legally drive by the time she graduated high school.

"What about you, though?" she asked Jay. "What's new with you guys?"

Before he could answer, Daphne came into the room carrying a giant tray with their three bowls of chili and little bowls with fixings—cheddar cheese, chopped green onions, corn chips, sour cream. Jay leaped from the couch to help her and set the tray on the coffee table in front of the couch.

"I'll tell you what's new. Hubby here got himself a promotion," Daphne said. She gave Jay a kiss on the cheek before lowering herself onto the couch in the slow way that pregnant women do.

Jay was a firefighter at Seattle's Station 8 in Queen Anne.

"Oh my god, that's amazing," Sasha said.

"He gets a fancy title. Driver engineer," Daphne said.

"That's awesome, Jay. Really. I'm so happy for you guys," Sasha said.

Jay gave Sasha and Daphne their chili and then sat back in the armchair with his own. They took their first bites, making the requisite "mmm" sounds in appreciation of Daphne's culinary talents.

"You guys still don't want to know the sex of the baby?" Sasha asked.

"One of us would really like to know," Jay said, pointing a thumb back at himself, "but one of us wants a *surprise*."

Sasha made a face like she'd smelled something bad. She hated surprises in life. Even the good ones were unsettling.

"I think it'll help during labor to not know the sex. I'll be so excited to find out," Daphne said.

"To each their own," Jay said.

"I could never wait to find out," Sasha said.

Daphne looked at her with a soft smile. "That's the difference between us, sis. You want all the knowledge. I'm happy not having it."

Daphne reached over and put her hand on Sasha's hand. Something about the gesture made Sasha want to cry. Daphne understood her in a way nobody else did. That had to be the crux of true love—feeling seen.

Sasha shook off her sentimentality and said, "Damn, Daph, this chili batch is really good."

"I've got leftovers in a Tupperware for you," Daphne said to Sasha. "Don't let me forget to give it to you."

"Homegirl has gotten so forgetful," Jay said with a laugh.

"Pregnancy brain," Daphne said.

"The struggle is real," Jay said.

"You got my email about the shower?" Daphne asked.

Sasha had gotten her sister's email about the shower and had promptly marked it unread to remind herself to come back to it. Sasha hated baby showers, as a rule. She hated how capitalism had turned a meaningful rite of passage into a Pinterest-board extravaganza with ridiculous games. In the email, she'd been asked to help out with one such game involving placing different candy bars into open diapers so that they resembled logs of shit. The guests would have to guess the candy bar based on sight and smell. It was the epitome of stupid, but Sasha loved Daphne, so she planned to arrive with a grocery bag of Milky Way, Snickers, Payday, 3 Musketeers, Butterfinger, Almond Joy, and Baby Ruth bars.

"The candy bar thing," Sasha said. "Got it."

"I know you think it's stupid, and I don't care," Daphne said.

Sasha just shrugged. Her sister knew her well.

"I think Mom's pissed that Krystal is hosting."

Krystal was married to a coworker of Jay's, and they lived in a nice house in Queen Anne, the type of house Daphne and Jay were saving to buy.

"I mean, Mom's place is so small," Sasha said.

"I feel a little bad. I'm trying to develop a better relationship with her," Daphne said. She sat up straighter as she said this, as if making a point, as if calling attention to some superiority.

"What does that mean?" Sasha asked, already annoyed. Sasha preferred bonding with her sister over how difficult it was to connect with their mother.

"I mean, she's going to have a grandchild. I want her to know my child," she said.

"Well, Mom only works one job now, so I guess your kid will see her more than we ever did."

Sasha couldn't help but have this chip on her shoulder. She knew her mother had had to work as hard and as much as she did. There had been no other way. But that didn't mean she was at peace with the fact that her mother had rarely been around. Even on weekends, she'd had shifts at the pharmacy. She wasn't there to shuttle the girls to birthday parties or sporting events or playdates. If they wanted to go to something, they had to learn the bus schedule and figure it out themselves. This early independence had probably made Sasha into who she was, but she wasn't always sure she liked who she was.

"It might be healing for you to resolve some of this stuff with her," Daphne said gently.

Healing? Resolve? This was not how Daphne usually talked.

"God, are you going to *therapy*?" Sasha asked.

Jay snickered.

"You know, it's not a bad thing to seek self-improvement," Daphne said.

"You *are* going to therapy?" Sasha asked.

Jay snickered more. "It's worse than therapy," he said.

Daphne balled up a napkin and threw it at him.

"She's a disciple of Angelini Luna," he said.

The name rang a bell, but Sasha didn't know why at first.

"It's *Angeni*. Not *Angelini*," Daphne said. "And I'm not a disciple. I just like her content."

"She's on Instagram," Jay said. "Like, all over the damn thing."

That was why Sasha recognized the name. Inspired by her sister's pregnancy, Sasha was planning a dissertation about how Motherhood, the institution with a capital *M*, was the final frontier of feminism. She wanted to investigate how society perpetuates the belief that women are not truly women unless they reproduce, leading many to have children as an assumed matter of course, only to realize that the same society that corralled them into this role offers no support infrastructure—no paid maternity leave, no subsidized childcare, nothing. Daphne was already talking about whether or not to continue working after the baby arrived, considering that day care would eat up 90 percent of her salary.

To Sasha, it all seemed like a patriarchal scheme to "keep women in the kitchen." Without support infrastructure, mothers have no choice but to suspend every other pursuit in their lives to raise their children. This takes many of them out of the workforce and redirects all their brain power away from things like personal fulfillment or fighting for equality—which is, of course, just fine for the white men at the helm. When Sasha tried to talk to Daphne about her thoughts, her sister scrunched up her forehead and said, "Oh, Sash, your brain never sleeps."

As part of her research, Sasha had been perusing various popular accounts on Instagram to see what kind of messages about femininity were being disseminated to the masses. It was a dark and dank rabbit hole, in which she discovered something called the "traditional wife" movement, #tradwife. This movement involved an endless parade of pretty, mostly white women in their twenties and thirties making meals for their hardworking husbands and talking about how they didn't want to "waste fertile years" pursuing college and careers. It was, in a word, horrifying. Then there were the all-in mother accounts featuring women who dedicated every moment of their days to abandoning their own needs and desires in service of their children and husband. Also horrifying. Sasha remembered scribbling down Angeni Luna's name after seeing that her account had a couple million followers. Someone with that much reach was exactly the type of person Sasha had to understand.

"I thought Angeni Luna was a motherhood content person," Sasha said.

"She has two accounts—her Conscious Couples account and her Mother Nurture account," Daphne said.

"I'm sorry, but you *do* sound like quite the disciple."

Daphne sighed and shook her head. "Whatever. I like her. I like what she has to say. It resonates with me."

Sasha looked at Jay, and he gave her a smile and a shrug.

"Happy wife, happy life, am I right?" he said.

"You're a good man, Jay," Sasha said.

"Wait, did she tell you about the giant tub?" he asked.

"I haven't told her about the giant tub," Daphne said.

"What giant tub?" Sasha asked.

"Oh shit," Jay said. He stood and set his bowl of chili on the coffee table. "You gotta see it to believe it."

He started walking down the hall, and Daphne got up to follow him. Sasha, behind the two of them, assumed they were going to the bathroom—giant tub?—but Jay went toward the garage door. He opened it, switched on the light, and said, "Ta-da!"

Sasha peered around Daphne to see a giant inflatable tub in the middle of the garage. So that was why their cars were parked out front.

"I don't get it," Sasha said.

Her first thought was that it was a play pool for the baby, but she couldn't figure out why they had this before they'd even acquired a crib.

"I'm going to have a water birth," Daphne said. "At home."

Sasha must have still looked confused, because Jay jumped in to clarify: "She's going to have our baby in this tub."

Sasha looked at her sister. "You serious?"

"I've done my research, and it's what I want to do," Daphne said. Sasha could tell by the tone of her voice and the way she jutted her chin slightly upward that there was no changing her mind.

"It's because of Angelini Luna," Jay said.

"Angeni," Daphne corrected.

"Is it safe?" Sasha asked.

"Of course it's safe. It's childbirth. It's a very natural process if people would let it be," Daphne said. She sounded rehearsed, unlike herself. Sasha knew she had to tread lightly. Her sister could be very stubborn.

"Are you going to have a midwife or whatever?" Sasha asked.

"Yes, we have someone," Daphne said.

"Daph found her on the internet," Jay said, dubious.

"Does Mom know?" Sasha asked.

Sasha knew there was no way their mother would agree with this.

"I haven't told her yet," Daphne said.

Jay couldn't suppress a laugh. "I hope I'm involved in that convo."

"This really isn't that crazy of a thing. Women do it all the time," Daphne said.

Sasha went to the giant tub, lifted a leg up and over the side, and stepped into it.

"Angeni Luna had a water birth," Jay said.

"If you're interested, I'll send you the birth video when she releases it. You'll see how beautiful it can be," Daphne said.

Sasha walked a lap in the tub and then climbed out. Then she said what she knew Daphne wanted to hear: "Sure, yeah, send it to me."

~

While Jay did the dishes in the kitchen, Sasha and Daphne sat on the couch, each of them scrolling on their phone. Sasha typed Angeni Luna's name into Instagram. She looked familiar. Sasha was sure she'd come across her before. She didn't appear to be a typical #tradwife, but she had some of their characteristics. She was a pretty white woman who looked to be in her early thirties. She spoke reverently of her husband, Erik, a very good-looking man by conventional standards. Clearly, Angeni Luna worked, though. With just a few taps, Sasha could see that she had somewhat of a social media empire with @conscious.co.official and @mother.nurture.official. Her link tree showed various course offerings and workshops, things she was selling to make enough money to live on a large amount of land on Bainbridge Island. Sasha guessed that had piqued Daphne's interest—the fact that Angeni Luna was a local, just across Puget Sound from Seattle.

Many of the posts showcased a kind of homesteading lifestyle, a glamorization of a slower pace and deep connection to nature. That all seemed well and good, in theory, though Sasha was always skeptical. She'd learned about tradwives who had this type of lifestyle, and their days were so occupied with making cheese and dusting baseboards with cloths—never paper towels—that they simply did not have time to think critically about the larger world. It was pitched as "wholesome," but ultimately supported a patriarchal agenda.

Angeni Luna was obviously obsessed with her baby, who had been born the previous month. This must have also appealed to Daphne—the nearness of their due dates, the parallelism of their paths. There were lots of posts about attachment parenting, which also concerned Sasha. She'd been following the resurgence of attachment parenting, seeing it as similar to the tradwife movement in that it encouraged women to put so much focus on caretaking that they had no choice but to sacrifice any other pursuit. Was this what her sister wanted, a life dedicated to making baby purees from scratch and washing cloth diapers? If that was what she wanted, could Sasha support it?

"Have you thought any more about if you'll go back to work after having the baby?" Sasha asked. She couldn't help herself.

Daphne looked up from her phone and sighed. "I don't know. I'll have to feel it out, I guess. Day care would be so expensive, and I'm pretty sure I'm going to want to be with the baby, you know?"

Sasha didn't know, but she nodded.

"I know you probably don't agree," Daphne said.

Sasha shrugged. "I just want you to be happy."

That was the truth. All her feminist theories fell by the wayside when she was sitting there next to her sister. She just wanted her to be happy.

~

Daphne and Jay walked Sasha out to the front porch. Daphne reminded her about the candy bars for the shower, and they made tentative plans to meet up at Kerry Park the weekend after the shower. Daphne and Sasha had always loved that park, with its views of the water and Seattle skyline.

Sasha hugged Jay, then Daphne. Her sister held her longer than usual.

"I love you so much," Daphne said.

Sasha felt Daphne's body tremble against hers. She leaned away to confirm her suspicion: "Are you *crying*?"

Tears started to roll down Daphne's cheeks as she waved Sasha off. "Shut up, it's the hormones!"

"The struggle is real," Jay said, shaking his head.

Sasha put a thumb to her sister's cheek, used it to wipe away the tears.

"I love you, you hormonal weirdo," Sasha said.

They all started laughing, though tears were still rolling down Daphne's cheeks.

"Sister date at Kerry Park, okay?" Daphne said. "Don't flake."

"I won't. I promise!"

But the Kerry Park date never happened. It rained the weekend after the baby shower, so they postponed the meetup. Neither of them firmed up a reschedule date as a few weeks passed with Sasha busy in her world of academia and Daphne busy in her world of impending motherhood. Then this terrible thing happened, and Sasha would never see Daphne ever again.

Chapter 5

Gwen

The day Gwen and June came home from the hospital, Gwen was overcome by the sheer unoriginality of her feelings. She thought what every new mother thinks: *How did they let me leave the hospital with her? I am not equipped for this.* It was an avalanche of self-doubt and dread that, despite its unoriginality, caught her by complete surprise. She had done so much research, so much prep work, for this. She had assumed she would transcend the usual insecurities by being so *ready*. But, of course, the things she was ready for were not the things that had happened.

She had a mental list of everything she needed to recover from a vaginal birth—witch hazel sprays and hemorrhoid cream, just in case; a freezer full of pads to stuff in her underwear; a donut-shaped pillow to sit on while the tender life-delivering parts of herself recovered. She did not know the first thing about recovery from a C-section and hysterectomy.

It hurt to move, but she hadn't wanted to take the painkillers since discovering that they made her extremely constipated. Two days into being home, her incision opened more than it was supposed to. She stared at the ooze and thought of herself as a filleted fish. She needed to go in and have the stitches reinforced.

With all the stress to her body, her milk production waned. Or she assumed it waned. There was no way to tell exactly how much she was producing, which was maddening. Why hadn't anyone invented a pacemaker-type object that could be implanted to measure the ounces? Was she supposed to just trust that her body was meeting her baby's needs? She didn't see how trusting her body would ever be in the cards again.

All she knew for sure was that June was inconsolable. She cried constantly. All mothers said this, but Gwen knew they didn't really mean *constantly*. They were exaggerating. But with June, it was constant.

"Do you think she's hungry?" Jeff asked on one of those first days home.

Do you think your body is failing her . . . again?

That was the question Gwen heard.

~

When they took June to her first pediatrician check-in, the doctor said, "Well, she's not back to her birth weight, and we like to see that by this point."

Gwen had selected this particular pediatrician, this Dr. Goodall (as in Jane), because she had excellent reviews online and was known to be very holistic and pro-breastfeeding and not the type to condemn co-sleeping. But now she hated this doctor.

"Her *birth weight*?" Gwen said, rage simmering inside her body. "You mean the weight she was when they cut her out of my body."

"Hon," Jeff said, putting his hand on her thigh.

Gwen stared at his hand there, atop the same sweatpants she'd been wearing for days. It didn't seem like her thigh, but like someone else's thigh, attached to her body. She stared and stared.

The doctor clasped her hands in her lap and said, "Mom, maybe we need to talk about how *you're* doing."

Mom.

Gwen wanted to slap her.

"I'm fine," Gwen said, nearly spitting the words.

The doctor cocked her head, considering, then took a deep inhale.

"I want you to come back at the end of the week, okay? I want to keep a close eye on June's weight . . . and on you."

Gwen said "Fine" again and stood up, clutching June to her chest. As she stomped—yes, stomped—out of the exam room, she heard Dr. Goodall say to Jeff, "Do you mind hanging back for a second?"

Gwen paced the waiting room with June for five minutes, waiting for Jeff to emerge. She knew they were talking about her—how inept and irrational she was. She had lost control of her own existence ever since they'd wheeled her into that operating room. Since then, she had become someone to be managed, someone who required the imposition of a stranger's expertise.

Jeff looked apologetic when he came out. She didn't ask him what they'd discussed because she didn't want to know.

~

Gwen scoured the internet for tips to improve her milk supply. She ordered a bulk pack of fenugreek tea from Amazon, paid an additional $2.99 to have it delivered the same day. She filled two sixty-four-ounce water bottles and made sure she drank both of them every day. Hydration was key, Google said. She offered June each breast whenever possible, whenever June was awake and alert. When she dozed off, Gwen used the pump, watched how little was trickling out through the tubes, furious with herself. Other women were producing so much that they had to buy an extra freezer to keep in their garage to store it all. They posted photos of frozen milk pouches literally tumbling out when someone opened the door in search of a popsicle.

Insurance paid for a lactation consultant named Mary to come for a half hour twice a week. Mary was fifty years old and talked very slowly. Gwen couldn't tell if she was talking slowly in an attempt to calm Gwen's noticeably anxious energy or if she was talking slowly because that was just the way she talked. When Gwen said that she didn't think her body was making enough milk, Mary did not disagree. Instead of assuring Gwen that her body was magical and that it knew exactly what to do to nourish June, Mary said, "Give yourself grace, dear. How is your body supposed to focus on producing milk with all you've been through?"

Mary suggested that Gwen consider supplementing with formula. Jeff was sitting on the opposite end of the couch from Gwen when Mary suggested this, and Gwen could see him nodding out of the corner of her eye.

"I'm not doing formula," Gwen said.

It was the first thing she'd said with any kind of conviction in days.

"It's just something to consider," Mary said.

"I've considered it," Gwen said. "I considered it throughout my pregnancy and read every fucking book on the planet and educated myself about every single benefit of breast milk."

"Babe," Jeff said.

"Everyone is acting like I don't know anything," Gwen said.

She stood then, June resting on her bare breasts, her nursing bra folded down over her possibly still-infected incision, and left the room, even though there were ten minutes left in their consultation session.

She didn't want them to see her cry.

She didn't want them to know that she was starting to realize that she actually didn't know anything.

~

It was sometime in the blur of these first days home when Angeni Luna began to feel like a beacon in the darkest night, a friend whispering in her ear, saying, "Dearest, you are her mother. Do not let the medical establishment and your clueless husband lead you astray. You know everything you need to know."

You know everything you need to know.

She began to whisper it to herself like a lullaby to soothe herself when nothing she did seemed to soothe her baby.

Miraculously, by the next appointment with the pediatrician, June had gained weight. The incessant feeding and pumping and fenugreek tea had worked. Gwen had never felt so fulfilled. The rush of dopamine that came with this accomplishment was unlike anything she'd ever felt in her high-achieving life. With just her body, she had corrected their course. June was on her way to thriving, which meant that Gwen was thriving too.

Until she wasn't. Again.

It started with June developing daily diarrhea that had a greenish tint to it. Per Dr. Goodall's instructions, Gwen scooped some of the poop from June's diaper into a Ziploc baggie and brought the sample to the doctor's office.

"You're eating something that doesn't agree with her," Dr. Goodall said.

Because of course it was Gwen's fault. Again.

"Do you drink coffee?" she asked.

Did she drink coffee? Who did this doctor think Gwen was?

"Um, no," Gwen said.

"Good. That's the issue for some moms. The caffeine, the acidity, it doesn't agree with the baby."

No shit, Sherlock, Gwen wanted to say, but instead: "Yeah, I know."

Dr. Goodall gave her a paper that had clearly been xeroxed about a billion times, with the title "Elimination Diet for Breastfeeding Mothers" at the top. The idea was to eliminate one common food culprit at a time, wait awhile to see if symptoms improved, then eliminate another food. This could go on for weeks until the offending food was identified.

"You can start with dairy. For most people, it's dairy."

Gwen thought of all the pizza she'd been consuming. Jeff had been ordering delivery regularly, multiple boxes, so they'd have leftovers for days. She thought of how she'd been starting every day with an organic yogurt smoothie that she'd mistakenly thought was healthy and nourishing. All that protein, all that calcium, all those probiotics. At night, as the sun set and she braced herself for sleepless dark, she dipped her spoon into a carton of ice cream as a sort of salve. It was a reminder that she was capable of experiencing pleasure. Dr. Goodall was reminding her that she was a mother now; pleasure was not a priority.

"Can't I just remove several things at one time instead of doing this drawn-out thing?" Gwen asked.

"You can. You have to consider how limited your diet would be. I know you want to keep breastfeeding, which demands a lot of calories. You have to think about your own health, not just your baby's."

She was using that same tone as when she'd said *Mom, maybe we need to talk about how you're doing.*

"I'm savvy with nutritional stuff. I can figure it out," Gwen said.

"I'm not just talking about physical health."

Gwen felt the rage simmering inside again.

"Thank you for your concern," she said.

She was not thankful at all, but she'd already learned that she had to be calm and smiley for Dr. Goodall, or Dr. Goodall would team up with Jeff to question every single thing she was doing as a mother.

~

That night, another night of half-hour stretches of sleep, Gwen googled recipes while feeding June. She'd decided she'd start by removing dairy, soy, and eggs. "It can't be that hard," she'd told Jeff, who looked skeptical. She used the Notes app in her phone to prepare a grocery list to give him the next day. When she was satisfied with her list, she tapped over to Instagram for her daily visit to the Mother Nurture page and saw that Angeni Luna had posted her birth story. There was an all-caps *TRIGGER WARNING* at the top of the caption with an explanation that said *If natural births disturb you in any way, shape, or form, I encourage you to skip this post and protect your emotional state.*

Gwen did not think she qualified as someone who would be disturbed by a natural birth, so she swiped away the "sensitive content" warning and watched the video. She had watched plenty of natural birth videos during her pregnancy, studying them with the same intensity she'd used to pass the bar exam on the first try.

The video was beautifully edited, nothing like those amateur iPhone videos on YouTube. Angeni Luna described it as "real and raw," but it was only two minutes long, representing just about 0.1 percent of the actual labor (Angeni Luna said it had been about twenty hours from first contraction to delivery). Still, it was enthralling—the close-ups of the pain on Angeni Luna's face, her eyes closed, her skin covered in a sheen of sweat, as she crouched on all fours in her giant birthing tub, her head resting on its edge. Her husband was behind her in the tub, his arms wrapped around her middle, his face contorted in a pain that mirrored hers. They cut to her still in the tub but squatting, her husband still behind her, his palms pressing into her thighs. Her breasts and her vulva were blurred in accordance with social media policies. After the next cut, she was there with the baby in her arms at some undefined period of time later. Angeni and the baby were both clean and calm, looking as if they had not been through any kind of trauma at all.

Gwen didn't realize that she was crying until she heard a voice, seemingly from another dimension: "You okay?"

Jeff was standing in the doorway, in his suit, which was extremely confusing until Gwen realized that it was no longer the middle of the night but the early morning. June was asleep on her chest, undisturbed by her mother's sobbing. Gwen was starting to realize that this was motherhood—giving every part of yourself to your child while they were completely oblivious to your sacrifice.

She wiped the tears from her cheeks and sat up straighter in bed, only then noticing that she had been in an awkward position all these hours, her back hunched, neck cricked.

"Where are you going?" she asked him, trying her very best to sound sane.

He looked at her like she was not sane at all.

"I'm going to work," he said. "Remember?"

She tried to laugh it off, playfully face-palmed herself. Of course he was going to work. They had been talking about this day—his first day back—for the past couple of weeks. His law firm had been progressive in offering him a month of leave—double what most companies offered, if they offered anything at all—and now it was time for him to return. She envied him, his ability to just go to this other place and dedicate his thoughts to this other thing.

"I remembered. I was just . . . not thinking straight."

He glanced at the phone in her lap.

"What were you looking at? Why are you crying?"

"It's nothing," she said. "I'm just emotional these days. Hormones and all that."

She wasn't sure why she couldn't be honest with him. They had always been so honest. She knew it would create a divide between them, this hiding of the person she'd become, but she thought that showing the person she'd become would create a divide too. There seemed to be no winning.

He came closer, peered at the phone. The video of Angeni Luna's home birth was still playing on a repeated loop.

He sat on the edge of the bed with a sigh.

"Hon," he said. "You can't be doing this to yourself."

She didn't want to resume crying, but she couldn't help herself.

"Maybe you need to talk to someone?" he suggested. "Or weren't you going to do a support group for new moms or something?"

She *had been* going to do a support group for new moms. She'd identified a popular one—there was a waiting list because they insisted on keeping the group to just ten mothers "dedicated to fostering intimacy"—and enrolled when she was halfway through her pregnancy. She'd envisioned herself showing up and serving as a sort of role model for the other moms, who would be emotional and harried and desperate for guidance. She would be the leader, the mother of all mothers, the Mother Hen. If she was lucky, a couple of them would become lifelong friends.

She couldn't imagine herself showing up to that group now.

"Or maybe my mom can fly in for a week or two?" he said.

This was an option they had never discussed. She thought about that doctor's advice—"tap into family." Everyone always assumed that people had family nearby, waiting in the wings to offer support and comfort, or at least bring a selection of casseroles. She and Jeff didn't have that. Jeff's parents had divorced when he was young, and he rarely spoke to his father. He was close to his mother, but she was in her seventies and living in a retirement community in Florida, clear across the country.

"You're not calling your mother," Gwen said.

"What about your mom?"

"No," Gwen said without a second thought.

Gwen's father had had a sudden-death heart attack when she was in middle school, and her mother had gone into a reclusive depression from which she'd never emerged. There is so much said about how hard depression is for the person who has it, but so little said about how hard it is for the people who depend on them. Gwen had only known her mother as someone completely self-absorbed, gazing at her own glum navel.

When Gwen was in the hospital after June's delivery, when she felt more fragile and vulnerable than she ever had before, she couldn't deny the craving she felt for her mother. Did every daughter feel this craving? She caved, called her mother, who had done nothing for her during the pregnancy except send a check for a hundred dollars as a shower gift.

"The baby is here *already*?" her mother said, seemingly offended by the news.

Gwen informed her that, yes, the baby had been born early. Then she took a risk by suggesting that her mother come visit. Gwen had visions of her mother transforming into someone she wasn't—someone generous with her time and energy, someone loving and helpful.

"Well, I wasn't expecting the baby to come in *May*."

"Neither was I, Mom."

"I had some days reserved for you in June, but May is just . . . well, it's packed."

"Never mind," she said.

"Maybe—"

"Mom, forget it."

She couldn't handle her mother's rejection, the implication that she was a burden. She wouldn't ask her for anything again—a declaration she renewed with herself anytime her mother let her down. When May turned to June, her mom texted regarding the "days reserved" for Gwen, and Gwen told her not to worry about it, that she was fine. She knew this was what her mother wanted to hear. After her father's death, Gwen had had no choice but to become the self-sufficient overachiever that she still was. Her mother had always praised that—not because she was proud, but because she was off the hook, released from any maternal duty.

There was no other family nearby. Neither Jeff nor Gwen had siblings—a first-date discovery that they'd added to the tally of their similarities. There were some cousins, a smattering, but nobody who was close—location-wise or otherwise. They were on their own. They had always taken pride in being on their own.

Jeff, sweet Jeff, was still trying to come up with a solution.

"What about Deena?"

Deena was Gwen's closest local friend. Her friends from high school and college and law school were scattered across the country. Gwen had met Deena at her first job out of law school, and they'd done dinner and drinks regularly until Deena had her first child and promptly vanished. She surprised Gwen with a text every now and then, but the communication was always sporadic—text conversations begun and then deserted. It wasn't personal, Gwen knew that. This was what happened.

"Deena has a kid of her own, and she's pregnant with another," Gwen said.

Had Deena struggled with new motherhood? Gwen assumed she hadn't, or she would have heard about it, but maybe that was the problem—nobody talked about it. They made blanket statements about being tired and "adjusting to a new norm," but nobody discussed the nitty-gritty. Each woman was wandering into this abyss, thinking that it must not be *that* scary or someone would have warned her. The lack of warning probably wasn't malicious. It was just that the abyss sucked you in, and you lost the ability to track time and organize your thoughts, let alone communicate them to others.

Gwen watched Jeff's eyes go to the clock on the nightstand, a little white clock with bunny ears that someone had bought off their baby registry.

"I'm sorry, hon, I gotta get going," he said. "How about you two go outside at some point today? Fresh air might be good."

Men and their endless solutions. One could never go wrong with fresh air.

"Sure," she said, because what else was there to say?

He kissed her on the cheek, then kissed June on the top of her head, and then he was gone, reentering the real world. A world Gwen thought she'd never again inhabit.

~

It was weird with Jeff back to work. Consumed in her bubble with June, Gwen hadn't thought his presence at home was that beneficial, but his absence revealed that she was wrong. The days seemed longer without an adult in the vicinity to inquire about her well-being or hold June while Gwen went to the bathroom. With each sunrise, she felt panic, wondering how the two of them could possibly get through another day—the crying, the feedings, the unpredictable naps. Gwen could not follow that basic advice and "sleep when the baby sleeps." Whenever June nodded off, Gwen was afraid to close her own eyes, afraid to sink into a peaceful slumber only to be awakened minutes later by a jarring shriek. She could not let herself relax. She was always bracing for the next moment requiring her to tend to June. It was relentless in a way nothing in her life had ever been relentless before. There were no breaks to look forward to, no daydreams of rejuvenation to sustain her. She would never be truly alone again. That was what it felt like. Jeff would tell her that wasn't true, that these were the hardest days, but he didn't know. Mothers are never truly alone again. Physically, yes, at some point. But a child will forever consume so much space in other ways.

Gwen started to check the Mother Nurture page several times a day. Angeni Luna had started doing these "Ask me anything" stories, inviting followers to send in their queries for her to respond to, and Gwen couldn't get enough.

ASK ME ANYTHING

did u vaccinate freya

I know this is a controversial topic
and I encourage all mothers to
trust their intuition. At the thought
of doctors putting needles into my
newborn daughter, I had a full-body
visceral response and that response
was NO. Absolutely not. I am open
to changing my mind at a later date,
but this is what my inner wisdom is
telling me right now.

Gwen looked down at June, sleeping on her right breast, nipple still in her mouth. Gwen hadn't even thought about the needles put into June's newborn body. She had been unconscious in the ICU when the doctors did whatever they did to June. Jeff wasn't the type to challenge authority. He would have agreed to whatever the doctors presented as the norm. Gwen hadn't planned *not* to vaccinate June, but she'd planned to ask questions, to perhaps space out the vaccine schedule to avoid any unnecessary overwhelm to June's little body.

She'd already failed at so, so much.

She couldn't stop thinking about her insistence on running during her pregnancy, her dedication to this selfish hobby of hers that might have caused her placenta to detach. Nobody would tell her that was the reason. In fact, they said that it likely was *not* the reason, but "likely" was no comfort to Gwen. In some ways, it was easier to see herself as at fault than accept a reality in which "these things just happen." If it was her fault, it (and other terrible things like it) could be prevented in the future. June, this human being literally attached to her, was like a constant reminder that Gwen was not in control in the ways she thought she was.

ASK ME ANYTHING

how do u and erik nurture
ur relationship now that
Freya is here?

I would be lying if I said it was
easy to maintain a deep partner
connection in the midst of new
parenthood. Since Freya's birth, I
have not been away from her for
more than 5 minutes. Personally, I

> do not understand parents who are anxious to resume date nights and the like. My commitment is to our daughter and ensuring she feels perfectly secure. Erik is supportive of this approach. it means we have less time for each other, but it is also beautiful to miss one's lover at times.

Gwen took mental notes.

Angeni Luna felt like the way back to the type of woman she wanted to be.

~

After Gwen had removed dairy, soy, and eggs from her diet, June was still having green-tinged diarrhea on a daily basis. So Gwen removed the next group of items on the list—gas-producing vegetables. These included broccoli, cauliflower, onions, and green peppers. She didn't eat much of these things, with the exception of onion, which seemed to be in almost any cooked dish. That didn't have a positive effect, either, so she removed all citrus fruits. Still no effect. The last item on the list was tomatoes, which she didn't think could possibly be the problem, but lo and behold, it was. Just a couple of days after Gwen had removed tomatoes, June's poops became a normal color. Gwen felt a rush of accomplishment. She had done it.

"Okay, so no tomatoes," Jeff said as they sat at the dinner table.

He'd been back at work for a few weeks and seemed like his chipper self again.

Gwen could see now that he'd been miserable while he was on paternity leave. She used to be his favorite person, but she'd become terrible to be around.

"That doesn't seem so hard to avoid," he said, shoveling a forkful of pad thai noodles into his mouth.

They were surviving on takeout nearly every night because Gwen still could not bring herself to cook anything. She didn't understand how these other mothers did it. Angeni Luna was simmering tomatoes—tomatoes!—for homemade sauces and making whole roast chickens.

"Avoiding dairy would have been hard, but this seems totally manageable," he said.

Gwen was irritated with his optimism, his sprightly *okay, that's solved* attitude.

"I mean, tomatoes are in a lot of things," she said finally, interrupting his cascade of positive thoughts. "Salsa, marinara sauce, ketchup . . . a lot of things."

Gwen watched him inhale a deep breath, his chest filling and expanding. He set down his fork and looked at her, his eyes pleading with her to *just please stop*.

"I don't know what to do anymore," he said.

As if on cue, June started crying, having woken up from her too-short nap in the swing on the floor. She would only sleep in the swing, going at full speed. The thing required D batteries and burned through a set every two days.

Gwen lifted her out of the swing and got her settled on her lap, unbuttoning the front of her shirt with one hand. She had become an expert at this, at least.

"Did you hear me?" Jeff asked her.

Did she? She didn't know. Had he said something? June latched on to her left breast and began suckling. Gwen stared at her baby's closed eyelids, her long eyelashes. She'd made this child. It shocked her every day.

"Sorry, what?" she said.

He looked at her like *Are you serious?*

"I said I. Don't. Know. What. To. Do. Anymore."

"With what?"

"You," he said.

There it was, finally—irritation. All this time, he'd been too kind, too concerned, too focused on solving her problems. This was what she deserved—his wrath.

"I'm sorry my struggling is so inconvenient for you," she said, her tone completely flat.

He rolled his eyes.

"Don't do that. Come on, hon. We're better than this."

They *were* better than this. Before. In their previous life. That life was over.

"I'm not better than this anymore," she said.

"I think you need to talk to someone. Try the support group. Something. You have to take some initiative to . . . improve things."

"Some *initiative*? You don't think I have enough initiative?"

She raised her eyebrows in genuine curiosity. How did he see her now? As a loser, a failure? What was it, if not initiative, that motivated her to tend to their daughter's every need, with so few seconds between the expression of that need and Gwen's maternal response?

"I just think you'll feel better if you take some steps to . . . feel better."

"You think I'll feel better if I take some steps to feel better."

He sighed, flustered. "You know what I mean."

"I don't know if I do."

"This is a hard phase. Everyone said it would be hard. This is the time to call in as much support as we can."

She resented the "we." He didn't seem to be calling in support. He was telling her to call it in, telling her to *take initiative*.

"What I'm going through is normal," she said.

He put his two hands up, palms facing her, as if showing her he didn't have a weapon.

"I didn't say it wasn't. Of course it's normal. That's my point."

"Well, you seem to think there are steps I should be taking that I'm not taking."

"This isn't a critique, Gwen."

She felt a chill at the mention of her own name. Not *sweetie* or *hon*, but Gwen.

"For one, I think this breastfeeding thing is too much," he said.

This breastfeeding thing.

"There is no shame in stopping. It doesn't work out for some people. You've lost too much weight."

She had. She was below her prepregnancy weight.

"It's working fine now. I just can't eat tomatoes. You said yourself that tomatoes aren't that hard to avoid."

He sighed again. "I just mean this whole process has been . . . a lot. It's taken a lot out of you, figuring out this diet thing. Nursing her all the time. If we do formula, I can give her some bottles at night, and—"

Formula? Did he not know her at all?

"We're not doing that," she said.

He threw his hands in the air dramatically, then let them fall onto the table with a thud.

"This is what I'm saying. I don't know what to do anymore. You don't want my opinion. You act like my thoughts mean nothing."

They did mean nothing.

"I have no say. You are clearly overwhelmed and having a hard time, and I have no say. You just want to dig your hole and sit in it."

"Dig my hole and sit in it? Is that what you call taking care of our daughter?"

"Don't do that. Don't twist what I'm saying. We could adjust certain things, like the breastfeeding, and still be taking care of our daughter just fine."

"Really? Did you read all the same books as me when I was pregnant?"

He stood from the table, took his dish to the sink, then started walking down the hallway, shaking his head.

"Where are you going?"

"There's no point in talking to you," he said from the hallway, his voice getting farther away. "You are hell bent on suffering. It's like you think that makes you a better mother."

She heard their bedroom door slam. She had never heard him slam a door before.

She switched June to the other breast. She was becoming so much more efficient at feeding lately. They finally had a rhythm. This wasn't suffering, was it? If it was, maybe Jeff was right. Maybe it did make her a better mother.

Chapter 6

Angeni Luna

When you look back, will you regret the time you spent with your babies or the time you spent away from them?

This is so good. I can't imagine being away from my babies. So happy I get to be home with them

💯 will never regret the time I spend with them, even on the hard days

Thank you for this reminder 🙏 You are a beautiful giver of perspective

Anytime I'm at the end of my rope, I remind myself that I'll miss this time one day. We mothers are so lucky

~

It had been two days since Angeni released the birth video, which was one of her most popular posts to date. Engagement was up dramatically. In forty-eight hours, the Mother Nurture account had gained ten thousand followers.

After watching comments come in on her latest post, she tapped over to check her email and saw that a literary agent had reached out to inquire about her interest in writing a book. The world needs content like yours, reminding all of us of the sacredness of motherhood in this wounded world.

Angeni had used those exact words before—*the sacredness of motherhood in this wounded world.* This agent had clearly done her homework. Angeni immediately googled the agent's name—Elizabeth Conroy—and discovered she was quite successful and well known, representing a roster of self-help and nonfiction writers who had become household names. This wasn't a scam; it was real.

A book.

Angeni Luna had considered a book, of course. While it was true that many people didn't read anymore and Instagram would remain her main vehicle for communicating her ideas, a book would lend her a certain amount of credibility. A published book was evergreen, inarguable proof of making it in the world. Currently under her name on Instagram was the title *public figure*. If she wrote a book, she could change that to *author*. That seemed more prestigious, more respectable. It would be a clapback to the haters.

Angeni was sitting in the rocking chair in their family bedroom, Freya on her breast. She tried to restrict her phone time to moments when Freya's attention was on feeding and Angeni could hold the phone behind the baby's head so she was blissfully unaware of the presence of this technology. To help protect against electromagnetic fields, Angeni had placed special harmonizing stickers on everyone's phones on The Land. When she'd given one to Sitka, explaining that it was a requirement for their living situation, Sitka had looked as if she'd handed her bird droppings. She'd had to explain that the stickers were infused with semiprecious gemstones emitting negative ions to help balance out the positive ions from phones. Angeni didn't know if it was perfectly safe, but it was safer than nothing. On her mental list of topics to bring forward on Mother Nurture, EMFs were near the top. She knew posting about them would get lots of eye roll emojis, but she didn't care. People should know.

Freya turned her head, as if trying to see what was behind her that had her mother's attention. Angeni put her phone down on the floor. At some point, Freya would become aware of the phone, of course. Angeni and Erik had already talked about how to navigate this. They planned to refer to the phone as a "work tool" so that Freya did not associate it with entertainment or stimulation.

"Sitka," Angeni called out.

She needed to discuss this book possibility with everyone as soon as possible.

When Sitka didn't immediately appear, Angeni called out again: "Sitka!"

As the last syllable was still vibrating in Angeni's throat, Sitka appeared in the doorway.

"Yeah?" she said, eyebrows raised in expectation.

"Sorry, I'm just a little excited. Do you think you can gather everyone for a family meeting in the kitchen?" Angeni asked.

"Sure," Sitka said. "Everything okay?"

"I have news."

From the rocking chair, Angeni heard the sound of her people gathering in the kitchen. She let Freya finish, watched the nipple pop out of her mouth as milk trickled down from the corners. It was the most satisfying thing to see her daughter so satisfied.

She rebuttoned the opening of her dress and went to the kitchen, holding Freya against her chest. When she entered, everyone went silent, all eyes on her. They were all seated in chairs around the island. Angeni sat in her own chair, and Sitka approached.

"Do you want me to hold her?" Sitka asked.

Freya answered for them, smiling at just the sight of Sitka's face. Her drowsy milk-drunkenness gave way to pure, ecstatic joy. Angeni nodded to Sitka, and Sitka lifted the baby against her chest. She started pacing the length of the kitchen, bouncing Freya in her arms.

"So Sitka says there's news?" Aurora said, noticeably rising from her seat. Aurora was always so easily excitable. "It's the birth video, huh? Did Oprah call you?"

Angeni watched Sitka pause her pacing to look at Aurora with the same pity or disdain she'd shown during the Abraham Lincoln debacle.

"No, not Oprah," Angeni said with a laugh.

Sitka resumed pacing.

"But," Angeni said, "I did get an email from a literary agent."

Aurora nodded enthusiastically, like *And? And?*

"That's great, babe," Erik chimed in.

"So great," Matt added.

"She asked if I was interested in writing a book. She said she can think of several editors at publishing houses who would be clamoring for it."

That was the word she'd used—*clamoring*.

"Wow," Sitka said, stopping again.

Was Sitka genuinely impressed, or just surprised? Angeni couldn't tell. She was bothered by how much she wanted the girl to be impressed. There was something about Sitka that seemed incapable of being impressed with anything.

"I know, it's crazy," Angeni said, her eyes locked with Sitka's. "I never would have thought I'd write a book."

Though she had thought this, had always known it in her bones. She was just waiting for the right time, the right opportunity, a calling from the universe.

"You are made for this," Aurora said, in alignment with Angeni's own thoughts.

"Just incredible," Erik said. "This will take you to a whole new level."

They were all talking over each other. Angeni felt like she was levitating.

"Did you email her back?" Matt asked.

"Not yet," Angeni said. "I wanted to talk to you all first."

"Us?" Aurora asked.

Sitka stepped away from the island, went to the giant beanbag cushion on the back wall of the kitchen. She lay down on it, held Freya up above her, arms outstretched. They were both smiling, giggling.

"Well, yes," Angeni said. "Because if I'm going to pursue writing a book, that's a huge time commitment, and I'll need the support of my community."

"We got you, babe," Erik said.

"Anything you need, Ang," Matt said.

"We are here to support you," Aurora said.

"I don't want to get ahead of myself. I haven't even responded to the agent yet, but I just want you all to know that I realize this would be a community effort."

"Totally," Erik said. He looked each of them in the face before saying, "And I think I can say, on behalf of our community, that we are here to do whatever we can to enable you to do this."

"This is what community's about," Jer said with his usual solemnity.

"Watch us rise to the occasion," Matt said with a theatrically deep voice.

Angeni laughed.

"Are you guys sure?" she asked.

They all nodded.

Angeni looked at Sitka in the beanbag chair. She had yet to say anything about the news. Angeni wondered if she didn't yet feel like one of them, part of the group, with a right to an opinion.

"The thing is, I do want the projects on The Land to continue, and I know you guys are knee deep in those," she said, looking at Erik, Matt, and Jer.

"I can help with Freya," Aurora offered, raising her hand high in the air like a kid in school.

Sitka was still not looking at Angeni.

"Thank you, Ror," she said. "Freya is so lucky to have such a loving auntie. I was thinking Sitka may help too. Freya seems to love both of you so much."

Sitka finally looked up, seemingly surprised to be included in the conversation.

"Oh," she said. "Yeah. I can help."

Angeni noticed Aurora's shoulders slump slightly. Always adept at reading a room and soothing hurt feelings when she saw them, she said, "Ror, maybe you can take on more of the meal prep and cooking I've been doing. We can come up with weekly menus together."

Her eyes lit up. "That sounds great."

"This feels good," Angeni said. "I think I'll respond to the literary agent later today."

"So happy for you, babe," Erik said.

She gave Erik a loving smile. He was so devoted to her. Her happiness was his. She felt sad for women who settled for anything less than this.

"Sitka, do you mind joining us at the island?" Angeni asked. "I think we need a community inhale."

They did these every now and then, when discussing any big decisions related to their lives on The Land.

Sitka pushed herself up with one hand from the beanbag chair, holding Freya against her with the other hand. She retook her seat at the island, Freya in her lap. The six of them held hands around the island and closed their eyes.

"Okay, everyone, let's exhale everything that isn't serving us," Angeni said.

They all exhaled loudly, some of their exhales transforming into drawn-out sighs.

"And now let's take a big inhale of all that is possible for us."

On cue, they all inhaled and held it for their usual count of eight. Then they opened their eyes and exhaled, their breaths mingling, a perceptible electricity in the air.

~

It was a rare sunny day, a break from the usual misty gray. It was as if the clouds had parted in celebration of Angeni's book prospects. She was already thinking of the structure of the book, the chapters she would create. She was already imagining the glowing reviews, the expansion of her online community.

Just as she finished an email to the literary agent, suggesting they set up a phone call to talk, Sitka came to retrieve Freya for their daily nature walk.

"Mind if I join you two today?" Angeni asked.

Sitka shrugged as she reached for the baby. "Sure."

The Land was eleven acres of forest, deep and dense enough to get lost in. Angeni loved this about it—the way it offered endless exploration, new discoveries. There were streams running through it, thin trickles of water in dryer months, gushing rivers after intense rainstorms. There were a few well-trodden paths weaving through the trees, foot-wide trails to keep them on course. She couldn't wait for Freya to walk these trails, to touch the blades of grass, to pick the flowers in spring, to search the branches overhead for nests. She couldn't wait to teach her daughter about all her favorite herbs and plants—motherwort, calendula, chamomile, lemon balm, feverfew. It was the ultimate gift to her daughter, this land. On it, Angeni could offer Freya an entire life.

"It's so beautiful today," Angeni said, face to the sky, skin absorbing the sun.

"It is," Sitka said.

Freya was in the wrap on Angeni's chest, and she started to whine. She wasn't due for another feed, but Angeni figured she needed comfort.

"Stop for a few?" Angeni said.

They sat on a log, a fallen pine tree that Erik and the guys would need to clear at some point. Tending to The Land was a full-time job, and without Erik, Matt, and Jer, Angeni could not have this life, this beauty. She reminded herself of this whenever she felt stress or resentment creep in over her role as the primary earner.

Angeni removed Freya from the wrap and lifted her shirt so the baby could rest directly on her skin. Freya calmed immediately. Sitka leaned back, tilted her face to the sky, also absorbing the sun.

"Are you happy here?" Angeni asked her.

Angeni had started to become self-conscious that Sitka wasn't happy. She'd become so quiet, so inward. She always seemed to be thinking about something, in another realm just out of reach.

"Me?" Sitka asked, looking over her shoulder, as if there were someone else with them.

Angeni laughed. "Yes, you!"

"Oh, sorry," Sitka said. "Am I happy?"

Angeni nodded.

"Yeah. I mean, I'm kind of taking it all in, you know?"

"I guess I just hope you don't feel like you're just my helper or something. I care about you. I value your presence," Angeni said.

"Oh, well, I appreciate that," Sitka said.

"You're so good with Freya. Do you want to be a mother someday?"

Sitka's eyes went wide at the question. "Oh, I don't know."

"Really? You're a natural."

"Did you always know you wanted to be a mother?"

"Not always, no," Angeni said. "I had to go through several stages of healing before I felt the pull."

There was more of a story to tell here, but Angeni wasn't ready to tell it to Sitka. It was a story of her own childhood. It was a story of an ache, a longing, to know what the mother-child bond was supposed to be.

"Your posts make it sound like you always knew, like it was your destiny," Sitka said.

"It was my destiny," Angeni said. "It just took me a while to realize it."

~

They sat in silence for a few minutes while Freya's tiny hands pressed on Angeni's breasts.

"Can I ask you something?" Sitka said.

"Anything," Angeni said.

"Do you ever worry about how your messages affect people?"

"What do you mean?"

"You have these followers who think you're, like, a god. They live their lives according to what you say. Doesn't that worry you?"

Angeni wasn't sure what she was getting at. She loved that she was influencing people to enrich their relationships. She loved how mothers turned to her for ways to better connect with their babies.

"Why would it worry me?"

"I don't know. Not everyone can . . . or should . . . do things the way you do, right?"

Angeni shrugged. "I don't know. I believe pretty strongly in what I do. I think I have every right to share what I've come to see as true."

"You do have every right," Sitka said. "I guess I just wonder if you feel a certain responsibility to people?"

"Responsibility? I see it as my responsibility to share what I know, to share my truth. It is the responsibility of others to receive it as needed."

Sitka nodded. She said, "I see," but she seemed distressed somehow. A silence followed, and it was tense, awkward. Angeni felt the need to shift the energy, so she stood. Freya was still against her bare chest, not feeding, just playing with her breasts.

"I have an idea," Angeni said. "The light is so beautiful right now. Maybe you can take some photos of Freya and me?"

Sitka had assumed the photographer duties on a couple of occasions before. She shrugged and said, "Sure."

"Are you okay if I'm naked?" Angeni asked her.

"Sure," Sitka said again. She had seen Angeni in various states of undress on a daily basis, after all.

Angeni handed Freya to Sitka and took off her socks and shoes. She stepped out of her leggings and pulled her shirt down over her hips, letting it fall to the ground. Though it was sunny, there was still a chill in the air, and goose bumps dotted her skin as she stood in her underwear before casting that aside too. She watched Sitka's eyes scan her body, the pooch of her belly where Freya had resided all those months, the full bush of hair beneath that.

Angeni extended her arms to receive Freya, unsnapped the baby's onesie and cloth diaper, and set them on the ground next to her own clothes. She held her naked baby over her head.

"Do you have your phone, or do you want to use mine?" Angeni asked.

Sitka took out her phone and started taking photos.

~

That night, Angeni, Erik, and Freya nestled together in the family bed—Angeni in the middle, the baby on her right side, Erik on her left. She'd decided that having the baby between them was too risky. Erik could roll on top of her. He was a typical man when it came to sleep—it took him approximately thirty seconds to fall into a deep slumber, and nothing short of a significant earthquake would wake him.

Angeni considered mothers to be like the orca whales that swam the waters around their island. They could selectively shut off one hemisphere of their brains to sleep, while the other hemisphere was awake and propelling their bodies through the ocean. The people who condemned co-sleeping were idiots. Mothers and babies had been sleeping together, body to body, since the beginning of time. It wasn't dangerous—it was natural, beautiful. She would never roll on top of Freya, never suffocate her. It just wasn't possible. Part of her maternal brain was always on watch.

Freya finished feeding from Angeni's right breast, so Angeni rolled on her side to offer the left breast. As she did, Erik rolled, too, spooning her body with his own. He kissed her neck, her earlobe. She used to love when he kissed her earlobes. It always awakened desire, sent a pulse of energy down her body. Now, though, it felt strange and unwelcome, as if he were kissing some completely unerogenous area—her nostrils, her eyelids. She shrugged a shoulder up toward her ear so it came in contact with his face, nudging him away.

"I miss you," he whispered.

"I know," she said.

Instead of leaning back into him, just a bit, she leaned forward into their daughter, stroking Freya's head as she suckled. As long as Freya was feeding, Angeni had reason to keep her husband at bay.

He wasn't taking the hint, though. He moved closer to her again, and this time, she could feel his erection at her back. It was embarrassing how men's needs were so obvious, so *out there*. It was infuriating that they felt no shame while women suppressed their every urge and desire in a never-ending quest to be seen as decent and good.

He kissed her neck, and she couldn't help but laugh. It tickled.

"You're laughing at me. That's not a good sign," he said. He sounded sad, but she could feel his lips part in a smile against her neck.

"I'm sorry," she said.

"Do you miss me?" he asked.

It had been a while since they'd been intimate. How long exactly, she didn't know. A month? Two? Whenever the last time was, it had been in the wee hours of the morning and obligatory. She was trying to be the woman she showed to the world—a woman who respected her husband's masculinity, who encouraged him to be his full self. But the truth was that his full self was a burden. She didn't have any parts of herself left to give. It wasn't fair to him, but it wasn't fair to her either.

"I've just been so busy with Freya and—"

He shushed her lovingly and kissed her neck again.

"You're such a wonderful mother," he said.

This was his version of foreplay now. Or a version he was trying out for her benefit.

"Sitka took some beautiful photos of us today—Freya and me," Angeni said.

He kept kissing her neck. "Oh yeah?"

"We were both naked."

"You and Sitka?"

She laughed, reached over her shoulder to playfully hit him in the head.

"Me and Freya."

"Oh, I was gonna say."

"I'll post them tomorrow, the photos."

"I can't wait."

"Did you want them to be of me and Sitka?" she asked, laughing to signal that she was joking, though she did wonder. Sitka was objectively gorgeous.

"I'd much prefer you and Freya, babe," he said. "I can't wait to see them."

Freya pulled off Angeni's nipple and tipped onto her back, eyes closed, sleeping. There was no real reason Angeni could not tend to her husband now.

"I know it's been hard to connect lately," she said, still curled on her side, his erection still against her back.

"We knew it would be this way. You are in an entirely new role. It's an adjustment," he said.

He was so kind. He knew all the right things to say. They had talked about this so much before having Freya—this phase when they would feel distant from each other, when their relationship would be challenged in ways it never had been before.

"Maybe we can start with a date night," he said. "Baby steps."

Had he not seen her "Ask me anything" story the other day? She was explicitly opposed to this "date night" concept, this rush for couples to get back to their time together and put their own needs first when their babies were still so little.

"I don't feel right being away from her," she said, though perhaps the true, full sentence was *I don't feel right being away from her to be with you.*

"But she's away from you at night sometimes," he said. "With Sitka."

"That's different."

"Why?"

There was no good answer. It wasn't different, not really. It was just that she was sleeping in those times of separation. She could wake up the next morning with the baby placed back beside her and pretend like it had never happened.

"I just feel like when I'm awake, I should be engaged with her."

"You *are* engaged with her."

She could hear what he wasn't saying: *I need you to be engaged with me too.*

"Sitka takes her on nature walks, so you have that time away from her too," he said.

"For, like, fifteen minutes." Her tone was argumentative, and she couldn't help it.

"I would take fifteen minutes alone with you," he said. "I'm easy. It doesn't take much."

She imagined the rushed sex, his body hot and sweaty with pent-up need, thrusting faster than she liked in the interest of time. It would be nothing like the long, tantric sex they had enjoyed before Freya, whiling away entire afternoons in each other's arms, making a game of tallying orgasms.

"I went with them today. On the walk. I go with them sometimes. It's not always just Sitka and Freya."

He sighed. "You don't have to defend yourself, babe."

She rolled over to face him now, took his face in her hands, pressed her lips against his. She didn't feel anything. It was like kissing a distant relative.

"I'm sorry," she said. Because she was. Of course he wanted more. He missed her. She should choose to see it as sweet instead of bothersome.

"You don't have to apologize," he said. "I just crave you a lot lately."

"I know."

His hands stroked her bare belly, then moved up to her breasts, the very breasts that had just been feeding their child. She envied his ability to compartmentalize, to forget about all her motherhood duties and see her just as a desirable woman.

"I'm so tired," she told him.

It was so trite, becoming this person. Shameful too. People turned to her for guidance on creating an ongoing spark with their partner, and here she was, extinguishing the fire she'd tended for so many years, snuffing it out as if it were nothing. Erik could easily call her out on her hypocrisy, but he wasn't mean spirited that way. Maybe he would be, eventually, if she let this go on too long.

"Maybe we can talk about this in our next State of the Union," she said.

They hadn't been keeping up with their weekly State of the Unions like they had before having Freya. It was something she had presented to her followers as a nonnegotiable, but, it turned out, it was very much negotiable. Forgotten, in fact.

"Okay," he said, and kissed her on the nose.

He took his hands off her body, and she felt her body relax, finally. He rolled onto his back and stared at the ceiling.

"I feel like I could lose you," he said, to the ceiling instead of her face.

"Lose me?"

He nodded but didn't look at her.

"You have Freya and now this book project."

"*Potential* book project."

"It'll happen. It's meant to be," he said. "And . . . I don't know. How could you possibly have space for me? How could I even expect you to?"

She didn't know what to say. His concerns were valid.

"It won't always be like this."

She spoke with certainty, though she wasn't at all sure it was true. It felt quite possible that it would always be like this.

"I shouldn't need your reassurance. I should be more emotionally mature than that," he said. "But thank you."

"Needing reassurance isn't emotionally immature, silly," she said. "It's human."

He took her hand in his and squeezed.

"I love you," he said.

He kissed the corner of her mouth and then rolled over on his side, away from her. From the rustling of the sheets, she knew he was tending to his own needs. She had given him no other choice.

Chapter 7

Britt

When Britt was ten, a new man came into her mom's life. Bill had mysteriously vanished. Or rather, it was mysterious at the time. Britt found out years later that he'd ended up in prison for sideswiping and injuring a bicyclist while driving his station wagon with a blood alcohol level of 0.30.

At first when Bill stopped coming around, Britt thought it was because her mom had finally had enough. Despite all evidence to the contrary, Britt persisted in seeing her mother as a smart and capable person. She needed to see her that way. Accepting the reality of her mom's ineptitude, not only as a mother but also as an adult in the world, presented a terrifying question for a ten-year-old: What the hell was she supposed to do?

Steve seemed like a decent answer to that question.

~

Britt and her mom met Steve when their 1978 Oldsmobile Cutlass had broken down yet again, necessitating a trip to the auto repair shop, where all the guys knew Britt's mom and knew how shamelessly she would flirt in attempts to get a deal. Occasionally, she managed to negotiate down a price, but she never got anything for free. She wasn't beautiful enough, or the men weren't dumb enough.

On this particular day, Britt watched her mom step into her very best dress, a pink flowery number with buttons up the front that barely closed over her midsection. She wasn't fat, but she was bloated from drinking more in the weeks since Bill had vanished from their lives. Britt watched the way the dress pulled at the buttons, giving glimpses of her mom's skin beneath. She was embarrassed on her mom's behalf, embarrassed by her mother's apparent unawareness of how she'd let herself go, gradually and then all at once.

Steve was new at the auto repair shop. He couldn't have known why his boss groaned audibly when Britt's mom walked in with her freshly glossed lips, her boobs in a too-small bra, busting out of the top of her dress. Even if they'd warned him, he would have still been kind. That was just how he was.

Britt's mom seized upon his newness, walking right up to him and sticking out her hand to introduce herself: "Hi there. I'm Monica Taylor. I don't believe I've seen your handsome face before."

Britt lingered in the background while her mom performed her usual sob story about how she was a single mother and this was their only car and if she didn't have a car, she couldn't get to her grocery store job, which was six miles from their apartment, too far to walk on a daily basis.

Steve nodded along while Britt's mom talked. He furrowed his brow in what appeared to be genuine empathy.

"Well, why don't we just look at what's going on with the car and then talk," he said.

Her mother swooned, taking Steve's hand in hers, squeezing it with a desperate kind of affection as she said, "Thank you, thank you."

"Is this little girl yours?" Steve asked, peering over Britt's mom's shoulder, his eyes meeting Britt's.

"Oh, yes, that's Brittney," her mother said. She beamed with pride, the way other mothers did naturally but she only did as part of a performance for a man.

"Hey there, Brittney," Steve said, giving her a wave.

Britt waved back, but she was dubious. She had no reason to trust any man. All the ones who had entered her mother's orbit were addicts with anger issues. Steve didn't seem like that. His demeanor was gentle and kind. Some of them were like that at first, before they got comfortable enough to be their terrible true selves.

"Say hello, Britt," her mom said with the giggly laugh that Britt only heard in these situations. Britt hated that laugh, the fakeness of it.

"She waved," Steve said. "She doesn't have to say hello if she doesn't want to."

"Well, it's kind of rude, in my opinion," Britt's mom said.

Britt rolled her eyes. Her mom did this sometimes—criticized Britt in front of people, as if to demonstrate her own superiority.

"I was shy like that when I was her age," Steve said.

He gave Britt a wink, and Britt couldn't help but smile.

~

The problem was the transmission. When Steve reported this, Britt's mom nearly collapsed in dramatic agony, saying how she knew the transmission was one of the more costly repairs. Britt saw one of the other guys at the shop watching her display and shaking his head. She tried to catch his eye so she could give him a shrug that said *I know, she's crazy, I'm sorry*. He wouldn't look at her, though.

Steve pulled Britt's mom aside and, in a whispered conversation, agreed to let her pay installments over time. Britt realized later that what had actually happened was that Steve fronted the money for the repair himself, expecting Britt's mom to pay him back in those installments. Britt knew her mother never would have done this. She was the queen of accruing debts. It didn't appear to upset Steve too much, because they started dating. He was the type to forgive and forget. That was the only reason they were able to stay together as long as they did.

~

It wasn't long after they started dating that Britt and her mom were kicked out of their apartment. This wasn't the first time this had happened. Britt was well accustomed to landlords banging on their door, yelling about rent checks, threatening eviction. Britt's mom took advantage of the fact that it was a notoriously long and difficult process to evict someone. This particular landlord did things the old-fashioned way—while they were out, he removed all their belongings from the apartment, placed them on the small strip of browning grass in front of the building, and changed the locks. "Well, fuck," Britt's mom said before calling Steve and asking if they could crash at his place "for a couple days." That couple of days turned into a couple of years, and that couple of years was easily the best of Britt's childhood.

Steve had a small one-story house that he had inherited from his mother, who had also been a single mother and was probably the reason why he took pity on Britt and her mom. His mother had died of lung cancer just a couple of years earlier, and he had framed pictures of her in every room of the house. Britt's mom thought it was weird, but Britt thought it was sweet to have a mother you loved so much that you wanted to see her face at every turn.

The house had two bedrooms, one of which Steve used to store boxes of his mother's belongings that he hadn't sifted through yet. Britt's mom moved her things into Steve's bedroom, and Britt assumed she would have to sleep on the couch in the living room before Steve said, "Don't worry, I'm going to clear out that other room for you." Britt's mom said, "Oh, you don't have to do that," but he insisted. Britt figured it might be an empty promise and told herself not to get her hopes up, but sure enough, by the end of that day, Steve had taken all the boxes to the garage and vacuumed up the dust before presenting the room to Britt.

“We’ll have to get you a proper bed and whatever else tomorrow,” he said, “but I have a blow-up mattress you can use tonight.”

While Britt’s mom got herself settled, unpacking and arranging her things, Steve got Britt settled. He didn’t have an extra set of sheets that would fit the twin-size blow-up mattress, but he gave Britt a blanket and throw pillow from the couch before telling her to sleep well.

“Thanks,” she said.

“You okay?” he asked.

Her unease must have been obvious.

“I just don’t understand, like, why you’re doing this.”

He looked at her, confusion all over his face.

“Nobody’s ever done this for me before.”

He put his hands on his hips like *I’m the new sheriff in town.*

“I’m very sorry to hear that,” he said. “I’m happy to help you feel at home, okay?”

She believed him. He seemed truly happy to help. Years later, she would look back on Steve and identify him as a classic rescuer. It was no wonder he gravitated to Britt and her mom. They needed so much rescuing.

~

Steve’s house was just one street over from Becky’s house, and Britt was so enamored with her new room that she began inviting Becky over instead of just going to Becky’s house. One Saturday, Becky arrived along with her mother, Rainbow. She usually came alone, was old enough to not need an escort, but Rainbow said she’d heard about Steve and wanted to meet him.

“The pleasure is all mine,” Steve said, extending a hand.

Rainbow acknowledged the hand with a nod but proceeded to hug him instead. Her usual greeting. Britt’s mom was sitting on the couch, watching the scene, and Britt caught the look of displeasure on her mother’s face. Of course her mother would be unhappy with Rainbow’s presence. Rainbow was beautiful in ways Britt's mother would never be. She was thin and lithe, her face bare of any makeup yet still glowing.

Rainbow must have sensed the tension, because she said, diplomatically, "Hello there, Monica. How are you today?"

Every muscle in Britt's body tensed as she watched her mother stand and go toward Rainbow. She got unusually close to Rainbow, just a few inches separating their bodies, and said, "Did you need something?"

"Mom, she's just saying hi," Britt said. She was so embarrassed.

"Well, she never came to say hi when we lived at our apartment," Britt's mom said. Then, to clarify: "Before I met Steve."

Britt had explicitly told Becky and Rainbow not to visit their apartment. She'd preferred to live in two separate worlds—the world of their apartment and the world outside it. Steve had arrived and straddled the worlds, serving as a go-between. With him, she felt she had an ally. With him, she felt like she could finally collapse her two identities into one.

"I'm sorry, Monica. I don't believe we were invited before. If I missed an invitation, I truly apologize," Rainbow said. She was her usual unruffled self, her smile as serene as ever.

"Did someone invite you today?" Britt's mom asked.

"Mom!" Britt said, at the same time Steve said, "Mon, it's okay. They're just being neighborly."

"I'm sorry—I'll go," Rainbow said. "Bec, do you still want to stay and play?"

Becky was clinging to her mother's side now. She grasped her mother's hands, and Britt stared at the way their fingers interlaced. Britt's mother had never held her hand like that.

"I don't know," Becky said.

She gave Britt a look, telling her with her eyes that she felt uncomfortable.

"You can always come to our house later if you want, Britt," Rainbow said.

"Maybe today isn't the best day," Britt's mom said.

The room grew quiet enough for all of them to hear Steve sigh. It was the first time Britt understood that her mother exhausted him too.

"Sorry," Britt muttered to Becky.

Rainbow knelt down so she was eye level with Britt and whispered, "There's nothing to be sorry for. We will see you soon."

And then they left.

Britt's mom made a show of stomping off to the master bedroom, and Steve went after her, closing the door behind him. Britt pressed her ear to the door and held her breath in anticipation of Steve telling her mother that she had to move out. Britt was prematurely furious with her mother for ruining this good thing they had.

Steve did not tell her mother she had to move out, though. Instead, he apologized for not being more sensitive to her feelings and assured her that he had no romantic feelings for Rainbow, which Britt thought should have gone without saying, given that he had literally just met the woman. Britt's mom's tone changed from angry to loving, and Britt stepped away from the door, unwilling to listen to any more of their nonsense. She was relieved that Steve wasn't ending things, but also disappointed in him for not saying what was true—Britt's mom was impossible.

When Steve finally emerged from the room, Britt was sitting on the couch, flipping through TV channels. He sat next to her.

"Sorry about that," he said.

"You're too nice to her," Britt said. It felt good to say it, to trust that Steve could handle this truth.

"She needs a lot of love," he said. "I don't mind giving it."

"You'll get tired," Britt said. "Eventually."

"I don't think so," he said. He sounded so sure.

Britt pretended to watch whatever was on TV and waited for him to leave. He stayed sitting next to her, though.

"Hey, I have an idea," he said. "You want to go shooting with me?"

Steve was a gun man. He owned several and kept them locked in a cabinet in the garage, taking one or two out with him each weekend to shoot at an outdoor range a half hour away. Britt had asked to hold one once before, and he'd let her. She'd loved the feel of it in her hands, the sense of power it gave her. It was rare for Britt to feel power.

"Seriously?" Britt asked.

"Seriously," Steve said.

"Mom will let me?"

Steve shrugged. "We'll just tell her we're going out for a bite to eat. She wants to nap anyway."

This, the white lie shared between them, gave her a sense of power too.

~

They took his truck out to Swakane Canyon, which he said was his favorite place to go shooting. He spent the drive telling Britt about the guns he'd brought with him that day—a Steyr AUG rifle and a 1911 handgun.

"The AUG is a real special one," he said. "Stands for Army Universal Gewehr. *Gewehr*'s the German word for 'rifle.' Came out in the seventies, but looks futuristic. You seen *Die Hard*?"

"The movie?"

"With Bruce Willis."

"No," Britt said.

"Well, that's another thing we gotta do. But anyway, the Steyr AUG's in that movie. That's why I wanted one. Stupid reason, I guess."

Britt shrugged. "I don't know. Doesn't seem that stupid."

"The price tag was stupid, that's for sure," he said with a laugh.

"Who taught you to shoot?"

"My granddad. When I was about your age, in fact."

Britt hadn't thought much about Steve's family, about the fact that there were people in his life besides Britt and her mother.

"Your dad didn't shoot?" Britt asked him.

"Never met him," Steve said. "Was just me and my mom."

He took his eyes off the road for a moment to wink at her, acknowledging that they had this in common.

Nobody else was at the shooting range when they arrived. There was nothing fancy about the place—a concrete slab with a wooden roof structure over it, five designated lanes for shooters, targets off in the distance.

"Which one you want to try first?" Steve asked.

Britt assessed what was in front of her—the large, intimidating rifle and the small pistol. She surprised herself by saying, "The big one."

Steve gave her a lesson on the different parts of a gun—stock, barrel, receiver, muzzle, action, sight. He showed her how to load the magazine, how to hold the rifle so that the butt of it was pressed into the meat of her shoulder. He warned her that she might have a bruise there later.

He put up papers with black silhouettes of human torsos as the targets, then handed her a pair of earmuffs, warning her that it would be loud. He put on a pair for himself too.

"You ready to take your first shot?"

"I don't know," she said.

"I'm right here," he said. "You're safe."

She nodded, believing him.

He kept one hand on the rifle, one hand on her to steady her.

"Now, look through your sight there. You see the red dot?"

She could hear her blood pulsing through her ears as she said, "Yes."

"Okay then, on three."

He counted to three, and she pulled the trigger with her shaky hand. The sound of it, the bang, was louder than she expected, even with the earmuffs.

"Nice!" he said.

She had no idea if the bullet had even hit the target. She was too busy assessing her own well-being. Had she somehow hurt herself? After a moment, she realized she was fine—still shaky, but fine.

"Right in the heart," he said.

That was when she saw that her bullet had gone right into the middle of the torso. It was an odd thing to be excited about—killing this representation of a person—but she felt elated to have Steve's approval. It had been a lucky shot; she didn't tell him, but she'd closed her eyes as she pulled the trigger that first time. But she decided she could be good at this, if she tried. She decided she would make him proud.

~

Shooting in Swakane Canyon became a weekly outing for them. They told Britt's mom they were going out for ice cream and then ventured out together for a couple of hours. Every time, Steve imparted some kind of wisdom—often about guns, sometimes about life.

Britt had been living in Steve's house, with her very own room, for nearly a year when he told her, during one of their shooting trips, that he was thinking of proposing to Britt's mom.

"Oh wow," Britt said.

In all honesty, she thought Steve was too good for her mom. Granted, her mom had cleaned up her act since meeting Steve. After witnessing a bout of The Darkness, he'd taken Britt's mom to the doctor. Britt didn't know what was prescribed, but whatever it was helped. Steve doled out the pills every night at dinner, and her mother took them without a fight. She didn't drink as much—a beer or wine cooler a few times a week. She didn't have as many wild outbursts. Still, Britt didn't trust it. She'd never known one of these good stretches to last long.

"I suppose I'm asking your permission," Steve said.

Britt raised her eyebrows at him. "*My* permission?"

She was just a kid. Since when did he need her approval?

"Well, yeah," he said with a laugh.

She was flattered, had to bite the insides of her cheeks to keep from smiling too big. It felt too vulnerable, too scary, to let him see how happy he made her.

"You have my permission," she said with a nod.

She wanted to ask if his marrying her mom would mean he would be her dad. Would he adopt her, make it official? Just thinking about it, she bit the insides of her cheeks again.

"Thank you, my dear," he said with a playful bow.

"When are you going to do it?"

"As soon as I get the ring. Put a down payment on it last week. Paying the rest next week."

"Wow," she said again.

They took a few shots—he with the 1911, she with the Steyr AUG.

"Not every woman has to get married, you know," he said. "But I think your mother is better off with me around."

"Oh, she definitely is," Britt said.

"I'm quite sure you will do just fine in life with or without a man by your side."

Britt hadn't thought much about her future at that point, hadn't considered marriage. She took note of what he was saying, though.

"Just look at you with the guns. You're a quick study," he said. "You're smart. You can do anything you want in this life. I'm not sure of much, but I'm sure of that."

She thought back to first grade, when she'd said she wanted to be famous. She shook her head at her younger self. But secretly, she still felt she was destined for something special, something she couldn't quite conceive of yet. Steve seemed to see it too.

"I hope you're right," she said.

"Just wait," he said. "You're going to do big things, and I'll be applauding on the sidelines."

Chapter 8

Sasha

The week before Daphne's due date, Sasha texted her to check in, not knowing those would be the last texts she would ever exchange with her sister.

Sasha: I'm gonna need a photo of the current bump situation
Daphne: get ur ass here and see it in person
Sasha: I'm sorry. This weekend? I'm a horrible sister
Daphne: U are, but I forgive u

Daphne texted a photo of herself sitting on the couch, her belly huge, taking up most of the frame. It would be the last photo Sasha would ever have of her sister.

Daphne: I feel like a whale
Sasha: You look beautiful
Daphne: Like a beautiful whale
Sasha: Any day now, right?
Daphne: That's what they say. My midwife thinks I may be late. No signs of action yet
Sasha: You better text me when there are signs of action

Daphne: Jay's on duty for that. Don't think I'm gonna wanna be texting anybody lol
Sasha: I'm excited for you ❤
Daphne: Thanks, boo. I'm excited too. Ur gonna be the best auntie

That was it. Sasha abandoned the text conversation to reply to an incoming text from Professor Williams, her faculty adviser. Days later, she would still be thinking about how she wished she'd ended with an "I love you" text. It was something small, silly, but it would have offered a bit of comfort.

~

Sasha got a text from Jay the very next night, just after 7 p.m. He sent it to Sasha and her mother.

Contractions started 👍

Sasha texted back with a party-hat emoji, something she would deeply regret later. Her mother responded with a barrage of questions: When did they start? How far apart were they? What was the pain on a scale of one to ten? How was Daphne feeling?

Jay didn't have time to get into details. He just wrote:

I'll keep y'all posted

Sasha knew that labor wasn't fast and dramatic like it was in the movies. It could take hours, days, even. Her mother had said she was in labor with Daphne for twenty-seven hours and with Sasha for ten hours—firstborns took their sweet time, she said.

Still, Sasha sat on the edge of her couch, awaiting any further information. After a few hours, she texted her mother to ask if she'd heard anything. She hadn't, but she said this was all normal. They were probably just in the beginning stages, focusing on managing the pains, preparing for the real battle ahead.

> We should both get some sleep. I wouldn't be surprised if she was still laboring in the morning.

Sasha took her mother's advice, going to bed around 11 p.m. She couldn't sleep, though. At the time, she chalked it up to excitement. In retrospect, it was anxiety. Her body could not rest because something didn't feel right—a sisterly premonition.

Sometime during the night, she did manage to fall asleep, because the next thing she knew, morning light was coming through the window in her bedroom, and her phone was buzzing with an incoming call. Her eyes flicked to the digital clock on her nightstand—she was someone who still had a digital clock, not wanting to tap her phone every time she wanted to know the time. It was just before six. When she glanced at her phone, Jay's name flashed on the screen. Her heart started pounding at the sight of it.

"Is the baby here?" she asked immediately.

It was silent for a moment, and she looked at the screen to see if the call had dropped. He was still there, though, the seconds of the call ticking by.

"Jay?" she asked.

She heard the sound of a pained animal, and it took her a second to realize it was him.

"Sash," he said.

His voice was high pitched, screechy, the voice of someone crying. Sasha felt a bolt of adrenaline through her body, readying her for whatever was coming.

"What is it? Is the baby okay?"

"Can you come?" he asked.

Later, she would determine that he couldn't bring himself to tell her, to say the reality out loud. He had to show her.

~

When Sasha pulled up to Daphne and Jay's house, her mother's car was pulling up at the same time. An ambulance was out front, lights flashing. A woman was standing on the front steps, a phone pressed to her ear. Her long cotton dress was covered in blood.

"Oh my god," Sasha's mother said as she slammed her car door shut and ran toward the house.

The baby had died. Sasha knew this in her bones as she ran after her mother. She braced herself for her sister's devastation, the unbearable pain she would be in, the way it would be evident on her crumpled-up face.

The woman with the blood-covered dress lowered the phone from her ear when she saw Sasha and her mother approaching. She opened her mouth as if to say something, but Sasha's mother just pushed right past her.

This woman was the midwife. Sasha would realize that later.

"Where is she?" Sasha's mother yelled, head turning one way, then the other. She was frantic. Sasha had never seen her like this.

Jay appeared, stepping out from the doorframe of their master bedroom into the hallway. He was wearing boxer shorts and a T-shirt. They were covered in blood. When he put his hands to his face, Sasha saw they were covered in blood too.

"She's gone, she's gone," he wailed when he saw Sasha and her mother.

The baby had been a girl. Sasha took in this information.

"Where's Daphne?" Sasha asked, peering around him.

He clung to Sasha and her mother as if he would fall to his knees otherwise. His desperation was terrifying. He was the drowning person; they were buoys.

"She's gone," he repeated.

Two medics came into the hallway then. They did not seem to be in a rush. Their faces were somber. They nodded toward Sasha and her mother.

"Oh dear God," Sasha's mother said.

That was when reality started to make itself known, despite Sasha's adamant refusal to know it.

The next several hours were completely erased from her memory—missing frames from a strip of film, snipped away, disposed of, never to be seen again. She must have seen her sister's dead body there in that bedroom, lying next to the dead baby's, pools of blood, but she has no image of this saved in her brain. She wonders if it will surface one day, this image, when she is going about her daily life, when she least expects it.

~

Things had gone horribly wrong. That was the unofficial cause of death. The baby had become stuck in the birth canal. The head had emerged, but not the body. The baby had gone without oxygen for too long, was dead when the midwife finally got him—the baby was a boy—out of Daphne's body.

When the bleeding started after the delivery, the midwife was in denial of the severity at first. By the time she realized she was in the midst of a catastrophic hemorrhaging event, it was too late. She called 911, and they came, but there was just too much blood. Daphne was dead before they could even transport her to the hospital for the requisite care, which, even if it had been done, might not have saved her life.

There was immediate talk of a lawsuit, but in the end, Jay wouldn't go through with it. It was his fault, he told himself. He shouldn't have just gone along with what Daphne wanted. He should have researched home birth, vetted the midwife. He had been so stupid. Everyone told him not to blame himself, but how could he not? He was the one person in Daphne's life who could have stopped this.

The funeral was a blur of condolences and tears, Daphne's casket next to the impossibly small casket for the baby boy named Theodore. That had been their pick for a boy name. They would have called him Theo.

People said things like "At least they are together in heaven," and Sasha decided that no statement starting with *at least* offered any real relief. Jay was a mess. He hadn't been eating or sleeping. When he approached the podium to say a few words, he promptly fainted. Everyone gasped, a few relatives in the front row rushing to his aid. While he came to in the back of the room, Sasha went up in his place. She hadn't planned to say anything, didn't think she'd be able to utter a word without breaking down, but she felt she owed it to Jay and her sister.

"Thank you all for coming. My sister was such a beautiful soul," she said. Predictably, her voice cracked, and she started to cry. The church was silent as people waited for more. What was there to say to sum up who Daphne was, the magnitude of her loss?

She stepped down, feeling unsteady on her feet, and took her seat next to her mother. Her mother grabbed her hand and didn't let go of it until the end of the service.

~

In the days right after Daphne's death, the funeral had been a welcome to-do item for Sasha to focus on. She excelled with a task, a project, always had. Once it was over, she didn't know what to do with herself. She tried to refocus on her dissertation, but Professor Williams advised her to take time off.

"I don't even know why you're here," Professor Williams said when Sasha showed up for their usual Friday meeting time.

"I don't know where else to be," Sasha said.

"This is a huge thing, Sasha. You need to grieve."

People kept saying this, but Sasha had no idea what that meant. There were the stages of grief—denial, anger, depression, bargaining, acceptance—but apparently, they weren't linear. They weren't a checklist. The experts said people tended to bounce between the stages, which had already proved true for Sasha. Some mornings, she woke up and told herself that her sister hadn't died. It was a bad dream. Daphne was still pregnant, delivering any day now. Denial. The next day, she would wake up heavy, weighed down by the awfulness of it all. Depression. Then one day, she was overcome by a tsunami of rage.

She didn't know what to do with this anger. She could not seem to get past how stupid this was. Yes, *stupid.* She could think of no better word to describe it. It was stupid that her sister had died. It was stupid that she had wanted this stupid home birth. Daphne would have survived, and the baby would have survived, if she'd gone to the hospital and been monitored appropriately, with skilled physicians at the ready to tend to any problems. Yes, the Black maternal mortality rate in the United States was appalling—more than double the rate for white mothers—but it was still highly likely that Daphne would have been okay. Sasha could not stop thinking about this, imagining this alternate reality with her sister on the maternity ward, the baby in a little bassinet next to her bed.

It didn't feel right to direct her anger at Jay. He loved Daphne. He'd trusted her judgment. He didn't know what he didn't know. He was the embodiment of an obnoxious trope—the bumbling husband, adhering to the "happy wife, happy life" philosophy. She felt terrible for him. He was blaming himself, and probably would for the rest of his life. For his sake, and her own, Sasha had to think of another target, someone else to blame.

She got the name of the midwife from Jay, who handed over some papers Daphne had signed when she hired the woman for her services. Her name was Rochelle, and she was young and not that experienced, but she hadn't lied to Daphne and Jay. She had told them that she was new in the field, which was why her rate was so low. Daphne, always trying to get a deal. *Stupid.* The paperwork Daphne had signed basically released the midwife from any liability. Rochelle, like Jay, was in a hell of self-blame, so it was difficult to hate her. She hadn't run from the situation, which would have been tempting and even understandable. She was calling Jay every day. She'd written a letter to Sasha and her mother, expressing her profound regret and sorrow.

Things had gone horribly wrong.

That was the crux of it.

There was one person Sasha decided she could hate, and that person was Angeni Luna. Sasha kept visiting her Instagram page, seeing how she portrayed her own home birth as this transcendental experience. There were so many comments from followers who praised her, who said she was inspiring them to pursue their own natural births, free of medical interference. It was here, on this stupid—*stupid!*—Instagram page, where Daphne had gotten the idea to buck convention and have her baby in a giant inflatable tub. Angeni Luna wasn't a doctor, and yet here she was, encouraging women to trust their bodies, seemingly oblivious to the fact that their bodies could betray them, that catastrophe was possible.

Sasha composed a message:

> Hello. I just wanted to inform you that my sister took your advice and had a home birth and she fucking died, as did her son. You are so irresponsible. So reckless. I don't know how you sleep at night.

It was biting and unfair, but she sent it anyway.

She stared at the screen, waiting for a reply from Angeni Luna, or whoever was in charge of her account. After an hour of just staring, she slammed her phone onto her nightstand, buried her head in a pillow, and screamed.

The next day, there was still no reply, and Sasha became increasingly agitated. How dare this woman just ignore her message. Did she not even read any of the messages from her followers? Did she think it was appropriate to just put her agenda out in the world and be closed to feedback? The entitlement, the arrogance, the self-centeredness. She hated this woman, and it felt good to hate her. Anger was energizing, the antidote to the heavy-limbed feeling that accompanied sadness.

She went for a run and felt like her feet were barely touching the ground. She was just gliding through the air, powered by her rage. At the end of her run, sweaty and breathing heavy, she texted Jay:

I hate Angeni Luna

He texted back.

I know. I shoulda talked Daph out of it

He couldn't stop bringing it back to himself.

She was brainwashed, Jay. It wasn't your fault.

He didn't reply. There seemed to be no convincing him.

Sasha began to fantasize about avenging Daphne's death. This seemed like the only way to stop her brain from looping over the same thoughts. There had to be some justice for Daphne if Sasha was ever going to have peace.

It seemed cut and dried: Angeni Luna needed to feel repercussions. People needed to see her for the self-righteous, reckless person she was. They had to realize her role in Daphne's death and shame her for it until she was canceled into oblivion. Sasha saw it as a kind of math equation. Daphne's death had created this huge sum of suffering. Right now, Sasha and her mother and Jay were the ones carrying it. The midwife too. Angeni Luna deserved her fair share. It stood to reason that if some of the burden, some of the weight, was put on Angeni Luna, the rest of them would have less to withstand. This was not how life worked, of course. But Sasha was desperate to believe it was.

Chapter 9

Gwen

Jeff had never been the silent treatment type, but after the door-slam incident, he withdrew, becoming sullen and dejected and mute. Gwen could sense his disappointment with her, with how the early days of parenthood had made them into their worst selves instead of their best. Or maybe it was just her that was her worst self. He seemed to be exactly the same person he'd been before June arrived, and maybe that was the problem.

After a few days of tense quiet, their bodies moving awkwardly around each other in their shared living space, as if they were engaged in some strange performance art about marital discord, Gwen decided a peace offering was in order.

Jeff was packing his leather messenger bag for the day, stuffing it with various folders and papers. He had a deposition, and he was running late.

"I was thinking," Gwen said as he snapped his bag shut, "you're probably right. I should try that support group."

When his eyes met hers, she could see the hope in them. It was a boyish, innocent kind of hope that told her he hadn't given up on her, after all. His faith in her, in them, was alive and well, and she felt suddenly like crying for ever doubting their ability to survive this.

He put his bag over his shoulder and came to her, put his arms around her middle, hugged her so tightly that she did start crying.

"I think that's a great idea," he said, his breath hot on her ear.

She clung to him. She didn't want him to go. She wanted to beg him to stay home, to call in sick, but that was never who she was. She was never needy. She was never that type of partner. He had married a strong, independent woman. Breaking down in front of him, requiring his presence on a random Tuesday, felt like a violation of their vows.

"I'm sorry," she said.

He kissed her cheek.

"Me too."

~

She watched his car pull out of the driveway and then let herself completely sob. June was on a play mat on the floor, a few stuffed animals dangling from a curved bar above her head. She stared at them in wonder and then stared at her sobbing mother in wonder. Gwen knew June wouldn't remember her mother's emotional fragility on days like this one, not consciously, at least. But would something be imprinted upon her? Something that wired her brain to see her mother as unpredictable and dangerous? Gwen was starting to hate that she'd read so many books.

She wiped her eyes and nose on the sleeve of her sweatshirt and sat on the floor next to June.

"Mommy's having a hard day," she said.

June was reabsorbed in staring at the dangling stuffed giraffe. She did not care about her mother's hard day.

Gwen tapped her phone screen to check the time. The support group was about twenty minutes away, at Virginia Mason Hospital, the same hospital where she'd had her C-section. If she wanted to actually go, and not just lie to Jeff about going, they would have to leave soon.

"You want to go on an adventure with Mommy?" she asked June.

~

They hardly ever left the house. For better or worse, Gwen could order almost anything they needed online. In this modern age, errands could become obsolete. When they did leave the house, Gwen felt like a bear emerging from hibernation, weak and ragged, muscles atrophied, eyes squinting in the daylight.

She strapped June into her car seat and pulled out of the garage. Throughout the drive, she peeked into the rearview mirror to see June's face reflected in the little mirror attached to the back of her rear-facing car seat. Whenever June was quiet, Gwen feared she'd stopped breathing suddenly. The night before, she'd googled *Can babies choke on their own saliva?* Since her own medical drama, she'd felt vulnerable to tragedy in a way she never had before.

When they approached the hospital parking lot, Gwen's palms got so sweaty that she had to take them off the steering wheel one at a time and wipe them on her sweatpants. It hadn't occurred to her that it might be difficult to return to the hospital for the first time since her surgeries. She wasn't the type to be so *affected* by things. But there was no denying that her body was on the verge of a panic attack while her brain was confused about what was transpiring.

She pulled into a spot at the far end of the parking lot, mostly because she didn't trust herself to navigate the more crowded area closer to the entrance. When she put the car in park, she willed herself to take deep breaths but felt like her lungs were the size of chicken eggs.

"Mommy's okay," she told June.

Not that June seemed to notice anything was amiss. Gwen's only witness in this new life was completely oblivious.

After ten minutes of jagged breathing, Gwen opened her car door with a shaky hand, then went to get June out of her car seat. The weight of the baby in her arms was a comfort. She thought of those dogs wearing weighted vests in thunderstorms.

Thankfully, the entrance they used wasn't the same entrance as the one Jeff had taken her through on that horrific day. She speed walked down a quiet hallway in search of the right room. They were a few minutes late, so there was no gathering of people outside a room to alert her to the right location.

When she found it, she peeked inside to see about fifteen women sitting in a circle of chairs, their babies either in their arms, in car seats next to them, or on floor mats in front of them.

"Are you looking for the moms' group?" a woman asked, seeing Gwen before Gwen could decide if she wanted to be seen.

"Um, yeah," Gwen said, taking a tentative step inside.

The woman stood. She was clearly the leader of the group. Gwen had probably emailed back and forth with her during her pregnancy, when she was making arrangements to attend the group. She couldn't remember the woman's name to save her life, though. It was like her brain had moved so many things to the recycle bin when June came along, then permanently deleted the files.

"Well, come on in," she said. "We're just getting started."

The leader woman pulled a chair into the circle for Gwen, and the other women shifted around to make room. Gwen felt ridiculous with all this rearranging on her behalf. She gave a little wave to the group but didn't make eye contact with a single person.

She kept June in her car seat, placed in front of her on the floor. She could feel everyone's eyes on her.

"I'm Karsha," the leader woman said. The name didn't ring any bells. "Why don't you introduce us to you and your little one?"

Gwen felt nervous in a way she hadn't since high school. In her years as a lawyer, she had mastered public speaking, no longer felt a tinge of discomfort about it. This surge of anxiety was new and overwhelming.

"Um, I'm Gwen," she said. Her voice was shaking. She didn't know why her voice was shaking.

"And this is June."

She felt the urgent need to swallow, her throat dry and pasty. She dared to look at the woman seated across the circle from her, and she had a pleasant but expectant smile on her face.

"And how old is June?" Karsha asked.

Duh, Gwen thought. *Say more, you idiot.*

"Sorry, June is ten weeks."

"Great, we have a few babies right around that same age."

Gwen did a quick scan of the babies, saw that a few did look to be the same age as June. A few were younger, just a handful of weeks old. Some were older—six months, nine months. If Gwen remembered right, this group was limited to mothers in their first year with their firstborn.

Karsha finally took her eyes off Gwen, turned back to the larger group, and said, "Okay, so does anyone want to start with a share today?"

A share. It was like they were in a twelve-step meeting, addicts looking for relief in each other's confessions. Maybe it wasn't that dissimilar, actually.

A woman a few seats over from Gwen raised her hand.

"Go ahead, Megan."

Megan's baby was one of the younger ones, a scrawny newborn swimming in his onesie.

"I just wanted to thank you all for your support last week. I think we've finally turned a corner with breastfeeding, and things are feeling better."

A couple of women chimed in with "Oh, that's so great" and "Yay!" This was clearly a group of breastfeeding enthusiasts, and Gwen was heartened to know she wasn't the only one who had struggled with it.

"It was hard for me in the beginning too," the woman next to Gwen said. "But I'm so glad we've stuck with it. We're almost at three months, and it's going so well now."

This woman's baby, a girl who was similar in size to June, was sitting in her lap, pawing at her mom's shirt as if wanting a boob right then and there.

"Have you had any supply issues?" Megan asked the "going so well" mom.

"Not anymore. We're all good now," the woman said with a nervous laugh. She had to know being "all good" would evoke envy, bordering on hatred, in any gathering of new mothers.

For the next hour, the women talked about exactly what one would expect a moms' support group to talk about—sleep (or lack thereof), going back to work, day care, introducing bottles, resuming sex with husbands. Gwen had been given the all clear to resume sex at her six-week appointment. It had seemed like that was the entire point of the appointment—for her male doctor to say, "All looks good. You can have sex!" Was there any woman alive who was eagerly awaiting that green light? At ten weeks, she still couldn't fathom having sex with Jeff. Her C-section scar still felt tender. She had zero interest in anything going on below that scar, would have been fine if her vagina had just been sewn shut like her belly, like *no need for this thing anymore*. Jeff had been patient, hadn't even brought up sex, but she knew he must want it. They had been a twice-a-week couple before June was born, with the rare exception.

At the end of the meeting, they all stood from their chairs. A few chatted among themselves, clearly having become friends over the time they'd spent in the group together. A couple introduced themselves to Gwen, shaking her hand and sharing their names, which she immediately forgot. Everyone seemed nice, but she didn't know if she'd come back.

"I think everyone here hates me now," the "all good" mom whispered to her as she collected her things alongside Gwen.

Gwen smiled. "*Hate* may be strong. Mild disdain, maybe. Personally, I like to hear it's possible for things to go well."

"*Well*? That may be strong. I'm slightly less psychotic than I was."

The woman lifted her daughter in her arms, and Gwen did the same with June. They faced each other, their babies between them, little human buffers.

"I'm Leigh," the woman said. "I completely forget your name."

"God, sometimes I completely forget my name. It's Gwen. I think."

They both laughed and started heading for the exit.

"What did you think of the group?" Leigh asked.

"I don't know. Something to do, I guess."

"That's why I started coming. Just a reason to get out of the house. Which is so sad, isn't it?"

Gwen shrugged. "Everything feels sad, honestly."

Leigh stopped, put her hand on Gwen's shoulder. So Gwen stopped too. "Are you okay?"

Her eye contact was unnerving. It was as if she was trying to see into Gwen's soul. Gwen had to look away.

"I'm fine. I think."

"Look, this shit is hard. If you need to chat or whatever," she said, fumbling around in her diaper bag with one hand, the other hand holding her daughter. She took out her phone. "What's your number?"

Gwen gave it to her, watched her tap it into her phone.

"There. I texted you so you have mine."

"Thanks," Gwen said, unsure what to make of this sudden kindness, this abrupt proposal of friendship. Or maybe it wasn't quite friendship, but simple camaraderie, a companionship based on circumstance. Whatever it was, Gwen felt herself wanting it. It had been so long since she'd wanted anything.

They continued walking through the hallway of the hospital, then out to the parking lot. Leigh had parked near the entrance, and Gwen watched as she went through the familiar mess of motions, trying to get her baby into the car seat without dropping any of her own belongings. Gwen would have helped, but her own hands were full. Leigh's baby started to wail, as if sensing her mother's discombobulation and feeling unsettled by it. You couldn't even have your own emotional experience as a mother without your child being affected.

"I wish we could stay and chat more," Leigh said. "But my kid is about to lose her shit."

Gwen wanted to hug this woman. She'd never felt such an urge toward a stranger before.

"I get it. I'm sure mine is going to lose her shit soon too."

"They're always about to lose their shit or in the process of losing their shit, aren't they?"

"Sometimes it's literal shit," Gwen said, proud of herself for the joke.

"That's our days, right? Literal and figurative shit."

Leigh closed the door so her baby's crying was now quieter, muffled.

"It was really nice to meet you," Gwen said.

"Likewise. I'll text you, okay? We can hang sometime."

The excitement Gwen felt was on par with what she'd felt in high school when a boy she liked dared to glance in her direction.

"I'd like that," she said.

She started finger-combing her hair behind her ear nervously, which was also something high school Gwen did. *Stop being a weirdo,* she told herself.

Leigh walked around to the driver's side car door and let herself in. Her baby was, as predicted, losing her figurative shit. As the car pulled away, Gwen waved, then lifted June's little hand to wave too.

"Look, honey, we made friends," she whispered.

~

That evening, Gwen decided to make a lasagna—with a pesto sauce, no tomatoes. She didn't have all the ingredients, so she placed an order with Instacart, and the goods showed up on her doorstep—oven-ready noodle sheets, pesto in a plastic tub, ricotta, mozzarella, a bag of spinach.

She texted Jeff that she didn't need him to pick up anything for dinner and included a playful chef emoji. He wrote back with heart eyes and said:

I can't even tell you how excited this makes me

He always loved her pesto lasagna.

She placed June in the baby lounger that someone—she couldn't remember who—had purchased off her registry. It was a glorified pillow with a bumper around it so the baby was penned in, secure, and it cost more than a hundred dollars. There were probably cheaper options, but she'd chosen the higher-end items. All these baby-equipment companies preyed on first-time mothers, seized upon their belief in *only the best for my child.* She had to assume the second-time mothers realized they'd been duped and would never buy a hundred-dollar glorified pillow.

Gwen hadn't cooked an actual meal since she was pregnant, when she was whipping up breakfasts and lunches and dinners chock full of superfoods. The most she could manage since June had arrived was slathering bread with almond butter and honey or, if she was feeling particularly energetic, microwaving a bowl of oatmeal. She hadn't had a conversation with Jeff about her sudden abstention from basic self-care, so bless his heart, he had kept the fridge stocked with various ready-made items—sandwiches and wraps and parfaits and those expensive juices that looked healthy but had fifty grams of sugar per sip. She hadn't thanked him because doing so would be admitting what she'd been failing to do herself. She would thank him tonight, she decided. She'd been so awful lately.

June didn't start fussing until after Gwen was done layering the lasagna—noodles, sauce, sautéed spinach, cheeses.

"Perfect timing, June Bug," she said, as she slid the casserole dish into the oven and set the timer.

When she went to retrieve June from the lounger, she felt a surge of warmth and affection for her baby that was like a light bulb going on in her head—*Ooh, this is what all the new moms are talking about.* She held June close to her and twirled—twirled!—around the living room. She was giddy, and she knew it was all because of that woman. Leigh.

~

The lasagna was done cooking and was resting on the stovetop when Gwen heard the garage door open. Jeff was home. June was just finishing feeding.

"Perfect timing again!" Gwen said to her.

She stood, June cradled in the crook of her arm, ready to greet Jeff. Had she not greeted him since he'd started back at work? She couldn't remember doing so. It was like he just appeared, standing in the living room, his tie loosened around his neck, looking tired, but a different kind of tired than she was.

"Oh my god, it smells delicious in here," he said.

He kissed Gwen on the cheek, then June.

"How are my girls? Good day?"

He seemed nervous to ask. It was her fault, this nervousness. He approached her like a grenade that could go off at any time.

"It was a good day," she said.

He set his work bag on the floor and stepped out of his shoes.

"And what made this one so good?"

"June and I made friends. At that support group."

He could have said "I told you so," but he just said, "I'm so glad."

"Me too," she said.

She was smiling too much. She looked down, embarrassed that such a small thing, the meeting of this one person, could shift her mood so dramatically.

"What are your friends' names?"

"The mom is Leigh. Shit, I don't think I even asked the kid's name."

She felt her heart rate accelerate. What an idiot. Had Leigh asked June's name? She couldn't remember. But Gwen had introduced June at the beginning of the meeting, so Leigh probably already knew June's name.

"Can I help set the table?" Jeff asked.

Gwen was suddenly distracted, looking for where she'd set her phone. There it was, on the island. She picked it up, tapped out a quick message to Leigh.

> Hey. Just wanted to say thank you for chatting today. And I feel like a moron because I don't think I even asked your daughter's name. I'm so sorry!

She stared at her phone, waiting for an instant response. What if Leigh didn't write back? What if she'd done her own replay of their interaction and been so offended by Gwen's self-centeredness that she had no interest in hanging out after all?

"Babe?" Jeff said.

She looked up. "Huh?"

"Can I set the table?"

"Oh. Yeah. Sure. Thanks."

He moved around her in the kitchen, taking plates and utensils and water glasses to the table. They would usually have wine with lasagna, a nice red, but he knew she wasn't comfortable drinking when she was breastfeeding. Her supply wasn't good enough for her to do the "pump and dump" that other lucky moms did. He could've opened a bottle on his own, indulged a bit, but he didn't. He was a good man, decent, and she'd been so awful.

"Who are you texting?" he asked.

"Leigh. The woman. I can't believe I didn't ask her baby's name."

"Hon, I'm sure it's fine," he said.

He came up behind her, wrapped his arms around her and June.

"I feel like they did a lobotomy along with the hysterectomy sometimes," she told him. "I've lost all social graces."

"You're just rusty. And sleep deprived."

He kept saying that he appreciated her feeding their daughter, but he wished he could help at night. If they introduced bottle feeding, Jeff could take some of the night shifts. But the thing was that she didn't have a freezer stash of milk to use for bottles. Formula was still out of the question. Even if she did miraculously increase her milk supply so that she had reserves, she wasn't sure about the bottle thing. There was the dreaded "nipple confusion" discussed on all the message boards. It was possible June could love the efficiency of the bottle and refuse her mother's breasts. Gwen couldn't imagine how terrible that type of rejection would feel. She'd tried to explain all this to Jeff, and his eyes had gotten that glassy, faraway look. She exhausted him.

~

They sat for dinner, June in the swing next to the table. Gwen kept her phone by her plate, willing it to light up with a text from Leigh.

"This is delicious," Jeff said upon taking his first bite.

It *was* good. Gwen felt like she'd lost so much competency, but she could still make a mean lasagna.

"How was your day?" Gwen asked him.

He started talking about a case he was working on right as her phone flashed, Leigh's name on the screen. She opened the message, though she could feel Jeff's eyes on her as he continued talking. She made the requisite sounds of an attentive listener—"uh-huh" and "right" and "oh"—as she read Leigh's text:

Omg. Don't even worry. I didn't even think to mention her name. Lol. Her name is Belle. Like from Beauty and the Beast. I have second thoughts about it every other day

Gwen smiled.

"Is that your friend from group?" Jeff asked, giving up on the recounting of his day.

She was already tapping a response.

Aww, I think it's pretty. My daughter, June, was supposed to be born in June, but she was born in May. I also have second thoughts

"Babe?" Jeff said.

"Huh? Yeah. Leigh. From group. Sorry. I felt so weird about not asking her daughter's name. It's Belle."

"Crisis averted."

She assessed his tone for sarcasm but found none. He was trying, so hard, to be supportive, and she loved him for it.

Leigh sent a laugh-cry-face emoji.

"It's good to see you smiling," Jeff said.

Gwen covered her mouth with her hand, embarrassed by this trivial thing that gave her happiness—a happiness that her husband had been trying to give her for weeks.

"I guess I didn't realize how friend starved I was."

Again, he could have reminded her that the support group was his idea. He could have said "I told you so," but he just returned her smile. He wanted her to be happy, above all else, above his own ego. If that wasn't love, she didn't know what was.

"You should invite her over with her husband and the baby," he said.

Gwen tried to picture it, all of them sitting together at the table, their babies in swings or loungers at their feet. It didn't appeal to her as much as Leigh's initial suggestion that the two of them hang out. She hadn't even thought about the existence of Leigh's husband, didn't see how involving their respective men would be that fulfilling.

"I should probably get to know her a little first, right?"

"Sure, yeah. Just throwing it out there for the future," he said.

Another text from Leigh:

I can't remember if you said in group . . . are you on mat leave from work? I'm not working now so if you wanna hang during the day sometime, let me know. The days can feel so long

Leigh sent a melting-face emoji to punctuate the text. It was Gwen's favorite emoji since she'd become a mother.

Gwen: Ya, I'm on leave for a few months. Longer if I can swing it. Would love to get together

Leigh: Ok cool. Do I sound too desperate if I suggest tomorrow?

Gwen's fingers were vibrating as she tapped back:

Let's do it!

Leigh quickly sent along her address, which was in Capitol Hill, the neighborhood southwest from theirs in Madison Park. It was one of the hipper Seattle neighborhoods—lots of bars and nightclubs.

When Gwen finally put down her phone, satisfied with the plan for the next day, she saw that Jeff had already finished his food.

"I'm sorry," she said.

"It's okay. Really."

June started to squeal in her swing, and Gwen reached to get her.

"I'll get her. You eat," Jeff said, standing from his seat.

He lifted her out of the swing, then resumed his seat with June in his lap. She clasped his ring finger with both of her tiny hands, sucked on the gold wedding band.

Gwen took fast bites. She'd grown accustomed to shoveling calories into her face, knowing she needed them for her body to continue to make milk and feed their child. Savoring had become a foreign concept.

"You can take your time," Jeff said. "I've got her."

But Gwen was already almost done. She took her last two bites and then brought her plate and Jeff's plate to the sink.

"I can do the dishes. Just sit. Relax."

She sat but felt uneasy with nothing to do. Was this what life had been like before? She just . . . *sat*? She honestly could not remember.

Jeff placed June on her play mat on the kitchen floor and went about clearing the table. She watched him at the sink, scrubbing the dishes by hand. That was always his preference. He said he found the warm water soothing. She was a rinse-and-throw-it-in-the-dishwasher type of person, trusting the appliance to sanitize better than she ever could.

She thought of Angeni Luna right then, wondered if she owned appliances. It seemed like she would be opposed to them, though Gwen couldn't think of a logical reason why. Probably something about how machines made it impossible for us to go at the slower pace we were intended to go, how they contributed to our culture's sense of urgency, prioritizing efficiency over all else.

Gwen picked up her phone and mindlessly tapped to Instagram, to Angeni Luna's profile. The little ring around her profile photo—a photo of her and her daughter touching noses—was lit up, indicating a new story was available.

ASK ME ANYTHING

Have you struggled at all with breastfeeding? I'm 3 weeks in and want to quit :(

Whenever women tell me they struggle with breastfeeding, my first question is if they had unnecessary medical interventions during labor, as that can disrupt the natural bond between mother and child and get breastfeeding off to a difficult start. If that was the case with you, give yourself grace as you recover and know that it may be harder at the start, but totally worth it. There is nothing more beautiful than breastfeeding, in my opinion. How amazing that our bodies make exactly what our babies need to thrive.

It was a little before eight. June wasn't whining to be fed, but Gwen suddenly felt like she had to feed her. Sometimes, she needed it more than June did, for the rush of accomplishment, for the reassurance that she was succeeding.

"I think I'll go feed June," she said.

Jeff was still at the sink. He looked over his shoulders, arms wet up to his elbows.

"Okay," he said.

She picked up June from the play mat, took her into the guest room, the room they shared at night. Usually, this would be her last feed before they attempted something like turning in for the night. There was never a clear break, though. June woke up every two hours, regardless of the time of day. She didn't yet understand that the purpose of the night was to sleep.

Gwen changed June into a fresh diaper and stuffed the soiled one into the special trash can someone had purchased for them for just this purpose. It was especially adept at masking odors. It was presently overfull, and Gwen knew it would weigh about twenty pounds when she finally pulled it out—a long snake of yellow plastic filled with her daughter's pee and shit. She made a mental note to ask Jeff to take it out. They had talked about that in the support group—delegating. Apparently, many new moms were "gatekeepers," placing themselves in charge of all the tasks because they did not trust anyone else to do them correctly, which then led to others being actually unable to do them since they'd been out of the loop so long. The eventual burnout was, essentially, the mother's fault.

Once she had June in her pajamas, she settled them into bed together and put June on her right breast. June closed her eyes and immediately went to work as Gwen felt the familiar tingle of the milk letting down. Angeni Luna was right—breastfeeding was rather incredible, at least after it stopped being so torturous.

June fed for about twenty minutes while Gwen stared at the ceiling, eventually closing her own eyes. At this point, she would usually let herself doze off. June was most likely to have her longest stretch of sleep at this time—three hours, max, but it was something.

But then Gwen heard Jeff in the kitchen. She saw the light under the guest room door go dark. He'd turned out the hallway light and was walking to their master bedroom, a room she hadn't slept in since the night before going on that stupid run that changed everything.

One of the women in group today had said she was afraid her husband was going to have an affair because she had no interest in having sex with him. She'd admitted she was sort of joking, but sort of not. It hadn't even occurred to Gwen to worry about Jeff's sexual frustrations. When she considered him having an affair, she was shocked that it didn't even bother her. Let another woman service him. It felt like outsourcing a task, like on Instacart.

She set June in her bassinet next to the bed. June rarely slept in there because she much preferred being on Gwen's body, but she seemed especially passed out, so Gwen took a chance. June squirmed for a few seconds in the bassinet, but then resumed her peaceful slumber. Gwen tiptoed out of the room and down the hall to the master bedroom. Jeff was sitting up in bed, one ankle crossed over the other, hands behind his head, watching a sports recap show on TV.

"Everything okay?" he asked.

He was still sitting on his side of the bed. It had been weeks, and he hadn't moved to the middle, hadn't claimed the bed as his alone. Her side looked so sad and empty.

"Yeah. She's in the bassinet, sleeping."

"Awesome. Nice job."

She got into bed, occupying her side for the first time since becoming a mother. Jeff looked surprised, and she hated that he looked surprised, hated that her wanting to be with him was such a novel occurrence.

"I miss this bed," she said, running her hands along the comforter.

He leaned over, kissed her cheek, put a hand on her thigh.

"It misses you," he said. "So do I."

He said it quickly, not in a dramatic, guilt-inducing way. It was enough to make her cry.

"Oh, babe, don't cry," he said.

It was what every man said to every woman—*don't cry, don't cry, don't cry*. Why didn't they understand that what women wanted was to be held and told to cry, cry, cry?

He pulled her into his side, and she rested her head on his chest. When she looked up, her lips found his, and they were like brand-new lips, lips she had never kissed before. She felt something awaken inside—not desire exactly, but a memory of her own body.

Soon, they were lying beside each other, both on their sides, facing each other, torsos pressed against one another.

"We don't have to . . . you know," he said. "I mean, I'd love that. But this is fine. Okay?"

She tugged on the waistband of his shorts, her telltale way of saying what she wanted without words. She took off his clothes, and then he took off hers. She watched his face as he did, looking for a sign that he was shocked by what he saw. Her body wasn't the same, would probably never be again. This was the first time she'd let him see it in its new state. She'd been closing the bathroom door when taking a shower, wrapping herself in a towel on the way to the closet, things she'd never done before. She missed the immodesty of her former self.

When they were naked, he felt inside her with two fingers, as if inspecting that things were the same. She felt a laugh bubbling up inside her. She'd had a C-section, but he clearly wasn't sure that her vagina was unaltered.

"What?" he asked. He'd no doubt felt the vibration of her chest as she suppressed the giggle.

"I feel like we're hooking up for the first time."

"We kind of are."

"I think I'm more nervous now than I was our first time."

~

Back in law school, Gwen and Jeff had been in the same torts class and had started hanging out at Friday happy hours with a group of people from the class. Gwen was dating someone at the time, another lawyer-to-be who was an arrogant asshole. She liked Jeff as a person. He was kind and funny and didn't seem like someone who should become a lawyer. There was another woman in the program—Melissa, went by Mel—who had a crush on him and made it very obvious. She was pretty in the conventional way—blond hair, generous boobs. Gwen watched her laugh at everything Jeff said and could tell that Jeff was not, for whatever reason, interested. It became cringeworthy over time, the way Mel threw herself at him. During one of the happy hours, after Mel had gone to the bathroom following a particularly heinous display of flirtation, Jeff leaned over to Gwen and said, "How do I get it to stop?"

That was when they started chatting more. Gwen was on the outs with the asshole, and Jeff was there, the good-hearted antidote. He didn't ask her out on an official date, but they found themselves talking between themselves at more of the gatherings. When he invited her back to his place, she said "Sure" and felt Mel's eyes on them as they left together.

By that point in her life, Gwen had slept with about a dozen guys. She'd had a few serious relationships lasting a year or more, and lots of not-serious relationships. That first time, she wasn't sure what Jeff would be—a serious or not-serious. But it meant something that she was so nervous, her hands trembling as he undressed her, blood whooshing in her ears. She was nervous because she cared. It was terrifying to care.

He took his time that first time, and the other times after. She knew good sex from bad, and the sex with Jeff was good. He was attentive and tender. He cared about her pleasure. Unlike many men, who hopped out of bed after as if their skin were on fire, he liked to linger and cuddle. Even after they'd been together a couple of years, when sex for most couples became rote, he lingered and cuddled as if it was their first time together all over again. He never seemed ungrateful.

She closed her eyes now as he went down on her, kissing and licking her between her legs. He always insisted on doing this for her, even when she told him he didn't have to. "I like it," he'd always say, and she did her best to believe him.

After a few minutes, she pulled at the hairs on his head, signaling him to come up to her, to kiss her on the mouth and put himself inside her. He obeyed. The moment he entered her, she gasped—and not in a good way. Something was wrong. It didn't feel right. He was suddenly bigger or she was suddenly smaller. His dick against the walls of her vagina felt like a thumb rubbing against the wall of a Tupperware container. All that was missing was the audible screech.

He continued to go through his usual motions, which in this new body were excruciating, so she placed her palms against his chest, pushed him off as best she could.

"What's wrong?" he asked.

She started crying over the fact that, once again, she was the only one aware that anything was wrong.

He pulled out of her, looked down at her vagina as if expecting a gush of blood.

"Oh my god, did I hurt you?"

He looked horrified, and that made her cry more.

"It doesn't feel right," she said. "It hurts."

She didn't mean to make him feel guilty, but she obviously had.

"Oh my god, I'm so sorry."

He lay next to her, his erection still there, waiting for attention.

"I don't know what's wrong with me," she said.

She was really sobbing now.

"Nothing. Nothing's wrong. It's okay."

These were all lies.

June, as if sensing that her mother needed an excuse to leave this godawful situation, started shrieking. She had never woken up without her mother right next to her.

"I have to go get her," Gwen said.

She stood, still naked, not bothering with re-dressing herself, and fled the room. He started to follow after her, wanting to talk and comfort and do all the right things that she wanted nothing to do with.

He was standing behind her as she picked up June from the bassinet, held her against her chest.

"Mommy's here, Mommy's here," she said.

Jeff's presence felt like a burden, something else to tend to. She just wanted to be alone with June again. It was the only relationship that made any sense.

"Let's just talk tomorrow, okay?" she said to Jeff as she bounced June in her arms.

"Okay," he said, "if that's what you want."

It was clear it wasn't what he wanted, but what was she to do?

"I'm sorry," she said.

He kissed her on the lips and then on the nose, then kissed the top of June's head.

"I love you girls," he said.

"Love you," she said back.

When he turned to leave, she stared at his naked butt, the muscles of his back. He was such a handsome man. She was just no longer a woman who cared about such a thing.

Chapter 10

ANGENI LUNA

A society that tells a mother she has anxiety because she doesn't want to be away from her child is a broken society.

In the caption, Angeni wrote about how natural it was for a mother to be with her baby around the clock. She explained how humans are born premature compared to other mammals—roughly twelve months too early, according to some research. In an ideal world, gestation would be twenty-one months—nearly two years. Horse foals, for instance, come out of the womb practically galloping. Same with giraffes. The problem is our brains. Human babies cannot gestate any longer because their heads would become too big to fit through the birth canal.

So humans are born earlier than would be reasonable in other parts of the animal kingdom, with the assumption that their mother will be tending to their needs 24/7. The bond between a mother and a baby is critical for the survival of the newborn, so the instinct to be close at all times is a good one. If mothers did not feel this instinct, the human race would not continue.

Angeni liked to educate her followers about how this intense connection doesn't just apply to the baby's first few months of life, but also to the first few *years*. In her "Ask me anything" stories, so many people inquired about Angeni's plans to have another child, and she always took this as an opportunity to explain that true infancy is a three-year process, so she would wait three years before considering adding another child to their family. She did feel like another soul, a boy this time, was calling her to be his mother, but these first three years of Freya's life would only be dedicated to Freya. If more parents operated with this mentality, more children would receive the care and attention they needed to thrive. If more people followed Angeni's teachings, the world would be a better place.

The response to this particular post was especially enthusiastic, which signaled to Angeni that she had again uncovered something about modern motherhood that required collective attention.

> Omg preach. I am so sick of people telling me I need to chill out and take time away from the baby. I WANT TO BE WITH MY BABY

> Was literally just telling my husband this. Our baby is two months old and he thinks we should start day care 🤯

> tbh I think moms who WANT to be away from their babies are the ones society should be worrying about

> my friend is going back to work next week and her baby is only 3 months old. I don't get it and am so happy I get to stay home

It was responses like these that eased Angeni's occasional imposter syndrome and assured her that, yes, she did have every right and reason to write a book. Angeni had a lengthy phone call with the reputable literary agent, Elizabeth Conroy, during which Elizabeth showered Angeni with praise that made her whole body feel warm, the hairs on her arms standing on end in excited anticipation. Angeni signed a contract with Elizabeth's agency the next day. "You are going to be huge," the agent said. "You already are huge. But this will be a whole new level."

Angeni had assumed she'd need to write a book proposal. In the past, when she'd toyed with the idea of writing a book, her Google research had informed her that a comprehensive proposal was the first step. Elizabeth said that wouldn't be necessary. Just two days later, there was a bidding war between two major publishers. All Elizabeth had to do was show them how many followers Angeni had between her personal account, the Conscious Couples account, and the Mother Nurture account. This was how the publishing industry worked these days, Elizabeth explained. The two publishers threw out six-figure offers like they were nothing. After a round of intense negotiations, Angeni accepted the slightly higher bid of $200,000. They told her she could have a year to write the book, which seemed like both an eternity and no time at all.

It had been gnawing at her how she'd been so adamant about having all her attention on Freya for the first three precious years. She had instructed herself not to commit to any major work projects during those years.

The night before, lying in bed next to Erik, she'd asked him, "Am I betraying myself? Am I betraying Freya?"

"I think you would be betraying all of us if you didn't write this book," he'd said.

She hadn't thought of it that way.

"Sometimes, life gives us opportunities that we did not expect. Spirit works through us in ways we could not imagine," he'd said.

"Freya won't remember this time," he'd said.

She never understood parents who said that—*She won't even remember this*. The body carried memories that the brain did not.

Would Freya feel her mother's divided attention, her dedication to something other than mothering? Erik wouldn't understand these kinds of concerns, so she didn't bother talking through them. She had to reason this out with herself.

"Think about how the universe brought us Sitka," he'd said. "We didn't expect that either. And look how beautiful it's been to have her here. Maybe the whole reason for Sitka coming to us was to support you during this time of creative production."

"Maybe."

Spirit had a way of doing this—bringing you what you needed before you knew you needed it. It was often only in retrospect that you saw the magic.

She needed to discuss a formal plan with Sitka for Freya's care while the book was in progress. They needed a structure that would feel right to all of them—Angeni, Freya, and Sitka.

~

They were in the kitchen together now, the three of them plus Aurora. Angeni was starting a batch of chicken-liver pâté for Freya. She put the chicken liver in a pot of bone broth and turned up the heat to a simmer. When it was cooked through, she would add raw butter and a pinch of sea salt before putting everything in the blender, then pouring the mixture into tiny glass jars to store in the fridge.

Whenever she posted these meals, she got a slew of comments from people like gross and you feed that to your kid? and I highly doubt your baby eats that. Her baby *did* eat it, though—not enthusiastically at first, but she ate it. And that was because Angeni was smart and intentional about how she introduced foods to Freya. She was focused on foods to help Freya's brain develop and give her a healthy microbiome and set her up for a lifetime of healthy eating. She had no plans to introduce anything sweeter than a yam for several months. This was a mistake most parents made. They gave their babies fruits and yogurts and then were mystified later when they refused to eat broccoli and chicken.

"I'm thinking I should include some recipes in the book," Angeni said.

Freya was in her bouncer on the floor. It was more of an activity center than a bouncer, the seat surrounded by various things to capture her attention—a spinning butterfly, an elephant rattle, a turtle mirror, a frog that lit up. Angeni worried it was too much stimulation, that it would wire her brain to crave increasingly higher levels of excitement, chasing the dopamine dragon like the brains of so many other small children. But it was a gift from Matt, and she felt awful not using it. He didn't have a lot of money, but a simple Google search told her he'd spent nearly a hundred dollars on this toy contraption. So she let Freya sit in it for about a half hour a day, max. It was obvious she liked it, which was both heartwarming and unsettling.

"Recipes would be such a nice touch," Aurora said.

"I'll have to ask my agent what she thinks."

"I mean, that's what you're about, right? *Nurturing.* Emotionally and physically," Aurora said.

Aurora knew her well, but she would always be a cheerleader, never a critic. Angeni turned to Sitka to seek her opinion.

"Sitka, what do you think?"

"About what?" she said.

Sitka seemed distracted lately. Angeni got the sense sometimes that she was itching to leave, that something outside The Land was pulling at her. She'd asked Erik if he'd noticed, but he said no. He wasn't nearly as intuitive as Angeni, though. He could be so blissfully unaware of things that Angeni saw so clearly. It was one of her greatest frustrations with him—she was often miles ahead, waiting for him to catch up to her.

"Recipes. For my book," Angeni said.

"Oh, yeah, sure," Sitka said.

"I think it's a great idea," Aurora reiterated.

They had reached a dead end on that topic, so Angeni decided to bring up the childcare arrangement for Freya.

"Sitka, I wanted to talk to you about a set schedule for you to help with Freya while I'm working on the book," Angeni said.

Aurora went to the stove to tend to the chicken liver, though it didn't need much tending. Angeni knew she was still a bit hurt that she wouldn't be the primary caretaker for Freya while Angeni worked. Aurora loved Freya, but Angeni sensed Freya had a more natural connection with Sitka. Besides, what better way to integrate Sitka more into their community than to have her help with the baby?

"Okay," Sitka said.

Sitka sat on the floor next to the bouncer, her flowy skirt hiked up to her upper thighs, long dark legs stretched out in front of her. Her skin always seemed to be gleaming, probably thanks to the vanilla balm Angeni had made for her and told her to use liberally all over her body.

"I'm thinking of turning the sunroom into my writing room. I'll just add a desk and make a little creativity altar," she said.

She would start collecting things from the forest for her altar—heart-shaped stones and leaves and bird feathers, anything she found inspiring.

"I love that idea," Aurora said, turning around to share her enthusiasm.

"Okay," Sitka said again. She was now playing with Freya, pulling back and releasing the little elephant rattle, much to Freya's delight.

"I don't feel good about being away from Freya, obviously," she added. "So I was thinking I could create a play area in the sunroom next to my desk, and you could sit and be with her for my writing time."

Sitka looked up, met Angeni's eyes. Angeni could not tell what she was thinking. Her stare just looked blank.

"Okay," she said. It seemed to be the only word she was capable of saying.

"I'll only write for an hour or so a day. I don't want it to be totally boring for you. Or for Freya."

"That's fine. I don't mind spending time with her," she said. Then, as an afterthought: "And supporting you with the book."

Was it disapproval Angeni was sensing? Did Sitka not think she should write the book? She decided to ask, practicing what she so often preached about authenticity.

"Can I ask . . . What do you think of me writing this book?"

Sitka's attention was back on Freya. When she spoke, she didn't look at Angeni.

"I think it's a great opportunity for you."

"But do you think I'm . . . I don't know . . . *worthy* of it?"

"Of course you're worthy of it," Aurora interjected. Angeni ignored her, kept her eyes on Sitka.

Sitka looked up, surprised. "*Worthy?* I don't think I'm one to judge that."

But that was exactly what Angeni sensed—judgment.

Angeni tried again: "Do you think my mission, my teachings, are deserving of a book?"

Sitka stood, her skirt falling to her ankles, hands on her hips.

"You've said it yourself. I'm not your target audience. I'm not a mother. So I don't really know. But you have millions of people who think so. My opinion shouldn't matter."

But it did matter. For whatever reason, it did matter.

"I'm not a mother either, and I'm absolutely sure your mission is deserving of a book, Ang," Aurora said.

"Thank you, Ror," Angeni said. "But Sitka, I don't want to ask you to support this project if it doesn't align with who you are."

Sitka shrugged. "I'm not sure I know who I am."

Freya started pressing her tiny feet against the ground, as if trying to launch herself out of the bouncer and into the arms of the women who loved her. Angeni knelt down, lifted her out.

"You know, I haven't asked you enough about you," Angeni said to Sitka.

Maybe the disconnect Angeni sensed was easily correctable. Maybe they just needed more heart-to-hearts, more intentional connection.

Sitka was now leaning against the island. When she reached her arms over her head, her loose-fitting shirt rode up, and Angeni could see the taut midriff that taunted her every day.

"What do you want to know?" Sitka asked, lowering her arms.

"Where did you grow up?"

"Just outside Seattle."

"Siblings?"

Sitka swallowed hard and said, "No." Angeni tried to figure out the look that crossed her face. Was it sadness? Regret? Maybe she was estranged from her family.

"Are you close with your parents?" Angeni asked.

"It's just my mom."

Angeni saw the chance to identify some common ground: "It was just me and my mom too."

Sitka seemed unfazed by this fact, so Angeni went on: "Are you two close, you and your mother?"

"I wouldn't say we're that close. We talk every couple of weeks or so," she said.

"I'm guessing you kind of had to raise yourself," Angeni said. Then, as a show of vulnerability, "Like me."

Sitka exhaled like she was exhausted by this inquisition.

"My mom had to work. Some women *have* to work to, like, *survive*."

There was an edge to her tone. She was taking Angeni's observations as criticism.

"Right. I know. I get it. My mom wasn't around much either," Angeni said. "I'm just saying I know it's hard to grow up like that."

Sitka stood up a bit taller, her shoulder blades pinching together.

"I think I turned out fine. I mean, my mother didn't make me chicken-liver pâté, but she was a good mom."

She said that—*chicken-liver pâté*—with a tinge of mocking.

"It's really good, actually, the pâté," Aurora said. "I was going to put some out with crackers for the adults before dinner later."

Sitka looked amused by Aurora, but before she could respond, Erik, Matt, and Jer appeared at the side door. Aurora let out a sound like an excited squeal and went to them, taking a tall pink box from Jer's arms. She opened the top of the box to reveal a round cake decorated with wildflowers.

"Oh my gosh, it came out so good," Aurora said.

They broke into song:

"For she's a jolly good mama, for she's a jolly good mama, for she's a jolly good mama, which nobody can deny," they hollered.

Freya started to cry—her poor sensitive ears—and Angeni held her tight, one of her tiny ears pressed to Angeni's chest, the other cupped by Angeni's hand.

They repeated their song as Aurora went to place the cake on the island. It was a beautiful cake—slathered in white icing that acted like glue for the wildflowers. Scrawled across the top in pink icing was the word **CONGRATULATIONS!**

"Oh my goodness," Angeni said. She was truly surprised.

Aurora started taking photos with her phone. Angeni turned Freya's body so she was facing outward for the photos. She was already thinking up the Instagram post, how she would write about her gratitude for the community they'd created on The Land. This would be the perfect way to announce the book deal too—*I am so thankful for the kind souls who will make me capable of embarking on this journey.*

Freya was not pleased in Angeni's arms, kept looking back at Sitka, who had retreated to stand against the back wall of the kitchen, out of the photos.

"We are all so excited for you, babe," Erik said over Freya's cries.

Angeni bounced the baby, shushed her gently. "It's okay, sweetie. Let's smile for the camera."

She whispered these words, ashamed at how naturally they came from her mouth. She didn't believe in parents demanding certain displays of emotions from their children. But she couldn't exactly post a photo on Instagram with her child noticeably distressed.

Aurora kept taking photos, seemingly oblivious to Freya's meltdown.

"Do you want me to take her?" Erik asked.

Angeni shook her head. "She'll settle. It's all the excitement."

"Ang, we are seriously proud of you," Jer said.

"Seriously. A book deal!" Matt echoed.

Angeni smiled despite the discomfort rising within her. Freya was not settling. Angeni could feel Freya's body getting more and more dysregulated, her little legs kicking against Angeni's belly, her face turning red, her little mouth widening so big to scream that Angeni could see the back of her throat.

"Shhhh," Angeni kept whispering without effect.

"Should I cut the cake?" Aurora asked. "It's from that little bakery you love."

The bakery with the all-natural ingredients, the bakery that used whole wheat and spelt flours, flaxseed paste instead of eggs, applesauce instead of butter, maple syrup and honey instead of sugar.

"I can get some plates," Sitka said from behind her.

Freya kept shrieking, but everyone else seemed able to treat it like white noise.

"So how does it work? They pay you now, and then you write the book?" Matt asked, his voice loud enough to rise above Freya's cries.

Angeni was starting to feel hot and nauseated, Freya's body like a ball of fire against her chest.

"Um, yeah. It's called an advance, and I use that to live on so I can write the book."

"So awesome," Matt said.

"This book is going to change lives," Aurora added.

Sitka put plates and forks on the island while Aurora cut the cake, carving out thin slivers and putting them on plates for Jer to pass around. Erik handed a plate to Angeni as Freya continued to cry and squirm. Angeni was appalled that he thought she could take her hands off their child at this moment.

He must have read her facial expression, one of complete annoyance. He set her plate on the island.

"Are you sure you don't want me to take her?" he asked. He looked sheepish and guilty.

She felt a wave of heat roll through her and knew this to be rage. She was someone who went to great lengths to avoid feeling rage in her body. She had become so adept with her somatic work, easing herself into a calm state with deep breathing and compassionate self-talk. This rage, it was the rage of her youth, the rage of a past her followers could never know. It was one thing to share the broad strokes of Erik's story—a soft-focus Monet of his trials, tribulations, and triumphs on the way to sobriety. Angeni's image was completely different. Society was always harder on women anyway. Men could be forgiven nearly anything. Women, no.

"I can take her," Aurora said upon noticing the tension between Erik and Angeni.

"Nobody needs to take her!" Angeni shouted.

It came out as a roar, something deep and guttural. Everyone quieted, almost instantly, including Freya, who had never heard her mother raise her voice.

Quickly, the rage dissipated and was replaced with shame, which was always how it went. This was the Jekyll and Hyde of every human being—rage and shame, shame and rage.

"I'm sorry," she said, looking around the room at the faces of the people she loved most dearly.

Matt and Jer looked dumbfounded. Aurora looked scared. Erik looked worried, so worried. Sitka was behind her, so Angeni couldn't see her. Freya kept staring into Angeni's eyes, transfixed and curious, like *Who was that, Mommy?* Or rather, *Who was THAT Mommy?*

She could smell Sitka approach from behind her, the vanilla scent of the balm.

"I'm sorry," Angeni said again.

The room was pin-drop quiet. She could hear her own breathing. She wanted to hand the baby to Sitka and run into the forest, be with the trees, which would offer her their branches like arms of a hug.

"Here," Sitka said, her voice gentle and kind, her hands already on Freya before Angeni could refuse.

Angeni let her take the baby, a passive allowance. Sitka had given her no choice, and that was a relief.

"We should have told you we were doing this," Aurora said. "Surprises are a lot to take in, energetically. I know how sensitive your nervous system is. Freya's too."

She shared this frequently with her followers: the magic of a child being your mirror, your guru. In Freya, she saw herself—the thin skin, the tendency toward overwhelm at just existing in this chaotic, messy world. Angeni's own mother had said she was "too much," and she swore she would never say that to Freya, never let Freya ever feel like too much. But here she was, handing her to Sitka, effectively saying *I cannot deal with you right now*. But maybe Freya could not deal with her either.

"Maybe you just need a breather," Erik said.

"I'll walk Freya around outside a bit. She loves the trees," Sitka said. Then: "Like her mama."

It was sweet of Sitka to say this, to remind Angeni that she understood her and Freya well.

"I'm okay. I was just overstimulated," Angeni said.

"Of course," Matt said.

They were all nodding at her.

"I might join you two in a minute," she said to Sitka.

"Sure," Sitka said.

Freya was back to her angel-baby self in Sitka's arms. Angeni watched them leave, saw them through the big picture window in the kitchen as they meandered down the path to Angeni's favorite tree, the one bearing Sitka's name—how uncanny that was.

"The book deal, it's a bit overwhelming. I think that's it," Angeni said.

She felt she had to say something, that the others were waiting for her to explain, to absolve them of any fault.

"I really do appreciate the gesture," she added.

"Dude, if I had to write a book, I'd be having daily panic attacks," Matt said.

Erik gave him a look. "I don't think that's helping, Matt."

"It's fine," Angeni said. "Guys, I'm fine."

Erik put his hand on her shoulder, squeezed the tense muscles.

"I'm going to follow my girls," Angeni said, jutting her chin outside toward Sitka and Freya.

"Fresh air does wonders," Erik said.

"Never fails," Aurora said.

~

Fresh air did do wonders. Angeni inhaled deeply the moment she stepped outside, felt her inner world make sense again, the ragged edges smoothing. She walked quickly to catch up to Sitka and Freya. From a distance, she saw they had stopped in the clearing up ahead. It was a perfect space between the trees, a space Angeni envisioned using for prayer circles and other rituals. She pictured groups of people visiting The Land for healing, sitting on stools made from tree trunks, flowers woven in their hair. In her visions, the gatherings were always in the open air, but she knew it would be wise to build a yurt as well. It rained so often. The Clearing Project, as Erik had dubbed it, was number two on their list of priorities. The first priority was their outdoor sauna and ice bath, what Angeni referred to as The Pharmacy because it offered what their bodies needed more than actual drugs made by greedy pharmaceutical companies.

Angeni stopped about a hundred feet from Sitka and Freya. She watched them, the ease they had with each other. Sitka seemed like a different person whenever Angeni witnessed her alone with Freya. She laughed with her whole body. She smiled so big, her white teeth gleaming. Around Angeni, Sitka's smiles were always tight; Angeni never saw teeth.

In this moment, Sitka was holding Freya above her head and spinning around. Freya giggled with a gusto that filled Angeni with a mix of joy and doubt. Was Angeni too serious with Freya? Did Freya prefer someone younger and more fun? Was this just the classic mother-daughter friction already revealing itself? Freya knew she had her mother's love, so it was less interesting than the love of this person who was a stranger until just recently. Freya would spend her life pushing against her mother's love, testing its fortitude, in a way she would never push against any other human being's. It was an honor and it was torture.

Angeni resumed walking, picking up her pace, nearly jogging through the grass.

"Hi, you two," she called out.

Sitka stopped spinning and held Freya against her chest. When Angeni got to them, she said, "Mommy's here" and reached for Freya. She analyzed Freya's facial expression, looking for disappointment. There was none that she could decipher.

"See how nature makes us feel better?" she said to Freya, lifting her over her head as Sitka had been doing, then sitting on the ground with Freya in her lap.

Angeni let Freya touch the dirt and the ferns with her tiny hands. This was her dream, to have her daughter create an intimate relationship with The Land, to know every inch of the forest, to be tuned in to nature in a way that so many children these days were not. Angeni was horrified by the realities of iPads and YouTube, couldn't believe that so many parents allowed their children to while away hours on devices. She had to be careful she didn't come across as judgmental, though. She'd received enough flak already:

> Your kid isn't even 1 yet. Wait til she's 2 and you need a fucking second to yourself

> You seem kinda clueless about your privilege. You don't work a regular job. You have all kinds of helpers living with you. If I had that, my kid wouldn't be on the iPad either

> I'm catching a whiff of mommy wars. Can we just not? We all have diff circumstances and we're all doing our best

> Single mama here and ya, I use the iPad. tbh u have no idea what it's like to not have help

Angeni didn't bother responding to any of these people. She'd learned that some people were just dead set on criticizing her. This was social media—a venue for people to vent their grievances and express their bitterness in. Angeni was a perfect target because she had this life that so many envied. Did that make her a bad person? She hadn't always had this life. She'd manifested it with care and intention. Too few people took responsibility for their existence.

Sitka placed a small pebble in Freya's palm, and Angeni watched as she, predictably, lifted it to her mouth.

"Oh, no, sweetie, we don't eat rocks," she said with a nervous laugh, taking the pebble from Freya's hand.

This led to the return of Crying Freya. Angeni cradled the baby in her arms, offered her a pinkie finger to grasp in place of the pebble. Within a few seconds, Freya settled, but Angeni still harbored irritation with Sitka for offering Freya the pebble.

"She will literally try to eat anything you give her," Angeni said.

She expected an immediate apology from Sitka, but Sitka said, "I was watching her. I wouldn't, like, let her eat a *rock*."

"She can be quick about it. She could swallow it, and you wouldn't even know."

"I watch her," Sitka said. "Carefully."

Angeni didn't like the defensiveness in her tone. Angeni was the mother. Angeni was in charge. She had a passing thought that she should check Freya's poop more carefully, in search of pebbles or whatever other evidence that Sitka did not watch as carefully as she should.

"I'm sorry, though," Sitka said as if reading Angeni's mind.

Angeni always softened in response to apologies.

"It's okay," she said. "Erik says I'm too protective."

This seemed to pique Sitka's interest. "Does he?"

"Well, yeah. He's always been more laid back than me, I suppose. Every relationship has to have one person who is more anxious and one person who is telling the other to be less anxious."

She laughed to alert Sitka to the fact that this was nothing to take terribly seriously. She and Erik, they were solid. They'd spent years together working through their differences and had arrived at a peaceful place of allowing each other to be authentically themselves.

"Have you had many serious relationships?" she asked Sitka.

"Not serious, no," Sitka said.

That was what Angeni had assumed. Sitka was so young. She had so much to uncover about herself, and if or when she had serious relationships, there would be even more to uncover. That was what Angeni talked about in her Conscious Couples Communicating webinars—how relationships revealed things that we simply could not know in the comfort of our own company. Relationships were our greatest teachers.

"You have very independent energy," Angeni said.

"I like to think so."

Angeni smiled to herself. Sitka had yet to realize that the independence she prided herself on might be her greatest hindrance, holding her back from true connection. Hyperindependence was a trauma response, a reaction to having to be so self-sufficient at such a young age. Angeni understood because she'd been this way herself once. She'd healed. Sitka did not even know she needed healing.

"Do you crave connection, though?" Angeni asked.

Sitka shrugged. "I'm not longing for a boyfriend, if that's what you're asking."

"The label isn't important. Anyway, I'm just curious. I'm sorry if these questions are intrusive."

"It's fine," Sitka said. "I just don't want to ever lose myself to a man."

It was a surprise, this offering, an honest confession that Angeni didn't expect.

"If you've been independent for so long, that's an understandable concern. Erik is my first serious relationship, if you can believe it," Angeni said, offering a confession of her own.

"Really?"

"Yeah. Before him, it was just casual sex with guys who were terrible for me."

Sitka raised her eyebrows.

"Oh god, don't tell my followers that."

"I don't think they'd believe me," Sitka said with a laugh.

It felt good to connect with Sitka, to capture her attention and get her to laugh, but Angeni couldn't deny the instant regret she felt about her disclosure. She had prioritized being liked by Sitka over protecting her inner life. It was juvenile; she wasn't acting in accordance with her higher self.

"There are some things I don't share," Angeni said, formalizing her tone, straightening her spine. "Things that would divert attention from the things I do want to share."

"I get that," Sitka said. "But I do think that's the danger of social media, right? It leaves out the whole picture."

"I don't think people truly want the whole picture."

"I do," Sitka said. "I like people keeping it real."

"Do you think I don't do that? Keep it real?"

Angeni felt her heart rate accelerate in anticipation of Sitka's response. It was strange how much Sitka intimidated her.

"I don't know," Sitka said. "I'm only just getting to know what's real for you."

Like the casual sex with guys who were terrible for me, Angeni thought but didn't say. She couldn't believe she'd said it the first time.

Angeni turned her attention to Freya, a pleasant distraction from the far-flung places their conversation could go.

"Can I ask you something?" Angeni said. She didn't wait for Sitka to respond, just went for it: "Do you think I'm a good mother?"

Sitka looked at her thoughtfully, mulling over the question for a length of time that made Angeni uncomfortable. Why didn't she respond with an immediate "Yes"?

"Your love for your daughter is obvious," Sitka said finally.

"But?"

"There's no 'but.' I don't really know what a 'good mother' is. That's what I'm struggling with, that definition," she said. "Like, how would you define it?"

Angeni hadn't thought about that, specifically. She didn't have a list of criteria in her mind for what made a good mother. It was instinctual.

"To me, *mother* is a verb. It's acting in service of your child, as a shepherd for them through the world," she said. "It's nurturing their bodies and minds in a consistent and dedicated way."

Sitka nodded. "If that is your definition, then you are a good mother."

"You sound like a philosopher," Angeni said. She forced a laugh to hide her uneasiness.

Sitka sat cross-legged on the ground, putting Freya in the space between her knees. She used Freya's finger to trace hearts in the dirt.

"Can I ask what your definition of a good mother is?" Angeni said.

Sitka didn't hesitate with this answer. "I think a good mother is, first and foremost, a fully realized woman, someone who loves herself and sets an example for her child of self-love."

Angeni found her answer interesting, the way it centered the mother in the mothering instead of the child. It made sense, considering Sitka's age. When Angeni was in her twenties, she could not see beyond herself either.

"I can appreciate that definition," Angeni said neutrally.

Freya's hands were getting filthy, and Angeni kept a close eye on her to make sure she didn't put them in her mouth.

"Should we get back?" she asked. "Freya might need a bath."

Sitka stood, and Angeni lifted Freya into her arms. As they headed back to the house, Sitka lingered behind Angeni and Freya instead of walking side by side with them.

"I think I should tell you," Sitka said, her voice soft and quiet.

Angeni stopped and turned. Sitka stopped then too.

"I don't know how long I'm going to stay," Sitka said.

So there it was.

"Oh," Angeni said. She was both surprised and not surprised at all. "Okay. I mean, you're under no obligation, of course. Do you have a timeframe in mind?"

"I don't know," Sitka said. "I've already stayed longer than I thought I would. I know you need help with Freya when you work on the book. I just—"

Angeni felt a familiar defensiveness arrive within her. It was the defensiveness triggered by her abandonment wounding. For so many years, the moment anyone had hinted at leaving her, Angeni had shut down and had to leave them first. She had thought she'd healed that wound, but here it was again.

"I don't want you to stay if you don't want to stay."

It came out childish. She turned, resumed walking. Freya started fussing in her arms. She took a deep breath, remembered that she couldn't let her fears overtake her.

She turned around, locked eyes with Sitka. "We can pay you," she said.

"Oh," Sitka said. Her brows were knitted together as she appeared to contemplate this unexpected offer.

Angeni thought of what Erik had said from the beginning, how they should pay Sitka. Perhaps it had been wrong of her to assume that living here, for free, would be enough of an incentive for a young woman like Sitka.

"I can write it off as an expense—childcare while I work on the book." She was sure many mother-writers used some of their advance for childcare.

"Okay," Sitka said. "Let's see how it goes, then."

"That will formalize our arrangement, which is probably best for both of us," Angeni said. "I don't want you to feel unappreciated."

"I don't, I just—"

"So it's settled?" Angeni asked. "I'll work out the weekly wage when I talk to Erik."

"Okay," Sitka said.

Angeni had already turned back around and was marching back toward the house as Sitka delivered a barely audible "Thank you."

Chapter 11

BRITT

Britt got her period for the first time a week after turning twelve. She knew it was coming because girls at school were always talking about it. Becky had gotten her period a few months earlier. Rainbow had made her a crown of daisies and her favorite sugar cookies in the shape of hearts. It was a joyous event at their house, celebrated as a crossing into sacred womanhood. At her own house, Britt crawled under the blanket on her bed, tucked her knees to her chest, and cried.

It was gross, this blood coming from her body, announcing so violently that she was no longer a girl. She had a stash of pads that Becky had given her. She didn't want to tell her mother that she was now a woman because she knew her mother would never commemorate it the way Rainbow had. Her mother would just sigh and say something like "Welcome to the worst years of your life."

When there was a knock at her bedroom door, Britt panicked that it was her mom, that she had seen the pad wrapping in the bathroom trash.

"Yeah?" she called from under the covers.

"Just wondering if you still wanted to go shooting today."

It was Steve. It was Saturday. They always went shooting on Saturdays.

"Oh," she said. "Okay."

Whenever she had a buildup of feelings, shooting seemed to help. It was like pushing a reset button on her psyche. She got out of bed and put on a pair of baggy jeans, looking at her backside in the mirror to make sure the puffy pad wasn't visible. Then she opened the door to Steve's smiling face, and off they went.

~

After they'd each fired a round with the Steyr AUG, Britt was already feeling better. She'd started to load a new magazine when Steve put a hand on her wrist. She looked up at him, scared she was doing something wrong, though she'd loaded magazines dozens of times by then.

"Kiddo, there's something I need to talk to you about," he said.

She knew, from just his tone, what he was going to say.

~

Steve had never proposed to Britt's mom. He had bought the ring. But the all-important question was never popped. Britt waited and waited, hesitant to ask Steve outright what was taking so long. The thing was, she didn't need to ask. She'd overheard enough arguments through the walls to know that her mother was backsliding. She'd stopped taking her medication, saying it made her feel like a zombie and she was tired of feeling like a zombie. At first, Steve tried to coax her, doling out the pills like usual at the dinner table. But after she made a scene a few times with Britt sitting right there, he took his attempts to persuade behind the closed door of their bedroom. When those attempts failed, he gave up, said, "I can't force you."

Predictably, her mother's wild mood swings returned. They seemed worse than ever, but maybe it was just that Britt now had a peaceful reprieve to compare them to. The contrast was stark. She started drinking more again, and Steve suggested AA, said he would go along with her. He made a show of going to Al-Anon for himself. When he kept going, saying the meetings helped him, Britt knew the end was near. The people in those meetings had people like Britt's mother pegged. They would make Steve see the light, and when he did, he would leave.

~

They sat at a wooden picnic table directly behind the shooting range lanes, Steve on one side, Britt across from him. He placed his elbows on the table, clasped his hands together, and let out a long exhale.

"I think this might be the hardest thing I've ever done," he said.

Britt was already shaking her head, denying what was coming. Her eyes were already filling with tears.

"You're leaving us," Britt said.

She couldn't bear for him to be the one to say it. She had to break her own news, to feel some sense of control over the situation.

"I'm not leaving you, Britt," he said.

Britt felt hopeful for a second before his shoulders visibly slumped. His eyes were cast down, staring at his hands.

"Losing a relationship with you is like an unwanted side effect of this," he said. "I would never want to leave you."

"But you are," she said.

"Things with your mother . . . they've just become untenable," he said.

She imagined he had rehearsed this line, searched for the exact right word. *Untenable.*

"So it's over, then? She knows?"

"I'm telling her tonight. I wanted to talk to you first," he said.

Before the shitstorm was what he meant.

"I've really tried," he said.

Britt stared off at the targets in the distance and said, "I know." Because she did know. He had tried harder and stayed longer than he should have.

When she looked back at him, their eyes met, and she had to restrain herself from grabbing his hands and shouting *Take me with you.* He must have noticed her eyes were pleading for something, though, because he was the one to reach across the table, to take her hands and squeeze them.

"I'm so sorry, Britt," he said.

A fat tear rolled down his cheek. It was the first time Britt had ever seen a man cry.

"I knew this would happen at some point," she said.

It wasn't a *should have known* situation. She had known, all along, that it was too good to be true. She was upset that she'd let herself get swept up in the goodness and been willfully ignorant to the truth.

"I'm sorry that your life with her up to this point has caused you to expect so little," he said.

It was the most poignant thing she'd ever heard.

"You've been like a daughter to me," he said.

He must have thought she would find that endearing, but it just made her furious. She wasn't really like a daughter to him. If she was, he wouldn't leave. Or he would take her with him.

"Where are we gonna go?" she asked.

He was leaving them, yes, in all the ways that mattered. But they were living in his home. Britt and her mother would be the ones doing the actual leaving.

"I'm going to tell her there's no rush. You two can stay as long as you need to. I'll help you find a place," he said, rushing to fill in the blanks. So many blanks.

Britt had become so settled into this life at Steve's house. She had made the mistake of getting comfortable, relaxing her vigilance, daring to calm her mind instead of always thinking ahead to the next potential crisis. She could feel the parts of her brain that had previously been dedicated to managing the chaos of her mother awaken again.

"The minute you tell her it's over, she's going to want to leave," Britt said.

Because her mother was never reasonable in these situations.

"I'm going to try my best to keep things mellow," he said.

"Famous last words."

That made him chuckle.

"Maybe we can still go shooting sometimes?" Britt said.

Her voice was small when she said this. She felt silly admitting her desire to stay in touch. She braced herself for his rejection.

"I'd love that, but I just worry about your mom finding out."

"She won't find out."

"I don't know," he said. "We should probably wait awhile, let things settle, then see."

She knew then that she would never see him again. Britt stood from the table, unable to see any point in continuing the conversation.

"One day, she won't be your problem to manage anymore," he said. "I hope you know that."

Britt stood, hands on her hips. "She's my mother," she said. "She'll always be my problem."

He shook his head in adamant denial of this.

"No," he said. "You're going to grow up and go off on your own and have your own life. You are meant for more."

Britt shrugged. "I don't know if it matters what I'm meant for."

"You can't let her drag you down, Britt," he said. "You just can't."

"I'll try to remember that over the next six years when she's having one of her phases."

Britt started walking back toward the car. The pad between her legs felt especially bulky. It seemed somehow appropriate that she was bleeding. The wounds weren't visible, but they were there.

~

The drive back was silent until they were a couple of blocks from the house.

"I want you to have the AUG," Steve said.

Britt kept her gaze out the window as she took in his offering. He wanted her to have the rifle—her favorite one, the first one she'd shot.

"And the 1911 if you want it," he said.

Her favorite handgun.

"You don't have to do that," she said.

She didn't want his pity gifts, his attempts to assuage his own guilt.

"I want to," he said. "I'm going to leave the bag with them in your room when we get back. Please take them. You can sell them if you want."

They were expensive. She could get at least a couple grand for them.

"Okay, fine. I'll sell them. We'll need the money," she said.

She was just trying to hurt him. She knew she would never sell them. She knew she would keep them forever.

~

Britt was right, of course. When Britt's mother got word she was being dumped that night at dinner, she told Britt to pack her things. Steve was kind and did his best to convince her to give it a few days so they could find an apartment, but she was stubbornly committed to making it worse than it had to be. Britt filled two trash bags with the possessions she'd accumulated under Steve's roof and threw them, along with the duffel bag with the guns, into the trunk of her mom's car. Within an hour, they were gone.

"Where are we going?" Britt asked as they pulled onto the freeway.

"I don't fucking know," her mother said.

Her mother was driving too fast, ninety miles per hour. Britt hoped they would get pulled over. She hoped her mother would get into an altercation with a police officer and get thrown in jail for a night or two. Britt would have to go to some kind of juvenile center for kids whose parents were fuckups, but that didn't sound so bad.

As her mother sped along, undeterred, Britt watched her face. It was a face that looked so much like her own that hating it felt wrong. She hated it, though. She hated her mother.

I wish you were dead, she thought.

It was only when her mother said, "What did you say?" that Britt realized she'd said the words out loud.

"What?" Britt asked.

Her mother took her eyes off the road.

"What did you just say?" she asked again.

"I didn't say anything," Britt said.

Her mother stared at her until a car honked at them, laying on the horn for several seconds. Her mother was drifting into the other lane.

"Mom!" Britt said.

Her mother corrected, and they were back in their lane, her mother's eyes on the road. She didn't ask again what Britt had said. Britt continued thinking it:

I wish you were dead.

Chapter 12

Sasha

Sasha made a point of visiting Jay every few days after Daphne's death. "He's not doing well," Sasha's mother said, following one of her own visits. Sasha snapped at her mother then: "Well, of course he's not fucking doing well!"

The fire department offered just a three-day bereavement leave, as if it was possible to resume functioning three days after losing a spouse and child. When Jay came back after the three days, he was such a mess that they insisted he take an additional month of leave. It was unpaid, which was a concern, since Jay had spent most of his savings on the funeral service. He and Daphne hadn't had a ton of savings to begin with, had earmarked what they did have for the baby. It seemed cruel to have to use that money to survive in the wake of the destruction of their dream.

Sasha worried about him, alone in the house he'd shared with Daphne, the house where she and their son had died. She texted him several times a day, always starting with a "good morning" text and ending with a "sleep well" text. She held her breath after the "good morning" texts, awaiting his response. She knew he was drinking a lot at night. She worried that after a few beers, he would do something stupid. She knew they owned a gun. Daphne had mentioned it once, saying she wasn't sure how she felt about "the thing" being in their house. Jay had taken her to the shooting range once in an attempt to get her comfortable using it, and she had said, "No way. If there's an intruder, you're in charge."

Sasha didn't know if she was the best person to be offering support to Jay. She, herself, was not doing well. On the days depression began to descend upon her, she distracted herself with her ongoing rage toward Angeni Luna. After all, she had to direct her anger at something. It couldn't just . . . fester.

She kept having this fantasy of taking the ferry over to Bainbridge Island and finding Angeni Luna. She would confront her, tell her what had happened to Daphne. She would record the interaction on her phone, post it later for all the world to hear. Angeni would receive an avalanche of vitriol in response. It would be justice—not enough, but some. She decided to talk to Jay about the idea. He would talk her out of it or into it, she wasn't sure which.

When Sasha got to the house, a disheveled Jay opened the door wearing the same hooded sweatshirt he'd worn the last time she saw him, the fuzz on his chin thickening into a beard. The living room was littered with beer cans. She had told him she was coming by, but he clearly hadn't felt the need to tidy up. She figured the cans were his way of telling her, without telling her, how awful he was feeling: *Look, here is evidence of me trying to numb this unbearable pain.*

"Hey, sis," he said.

It was his usual greeting, previously said with enthusiasm and accompanied by a fist bump, now said slowly and softly, as if it were a struggle to manufacture the two words.

"Hey," she said, walking past him into the living room.

Someone—Sasha's mother, most likely—had collected all the baby-related items and put them in piles by the front door. It would be like her mother to arrange for Goodwill to come do a pickup. Sasha assumed the crib was still in the nursery, too big for her mother to move without assistance. Jay was not in a place to offer assistance with much of anything, but especially with that task.

They sat on the couch, the same couch they'd sat on with Daphne so many times before.

"You said you wanted to ask me about something?" he said.

"Yeah. Basically, I need you to tell me if I'm crazy."

He managed a smile and said, "You definitely are."

It felt good to tease each other like they usually did.

"For real, though. I have this idea," she said.

"Oh no. It's never good when you have an idea."

"I want to go to Bainbridge Island and see Angeni Luna."

He sighed and threw his head back so it hit the back of the couch.

"God, I'd be happy to never again hear that woman's name," he said. "Is that even her real name?"

Sasha had gone down rabbit holes trying to decipher the real Angeni Luna, who was as white as white could be but said that her name had been *bestowed* upon her, presumably by Indigenous people. Angeni was not even a true tribal name—just the Algonquian pronunciation of "angel." Luna was of Latin origin, meaning "moon." This woman was as inauthentic as you could get.

"I don't know. It's probably Karen."

He didn't laugh. With his head still tilted back, he said, "Sis, that woman can't bring Daph back."

"I know," Sasha said.

"So what are you trying to accomplish?"

"I want to confront her about Daphne's death. I want people to know what happened. She can't just go on living her smug little life as if nothing happened."

He lifted his head so he was sitting upright again.

"I mean, who am I to judge? If it helps you feel better, do it," he said. "Just don't end up in jail over there, okay? If I have to come over on that fucking ferry, I'm gonna be pissed."

He stood from the couch and went to the kitchen. Sasha followed him.

"I'm not going to end up in jail," she said.

He took a carton of orange juice from the fridge, poured himself a glass. He lifted the carton toward her, offering, but she shook her head.

"When are you doing this crazy stunt of yours?" Jay asked.

Sasha didn't have an exact day in mind. The sooner, the better. Otherwise, the fantasy would keep nagging her. She'd had it in her head that this confrontation of Angeni Luna would assuage her grief, at least a little. She had to believe something would. She couldn't just spend the rest of her life feeling like she was walking through molasses.

"Soon," Sasha said. "I'll text you."

He drank down the rest of the juice and put the empty cup in the sink, then headed back to the living room.

"Jay, are you going to be okay?"

She directed the question to the back of his head. She didn't know if she could ask it while looking at his sad face.

He sat on the couch and looked up at her.

"I have no idea," he said. His eyes were dark wells, filled to the brim.

She sat next to him on the couch.

"I need you to stick around for me," she said, her voice shaky.

"I'll at least stick around to find out what happens with Angeni Lunatic."

Sasha laughed, and he laughed, and Sasha felt for a second that both of them would be okay.

He walked her to the front door, and she hugged him, long and tight. Ever since Daphne's death, this had been how she'd hugged him. She would never again be able to hug someone without wondering if it would be the last time.

"I'll keep texting you every day," she said. "And if you don't respond, I'm gonna have to call your ass."

Daphne had loved talking on the phone, and they'd always made fun of her for it—*Okay, boomer.*

Jay strengthened his hold of Sasha, then let go.

"Please don't call my ass."

~

That night in bed, Sasha tapped the Google icon on her phone, typed in hippie names. When she visited Angeni Luna, she'd need a fake name, a name that would endear her to Angeni Luna and get her welcomed inside her home.

Indigo
Lark
Daffodil
Willow

Willow. That gave her an idea. Angeni Luna wrote often of her love of trees, spoke of the ones on her property as if they were resident friends. Sasha remembered there was one particular kind she'd mentioned as a favorite.

Sasha scrolled through Angeni's Instagram posts, looking for the one she remembered, the one taken from inside Angeni Luna's magazine-worthy kitchen.

There it was. The big picture window perfectly framing the giant tree outside.

The caption:

> This, my friends, is the tree whose branches feel like arms, holding me up as I walk through this world. This, my friends, is the Sitka spruce.

There it was.

It was perfect.

Sitka.

Chapter 13

Gwen

After showering, Gwen applied makeup for the first time since June was born, all in preparation for her visit with Leigh. She had the diaper bag stocked and June secured in the car seat with a half hour to spare. According to the map app, Leigh's condo was only twelve minutes away.

She stood at the kitchen island, the car seat on the floor by her feet, and scrolled through Instagram, pausing on Angeni Luna's latest post about a book deal. She watched the video of her people presenting her with a cake, singing to her. The baby, Freya, squirmed in her mother's arms, and when Gwen zoomed in closer, she thought she detected a touch of annoyance on Angeni's face. So she was human, after all.

June started to grunt, little expressions of impatience or discomfort, and Gwen put her foot on the edge of the car seat and rocked it back and forth while she continued passing time on her phone. She couldn't help but look up Leigh's address on Zillow. It was a condo in an eighteen-unit building in a great location, half the value of Gwen and Jeff's house, despite being about the same square footage. When Gwen and Jeff had bought their little house in Madison Park, one of the nicer Seattle neighborhoods, Gwen had been so sure of the decision. It was a good investment in an area that would always be desirable. Their daughter would have access to top-notch schools. They would be surrounded by successful, well-off people who shared their values. But now, Gwen envied Leigh, even though she hadn't even seen her home yet. She envied that she was just steps from restaurants and bars, able to keep one foot in her old life. Plus, if Gwen and Jeff had stayed in their apartment instead of taking on an enormous mortgage, Gwen wouldn't have to go back to work full-time. She and Jeff hadn't even discussed that yet—the coming-too-soon end of her maternity leave, her accompanying dread. She had been quite certain that she would slip back into her full-time work life with ease. She'd always loved her job. Hadn't she? She didn't even know who she was anymore.

~

"Okay, June Bug, ready to go see some friends?" she said in the singsong voice she'd acquired, another surprise of new motherhood.

June looked at her with faint interest, and Gwen lifted the car seat and lugged it out to click into the back seat of her car.

They arrived in front of Leigh's building on Eleventh Avenue just before two o'clock, right on time. They'd decided on an afternoon meetup, agreeing that the mornings were somewhat routinized and smooth, while the afternoons were marked by frayed nerves and meltdowns (for both the babies and the adults).

The building was a modern but cozy three-story, painted sapphire blue, right across from Cal Anderson Park. Gwen used to run on the park's jogging path when she and Jeff lived downtown.

When Gwen got out of the car, she heard her name: "Gwen! Hi!"

She turned to see Leigh on one of the third-floor terraces, the corner penthouse, waving frantically as if she'd been stranded there for months and Gwen was her rescue boat. Gwen waved back, just as frantically, caught up in their mutual excitement.

Gwen unlatched the car seat and held it up for Leigh to see, as if saying *Look, I have a baby!* Leigh bent down, disappearing from view, before reappearing with Belle in her arms, holding her overhead in a hilarious reenactment of the Mufasa-Simba moment from *The Lion King*.

"Let me buzz you in," she called down to Gwen.

Gwen was relieved to see an elevator in the lobby so she wouldn't have to carry June in the car seat up three flights of stairs. When the elevator doors parted, Leigh and Belle were there. Leigh, like Gwen, was wearing makeup, which made Gwen feel less self-conscious about the time she'd spent pulling herself together for this little meetup. Belle looked like she was about to start wailing any second but was waiting for just the right time to have maximal impact.

"We've had a bit of a morning," Leigh said.

"Isn't every morning a bit of a morning?"

Leigh led them down the hall to their unit and opened the front door. The inside was immaculate and stylish—white walls adorned with huge, colorful abstract paintings; wood floors done in a herringbone pattern; furniture that appeared curated for the space instead of transported from past homes over many years (like Gwen and Jeff's furniture). Gwen's eyes went straight to the floor-to-ceiling windows in the living room, the giant sliding door that went out to the terrace where Leigh had greeted Gwen.

"Wow, you have such gorgeous views," she said, setting down the car seat and wandering into the living room to stare out the windows.

"Yeah, on sunny days like today, it's pretty amazing," Leigh said.

June started crying, and Gwen turned around, remembering that she'd left her in the car seat by the front door. For the briefest of moments, she'd allowed herself to be lured by the views and completely forgotten her responsibility for this tiny human being.

She lifted June from the car seat, held her against her chest, patted her back.

"Was it an easy drive?" Leigh asked.

"Oh yeah, we're just in Madison Park."

Leigh's eyes grew wide for a second, long enough to express surprise at Gwen's financial status. In her ratty old sweatpants, Gwen certainly was not dressed like someone who could afford a house in Madison Park.

Belle started fussing in Leigh's arms, and Leigh sighed.

"Like I said, we've had a morning," she said. "Do you mind if I try to feed her again?"

"Not at all. I might try with June too."

Both of them sat on the couch facing the terrace. It was an oversize couch with deep cushions. Gwen felt like she could sink into it and never come out. They lifted their shirts and unfastened identical nursing bras. The babies latched in what looked like choreographed synchronicity.

"There we go," Leigh said with an exhalation of relief that Gwen knew well.

"How long have you guys lived here?" Gwen asked.

Leigh's eyes rolled up in mental calculation. "Almost two years," she said. "Nathan's parents used to own it, so we sort of inherited it from them."

Nathan. So that was the husband's name.

"Oh, I'm sorry. Did they pass?"

Leigh's mouth formed a big O. "Oh my god, no. I didn't phrase that well. They wanted to move to Oregon. Cannon Beach. We were living in Santa Cruz at the time, but it was a good time for us to move."

"I've heard Santa Cruz is beautiful," Gwen said.

"It is. I didn't really want to leave, but Nathan did. So . . . yeah."

Gwen sensed Leigh didn't want to say more on that particular topic, so she switched to another: "Are your parents nearby?"

Leigh shook her head. "They're in Santa Rosa. We were close to them when we were in Santa Cruz, but not now."

"Jeff and I don't have grandparents around either. I always envy people who have grandparent help."

"Same. But even if my parents or Nathan's parents were close, I don't think they'd want to be that involved in the day-to-day stuff, honestly. My parents like to travel a lot. Nathan's parents raised eight kids, so they're pretty done with all that."

"Eight kids?"

"I know. Insane. Can you even imagine?"

"I literally cannot."

"I keep telling Nathan he needs therapy. He was the seventh. Basically raised himself. He absolutely cannot understand why I want to, like, *tend* to our child."

"My husband's an only child, very tended to, and still seems mystified by the whole thing."

"I really don't see how we're supposed to do this together."

Gwen wasn't sure if she was talking about the two of them or what.

"Men and women. Raising a child," Leigh clarified.

"I think that's why they say it takes a village."

"Except none of us have villages. We just have our stupid partners," Leigh said. "I told Nathan we need to create some kind of commune situation like Angeni Luna's so I don't kill him."

"Oh my god, you follow her too?"

"Who doesn't?"

"I don't know, I would think she's too crunchy for some people."

"All the good mothers are too crunchy. And we all want to be good mothers."

She had a point.

"I can't decide if I have a crush on her or on her hot husband," Leigh said.

Belle pulled off her boob, and Leigh cradled her head and pressed her back on.

"Her husband *is* hot," Gwen said.

"He seems so . . . *helpful*."

"I think that's what's hot."

All the joke memes about gender roles had suddenly become relevant in Gwen's life, and she wasn't sure what to make of it. Before having June, if she'd seen a cartoon of a man doing the dishes and a woman swooning in the background, she would have rolled her eyes. But she understood it now. Her definition of romantic gestures had changed.

Leigh looked thoughtful. Finally, she said, "I think I'd want a threesome with both of them. Angeni Luna and her husband." She nodded, as if confirming this choice after much deliberation, and said, "Yeah, a threesome."

Gwen laughed so hard that June stopped suckling and stared at her, so unfamiliar was she with the sound of her mother's amusement.

"What? You don't agree?"

"I hadn't really thought about it," Gwen said.

"They would both be so . . . *attentive*."

Leigh appeared lost in a fantasy, her eyes glassy, a soft smile on her face. Gwen could not stop laughing.

"I'm impressed you can have any kind of sexual fantasy at all," Gwen said.

"I mean, I have to keep things interesting for myself, don't I?"

"Are you and Nathan . . . you know?"

Gwen felt her face flush. She was embarrassed that she was so embarrassed to talk about sex. What was she, a fifth grader? Then again, she barely knew Leigh. Leigh might be the kind of person to tell any joe on the street about her desire for a threesome with a social media momfluencer, but Gwen was not that kind of person.

Leigh sighed dramatically. Belle pulled off her nipple again, and Leigh switched her to the other boob.

"Nathan would love to return to regularly scheduled programming, but I am not there yet."

Gwen didn't realize she'd been holding her breath until she finally let it go.

"I'm so relieved it's not just me."

Leigh looked at her, disbelieving. "Of course it's not just you. No new mom wants to have sex with her husband."

"I bet Angeni Luna does."

"That woman is not normal," Leigh said. "She is some ethereal goddess being, not of this world. I'm sure they have the hottest sex."

"Jeff and I . . . we tried for the first time since I had June. It was so bad."

"Painful, right?"

Gwen wanted to hug this woman, to hold on for dear life.

"Yes. Why didn't anyone tell me about that?"

"Like you're being stabbed in your vagina with a switchblade, right?"

Gwen felt her eyes well up with tears.

"Are you *crying*?" Leigh asked, astonished.

Gwen *was* crying. Weeping.

"Happy tears," she said, using her free hand to wipe her eyes. "It's just nice to talk to someone."

Leigh reached over, placed a hand on Gwen's shoulder. It was the simplest touch, but it made Gwen weep more.

"I didn't even have a vaginal delivery, so I don't know why sex hurts so much," she said.

"It's the hormones," Leigh said, removing her hand from Gwen's shoulder and placing it back on Belle. "As long as you're breastfeeding, you'll be dry as the Sahara down there. That's what makes it hurt."

This felt like something Gwen should have known, but it was news to her.

"Oh, is that it?"

Leigh nodded. "Yep. It's like Mother Nature telling you not to have any pleasure when you should be completely focused on feeding your infant. What a cunt, right?"

Gwen laughed again.

"Lube helps. Try lube," Leigh said.

Gwen nodded.

"I only know this because I have a friend in Santa Cruz who has four kids and she tells me everything," Leigh said.

"Four? Wow. That's . . . ambitious."

"She loves chaos. Like, thrives on it."

"I wish I loved chaos. Seems like that would come in handy at this stage of life."

"I just read this article about these luxury postpartum hotels in Taiwan," said Leigh. "Like, you go there for a full month after you give birth and relax while people pamper you and take care of your baby."

"That sounds like a dream."

"Right? Although the woman who wrote it said it was kind of a shock to then go home and have to do everything herself."

"It's always a shock to go home after having a baby, isn't it? Better to delay it by a month, I'd say."

"Agree," Leigh said. "Anyway, I'm pretty sure Nathan and I will be a one-and-done family. I used to think I'd want two kids, but I don't know. It's so much."

Gwen felt her grief overhead like a cloud, slowly descending upon her. She wished the couch would just swallow her whole.

"Yeah," she said.

She knew what question was coming next.

"Do you guys want more kids?"

When Gwen swallowed, it felt like an enormous walnut was lodged in her throat. Her eyes prickled with tears again, these not of the happy variety.

"We can't have more," she said.

"Oh," Leigh said, her eyes scanning Gwen's face, trying to understand. She could almost read Leigh's thoughts: Could they not have more for financial reasons? Was it an IVF situation, where they only had the one embryo? Were they getting divorced?

"I had a C-section. It was an emergency thing," Gwen said.

She hadn't told anyone about what had happened. She knew that the support group was the appropriate venue for sharing this, but she couldn't imagine telling that room of strangers these intimate details. It still felt like admitting to a colossal failure.

"Oh, sweetie, that's traumatic," Leigh said, again taking the hand that had been cradling Belle and placing it on Gwen's shoulder for a quick, comforting moment.

Leigh thought that was the entirety of it—Gwen had had a frightening ordeal with the C-section and did not want to go through that again.

"There was a lot of bleeding. Jeff says I almost died," she said. She had to phrase it that way—*Jeff says*. As if it were his opinion and not a terrifying fact.

Leigh looked stricken. "Oh my god. That's so scary."

Gwen swallowed again, another walnut in her throat.

"They had to do a hysterectomy," she said. She stared at June's sweet, soft face as she said it, willing herself to be grateful for what she had instead of lamenting what she'd lost.

"Oh, Gwen. My god."

She couldn't meet Leigh's eyes, but she heard her sniffle and knew she was crying.

"Yeah," Gwen said. "I haven't, like, dealt with it well."

"Who the fuck would deal with that *well*?" Leigh said.

Gwen started weeping again.

Leigh stood from the couch, her nursing bra unclasped, her huge breasts exposed. Belle's little mouth finally released the nipple she'd been using as a pacifier. Leigh set her on a lounger on the floor, very similar to the lounger Gwen had at home. Belle opened her eyes in confusion, and there was a moment when it appeared she might start wailing, but she closed her eyes again and drifted off.

Leigh re-dressed herself and sat on the couch again, this time closer to Gwen, so that they shared one of the giant cushions and the couch threatened to swallow them together. She put an arm around Gwen's body, pulling her into her side.

"I'm so sorry," Leigh said.

And Gwen felt it—Leigh's sorrow on her behalf. She didn't think she had felt this from anyone. Not even Jeff.

"Thank you," Gwen said. "That means a lot."

She expected Leigh to release her hug, but she didn't. She continued holding Gwen, pulling her into her side.

June started to stir, as if sensing an unexpected loving presence and wanting to check it out. She opened her eyes and looked up at Gwen, then at Leigh, their two faces so close together.

"She's such a beautiful baby," Leigh said.

"She is, isn't she?"

"Just gorgeous. She has your eyes."

Leigh stroked June's cheek with her index finger, and June smiled her gummy smile.

"Yes, sweet girl, we're talking about you and what a beauty you are," Leigh said in the same singsong voice that Gwen used when talking to June.

"It hurts, sometimes, to look at her," Gwen said as they both continued staring at June. "Like, I love her so much it scares me. Losing her . . . it would kill me. I almost can't handle how huge it is, the love. Is that normal?"

"I don't know what's normal, but I feel that too. And you've been through so much. The fear of loss is, like, ingrained in you now."

That was it, Gwen thought. That was exactly it.

"I try to remember how lucky I am," Gwen said.

"Gratitude doesn't cancel out the fact that what happened sucks. You know that, right?"

Did she know that? Logically, yes, but in her bones?

"You can be lucky *and* devastated," Leigh said. "That's what I'm saying."

"You should be a therapist," Gwen said, feeling the need to make a little joke instead of bursting into additional tears.

"That was actually the plan," Leigh said, dead serious.

She leaned away from Gwen and moved to her own cushion, and Gwen felt a pang of sadness at the abrupt separation of their bodies. Leigh slid off the couch to be on the ground next to Belle in her lounger. She placed a hand on Belle's little belly as it rose and fell with each of her breaths.

Gwen decided to join her on the floor. The hardwood was covered in a plush shag rug that looked like it'd be plenty comfortable for June. She laid June on her back. Her eyes were wide open as she took in her new surroundings, her tiny fingers grabbing at the burnt orange threads of the rug.

"You really wanted to be a therapist?" Gwen asked. She immediately regretted the surprise in her voice that made it sound as if Leigh's career aspirations were absurd.

"I had just finished my clinical hours when I found out I was pregnant with Belle," Leigh said. "Told myself that was good. I'd done the hard part. I could take a break, have Belle, and then get started with my own practice. We'd moved from Santa Cruz. Seattle is a great market for therapists. So dreary, lots of depressed people. I had it all planned out."

This would have all sounded perfectly reasonable to Gwen before she became a mother. Now, though, she understood why Leigh spoke with a kind of grief. Embarking on a new career with an infant seemed impossible. Gwen wasn't even sure she could reembark on her already-established career.

"I just don't know how it could happen now," Leigh said with a wistful sigh. "Nathan says to give it time, but the more time I give it, the more my former career ambitions seem completely unrealistic."

"I get it," Gwen said.

"I feel like a bad feminist, you know? Giving up on my career or whatever. But it feels like the alternative is being a bad mom."

Gwen nodded. "I know. I mean, even just breastfeeding. Pretty much everyone agrees that's best, right? But when I go back to work, I don't see how I'm going to be able to do that."

Leigh looked her dead in the eyes. "You won't be able to. That's just the truth."

"I can pump. I know it's not the same, but—"

"It's not the same," Leigh said, interjecting a surprising amount of adamance. "Your baby still gets milk, but not the touch, not the closeness."

Gwen felt herself get teary eyed again. How was she possibly going to return to work?

"Oh, sweetie, it's okay," Leigh said, taking her hand off Belle's belly and putting it on Gwen's back. She moved her hand up and down over the bumpy landscape of Gwen's vertebrae.

"It's not, though," Gwen said, her voice catching.

"Yeah, I know. It's not."

Then they were both crying and, upon realizing this, both laughing, shyly at first, then hysterically, the maniacal type of laughter that signifies the release of something held within for too long. Leigh lay flat on the floor next to Belle, clutching her stomach as she laughed. Gwen did the same, lying flat next to June, staring at the ceiling, thinking how strange it was to be in this woman's home, crying and laughing and feeling better than she had in weeks.

There was the sound of the front door opening, and Leigh quickly jumped to her feet. Gwen was slower to get up, pushing herself into a seated position just as a man, presumably Leigh's husband, walked into the living room.

"Well, hello," he said.

He had a British accent, which was unexpected. He was excessively tall, six and a half feet probably, and thin, with auburn hair that explained the orangey tint to Belle's wisps.

Leigh had hurried to greet him.

"Gwen, this is Nathan," she said. "Nathan, Gwen."

Was Gwen right to feel an odd tension in the room? Was Leigh nervous around her own husband?

Gwen waved from her seated position on the floor. June flailed her arms, as if also trying to wave.

"Oh, so you're Gwen?" Nathan said, eyebrows raised in interest.

Gwen couldn't help but smile at the thought that Leigh had discussed her with Nathan, just as Gwen had discussed Leigh with Jeff.

"I'm Gwen," she said. "And this is June." She lifted June from the floor and stood for a proper greeting. He came to Gwen, stuck out his hand.

"Such a pleasure," he said, shaking her hand. His grip was firm, his eye contact intense. It was like he was trying to ascertain something about her just by staring at her, and she didn't know what it was.

"You got off work early?" Leigh said.

It was just after three o'clock.

He turned his attention back to his wife as he loosened the tie around his neck.

"I did. Sorry, forgot you were having company. I'll just jump in the shower and make myself scarce," he said. He gave her a quick peck on the cheek before jogging down the hallway.

"Maybe you can make a trip to the grocery store instead of making yourself scarce," Leigh called after him.

He grunted in return and then closed the door to what Gwen assumed was their master bedroom.

"He's usually not home until six or so. I think he goes out of his way to miss the witching hour," Leigh said. "But he knew you were coming, so."

So what? He'd wanted to meet Gwen? She couldn't imagine Jeff caring enough to meet one of Gwen's new friends, especially in the context of a baby get-together.

"Oh, that's nice," Gwen said, unsure if this was the correct response.

"He said he forgot I was having company, but he totally remembered."

Leigh seemed irritated by this, and Gwen waited for her to say more.

"There was this . . . thing . . . when we lived in Santa Cruz," Leigh said, waving her hand in the air, as if this "thing" were as silly and innocuous as a buzzing-about housefly.

Leigh sat on the couch again, while Belle continued hanging out in the lounger. Gwen resumed her seat on the couch next to Leigh, June in her lap.

"Nathan refers to it as my *indiscretion*," she said, using a British accent for "indiscretion."

Gwen still had no idea what she was getting at.

"This woman in my psychology program. It was nothing, but Nathan freaked out about it."

The gears in Gwen's brain turned slowly. A woman in her psychology program. An indiscretion.

"It was a brief fling situation. It didn't *mean* anything. Nathan saw a text from her on my phone. Freaked out."

Gwen understood now.

"That's pretty much why we moved," she said. "He was that bothered by it, said he couldn't stomach living in the same city as this woman."

Gwen had so many questions, but none she felt comfortable asking.

"Anyway, that's why he was a little unnerved when I mentioned you were coming over," she said.

"Oh" was all Gwen could say.

"I told him you're *married*, that you have a *kid*, that we are in a *support group* with moms. I guess he still felt he had to come home and see for himself."

"Oh, well, I guess I understand that," Gwen said.

Leigh seemed to think this was all dumb, but Gwen understood her husband's angst. Leigh had cheated on him. The fact that it was with a woman, that it "didn't mean anything," likely did not provide much comfort.

"He knew I was bi when we met," Leigh said. "I didn't hide it from him or anything."

Gwen took in this information and tried to keep her face neutral, though she was a little surprised that Leigh was discussing her sexuality when they barely knew each other.

"Anyway, this is all TMI, I'm sure. Sorry, I'm an oversharer," Leigh said. "I'm sure you could feel some weirdness, so that's why."

Gwen bounced June on her knees, thankful for her baby's giggles to distract her from the awkwardness of this situation.

"I appreciate your sharing," Gwen said diplomatically.

"Oh god. I've made it so weird," Leigh said. She knelt down to her own baby, probably seeking her own distraction.

Nathan appeared in the hallway, now wearing a pair of expensive athleisure pants and a T-shirt, his hair slick from the shower.

"Did you say you needed something at the store?" he asked Leigh. "I have a call at four, but I can run out now."

"Really? Would you? That would be amazing," Leigh said, jumping to her feet and running to the kitchen. She pulled out a notepad from a drawer and started writing frantically.

"So Gwen, Leigh said you two met in a moms' group?" Nathan said. He bent down to lift Belle from the lounger, held her against his chest.

"Yes. At the hospital. I just went for my first time."

"I told you this, Nathan," Leigh said with undisguised annoyance.

She ripped off the paper from the notepad and handed it to him.

"You're reminding me that I need to send my husband to the grocery store too," Gwen said, feeling the need to mention Jeff.

Leigh took Belle from Nathan, and the baby whined her disapproval.

"Right, okay. I'll run to the store," Nathan said, turning to collect his wallet and keys from the kitchen counter where he'd left them.

"I doubt I'll be here when you get back. Have to head home soon," Gwen said, still desperate to offer him reassurance. "So it was nice to meet you."

"You as well," he said, before closing the front door behind him.

Leigh gave Gwen a pouty lip once Nathan left.

"Do you really have to go so soon?"

Gwen didn't have to go, but she felt like she should.

"I'm sorry," Gwen said, standing from the couch, transferring June into the car seat.

"I totally made it weird."

"You didn't, I promise," Gwen said.

The situation was objectively a bit weird, but Gwen wasn't put off. A former version of herself might have been, but now she took comfort in another mother who didn't have all her shit together, another mother who had made mistakes. These new facts—that Leigh was bi, that she'd had a past "indiscretion"—had no bearing on their budding friendship. It was not like Leigh was attracted to Gwen. Even if she was, Gwen wasn't attracted to her, had never been attracted in that way to a woman.

"Okay, well, I hope we can do this again," Leigh said.

"We will. Of course," Gwen said with a burst of enthusiasm. "At my place next time?"

Leigh's face brightened. "Yes. Please. I'd love that."

Leigh opened the door for Gwen and asked if she needed any help to the car. Gwen assured her she was fine, and then she and June took the elevator down. As she put June in the back seat, she glanced up at the terrace, and Leigh was there. Gwen went around to the driver's side and waved up at Leigh.

"Thank you for coming," Leigh shouted down. "I couldn't remember if I said that."

Gwen laughed to herself and shouted back, "Thank you for having me."

Then she got in her car and drove home. It was only when she parked in the garage that she realized she'd been smiling the whole way.

Chapter 14

Angeni Luna

What a privilege to have a sleepless night, not because of woes or worries, but because of a sweet baby's need for love.

Angeni sat on a stool in her master bathroom, watching the comments on her latest post accumulate while Aurora stood behind her, styling her hair in preparation for Angeni's appearance on the Wellest podcast. News of her book deal was spreading, and people in the healing community wanted to talk to her. She figured it was good to start publicity sooner rather than later. Most of the time, she preferred her appearances to be audio only, but the people at Wellest had requested to have her on camera to boost engagement.

"God, your hair is gorgeous," Aurora said.

So many women lamented hair loss in the postpartum period, but it seemed like Angeni's hair was getting thicker and lusher by the day. She had to believe it was something to do with her diet, with the way she nourished her body with hearty organ meats and organic produce from The Land. And also, her own placenta.

She'd had her placenta steamed, dehydrated, ground into a fine powder, and placed into pill capsules by a Native woman on the island who specialized in this. She'd been taking the pills daily since Freya was born and had enough left for a few more months. It was supposed to help with general rejuvenation of mind, body, and spirit, and Angeni was a wholehearted believer. She made a mental note to discuss this practice more often on the Mother Nurture account and in her book.

"You want me to do your makeup too?" Aurora asked.

Aurora looked excited by the prospect, like they were little girls again, having a sleepover.

"I've got it," Angeni said, taking out the pouch of products she rarely used. She preferred to be barefaced, to keep any unnecessary contaminants away from her skin. All the makeup she owned was organic, of course, but still, the skin was so delicate, so porous. She didn't understand how people were so flippant about how they treated the largest organ in their body.

She set her phone on the counter in front of her and patted her face with powder, still watching comments come in.

Most of the comments were just heart emojis of different varieties and colors, with a few comments like these:

> Needed this. We had just a rough night last night over here and this helps me remember how lucky I am

> Thank you for always keeping things in perspective for us tired mamas. We love you

> It IS a privilege. All of it. How often we forget this 🙏

"So is today's podcast mostly about the book?" Aurora asked with her usual zeal.

"Yes, I think so," Angeni said.

Angeni felt a couple of strands of hair break as Aurora yanked them into the submission of the French braids she was creating on either side of Angeni's head.

"So exciting," Aurora said. "I don't know if I say it enough, Ang, but I'm so proud of you. I always knew you would be something."

"Aww, thank you."

The previous day, Angeni had had a call with her book editor, Trish, about her "vision" for the book. Angeni had shared various topics she planned to incorporate and tried to hide the doubts she was starting to have about her ability to put together an entire book. She was confident in her skills as a short-form writer—Instagram posts, for example. She knew she was great at hosting webinars and creating workbooks full of prompts to shepherd people through their own inner landscapes. But writing a book was something else entirely. It required big-picture thinking and organization that Angeni hadn't tapped into before. But she was trying to give herself grace. She'd only just begun. She would find her rhythm. She had to trust Spirit to guide her.

What made her especially nervous was her editor's suggestion that the book include more personal content: "I want to make sure the book includes a great deal about YOU—your upbringing, your life, the story behind Angeni Luna. Everything else is content people can find on your social media already. It's great that it will be gathered in a central location for the book, but I want to offer something more too. I want you to go deeper."

To this, Angeni had said, "Yes, of course," but the truth was that she was hesitant to go deeper, to share more of her past. It was a past that few knew. Aurora knew more than anyone because she had been there. Erik knew what Angeni had recounted to him, which wasn't everything. Matt and Jer knew bits and pieces. She would have to figure out how to share enough to seem vulnerable and real while concealing the problematic details.

Aurora slid a couple of bobby pins into Angeni's hair while Angeni used her finger to spread gloss across her lips. Erik appeared in the doorway and rapped his knuckles on the doorframe. His eyes grew large at the sight of Angeni.

"Wow. You look gorgeous, babe," he said.

"Doesn't she?" Aurora gushed.

"Ror, can you ask Jer to make sure the recording equipment is ready?" Angeni asked.

Once Aurora left, Erik came up behind Angeni, one hand on each side of her neck, his fingers massaging into muscles she didn't even realize were tense.

"You okay?" he asked.

He knew her so well.

"Just feeling a little anxious," she said.

"About the podcast?"

He bent down enough to give her a kiss on the cheek, then continued rubbing her shoulders.

"The podcast. The book. Us."

Just the night before, they'd had another discussion about her disinterest in sex. He had suggested that maybe they just needed to go through the motions of it to start, that maybe she would enjoy it once they got going. She had felt that as pressure, and told him so, and he had said, "Maybe it is pressure. I miss you, Ang." And yet she still couldn't give him her body. She felt stubbornly possessive of it, her heels dug in.

"Babe, I think you're doing that thing where you're nervous about one thing—probably this podcast—and then you decide to contemplate every other thing in your life."

She smiled. She *was* doing that thing.

Angeni stood, wrapped her arms around his middle. He craned his neck down to kiss the top of her head.

"Thank you," she said.

Aurora called for them from the living room: "Five minutes till showtime!"

"Come on," Erik said, putting his hands around Angeni's waist, lifting her off the ground and into his arms. "Let's do this thing."

~

When the Wellest team had contacted Angeni, she'd asked them if they wanted just her on the episode, or if they wanted her and Erik. They said they'd love to have the two of them, which was just fine with Angeni. He was a calming influence for her. If she got nervous or tongue tied, he stepped in. He kept things light. He was good at making jokes at appropriate times, changing subjects when necessary, all to protect her.

The hosts were Michael Hsu and Adriene Aguilera, thirtysomethings who had built a respectable fan base in a relatively short period of time—more than a half million subscribers. Angeni couldn't say no to these types of opportunities. These were the opportunities that would amplify her voice and expand her reach beyond what she could do on her own.

Aurora had set up a special circular light in front of Angeni and Erik, making them look bright faced despite the gray day outside their windows. Jer and Matt were manning the audiovisual equipment.

"You might not even need these, but let's attach in case," Matt said, affixing tiny mics to the collars of Erik's shirt and Angeni's blouse.

"You guys look great," Aurora said.

Jer positioned the screen, and Michael and Adriene appeared, sitting side by side at a desk, like news anchors. They were wearing matching smiles, bright-white teeth gleaming.

"Oh my god, Angeni Luna, hi!" Adriene said with a level of enthusiasm that overwhelmed Angeni.

"And Erik!" Michael said with an equal amount of enthusiasm.

Angeni and Erik were sitting on the living room couch. Erik took her hand, squeezed it. He could probably feel the energy humming through her body.

"We're just going to start the recording on our end if that's cool?" Adriene said.

"Sounds great," Erik said while Angeni cleared her throat.

"Okay, all set," Adriene said. "Hi, everyone! We're here today with two very special guests that we've been wanting to get on an episode for months."

"Years, actually," Michael said, and they all laughed.

"Angeni Luna is the creator of the Conscious Couples Instagram account, as well as the Mother Nurture Instagram account, which each have a following of more than two million people. Just incredible," Adriene said. "Her husband, Erik, is her partner in crime, and they recently welcomed a little girl to the world—"

"She is the most beautiful creature I've ever seen," Michael interjected.

"Legit the most beautiful," Adriene said. "And Angeni, for our followers who don't already know, why don't you share your recent news?"

"The recent news is that I'm writing a book," Angeni said.

Adriene did a little squeal, and Michael clapped his hands twice.

"As you can tell, we are a little excited about this," Adriene said. "Can you tell us about the book?"

Angeni felt heat rising in her chest. She shifted on the couch, and Erik moved his hand from her hand to her thigh. He was attempting to ground her.

"Well, it's just taking shape as I get into a rhythm with the writing," Angeni said. "But what's close to my heart is helping other women become the mothers they want to be, helping them establish a deep and rich connection with their children, starting in pregnancy."

"So beautiful," Adriene said.

"We're hoping you also continue to share the magic of the relationship you two have, especially as new parents," Michael said.

Angeni and Erik turned toward each other and couldn't help but laugh nervously.

"What do you think, babe? Is it magic?" Erik said to Angeni, giving her thigh a squeeze. This was their schtick, and they knew it well.

"It sure seems magical to us," Adriene said. "In a nutshell, what are your secrets to staying so connected? It must be harder now that you have a baby."

Angeni wasn't sure how to answer, and was grateful when Erik jumped in: "I think it helps that we truly respect each other. I want the best for her, and she wants the best for me. It starts there. We understand there are ups and downs with intimacy, and we do our best to talk through those, with this baseline understanding that we are each other's person."

"That's truly so sweet," Michael said.

"If you don't mind, we have a couple people on standby who are big fans of yours and want to ask some questions," Adriene said.

They had not mentioned this to Angeni ahead of time. Generally, she liked to know the topics that would be discussed. She didn't like surprise appearances, unexpected questions. But they were live on air, and she couldn't exactly show her disapproval now.

"Sure," Erik said, "let's hear 'em."

She would let Erik take the lead here. He had to know she was uncomfortable with this.

"Okay, first we have Sue. Sue, go ahead with your question!" Michael said.

"Yes, hello," a woman's voice said. It sounded odd, muffled. "My question is . . . will this book of yours include any information about your shocking past?"

Erik tightened his grip on Angeni's thigh. She felt her heart pounding in her chest. Before she or Erik could say anything, Adriene's face fell, and she said, "Oh my god."

"Angeni, we're so sorry. That is not the question she said she was going to ask," Michael said.

The hosts were clearly flustered.

Angeni's mind raced. Who knew about her *shocking past*? Aurora knew, but . . . Angeni looked around the room. Where was Aurora?

"Sadly, we're used to the crazies," Erik said, sounding unfazed by the whole thing. To him, it was just another troll. For all he knew, her past wasn't that shocking. She'd always pledged allegiance to radical honesty and transparency in relationships, but she hadn't applied those principles to her own marriage.

"Let's shift to another question. This one came as a write-in, and we thought it was interesting," Adriene said. "How do you balance your own pursuits with being such an involved mother?"

"Oh, that is a good question," Michael said.

Erik could not answer this one for Angeni. This question was for her. She cleared her throat, tried to regain her composure.

"Freya is always my number one priority," she said. "Whatever else I do is secondary to her."

"You'd be amazed at her juggling skills," Erik said.

Aurora came back into the living room then. Where had she been? Was she the person who had called in? Was that logistically possible? It hadn't sounded like Aurora. Angeni tracked her across the room, willing Aurora to look at her. When she did, she gave Angeni a thumbs-up. There was no betrayal on her face that Angeni could see. Was it possible someone, a stranger, was just taking a guess at her "shocking past," trying to rattle her?

"You totally don't have to put her on camera," Adriene said, "but is little Freya nearby?"

Angeni took her eyes off Aurora.

"Sorry?"

"Is little Freya nearby?" Adriene repeated.

Freya.

Where *was* Freya? Angeni didn't even know. She felt the color leave her face as she remembered how she'd told Sitka to watch her while she got ready for the podcast. Sitka had likely taken her outside for a walk.

But Angeni didn't know for sure. She'd been completely unaware of her child's whereabouts for at least an hour.

"We are fortunate to live in community on our land, and Freya is with our community right now," Erik said.

Angeni felt like someone had set a match to her skin and the flames were traveling to consume her body. It was just like when they'd all brought her that damn cake. Aurora, standing behind the screen, mouthed *Are you okay?*

"I'm sorry, can we pause? I need to get some water," Angeni said.

"Sure, of course," Adriene said.

But when Angeni stood from the couch, the world tilted on its axis, and she felt her body collapse as Erik said, "Oh shit."

~

When she came to, she wasn't sure if a few minutes or a few hours had passed. Erik, Matt, Jer, and Aurora were hovering over her, a circle of faces with identical looks of concern. In the background, the screen was dark. Adriene and Michael were gone.

"Babe?" Erik said.

"Oh my god, she's okay," Aurora said.

"What happened?" Angeni asked them.

"I'll get some water," Jer said. His face disappeared from the circle of faces.

"You passed out," Aurora said.

Angeni pressed herself up to her elbows.

"Whoa, whoa, whoa," Erik said. "Take it slow."

"Is your arm okay? You kind of hit it on the table when you went down," Matt said.

"I'm okay," she said, though everything was numb. She wasn't aware of any feeling in her arm at all. It was the shock, of course. Later, she would feel a throbbing near her elbow. There would be a bruise.

As Erik helped her up onto the couch, Angeni saw Sitka come in from outside, baby Freya in her arms. As she took in the scene, with everyone tending to Angeni, the pleasant smile on her face vanished, and her brows knitted together.

"What happened?" Sitka asked.

"Can I hold Freya?" Angeni asked her, stretching her arms out in front of her, clenching and unclenching her fists, just as Freya did when she wanted something.

Sitka sat next to her on the couch, transferred the baby into Angeni's arms. Angeni pulled Freya against her chest, kissed her head and cheeks. There was this mysterious force between mother and baby, this ability to coregulate, to bring each other's nervous systems into alignment. She felt her body absorb Freya's simple joy and cried tears of relief.

"Oh, my baby," she said.

"She passed out during the podcast episode," Aurora whispered to Sitka.

Jer sat on the other side of Angeni, offered her a glass of water and sliced apple on a plate.

"Maybe you need some sugar in your system," he said.

"She had breakfast not that long ago," Aurora said.

"Can I just have some space, actually? Just me and Freya?" Angeni asked.

When she looked up at the group of them, they were a giant blur, her vision obscured by the tears in her eyes.

"Of course, babe," Erik said. Then, to the rest of them: "Come on, guys."

Most of them went outside. Sitka vanished down the hallway toward her room. She wasn't one to hang with the group.

Angeni stayed on the couch with Freya. She took off her blouse and let Freya latch on to her breast. Angeni felt peace come over her. This was the power of breastfeeding—it calmed both parties. Mother and daughter, a symbiotic ecosystem.

While Freya fed, Angeni ate a few slices of apple, downed a glass of water, and tapped out an email with an effusive apology to Adriene and Michael: I've been feeling a little under the weather, I'm so sorry.

When she stood from the couch, she felt a bit weak, but mostly fine. She'd had a visceral reaction to Adriene and Michael's question about Freya's whereabouts. Her mama heart had panicked. That was all this was—a needed reminder of her priorities, a wake-up call of sorts.

"Mama loves you," she said to Freya, who responded with a gummy smile.

As she headed outside to find the group and explain her interpretation of what had happened, Erik was coming down the path back to the house.

"Hey," he said. "You feeling better?"

He put one hand on each of her shoulders, looked her in the eyes.

"Yeah. That was so weird."

"I'm just glad you're okay. I'm going to get some snacks for everyone. You want anything in particular?"

She shook her head. He kissed Freya's cheek, then the tip of Angeni's nose, and jogged past her toward the house.

The rest of the group was hanging out by the firepit, sitting in a semicircle around it, facing away from her. Erik, Matt, and Jer had recently completed an item on Angeni's wish list by turning fallen tree trunks into ten stool seats to surround the firepit.

As she approached, she heard them talking, her own name mentioned. She stopped, stood behind the trunk of a pine. It was wrong to eavesdrop, but she couldn't help herself.

"Something is clearly going on with her," Aurora said.

Angeni still couldn't get it out of her head that Aurora was the one who'd called in on the podcast. Who else knew about Angeni's history? Angeni had made that stupid casual-sex comment to Sitka in a foolish attempt to bond with the girl, but it couldn't have been Sitka who'd called in. Sitka had been with Freya outside.

"It's probably the stress of the book," Matt said.

"I'm picking up on some tension with Erik too," Aurora said.

How many times had Angeni talked about not gossiping within their community? Why was Aurora doing this? It was not that she was wrong to pick up on some marital tension, but it wasn't her place to talk about it like this. Maybe Aurora did have some ill will toward Angeni. But why? Was she still upset about Sitka's arrival, her growing presence in Angeni's life?

"Erik will be back in a few," Jer said. "I don't want him to know we're talking about this."

"Yeah, I'm not trying to be gossipy," Aurora said. "Just a little worried."

"On another note, Ror, I saw that painting you're working on at your house. It's freaking amazing," Matt said.

"You think? I'm in an abstract phase."

"It's a good phase," Matt said.

"How are things going with Annika?" Aurora asked him.

"Good. I'm helping her at the farmers market this weekend. Selling her candles."

"The soy ones. Right. That one you brought me has lasted so long."

Now that they had moved past talking about her, Angeni emerged from behind the tree.

"Hey, guys!" she called, putting on a pleasant smile.

"You're up!" Aurora said.

They all stood, as if welcoming a queen. The joy on their faces seemed genuine. She tried to shake off her doubts and fears. These were her people . . . weren't they?

"How are you feeling?" Aurora asked.

Angeni sat on one of the wood seats, set Freya on the ground.

"I'm fine, really," Angeni said. "More embarrassed than anything."

"Oh, don't be embarrassed," Aurora said.

Angeni studied her. Aurora seemed like her usual self, loving and attentive and kind. She wasn't capable of betrayal, was she?

"It was hot in there with all the electronics running," Jer said.

It was kind of them to make excuses for her.

"Guys, really, I'm fine. Just a fluke thing," Angeni said.

Erik approached with a tray of food, a makeshift charcuterie board by the looks of it, complete with slices of meat, crackers, cheese, fruit, and nuts.

They all oohed and aahed at the effort he'd put into their snacks and started reaching for various things. Angeni felt the weirdness in the air dissipate and the usual tranquil energy return.

Erik sat next to Angeni, leaned over to kiss her cheek. She and Erik would be fine. They were solid. Weren't they? She did her best to quiet the questions, to calm her nervous system.

"You okay, babe?" Erik whispered in her ear.

Yet another question she wasn't sure how to answer.

"Yeah," she said. "I'm fine."

Chapter 15

Britt

After Britt and her mother drove away from Steve's house, they stayed on the freeway headed east for over an hour, not saying more than a few words to each other. Britt had no idea what the plan was and had to assume there wasn't one.

Her mother pulled off the freeway at an exit that was totally unfamiliar to Britt.

"I took some of his cash. We'll stay here tonight," she announced as they pulled into the parking lot of a motel flashing a neon VACANCY sign.

They hadn't even gotten out of the car before Britt realized this motel was one of those places that charged by the hour. A couple of women lingered near the entrance, wearing tight-fitting crop tops and miniskirts, making no attempt to hide their profession. Britt's mother just walked right by them.

"Isn't there somewhere else we could go?" Britt asked.

Her mother whipped around, eyes bulging with impatience and anger.

"Britt, seriously. You are too much. What more do you want from me? You're lucky we're not sleeping in our car."

~

The room was dingy—stained carpet, faded floral bedspread, rusted bathroom fixtures. There was only one bed—a queen. Britt and her mother lay next to each other, not touching. Britt stared at the cottage cheese ceiling and marveled at how quickly her life had gone from decent to destitute.

They spent two days in the motel before Britt's mother ushered her to the car again and they drove back on the highway the same way they'd come. At first, Britt thought she was returning to Steve's house, and she cringed at her mother's desperation. She couldn't bear seeing the pity on Steve's face when they showed up.

They didn't go to Steve's, though. They went to the mobile home park instead, which was a few blocks from their old apartment. Britt got her hopes up, tentatively. If they were staying there, she could continue going to the same school and hanging out with Becky and Rainbow. There could be some stability in the midst of her mother's chaos.

"I've got a lead on a place here," her mother told her.

The place was a dilapidated home at the back of the park. It had a FOR RENT sign out front. Britt stayed in the car while her mother went to knock on the door. A middle-aged man with an enormous belly answered. They exchanged words, and then her mother turned around and gave Britt a thumbs-up. This would be their new home "for the time being," her mother said.

Turned out, it would be the last home they would ever share together.

~

When Britt turned thirteen, Rainbow threw her a party to "usher in a new era" (Rainbow's words). Britt resumed spending most of her time with Rainbow and Becky, who had come to understand her plight better than anyone. Rainbow was less of a mother figure and more of a friend—both to her own daughter and to Britt. Rainbow allowed the girls to smoke weed with her, reasoning that they were teenagers on the cusp of adulthood and she'd rather they experimented with her than with kids their own age.

"It's not just about getting high," Rainbow told them. "It's about seeing where this plant medicine can take you within yourself."

Britt nodded, but for her, it really was just about getting high.

She loved weed from day one—the way it softened the edges of her everyday life, muted the cacophony in her head. Rainbow encouraged her to talk about her feelings when she smoked, said that marijuana could help her process the strife with her mother and find her way to peace. Even in an altered state, though, Britt was uninterested in wasting any time thinking about her mother.

When she was home, which wasn't often, Britt saw past versions of her mother resurrected. She was a drunk, again. She was dating drunks, again. She was unemployed, again. She was struggling to make rent, again. Britt thought about selling the guns, not to help her mom so much as to prevent them from being evicted, again, but she couldn't bring herself to do it. The guns were all she had left of Steve.

She walked by his house once, a few months after she and her mom had moved out. She saw him through the front window. He was vacuuming the living room. She wanted to go to the door, knock. She wanted to suggest they go shooting, because that was less vulnerable than suggesting he resume being her pseudo father. Then she saw a woman come into the living room, and this woman sat on the couch with a kind of comfort and ease that implied she'd been in his house many times. Did she live there already? Was she the real reason Steve had ended things with Britt's mom? Britt couldn't blame him, but she also couldn't shake the feeling of complete rejection.

She decided to go shooting by herself. Without a ride, she couldn't get all the way out to Swakane Canyon, so she wandered the trails in the woods near the mobile home park until she found a far-enough-away clearing. She didn't know anything about the legality of shooting outside a designated range, but she didn't think anyone would care or report her. She figured the cars on the nearby highway would drown out any sound.

Becky thought it was weird, the shooting. In true hippie fashion, Rainbow wasn't supportive either. "The only purpose of guns is violence," Rainbow had said. Britt disagreed. She tried to explain how shooting made her feel better, like hitting a punching bag. She could channel all the anger and sadness in her body and direct it to her finger as she pulled the trigger. The expulsion, the bang, was the ultimate release. She created her own targets on the trunks of trees. Sometimes, she took out the rifle, but she mostly used the handgun. Seeing her bullets hit the makeshift bull's-eyes was validation that this mess of feelings inside her, scattered and chaotic, could be channeled into a straight line. The precision, the perfection, gave her a sense of calm. It was probably similar to how her mother felt when she drank. They were chasing the same sensation, the same peace, just with different methods.

~

On the last day of eighth grade, Britt spent the night at Becky's place. They stayed up late smoking on the back patio and talking about their summer plans. Britt wanted to get a summer job, intent on starting to save up money for her eventual escape from her mother. The moment she turned eighteen, she wanted to rent her own place.

The next morning, a Saturday, they slept in until ten. Rainbow had already left for the day. She was still working as a Reiki masseuse, had accumulated enough clients to open her own small clinic in a business park by the school.

"We should go to the pool today," Becky said as they sat at the table, eating their usual bowls of Rainbow's homemade granola, drinking the sweet milk when all the cereal was gone.

The pool she was referring to was the public pool next to the library. It was a prime hangout location for all the teenagers, likely to be packed on the first day of summer break. The sun was bright, the forecast promising a high of seventy-two.

"Okay, I just gotta stop at my house for my bathing suit," Britt said.

The girls had gotten matching used bikes at a secondhand shop the month before—twenty-five dollars for both. "My treat," Rainbow had said. The bikes were teal with pink handlebar tassels. There weren't many exciting places to go in the neighborhood, but just the ability to go somewhere, anywhere, gave them a sense of newfound freedom.

Britt rode in front as they made their way to the mobile home park. On the way, they passed the pool, where two boys from their class stood outside in their swim trunks, eating Snickers bars. Britt was beginning to understand what it meant to like boys. She didn't want to like them, but felt herself being pulled toward this seeming inevitability.

"Hey, you girls coming to the pool?" one of the boys, Travis, asked.

"In a bit," Becky said.

"Glad to hear it," the other boy, Reed, said.

Britt felt herself blush and was grateful to be on her bike, riding past them before they could notice.

~

Britt's mother's car was in the driveway, which meant she hadn't gone to work, again. She had just started a job as a gas station clerk. Britt guessed she wouldn't have it for long if she was already missing shifts.

They parked their bikes on the sidewalk, and Britt said, "Be right back."

Usually, during these brief stops at the house, Becky would wait outside. There was no need to go in, especially if Britt's mother was there. It was like walking into a storm, the intensity of which was never known.

"I kind of have to pee. Can I come in really quick?" Becky said.

Britt nodded, and the girls walked in together. The door opened directly into the living space, where Britt's mother was sitting on the couch, looking completely disheveled, her hair a tangled mess, remnants of mascara smeared under her eyes. There was a near-empty bottle of tequila on the table in front of her. It was a scene that appeared staged for a play titled *The Alcoholic in Despair*.

Britt didn't see the gun right away. Her eyes were locked on her mother's face. She was trying to get her mom to look at her, but her mom's eyes were shifting all over the place, refusing to focus. Britt knew this meant there was no reasoning with her, that it was best to just leave.

"Is that a gun?" Becky said in a whisper, taking an instinctive step back toward the door.

That was when Britt saw it. It was the 1911 handgun Steve had given her, on the couch, next to her mother's thigh.

Her mother picked it up and held it in her right hand.

"This?" she said. "Yes, this is a gun."

She was slurring. Britt watched the gun waver in her grip.

"Mom, put it down," she said.

Britt put one hand behind her and gently nudged Becky, telling her to go. Becky didn't move, though. She took Britt's hand in hers, squeezed it. The phone was in the kitchen, which might as well have been another county.

"Is this Steve's?" her mother said, incredulous.

Britt chastised herself for not hiding the duffel bag better the day before. She'd gone shooting and had come home in a rush to get to Becky's for their end-of-school dinner and sleepover. Had she even shoved the duffel bag back into her closet, or had she left it just sitting there in the middle of her room? She couldn't even remember.

"Mom, just put it down and we'll talk, okay?"

"I can't believe he gave you this," she said. "And the other one."

It was unlikely her mother had been able to figure out how to assemble the AUG, which was a blessing. Had she loaded the handgun? Would she have figured out how to do that? Britt started to panic as she considered that maybe she hadn't emptied the chamber after yesterday's shooting session. Steve had always told her to be especially meticulous about that. He would be so disappointed in her.

"You didn't even tell me. Just some little secret you had with him?" she said.

Now she was waving the gun around. Britt crouched down, and Becky did the same.

"Mom, please," Britt said.

"What other little secrets did you have with him?" her mother said, standing from the couch now.

"Becky, go. Call someone," Britt said.

But Becky didn't move. Either she was paralyzed by fear or she didn't want to leave her best friend.

"Is that why he left me? Because of *you*?" her mother said.

She was right in Britt's face now, spittle flying from her mouth. The gun dangled from her hand, as if she'd forgotten she was holding it. All it would take was one wrong movement, one fumble, one accidental bump against the trigger, and all their lives would be in danger.

"Mama," Britt said.

She never called her *mama*. She was desperate for the term of endearment to take her mother out of whatever trance she was in.

"Mama," she said again, still trying and failing to establish eye contact.

Her mother took another step toward Britt and stumbled enough that the gun fell from her hand. Britt held her breath, expecting a shot to go off. When there was nothing, she lunged for the gun, picked it up before her mother could.

It all happened so fast.

Her mother was on top of her, wrestling her for the gun, or just wrestling her to wrestle her, taking out all her anger on this child she'd birthed, her long fake nails clawing at Britt's face. Britt would spend the rest of her life trying to understand how she could have done this, but in the moment, she was only trying to survive.

Becky screamed when the gun went off. The single blast was followed by a dreadful silence.

Britt's ears rang. She had pulled the trigger, yes, but not with the intention of shooting anyone. She'd just wanted her mother to get off her. It had worked. Her mother had gotten off her.

Britt stood, surveying herself. Had she shot herself? She didn't feel any pain, but she was in shock. She looked for red on her body, saw none. She looked to Becky next, Becky who was now standing against the door, her face white with terror.

"Are you okay?" Britt managed to ask.

Becky nodded and raised a shaky hand, pointing at Britt's mother there on the floor.

She wasn't moving.

Britt had seen her mother unmoving in the midst of so many blackouts that she wasn't scared at first. Her mother was lying face down, and as Britt went to her, she saw it—a pool of red blooming from underneath her mother's chest.

"Oh my god," she said.

She rolled her mother over, saw that she had been shot. Britt's mind flashed to the targets with the black silhouettes of human torsos. She had hit her mom just above her left breast, likely directly in the heart.

"Should I go call someone?" Becky asked.

Britt put two shaky fingers to her mother's neck, like she'd seen people do in the movies. She didn't think she felt a pulse, but she didn't know. She was just a kid—how was she supposed to know?

"Yes," Britt said. Then: "Wait."

Becky turned, one hand on the door.

"She shot herself," Britt said.

Becky furrowed her brow, confused.

"She did?" Becky said, her voice low and meek.

"She shot herself," Britt repeated. "Right? I didn't shoot her, right?"

Becky stared at Britt's mother, then the gun, then nodded.

"Right," Becky said. "She shot herself."

Britt nodded, and then they were both nodding.

"Go," Britt said.

Becky left and returned a few minutes later with a neighbor who had called 911 from her house. The neighbor said, "Oh my god," and covered her mouth. Upon seeing this stranger's distress, Britt vomited.

What had she done?

The sound of sirens came, first far away and then closer and closer before a parade of emergency responders descended upon the mobile home park. Britt and Becky huddled together, hands clasped, waiting to be asked what the hell had happened.

Chapter 16

Sasha

On a Friday afternoon, a month after Daphne died, Sasha boarded the ferry to make the eight-mile voyage across the water to Bainbridge Island. It was June, on the cusp of the official start of summer, but this was Seattle with its ubiquitous cloud cover and damp air. Sasha drove her car into the underbelly of the ship, then took the stairs up to the main deck. She got herself a coffee from the refreshments stand and then went outside to lean against the railing and watch the water pass beneath her.

It was a relaxing trip, and she regretted not having done it with Daphne. They'd never done a sister trip. Sasha expected the rest of her life to be riddled with "we never . . ." thoughts. Daphne would have liked the ferry voyage. She'd always been up for some kind of adventure. Sasha whispered into the wind: "Daph, if this is a totally stupid idea, give me a sign." She waited for something, anything—an orca making an unexpected appearance, someone bumping into her and spilling her coffee. There was nothing, though. She was left to assume that Daphne wasn't opposed to her harebrained scheme after all.

Sasha figured it wouldn't be hard to find Angeni Luna's property. Her Instagram posts alone had given enough clues as to the location. There was mention of having a Christmas tree farm as a neighbor, for example. How many Christmas tree farms could there possibly be on the island? If she ran into difficulty, she figured the island was small, a place where everyone knew everyone. Any convenience store clerk could probably point her in the general direction.

Her idea was to show up at the property, pretending to sell jewelry. She didn't want to let on that she knew the property was home to the infamous Angeni Luna. She would be irresistibly innocent and charming. She would say she was new to the island and hope that Angeni welcomed her inside to chat. Angeni Luna seemed like someone who wanted to be seen as hospitable and loving, a warm Mother Teresa goddess figure. In her fantasy of their confrontation, Sasha saw herself inside Angeni's home, infiltrating the beloved sanctuary.

There were several farms on the island, but only one was specifically referred to as a Christmas tree farm. Sasha found an Airbnb listing near the farm that offered a small, affordable guesthouse, perfect for what she needed. She booked it for the weekend using money she'd squirreled away from tutoring.

The drive from the ferry terminal to her Airbnb was just fifteen minutes. The listing hadn't done the property justice. It was huge—acres of ponds and pastures butting up against a forested area called Manzanita Park. Sasha drove down a gravel road past the main house to the tiny cottage she would call home for a couple of days.

Before leaving Seattle, she'd bought some cheap turquoise jewelry. Angeni had revealed her love of turquoise in various Instagram posts. She was almost always wearing a teardrop turquoise necklace and a turquoise beaded bracelet. In one of her posts, she talked about how "ancient peoples" believed turquoise had a "profound power to protect" and was "infused with tranquil energy" and representative of "enduring love." Sasha couldn't have rolled her eyes harder, but she was grateful for these little nuggets of insight into Angeni's interests and potential vulnerabilities.

Sasha laid out the jewelry pieces—an assortment of earrings, bracelets, necklaces—in the three tiers of a little cart she'd purchased at

Walmart. This would be her jewelry-peddler setup, which she hoped would pique Angeni's interest.

She figured there was no use wasting time, so she put on a flowy bohemian-style dress that she thought Angeni would appreciate, packed up her car with her jewelry, and headed out to explore the nearby properties, hoping Angeni Luna or one of her people would answer the door at one of them.

Thankfully, there weren't that many nearby properties. Everyone on the island seemed to own large pieces of land, their homes acres apart from one another. There was so much forest, so many trees, that it was impossible to tell where one property officially ended and another began. Only the mailboxes on the side of the road alerted Sasha to the demarcation of a new residence.

Just beyond the first mailbox was a gravel road that Sasha guessed led to a house. She took the road until a home emerged among the trees. There were no cars out front and no lights on in the house. This wasn't it. She reversed down the gravel road and continued on the main road until she saw a signpost with an address on it. Next to the signpost was a dirt road. She turned onto it and drove until a home appeared. There were a few cars parked in front of this one and lights on in the house. She had seen enough glimpses of Angeni Luna's home on Instagram to know that this was it. If there was any doubt in her mind, that vanished when she saw a familiar man coming from the other direction on the dirt road, carrying a bundle of wood. She knew this man to be Matt, one of the guys who lived on the property.

Matt squinted at her, and she was worried he would confront her, ask her what the hell she was doing here. She had to assume Angeni Luna was well known enough to get some unwanted visitors. But as he came closer, he simply waved.

She waved back as she put the car in park.

"Hi there, can I help you?" Matt asked when she stepped out of the car. He was friendly, not at all suspicious or wary.

"Oh, hi," she said. She felt self-conscious, as if her intentions were written all over her flowy dress. Instinctively, she crossed her arms over her body, hiding herself. "I'm, uh, new to the island and wanted to see if anyone was interested in my turquoise jewelry."

"New, eh? Welcome, then," he said.

"Thank you."

His eyes shifted up and down her body. He was assessing her—for what, she didn't know.

"You know, Angeni may be interested," he said finally. "She loves turquoise."

He said her name so easily—Angeni. Just the sound of it, the knowledge that she was somewhere nearby, made Sasha's heart hammer in her chest.

"Oh, wonderful," Sasha said. "Thank you."

She went to the trunk of her car and withdrew her little cart. She arranged the jewelry on each of its tiers and then stood at the ready. Matt looked pleasantly amused with her setup. He set down his bundle of wood and said, "Follow me."

She did as he instructed, following him to the front porch of the house, pushing the cart as she went. It was a beautiful wood-paneled house—unpainted, the natural grains of the wood visible. Matt knocked on the front door, and then there she was—Angeni Luna.

She was much shorter than Sasha had expected. For the past month, Angeni Luna had loomed so large in Sasha's mind, an Amazonian woman. In person, she was significantly shorter than Sasha's five feet, seven inches. Sasha guessed she was five two, if that. Her hair was in a braid that hung over her shoulder. She was wearing her usual turquoise necklace and bracelet. Her face didn't appear as bright and glowing as it did on Instagram. It was clear she was not above the use of filters. There were dark circles under her eyes, a smattering of sun spots on her cheeks and forehead.

Angeni's eyes went from Matt to Sasha.

"Ang, this young woman just moved to the island and is selling turquoise," Matt said. "Thought you might be into it."

"Oh," Angeni said. "My goodness. Sure, come on in."

It was that easy. Sasha had not been prepared for it to be so easy.

Matt started to walk away and then turned back suddenly. "Wow, I'm an idiot. I didn't even get your name."

It would be the first time she would say it out loud. She cleared her throat.

"It's Sitka."

"Sitka," he repeated. "Such a cool name. Nice to meet you."

Then he was off, disappearing down the dirt path.

"Sitka? Like the spruce tree," Angeni said.

There was a twinkle in her eye when she said it, and Sasha knew she'd selected the perfect name.

"Yes, like the spruce tree. Not many people know that."

"It's my favorite tree," Angeni said.

"No way!"

"And turquoise is my favorite jewelry," she said.

"It's almost like we're meant to meet," Sasha said.

She immediately regretted it, wondering if she was going too far, showing her hand. But Angeni didn't seem alarmed in the slightest.

When Angeni turned to lead them inside, Sitka hit the record button on her phone so she could capture the confrontation she'd been fantasizing about. The house was filled with natural light from several floor-to-ceiling windows. The kitchen, dining area, and living room were all one large space, with no walls between them. Sasha's eyes went to the big picture window above the kitchen sink, out of which she could see her namesake tree.

"This is beautiful," Sasha said, a compliment that was genuine, not part of her performance.

"Thank you," Angeni said, placing a hand to her heart as if in deep gratitude. "I have spent so much time tending to this space, making it reflect who I am as a person, you know?"

Sasha didn't know, but she did know that this was exactly the type of thing Angeni Luna would say.

There was a hallway off the living room that Sasha guessed led to the bedrooms. From that hallway, a woman emerged who Sasha quickly recognized as Aurora, the woman Angeni described as her "soul sister," whatever that meant. She was holding in her arms the beloved baby—Freya Odina.

The baby was undeniably beautiful, even without whatever Instagram filters Angeni used. It was her eyes—large and blue, accented by long, stark-black eyelashes. She stared with the intensity of a much older, wiser human.

"Ror, this is Sitka," Angeni said when Aurora came into the room and handed the baby to Angeni.

"Hi," Aurora said, giving a little wave.

"Aurora is my dear friend who lives with us here on the land," Angeni said.

"How wonderful," Sasha said, quickly chastising herself for using that word for the second time since arriving. Wonderful, wonderful, wonderful—everything was just damn *wonderful*.

"We really believe in building community here," Angeni said. Which was another thing that Angeni Luna would definitely say.

"I'm going to help the guys out back," Aurora said before excusing herself.

Angeni invited Sasha to sit on the couch in the living room. She offered tea, and Sasha accepted.

"Do you mind holding her for a minute?" Angeni asked.

Sasha was surprised by the request, had not planned on holding Angeni Luna's baby, but she found herself saying, "Sure."

Angeni handed the baby to Sasha, and Sasha almost said, "Hi, Freya!" before remembering that she was not supposed to know her name.

"What's her name?" Sasha asked.

"Freya," Angeni said. She scooped loose-leaf tea from a small ceramic pot into a kettle of water on the stove, turned on the burner.

"What a beautiful name."

"Thank you," Angeni said, again putting her hand to her heart in that display of exaggerated gratitude.

Sasha was overcome by a rush of unexpected emotion with the baby in her arms. She'd never been a baby person, never felt any kind of emotion toward a baby before. It had to be related to Daphne, to the nephew she'd never know. Freya seemed so small, but she was already nearly four months old. Theodore would have been so much smaller.

"Are you okay?" Angeni asked.

It was only at this question that Sasha realized her eyes were welling up with tears.

"Sorry, yes," she said. Then, seizing the moment: "It's something about holding your daughter. She seems truly special."

Angeni looked at Freya with such love and said, "She really is."

After the tea had steeped and Angeni had poured it through a strainer into their two cups, they went to the couch. She took Freya from Sasha then, and Sasha felt a pang of loss.

"So tell me about this jewelry. I love pieces that have a story," Angeni said.

The story is that I got this from a cheap knockoff shop in the city and nothing you see here cost more than twelve dollars, Sasha thought to herself.

"Why don't you look at the pieces and tell me which ones speak to you," Sasha said, hoping she sounded like the type of woo-woo person that Angeni Luna would like, "and then I'll tell you the stories."

As Sasha wheeled the cart in front of Angeni, she thought about why she was really here, what she had to say. The rage that had propelled her onto the ferry had fizzled in the presence of this small woman who seemed so ordinary, so unworthy of all the worship she received from women like Daphne. Sasha thought of the recording underway on her phone, the opportunity before her. Her resolve was shaky now, especially with the baby present. It didn't seem right to unleash on Angeni Luna in front of her child.

Sasha watched Angeni peruse the jewelry, fingering each item gently, as if in deference to its worth. She clearly had no idea that the pieces were worth next to nothing. Angeni Luna wasn't wise. She was naive, clueless. Maybe Sasha could post the audio recording of this interaction with the fake jewelry to embarrass Angeni. Would that be enough damage done? She thought of the account she could create—@exposingAngeni or @therealAngeniLuna.

"I simply adore this one," Angeni said, holding a ring between her thumb and index finger. It was a silver band with an oval-shaped stone perched atop it. "The simplicity of it is beautiful."

"That one belonged to my grandmother," Sasha said, a lie that came so quickly and easily that she surprised even herself. Angeni appeared deeply moved. Sasha couldn't help but delight in her foolishness.

"Oh my goodness, are you sure you want to sell it?" she asked.

"You know, I'm not sure I want to sell it."

Angeni extended her arm, offering the ring to Sasha, saying, "I totally understand."

"No, I think I'd prefer to give it to you," Sasha said. She was proud of herself for the orchestration of this moment. She had come to know enough of Angeni so far to predict that she would, again, put her hand to her heart.

"Really?" Angeni asked.

Were those tears coming to her eyes? Was she going to cry over the offering of this eight-dollar ring?

She was.

"I just feel like you should have it," Sasha said with a shrug.

"I'm truly honored," Angeni said.

"Let's make sure it fits," Sasha said. "I can always have it adjusted if need be."

She had no idea how to go about having a ring adjusted and wasn't sure she could follow through on such an offer, so she was grateful to see that it slipped onto Angeni Luna's middle finger for a perfect fit.

"It's like it was made for you," Sasha said.

Angeni stared at the ring on her finger, tilting her head one way and then the other, considering.

"I love it," she said.

She placed her hand in front of the baby's face, showing it to her. "What do you think, Freya?"

Freya just stared with those eyes of hers, a small smile on her chubby face.

"She's adorable," Sasha said. She was glad to mean this, wasn't sure how many lies she was capable of telling.

"Thank you," Angeni said. "Do you want to hold her again?"

There was a type of triumph in holding this woman's baby, her prized possession, especially after all Angeni had taken from Sasha.

Daphne, this woman is a fool, see?

"Sure, I'd love to hold her, if that's okay with you."

Angeni placed Freya in Sasha's lap, the weight of the baby atop Sasha's thighs. Her skin was so soft. Was all baby skin this soft? Had Theodore's skin been this soft? Sasha felt her throat constrict as she thought about Theodore. She must have seen the baby on that horrible day, but her mind had taken the memory from her. She wished she'd been able to touch him.

Now would be an appropriate moment to shift the conversation to what Sasha really wanted to say. *I was supposed to be an aunt recently. My baby nephew died. That's actually the real reason I'm here . . .* Her palms started to sweat. Before she could muster up the courage to speak, Angeni said, "So what's your sign?"

"My sign?" Sasha asked.

"Your astrological sign."

Sasha had never been a believer in astrology. Seemed like a bunch of hocus-pocus to give people some semblance of control over their lives. There was no science to it—how could there be? She knew Angeni was very into astrology. She often talked about planetary shifts and other bullshit that people seemed to eat up with the same gusto with which they ate up her views on conscious coupling and motherhood.

"I'm a Scorpio," Sasha said, because of course she still knew her sign, even if she thought it was meaningless. She also knew that Scorpios were said to be obsessive, with a venomous sting when wronged. Maybe it wasn't wholly inaccurate.

"I knew it," Angeni said, looking smug.

"You did?" She was genuinely curious what nonsense would come out of Angeni's mouth in explanation.

"You're a water sign. Just like Freya. Freya's a Pisces. Water signs have such an affinity for each other. I can tell you two just . . . *connect*."

"Oh, well, it's easy to connect with such a sweet baby," Sasha said.

"Have you done your Human Design profile?" Angeni asked.

"My what?"

~

For the next half hour, Angeni helped Sasha determine her Human Design profile, which was 6–3, the same as Freya's, according to Angeni. Angeni read aloud something on her phone: "You are someone who spends her life in experimentation. You may feel restless, always searching for the right thing. You are responsible and wise. Your challenge is learning to balance the structure of what you've learned with the natural ebbs and flows of being human."

This all sounded extremely abstract to Sasha, but she said, "Oh wow, that tracks."

"It's incredible that you and Freya have the same profile. I feel like you two are meant to have met, that you were meant to have come here today."

I was *meant to come here today,* Sasha thought to herself. *I planned it, in fact.*

"What are your plans now that you're on the island?" Angeni asked her.

This was another chance for Sasha to reveal the truth of her visit. But again, she found herself unable to do it.

Freya started to fuss in Sasha's lap, and Angeni reached both arms toward Sasha, asking for the baby. Sasha handed the baby back and watched as Angeni unbuttoned her blouse, baring her immensely full breasts without hesitation and placing Freya on to feed. All the while, she kept her eyes glued on Sasha.

"Do you plan to sell jewelry? The farmers market in town would be great for that," Angeni said.

"Oh. Well. Maybe. I'm not really sure," Sasha said.

My sister died because of you.

The words were right there and yet so far away.

"This may be kind of random," Angeni said, "but I feel like you'd be a great addition to our community."

Sasha was dumbstruck.

"What?" Sasha said.

"Our community. We have six of us here on the land right now. There's me and my husband, Erik. You met Matt. And Aurora. Jer is out back. I'll take you to meet him. And then there's Freya, of course. I wasn't really looking to grow the community just yet, but this feels strangely . . . *right*."

Sasha was speechless. She hadn't even considered this possibility. Her mind raced with thoughts as she considered the proposal. Spending more time with Angeni Luna would allow her to dig up more dirt, amass more recordings. It would be research to prove her hypothesis that Angeni Luna was a fraud. She would confront Angeni about Daphne when the time was right, then present the world with the dark truth of this woman. She could even rationalize this as a side project related to her dissertation, a deep dive into the world of intensive mothering and how it was threatening feminism. She was in no rush to get back to Seattle. She'd just started summer break, could easily reschedule her tutoring clients for when she returned to the city. Professor Williams, her faculty adviser, had said herself that Sasha should "take some time." This was one way of doing that. She only had enough clothes for the weekend, but that wasn't a big deal; there were shops in town.

"I can tell you think I'm crazy," Angeni said with a laugh.

Sasha could feel that her face was scrunched up. She did her best to relax it and gave Angeni a smile.

"I'm just surprised, that's all," she said. "It would be amazing to join your community."

Angeni looked delighted. "Really? I don't want to pressure you. I just have a good feeling about you."

That, right there, was proof that Angeni's self-proclaimed intuitive gifts were bullshit.

"I'm honored to be included," Sasha said.

"Okay then. It's settled. I can't wait to tell everyone."

Angeni stood from the couch. "Come," she said. "Let me give you a tour."

~

After meeting everyone and touring the property, Sasha had gone back to her Airbnb, gathered her belongings, and texted the host to say something unexpected came up—truly unexpected—and she would be leaving the property early. That was that. With very little effort, she had become part of Angeni Luna's community.

In the weeks since her arrival, in true scorpion fashion, she'd been lying in wait. She was observing, gathering information, trying to understand this strange woman and the cultlike community that had led Daphne so astray. Some days, she found Angeni Luna insufferable. Some days, she felt sorry for her. This woman had nobody around her to challenge her belief systems. She had only her followers—on the land and online.

It was difficult for Sasha to continue her performance as the eager young woman who was happy to help Angeni Luna however she needed. She couldn't help interjecting her true self at times, like speaking up about the Abraham Lincoln quote—such a great example of Angeni Luna's idiocy. Sasha had captured that on audio recording. She'd called into that podcast with that question about Angeni's past, which had upset Angeni so much that she'd *lost consciousness*. Sasha couldn't say she'd expected that—she'd just been trying to force cracks in her facade. This woman was so attached to this idealistic version of her own self that she couldn't bear to face the reality that she was human, that she'd once had meaningless sex and stupid relationships, that she needed help taking care of her child.

Oh, the child. Sasha's love of Freya was a complicating factor that she never could have anticipated. The baby had none of her mother's hubris. She was pure and beautiful. When Daphne had gotten pregnant, Sasha had known she'd care about her nephew, but she had been doubtful of her ability to feel the kind of love everyone talked about. Now that she knew Freya, a baby not even related to her, Sasha was certain she would have felt heart-exploding love for Theo.

Sasha had never done a single minute of babysitting in her life, but she took to it easily. She couldn't help but relish the irony of Angeni Luna talking about the importance of constant connection with one's offspring while handing off the baby to Sasha. Sasha kept a log of every babysitting hour, something she planned to share with the public eventually. Every so often, Angeni included a photo of Sasha with the baby on Instagram—Freya with her auntie Sitka—but Sasha suspected it was because Angeni wanted to showcase the token nonwhite person in the community. Angeni never, ever mentioned that Sasha was basically the nanny both day and night. Angeni made it seem like she was writing the book with Freya strapped to her chest. She posted several photos of that—Just me and my coauthor! The book was a laugh. Sasha could not imagine how Angeni would succeed in finishing it. Whenever she peeked at the computer screen, she saw only fragments of sentences, random notes, nothing of substance.

It didn't take long to gather evidence of who Angeni Luna really was. Jay encouraged Sasha to come back, to leave the strange vortex in which she'd found herself. She was building up to delivering her big speech about Daphne, mentally planning for her departure. But then

Angeni offered to pay her, to formalize their nanny-like arrangement, and Sasha could feel her desperation. It was a desperation that piqued her curiosity even more. Angeni Luna seemed shaken lately. There was a general sense of foreboding. Whether Sasha was the cause of whatever was imminent, or simply a witness to it, she didn't know. But she wanted to stay to find out.

When she told Jay she was going to stay a bit longer, he sent a facepalm emoji and wrote:

be safe, k? i can't lose u to angeni lunatic too

Every night, sitting in bed in her room with baby Freya asleep next to her, Sasha whisper-talked to Daphne: *I'm trying to understand, sis. How did you think she had all the answers?* She wondered if Daphne could hear her, in whatever realm she now occupied. She waited for some response—the flickering of a light, a whoosh of wind against the window. There was nothing.

Sasha texted her mom every few days, bland exchanges of pleasantries. She didn't tell her mother where she was, just said she was busy tutoring and working on her dissertation and trying to enjoy some summer downtime. Her mother had proved incapable of talking much about Daphne, saying it was too hard. Without Daphne to talk about, they were left with the weather, work.

It was possible Sasha was staying on Bainbridge Island to be farther away from the loss of Daphne. Her brain was busy taking in these new surroundings, and she couldn't deny that the distraction was a reprieve. She knew she couldn't stay forever, obviously. She would have to tell Angeni about Daphne soon and then exit the scene as gracefully as possible.

But then a new complicating factor arose. One night, as Sasha sat in her bed with baby Freya, Erik appeared at her doorway. "Do you mind if I come in?" he asked. And Sasha didn't mind at all.

Chapter 17

Gwen

In the wee hours of the morning the day after the visit with Leigh, Gwen was up breastfeeding June while googling the best sex lube. She couldn't focus, though, because her breasts were killing her. There were lumps in both—a first-time occurrence since she'd embarked on this experience of being a milk factory.

She pressed on the lumps, figuring she had clogged ducts. It sounded like a plumbing mishap because it was, essentially. The milk was not moving through the channels properly; there was a backup. She switched her Google search from sex lubes to clogged ducts. One had only to investigate a new mother's Google search history to understand all she was up against.

Her research confirmed what she already knew—the best cure was for the baby to breastfeed, pulling the trapped milk through the ducts with the magical sucking reflex. A few posts said to get on all fours and have the baby latch so gravity could do its thing. Gwen slid a finger into June's mouth to get her to release the nipple. She wasn't done feeding, so she was understandably annoyed with this interruption. As June whined, Gwen got on all fours and then did her best to hold June against her breast with one hand. How did women do this? This seemed like it would only work with a toddler that could stand on her own and lift her head to the nipple, like a calf to a mama cow.

She considered calling Jeff to come help. He could prop up June underneath her. But she knew he would think this was crazy, and she didn't want the burden of his judgment. She gave up and rested back into the usual position, holding June like a football across her chest as she resumed feeding. Somehow, despite the discomfort, Gwen fell asleep.

~

She wasn't sure what woke her—the sun peeking through the curtains or the chills running through her body. Was she sick?

Jeff opened the door to the room, already dressed in his best suit, his travel mug of coffee in one hand.

"Good morn—" he said, before realizing something wasn't right. "Are you okay?"

He sat on the bed next to her. She felt clammy, her whole body covered in a thin sheen of sweat.

"I think I've got some kind of bug," she said.

"Oh no, sweetie."

She put the underside of her wrist to her forehead. It seemed hot, but she wasn't sure how a forehead was supposed to feel.

"Do I seem hot to you?" she asked him.

He touched her forehead and said, "A little. Let me get you some Tylenol."

She heard him open the cupboard in the hallway where they kept all their medicines. She knew exactly where the Tylenol was, but he didn't. She could only take so much of hearing him rummaging around.

"It's on the right, by the Pepto-Bismol," she said.

"Aha!"

She stared at the two white pills in his palm. She knew over-the-counter pain medications were considered safe to take while breastfeeding, but was anyone really sure? There were so few studies on pregnant and breastfeeding women—no pharmaceutical company wanting to risk being blamed for damaging a baby.

"Babe," Jeff said. "Take them."

He knew exactly what she was thinking, and he had no patience for it.

She exhaled and took the pills. She was sure Angeni Luna would judge her for it.

"Should I stay home today?" Jeff asked.

It was nice of him to ask, but she knew this was a big day for him. He had to be in court, and Judge Barkley was presiding, and Judge Barkley did not take kindly to last-minute schedule changes.

"No, no," she said. "I'll be fine."

"Are you sure?"

She wasn't sure at all. She hadn't felt this sick in years. But it was probably just the flu. Her immune system was shot from lack of sleep. Viruses probably had a field day with new moms, feasting upon their vulnerability, capitalizing on their fatigue.

"I'm sure. We'll just take it easy today," she said. "Right, June?"

June, of course, did not give a shit if her mother was ill, but it was nice to pretend that she did, to entertain the idea of their relationship having some reciprocity. It occurred to Gwen that it would probably never be that way, that this was what motherhood was, that this was what she'd signed up for.

She caught Jeff looking at the clock. She knew he had to go. Judge Barkley also did not take kindly to tardiness.

"Will you call if you need me?" he asked.

She definitely would not call him out of court.

"I will," she lied.

He kissed her on the forehead.

"Wait," he said.

He went back into the hallway and returned with the bottle of Tylenol.

"In case you need more," he said, shaking it like a rattle before setting it on the nightstand with a satisfied tap. She had no plans to take more of this possibly damaging medication, but she thanked him anyway.

"We'll see you when you're home," she said.

He kissed June and said, "Be nice to Mama," and then he was gone.

Gwen stared at the clock, wondering how she was going to get through an entire day with an infant while feeling like she'd been hit by a truck. She set June in the bassinet and went to find the "baby care kit" that someone had given her at her shower. She knew it included a thermometer because she remembered telling Jeff that if they ever had to take their baby's temperature rectally, he would be in charge. They had laughed the way parents-to-be laugh when they have no idea what's coming.

She unzipped the kit and found the thermometer, stuck it in her mouth. She felt dizzy standing up, so she crouched down on the floor, easing herself into child's pose, resting her forehead against the cool hardwood. When it seemed like a couple of minutes had passed, she removed the thermometer from her mouth and willed her eyes to focus on the number.

104.

Did it really say 104?

She couldn't remember ever having a fever so high. Was it possible she'd gotten something from Leigh and Belle? Could a virus transmit that quickly? She crawled on her hands and knees back to the bed, reached up for her phone.

Hey. Sorry to text so early, but are you sick? I've got some kind of virus going on

The three dots of an incoming response appeared right away.

Leigh: Girl, I don't even know what normal hours are anymore. Ugh, being sick with a baby is the worst. Shouldn't be allowed. We are ok over here. What are your symptoms?
Gwen: I've got a 104 fever, aches, etc
Leigh: Shit. That's high. Do your boobs hurt?

Gwen: Ya they're killing me
Leigh: Shit. You might have mastitis

Of course, Gwen knew what mastitis was. But like most people when it comes to bad things, she didn't think it could happen to her.

Gwen: What do I do? Warm compresses? Cold? I can't remember
Leigh: I think you gotta call your doc. Fever is too high

Gwen scrolled through her contact list until she found Dr. Blake. She made her way past various prompts before getting the emergency answering service. When she told them what was going on, they sounded alarmed by the 104 fever and said they would put the doctor through.

"Ms. Fisher?" Dr. Blake said.

"Yes?"

"If your fever is a hundred and four, you need to go to the ER."

"What? Really?"

"Do you have someone to drive you?"

Jeff was likely in traffic, halfway to the court. She texted Leigh.

Gwen: Doctor says I should go to the ER. I know this is a lot to ask, but can you take me?
Leigh: Of course. Send me your address

She texted the address and told Dr. Blake she would be going to the ER. He said he would check in with the staff there in an hour.

She knew she should pack a bag for this unexpected outing, but she couldn't think straight. When had she taken the Tylenol? Had it kicked in yet? She felt suddenly cold, her teeth chattering. She pulled the comforter off the bed and wrapped it around herself. Her only solace was that Leigh would be there soon enough.

~

It seemed like just a minute later when Gwen opened her eyes and saw a woman dressed in white coming toward her. The figure was blurry, ethereal—an angel? No, not an angel. But Angeni Luna.

"Angeni?" Gwen whispered.

"It's me," the voice said. "I'm going to help you up, okay? Nathan's with Belle, so I've got June in Belle's car seat."

Nathan. Belle. The names were familiar. This woman wasn't Angeni Luna. This was Leigh.

"June?" Gwen managed. Had she passed out? How long? How had she not noticed her own baby being whisked away? She looked around to confirm that, yes, her baby was not in the vicinity.

"She's in the car already," Leigh said. "I've got the passenger door open. You just gotta get to the car, okay?"

But getting to the car seemed like an outrageous trek, on par with summitting Everest.

Gwen instructed her legs to move, but they no longer felt like they were under her jurisdiction. They were just these things attached to a body that felt increasingly unlike her own. But if her body wasn't her body, then how did she exist? Was this what it was to die?

"One step at a time," Leigh said.

They were in the hallway, making their way toward the front door, which was halfway open, letting in daylight from the outside. Gwen was, quite literally, going toward the light.

"You're going to be okay," Leigh said, as if reading Gwen's morbid thoughts.

Somehow, they got to the car, and Leigh buckled her into the passenger seat. Gwen had forgotten about June until she heard her cry in the back seat.

"Fuck," Leigh said. "Do you have any bottles in the fridge? Freezer bags?"

Gwen wasn't sure who Leigh was talking to. Was she talking to her?

"Gwen, is June hungry? Do you have milk?"

"What?" Gwen said.

"Never mind, we have to go. We'll figure it out at the hospital," Leigh said.

~

Gwen didn't remember the car ride. She closed her eyes for the entirety of it, and then they were there. Someone in scrubs opened the passenger-side door and helped her into a wheelchair while Leigh spoke in the background, her voice sounding far away, underwater. Then Gwen was inside, and more people were talking in concerned voices around her. It felt eerily similar to the day she'd been sliced open. Panic descended upon her body.

"What's happening?" she said, grabbing on to the sleeve of Leigh's sweatshirt, pulling at it.

"You're going to be okay," Leigh said, taking Gwen's sweaty hand in her own. "We're here now."

~

It was only later that Gwen was told the chain of events. She didn't remember anything, the fever having transported her out of reality and to some holding area, an antechamber to death. They admitted her to the hospital shortly after she arrived and started IV antibiotics. Both breasts were infected with methicillin-resistant *Staphylococcus aureus*, which Gwen hadn't heard of, though she had heard of its nefarious nickname—MRSA. It was one of the bacterial infections you didn't want because it was so resistant to antibiotics. But apparently, whatever they had her hooked up to would take care of it within a couple of days.

Both breasts had abscesses, one of which was the size of a kiwi and needed to be cut open and drained. They had hoped to just aspirate it, but it was too big and required surgery. She was, apparently, someone who always required surgery, someone to cut open against her will.

~

On day two in the hospital, she was starting to feel okay. Her right breast was heavily bandaged, so she couldn't see the wound left behind by the surgery. The left breast was sore, but softened from the rock-hard state it had been in. The full-body chills, the fever, those were gone. She could think clearly again, which was when it occurred to her that she hadn't fed June since this ordeal began.

"Hey, you," Jeff said as she stirred in bed, awakening from a midday nap or overnight sleep, she wasn't sure.

He was sitting in a chair next to her bed, June in his arms. Gwen had been too out of it to give Leigh the unlock code for her phone, so Leigh hadn't been able to get ahold of Jeff. But the hospital had had him listed as Gwen's emergency contact and called him. He'd left court to be with her and tend to June.

"Has June eaten?" Gwen asked.

It was a stupid question. Of course they wouldn't have let June starve until Gwen recovered.

"We gave her some food," Jeff said.

What was he talking about? And who was "we"?

"*Food?* She's not old enough for *food*," Gwen said with a laugh that came out tinny and made her sound insane.

"Nutrition," Jeff said. He cleared his throat. "We gave her nutrition."

He was looking down at June, not meeting Gwen's eyes. It felt so much like that day he'd told her she no longer had a womb.

"What did you give her?" she asked him.

Though, in her heart, she knew.

He sighed, heavily.

"Some formula," he said. "I know that's not what you would have wanted, but she needed to eat."

The tears came suddenly and with a surprising intensity. She understood, logically, why this had to happen. Her baby was hungry. Her baby needed to eat. She was unable to feed her. But she was still upset, betrayed by her husband and these doctors who were making decisions without her . . . again.

"I know that's upsetting for you," Jeff said.

She resented the "for you." It was like he was drawing attention to the fact that it wasn't upsetting *for him*, that it wouldn't be upsetting for any rational person. He'd been pro-formula since day one, when breastfeeding had proved to be an unrelenting challenge. He'd never truly valued the commitment she had to it, despite all the information she shared with him about why breast was truly best. He just didn't get it. He wasn't saddled with the same pressures she was as a mother. He didn't feel the same sense of duty to their child. *Must be nice,* Gwen thought.

"Can I hold her?" she asked.

He placed June on her chest, and Gwen sobbed, silently apologizing to her daughter for failing her, yet again. What kind of formula was it? Did the hospital supply it? Did Jeff get it? In either case, it was probably standard and cheap, definitely not organic or tailored for sensitive tummies like June's.

"So she took a bottle?" Gwen asked.

It was a stupid question. How else would June have consumed formula? But she needed confirmation of this calamity.

"She did," Jeff said. "Like a champ!"

His celebration of this fact made her feel even more alone. June taking a bottle hurt her feelings more than the actual contents of the bottle. She had wanted to believe that June would reject a bottle, would turn her tiny nose up at anything that was not her mother's body. But no. It turned out June was completely content with this alternative to her mother. She didn't really need her mother, after all.

Gwen kept sobbing, and Jeff put his hand on her shoulder.

"Oh, honey," he said.

He sounded less like he was heartbroken on her behalf, and more like he was impatient with her being heartbroken.

"You're coming off a pretty serious medical event," he said in his lawyerly tone. "You're going to feel better about everything once your body is recovered."

He'd said something similar after June's birth, after the hysterectomy, and he was wrong; she didn't feel better. And now this, compounding it all.

"When can I feed her?" she asked.

"I don't know, hon," he said. "We can ask the doctor."

She had a feeling he did know, though; he just didn't want to be the messenger.

~

The doctor explained to her that breastfeeding with her right boob was not possible until the incision healed. She would be able to breastfeed from the left boob.

"What about the medications I'm on?" she asked him.

"Perfectly safe while you're breastfeeding," he assured her.

She didn't trust him, though. She would never again trust doctors.

"What's it called?"

"The IV antibiotic?"

She nodded.

"Vancomycin," he said. "I'll be sending you home with ten days of Bactrim. That's also safe while breastfeeding."

She made a mental note to do her own Google research.

"Okay, so that's promising," Jeff said when the doctor left.

"Can I have my phone?" she asked.

Vancomycin, Bactrim, vancomycin, Bactrim. She repeated the names to herself so she wouldn't forget.

He handed the phone to her, and she began her research. At first glance, both medications appeared safe-ish for breastfeeding, but then she saw that Bactrim was discouraged for babies under two months because it can raise bilirubin levels. She didn't know what bilirubin levels were, which led to another Google search. They were related to the liver. June was older than two months, but Gwen couldn't risk messing with her liver.

"Maybe you can feed her from the left breast, and we can just use formula as a little boost," Jeff said.

He sounded entirely too chipper.

"I don't know if I feel good about feeding her while I'm on these meds," she said.

"Okay, then formula it is. Easy enough."

Sometimes she felt like he didn't understand her at all. When she'd been really struggling with breastfeeding, he'd brought a Costco pack of formula home "just in case." She'd told him to throw it away, but he hadn't. He'd just put it in the garage. She'd seen it on their "home goods" shelf, next to the batteries and light bulbs. He was just waiting for her to officially fail so he could swoop in, the hero.

"I think I should just pump and dump for now, then resume breastfeeding when I'm done with the antibiotics," she said.

"Pump and dump?"

"Pump my milk . . . with a breast pump," she said. Did he not even know what that was? Was it her fault for shielding him from so much of her mental load, or his fault for not making more inquiries? "And then dump it because it may not be safe."

He looked confused.

"So that my body keeps making milk," she explained.

"Oh," he said, still looking confused. "Okay. Yeah. Whatever you think is best, hon."

"Can you bring my pump from home?" she asked.

She rubbed her left breast, felt its increasing fullness.

"Sure. Where would that be?"

She thought of him rummaging in the cabinet for the Tylenol, clueless.

"It's in the nursery closet, next to the box of diapers," she said.

"Okay, yeah, sure."

He stood, glanced at his phone. "Oh, Leigh just texted. She'll be back with her daughter to visit soon."

This bothered Gwen—that they'd exchanged numbers, that Leigh wasn't wholly Gwen's anymore. She wasn't even sure she wanted to see Leigh, with her perfectly healthy tits and her nonpoison milk and her nipple-loving baby.

Jeff must have perceived her hesitation, because he said, "I can tell her not to come if you're not up for it."

"No, it's okay." Maybe Leigh's company would be nice. Leigh would get it, better than Jeff ever would. Leigh would make her feel sane.

Jeff glanced again at his phone, no doubt checking messages from his firm. In their line of work, nobody cared about medical emergencies.

"Work piling up?" she asked.

He jammed his phone into his pocket and said, "Work is not important right now."

It was a kind lie.

"All right, I'll get the pump and some food and then come back?" he said. "Do you want me to leave June with you?"

She nodded. Of course she wanted him to leave June with her. The fact that this medical emergency had presented the possibility of June being away from her was a trauma in itself.

"Okay, I'll be back with burritos from Lupe's. Sound good?"

Nothing sounded good, but she nodded.

"Okay, love you," he said with a hurried kiss on her cheek.

Then he was gone. It was like he couldn't get out of there fast enough.

~

Leigh arrived a short time later with Belle strapped to her chest. She looked exhausted, dark circles under her eyes, and Gwen felt simultaneously guilty and grateful for the time and energy Leigh had been giving to Gwen. They barely knew each other, really, and yet Leigh felt like someone Gwen loved—or needed. Was there a difference between the two?

"Oh my god, you poor thing," Leigh said, hurrying to Gwen's bedside.

Gwen started crying, happy tears this time, in response to Leigh's care and empathy. That was what she hadn't felt from Jeff—empathy.

"How are you feeling?" Leigh asked.

"Better physically. Mentally, I'm a wreck. I can't feed June. They gave her formula," Gwen said.

Leigh looked appropriately horrified.

"Oh, sweetie, I'm sorry."

"I can't feed from the right boob. I'm afraid to feed her when I'm on these antibiotics. I don't know if my supply has totally tanked."

The tears were coming faster now, sliding down her cheeks in two rivers.

"Okay, deep breaths," Leigh said.

Leigh took her own long inhale, demonstrating, then exhaled.

Gwen did her best to follow along.

Just then, a nurse came in to change out the IV bag. She either didn't notice that Gwen had been crying or didn't care.

"Hi there," she said with a robotic smile.

She unhooked the bag that was currently on the hook and replaced it with another.

"You're looking better," the nurse said.

Gwen didn't remember seeing this nurse before, but most of the previous hours were lost to her.

"Is the doctor coming soon?" Gwen asked.

She needed to see the doctor. She needed to ask questions, find out when she could get out of here, when her life could go back to normal. So many days she had agonized about the long hours home alone with June, doing nothing but breastfeeding and tummy time and napping (well, June napped, only in the swing, while Gwen used the "free time" to do chores or shower). She would give anything for those days now, anything to just return to the rhythm that had previously felt so dull and soul crushing.

"Doctor should be doing rounds soon," the nurse said with another robotic smile before turning to head out.

"Thanks," Gwen managed.

"Can we ask you a question?" Leigh said.

The nurse turned around and made a show of exhaling.

"Sure," she said.

"Women breastfeed after this, right?" Leigh asked.

The nurse took a moment to respond, and Gwen could imagine the wheels turning in her brain. Did she even remember why Gwen was there? The nurse's eyes landed on June, and she seemed to suddenly understand.

"Oh, you'll have to ask the doctor," she said. "But I'm not sure it'll be feasible to breastfeed after this."

Gwen stared at her name badge—Mari. She hated Mari and her use of the word *feasible*. Mari was young. Mari probably did not have children. Mari didn't understand. She wanted to punch Mari.

"But women do, right?" Leigh asked.

"I honestly don't know," she said, looking at the watch on her wrist, alerting them to her busy schedule. "But from what I've seen, it's usually a formula situation after something like this."

A formula situation.

Leigh rolled her eyes aggressively, and Gwen's heart swelled in appreciation for her friend's annoyance.

"Okay, we'll ask the doctor," Leigh said.

Gwen was so thankful for this "we," for the way Leigh made the two of them a team, figuring out this situation together.

When the nurse had barely left the room, Leigh said, at louder-than-normal volume, "Well, she was a bitch."

"Leigh!" Gwen said. She couldn't help but laugh.

"What? She was. So uncaring. 'First, do no harm.' Isn't that in their oath? Her very presence did me harm."

Gwen kept laughing, pleasantly surprised at her ability to do so.

"'Formula situation,'" Leigh muttered. "What a cunt."

"Leigh!"

Leigh shrugged. "Sorry not sorry."

The word continued to roll around inside Gwen's brain—*cunt, cunt, cunt*. She was in near hysterics, while Leigh sat with her arms crossed.

"Listen, this is bullshit," Leigh said. "You are going to feed your baby how you want to feed your baby. End of story."

There was something seductive about Leigh's resolve, though Gwen wasn't sure how realistic it was. She didn't have the energy to google herself down rabbit holes of information about recovery from severe mastitis. She was afraid of the message boards full of bad news, all the women before her who had had to accept their formula fates.

"Jeff's gonna bring my pump. I'll see what my left boob has to offer. Pump and dump while I'm on the antibiotics."

Leigh nodded. Unlike Jeff, she was following along with the plan easily.

"How long are the antibiotics?"

"Ten days."

"Okay, that's not so bad. Your boobs can bounce back. This must happen to women all the time, and I'm sure they resume breastfeeding."

Belle squirmed in her carrier, and Leigh lifted her out.

"Fuck, I'm sorry. I meant to feed her before I came, but I totally spaced," she said.

Belle was pawing at Leigh's shirt. It was amazing how babies were so clear on their desires.

"I can, like, go in the hall," Leigh said, starting to stand.

"It's okay," Gwen said, meaning it. "You can stay."

Leigh remained standing. "Are you sure? I feel like it will be triggering."

Just the fact that Gwen had acknowledged this lessened the awfulness of the situation.

"It might be, but it's okay. Please, sit."

Leigh sat with reluctance and looked Gwen in the eyes.

"Are you sure?"

"For the love of god, feed your damn kid."

Leigh sighed. "I didn't even wear the right shirt."

It was a tight cotton T-shirt, not ideal for breastfeeding. Button-downs or flowy tunics were best. Gwen watched as Leigh lifted the T-shirt up and over her breasts, exposing her nursing bra. She unlatched the bra and stuck her right boob in Belle's mouth. Belle latched on effortlessly, and Gwen felt like she was going to cry all over again.

"See? It's too much, isn't it?" Leigh said.

She looked so pained to witness Gwen's pain, and Gwen thought that must be a definition of true love.

"It's okay," Gwen assured her. "Just because I can't breastfeed doesn't mean I don't want you to."

Leigh relaxed back into the chair.

"You're a better person than me, I think. If the roles were switched, I'd probably tell you to go in the hall."

"But would you call me a cunt?"

They both started laughing before settling into a peaceful quiet. The only sounds in the room were the occasional beeping of one of the monitors attached to Gwen, and baby Belle's sweet suckling. June was lying happily on Gwen's chest, not even rooting around for a nipple.

"Maybe she likes formula better," Gwen said. She felt the sting of coming tears.

"Oh, Gwen, don't be like this to yourself," Leigh said.

"I feel like I'm not producing anything right now."

"Probably because of the stress of everything. Making milk is, like, the last thing your body is focused on right now."

Her stupid body, always going rogue.

Gwen couldn't help but wonder what Angeni Luna would say. She was so against the use of formula. But this was a unique situation. Angeni wanted to support mothers, ultimately, didn't she?

"What would Angeni Luna do if she were me?" Gwen asked. Her voice was soft. She was embarrassed with herself for the question.

"She would use the damn formula and not tell anyone about it," Leigh said.

"You think?"

"I mean, what's the alternative? Letting her baby, like, *die*?"

"That makes me feel better. It's so silly, but it does."

"You said her name, you know. Do you remember?" Leigh asked.

"What? When?"

"When I came to take you to the hospital. You were in and out. It was terrifying, honestly. I put June in the car and came to get you, and you called me Angeni Luna."

Gwen didn't remember that, but she remembered the vision of the woman coming toward her.

"You were wearing white?" Gwen said.

"Yeah, this tunic thing. Why?"

"I thought you were an angel," Gwen said. "I was so out of it."

"I'm so glad you're okay," Leigh said.

"I'm so sorry it was terrifying."

"Oh, stop. I'm quite sure it was more terrifying for you," Leigh said. "And look, just use the formula for now. You'll get back to breastfeeding. This will all be a blip on the radar."

Gwen started crying more.

"Oh, honey. It's okay. I promise it'll be okay. Here's what we're going to do. You're going to come over every day with June so we can hang out and get you through this rough patch. Okay?"

Gwen nodded.

"Thank you," she managed to say in the midst of her tears.

Leigh came to her bedside, took her hand, squeezed it. She stared into Gwen's teary eyes with such meaningful compassion that Gwen couldn't stand it, flicked her eyes downward.

"We should probably get going. Have to get home and do dinner," Leigh said.

"Okay, yeah. Thank you again," Gwen said, resuming eye contact.

"I know we've only been friends for a short time, but I really care for you," Leigh said.

Now Leigh's eyes welled up with tears. Gwen had to look away again. She couldn't handle such a strong dose of intimacy like this.

"You're a godsend," Gwen said.

Leigh squeezed her hand again. "Okay, sweetie. Rest well. Feel better. If they don't let you out soon, I'll bust you out."

"Sounds like a plan."

"I feel like we have a very Thelma-and-Louise vibe, don't you?"

Gwen laughed. "Minus the driving off the cliff at the end."

"Right, minus that."

Leigh blew her a kiss and then left the room. Gwen felt her absence immediately and acutely. Before she had a chance to analyze the depth of this unexpected ache, Jeff appeared, a brown take-out bag in one hand.

"How's the patient?" he asked.

"I'm good."

"Sorry it took so long. Lupe's was packed. Did Leigh stop by?"

"She did."

Gwen didn't want to bother trying to recount how much the visit meant to her. Jeff wouldn't get it, and maybe that was fine. Leigh got it.

"She seems like a good friend," he said.

He took out Gwen's burrito, placed it on the tray, and swiveled the tray in front of Gwen. She was suddenly starving and knew she would enjoy every bite.

"She is," Gwen said. "She really is."

Chapter 18

Angeni Luna

Now, more than ever, be
grateful for your commitment
to keeping your babies close.

Angeni cradled Freya against her naked chest with one hand, her other hand holding her phone behind Freya's head, her eyes glued to the screen. There had been another school shooting, this one in a suburb outside Cincinnati. A young man had taken an AK-47 into a public elementary school, driven by rage over a breakup with a woman who taught second grade there. He'd opened fire in her classroom, killing six children before killing her and then himself. It was horrific.

Angeni could not stop thinking of those six children, could not stop scrolling the news for information about them. The media began releasing their names and school photos—the boys in their collared shirts, the girls in ruffly dresses. Madison, Carter, Jocelyn, Emma, Jacob, Miguel.

Her Instagram post was a response to this tragedy. In the caption, she wrote:

> My heart aches. Events like this one remind me why it's so important for us to revisit our social norms. I

> feel awful for the mothers who have no choice but to send their children to schools that have become battlegrounds. We must all have the right to be with our children, teaching them within the safe walls of our homes 🙏❤️

Most of the commenters applauded her words:

> Homeschool FTW. I cannot imagine sending my children out into this world we live in. I don't judge parents who do, I just don't understand how they can. How are these parents of these poor six children going to live with themselves now?

> 😭 These shootings need to stop. Until they do, I'm homeschooling. It's not always easy, but at least I know my kids are safe.

> I'm so lucky to be able to stay home with my kids. Feel so sad for moms who have to go to work and send their kids to school. I can't imagine the daily worry

But there were a few of the usual haters:

> R u fucking serious right now? It's not the schools that are the problem, it's the guns. Wow. Unfollow.

> Ummm, hi, some women want to work. And some kids want to go to a regular school and spend time playing with kids instead of just interacting with people at their weird commune

> This is a really strange post. Somehow, you've found a way to shame working mothers in the midst of a national tragedy. Fascinating.

Shaming mothers? That wasn't what she was doing. She was speaking out for the safety of children. Why weren't more people up in arms about what was best for the children? This was what was wrong with society. If more people prioritized children and the nurturing they needed on a daily basis, so many problems would be solved. There would be no more of these shootings, for one thing.

The account handle for the last comment was @nurture.mother.official, a clear copycat account. Angeni tapped over to view the page. There were only a few posts so far, and they all looked exactly like the posts on her own page—same background, same text font. But the content of the page wasn't copying Angeni; in fact, it seemed to be opposing her.

> You are not a bad mother if you want time to yourself. You are a human being and your needs matter, too.

> Fed is best. Feed your child in a way that supports your happiness too. Happy mom, happy baby.

Angeni felt attacked. It was just so blatant. Was this even legal?

"Erik!" she called.

Things still felt off with Erik. She'd told him that morning that they should have their long-postponed State of the Union chat after dinner. She'd said it could be followed by "other things," and when she'd waggled her eyebrows suggestively, he'd smiled and said, "I'm definitely in." She was trying.

Erik appeared in the doorway. "You call me?"

"Yeah. Take a look at this."

She showed him the @nurture.mother.official account page.

"What is this?" he said, brow furrowed.

"Someone copying my page but with counter messages," she said.

"What in the world?"

"Can we report them?"

He shrugged. "I'll try. I guess there's nothing proprietary about your design, but this is pretty egregious. I can't remember—did Jer create the background?"

Jer did some small design tasks for the business, mostly related to their website. But he hadn't made the background.

"No. It's just something I found online."

"Hmm, I don't know if there's anything we can do, then. We could hire someone to make a custom design for us, change our colors."

"What? Why should *we* have to change anything? *They're* the problem. People know my brand. I can't go changing everything anytime someone like this comes along."

"Okay, okay," he said. "Let me see what I can do."

"It's clearly a new page. They only have a couple thousand followers. But we need to nip this in the bud."

He handed the phone back to her.

"I'm on it," he said. "Sorry, babe. Haters coming out of the woodwork."

He was right. She'd heard it all at this point—*Angeni Luna is tone deaf, Angeni Luna is the death of feminism, Angeni Luna is a witch.*

"We knew there would be some backlash from the book deal," he reminded her.

There had been backlash. Most people were genuinely supportive, but it was the negative comments that stuck with her:

is the title of the book 'how to make motherhood much harder than it needs to be'? if not, that's my suggestion. you're welcome

if ur writing a book, whenever will u have time to can tomatoes?

You know what bugs me? The type of mothering you're promoting would require most women to drop out of the workforce completely, meaning they would become financially dependent on their partner, thereby severely limiting what's possible for their freedom and future. What you're not saying in the image you're selling (yes, selling) is that you, in fact, make significant money from book deals like this. You are telling women there is only one right way to mother, but you are really having it both ways. Do you see the hypocrisy?

"I suppose this is just testing my resolve," she said.

"Exactly. Spirit is giving you obstacles to see how willing you are to overcome them."

He was right. He always reflected back to her the core beliefs she held dear. He reminded her who she was.

"Thank you," she said.

"I love you," he said back to her.

He leaned over sleeping Freya and kissed Angeni on the mouth.

"I'm looking forward to later," he said.

"Me too," she said, though she wasn't, not really. She would give him her body, out of obligation, which was something she'd sworn she'd never do again after too many episodes of meaningless, self-disrespecting sex in her younger years. Not that this was meaningless. Maybe, in marriage, obligatory sex was especially meaningful.

~

After some trial and error, Angeni determined that afternoons were her best creative windows. She wasn't pleased with her progress on the book. Mostly, she'd been putting different ideas into a Word document titled "Book Stuff," but she wasn't sure how these thoughts would make themselves into a cohesive manuscript. She was doing her best to trust the process, to let Spirit guide her. It was still early days, and the mental energy needed for a book was immense. She couldn't expect too much of herself. She had to practice the self-compassion she so often preached.

Freya was thriving. That was what mattered most. If Freya was thriving, Angeni was a success.

She breastfed Freya, then gave her some bites of chicken-liver pâté for her lunch. For at least the first two years of Freya's life, Angeni wanted breast milk to be Freya's primary source of sustenance, with food being more for practicing different tastes and textures. Her plan was to breastfeed through three years, or longer if Freya wanted. Angeni knew people thought it was strange when children breastfed beyond babyhood.

> Once they can ask for the boob with words, they're too old.

There were comments along those lines in every post in which she mentioned her intention to breastfeed long-term. This was what was wrong with society—rushing women through these precious moments of motherhood, encouraging them to have their babies sleep independently and find other sources of nutrition beyond the breast as soon as possible.

"Hey," Sitka said, coming into the kitchen to prepare her own lunch.

Every day, Sitka ate the same thing—two slices of Angeni's homemade sourdough bread, slathered in peanut butter and raspberry jam from the farmers market. Angeni had made the mistake once of offering Sitka a glass of raw milk with her meal, explaining how it contained more amino acids and natural probiotics than the altered milk most people drank. Sitka had looked at Angeni like she was the stupidest person on the planet and said, "I'll skip the listeria juice, thanks." Angeni didn't bother trying to defend her choices, but she did make a mental note to share more about raw milk on Instagram.

"Do you mind feeding her a few more bites of pâté?" Angeni asked Sitka. "I think I'm going to heat up some of that chili I made the other day."

"Sure," Sitka said.

Sitka scooted her stool next to Freya's high chair and lifted the tiny spoon, moving it around Freya's face and making airplane noises before saying, "Coming in for a landing" and putting the spoon in Freya's mouth. Freya thought it was hysterical. Was Angeni playful enough with Freya? She was so often consumed with tending to Freya's basic needs. She needed to focus on infusing more play. She added this topic to her list of future Instagram posts.

Angeni put the leftover pot of chili on the stove and turned on the burner. She was debating whether or not to ask Sitka about her post this morning. She both craved and feared Sitka's opinion.

"Horrible about that shooting in Cincinnati, right?" Angeni started.

Sitka was still doing the spoon-airplane thing with Freya, the two of them in their own little world.

"Shooting?" Sitka asked, eyes still on Freya.

So she hadn't seen the post. If she'd seen it, she would have read the caption and comments and known about the tragedy.

"A school. Six children were killed."

"Oh, that's awful."

"Yeah, it is. I posted something about it. Anyway," she said, stopping short of asking Sitka to read the post and give her thoughts right there on the spot. Since when was Angeni so insecure? It was the book project getting to her, making her question her abilities and worth.

"I'll probably take Freya into the forest today while you write, if that's okay," Sitka said. "It's so beautiful out."

"Okay, that's fine," Angeni said. "Send me photos. I like to feel like I'm there too. It's so hard to be inside when it's beautiful out."

"How's the writing coming along?" Sitka asked.

"Can I be honest with you?"

Angeni needed to be honest with someone, and she surprised herself by deciding that person was Sitka.

Sitka finally looked up from feeding Freya and said, "Of course."

"I'm struggling with it. The book."

"Oh," Sitka said. Her face morphed from surprised to pensive. "Well, it is a *book*. I don't suppose you've written one before?"

Angeni shook her head.

"I mean, that's quite the undertaking, writing a book. I can't imagine you thought it would be . . . *easy*?"

Angeni had a hard time deciphering if Sitka was empathizing with the difficulty of the task at hand, or if she was calling Angeni foolish for attempting it.

"Maybe not easy. But I thought it would be easier than it is."

"I'm happy to read anything if you want feedback," Sitka said.

But that was the problem—Angeni didn't have much of anything for her to read.

"Thank you, I'll keep that in mind," Angeni said.

A brief silence followed, and Angeni felt compelled to fill it. "My editor wants me to include more personal information in it. I think that's what's tripping me up."

"Oh," Sitka said. "I can see how that would be new territory for you."

"Not *new*," Angeni said, defensive. "I share so much about my life with my followers."

Sitka shrugged like she didn't agree.

"What?" Angeni asked.

Sitka shrugged again. "You share what you want people to see. You've said so yourself, right?"

Angeni had said something like that, but Sitka's phrasing made her sound disingenuous.

"I don't see how my personal story should matter as much as my teachings," she said. "My personal story could be a distraction."

"It would sell more books," Sitka said. "I'm sure that's what your agent is after."

"I mean, it's not like my personal story is that interesting."

Though it was.

Sitka gave her a hard stare. "I wouldn't know," she said.

As Angeni was trying to understand her cold tone, her hidden meaning, Sitka's face rearranged again. She smiled and said, "You said you and Erik are having a date tonight, right?"

Angeni had asked her to watch Freya after dinner so that she and Erik could have their time together. She'd called it a date because that sounded better, more romantic, than "sex appointment."

"Yes, if that's okay. Erik and I haven't spent true quality time together in ages," Angeni said. "If you can watch her, then bring her to me to eat at bedtime, that would be great."

"Okay," Sitka said.

Sitka continued feeding Freya, who was enjoying every bite, tapping her fingers together in the way they'd taught her to request "more."

"Can I ask how you two met?" Sitka asked.

"Erik and me?"

"Yeah."

It wasn't a story Angeni and Erik shared publicly because it didn't paint either of them in a great light. Erik had just gotten out of rehab and been told by his sponsor not to pursue any romantic relationships for at least a year. Angeni was in her own recovery program of sorts, a group of Indigenous natural healers who had taken her under their wing. It was this group that introduced her to shamanic rituals using a psychoactive brew called ayahuasca. And it was on one of her ayahuasca journeys that she committed to a year of celibacy as part of decentering men in her life and finding her way back to herself. Three weeks into that commitment, she met Erik.

It was at a spiritual retreat on Orcas Island. Erik was there with Matt and Jer, who he'd met in rehab and come to consider his brothers. Angeni was there alone. She had actually planned for it to be a silent retreat for herself, the ultimate exercise in going inward. The organizers of the retreat knew that was her intention and had said they would support her. On the first day, everyone was informed of her planned silence. Erik flashed her a smile, his white teeth gleaming, and she smiled back at him. A handful of hours later, they were already talking.

It was in the buffet line for dinner. Erik stepped behind Angeni and, as she dished out a helping of salad onto her plate, whispered, "I know you can't talk to me, but I just have to say I feel so pulled to talk to you."

Just those words sent a pulse of electricity through her body. She felt her cheeks redden, revealing to him wordlessly that she found him charming.

"If you want to talk to me, meet me behind the yoga studio after dinner," he said. "It can be our secret. If not, no worries. If we're meant to be, we'll find each other another time."

He stepped around her then, his arm grazing her side as he did, sending more of that electricity through her. She watched him at the end of the line as he placed a brownie on his plate. He didn't look back at her, though she was sure he could feel her eyes on him. For a second, she wondered if she'd heard him correctly, if this movie scene of a moment had really happened.

She sat at a table alone to eat, glancing up every now and then to see him eating his meal. The idea of meeting him was tantalizing. *Our secret.* When he rose from his table and took his plate to the bin of dirty dishes, he looked over at her, flashed that smile again. As if under a spell, she stood and took her own plate to the bin. Then she followed him outside.

The yoga studio was a yurt structure at the far end of the retreat property. She watched him disappear behind it and, after looking around for any witnesses, went to find him. He was sitting on a wooden bench, one leg crossed over the other, looking satisfied with himself in a way that made her doubt coming. He'd asked for her presence, and she was just giving it to him, demonstrating to him that she was willing to abandon her principles for a stranger. This wasn't who she wanted to be.

"You came," he said.

She nodded, not sure if she should break her silence for him just yet.

"You're so gorgeous," he said.

She finger-combed a strand of hair behind her ear. Men had always told her she was gorgeous, and she had always mistakenly considered that enough of a reason to fall madly in love. When you grow up feeling unloved by your primary caretaker, you assume you are unlovable. In this year of celibacy, she was supposed to be focusing on healing and seeing herself as worthy of love. She was supposed to be tending to her wounds, caring for herself for once.

"I don't know why, but I feel this attraction to you," he said. "I mean, you're beautiful, but it's more than that."

She sat next to him on the bench, communicating her willingness to hear him out.

He told her his story, how he'd started drinking when he was thirteen as a way to cope with a stressful home life, two parents constantly fighting, one of them always leaving for days at a time without any assurance of a return. She nodded enthusiastically so he would know she understood the pain of a fleeing parent. That was when he took her hand, held it in between his two hands.

He told her that he'd been numbing himself for his entire adult life and now, after rehab, he had a clarity he'd never had before. His sponsor had reminded him that his growth had been stunted starting at the age of thirteen, when he effectively chose alcohol and checked out of life. Despite his adult body, he was a quasi-teenager, going through phases of rebellion and discovery on his way to mature adulthood. He was not supposed to pursue a relationship while in this stage of his life. It was only fair to his partner to have that mature adult version.

"That may have been too much information," he said. "But I felt you should know."

He was still holding her hand, tightly, like he intended to never let go.

Angeni spoke. "It's not too much information. Thank you for sharing."

"She speaks!"

She shushed him. "I'm on a silent retreat."

"Right, right," he said. "Well, anyway, maybe we can stay in touch, and when my mature adult self is ready for action, I'd love to take you to dinner."

Angeni nodded.

But the next day, they met at the same bench and kissed for two hours.

Erik confided in her that while his primary addiction was alcohol, there had been "a thing with sex." An addiction, he meant. He said the two went together—the booze and the bodies. There was rarely one without the other. He was a changed man, though, no longer interested in sex outside a committed, growth-oriented relationship. "I want the physical, mental, emotional connection," he'd said. "The trifecta."

The day before the end of the retreat, they sneaked into the yoga yurt and had sex on a stack of mats. They looked into each other's eyes the entire time. This was new for Angeni, who was accustomed to closing her eyes and going somewhere else in her mind. This was *connected* sex. It was something she hadn't had before. She usually faked orgasms, but she didn't have to use her acting skills with Erik. They came together, something Angeni hadn't thought was really possible.

They kept their intimacy a secret from most of the people in their lives who were invested in their well-being. For Erik, that included his sponsor, Matt, and Jer. Angeni told Aurora about Erik, because Angeni told Aurora everything, but she didn't disclose the relationship to anyone else. She told her community that she and Erik were building a friendship, something rooted in integrity and patience. When a year had passed, Angeni and Erik announced to their onlookers that they were embarking on a romantic relationship. Everyone praised the care they had taken with their evolution individually and as a couple. In the privacy of each other's arms, Angeni and Erik promised each other that their true origin story would never be known.

~

Sitka looked at Angeni expectantly, awaiting her response to the question of how she and Erik had met.

"We met at a retreat," Angeni said.

This they had shared publicly, generating responses like "Aww" and "Of course you did."

"Was it a love-at-first-sight type of thing?"

Sitka was still spoon-feeding Freya, coming close to finishing the entire jar of liver pâté. Angeni noticed an increasingly familiar feeling of panic rising within her.

"It was something like that, yes," she said.

Had it been love at first sight? Angeni didn't know. They'd had instant chemistry. They were both fire signs, intensely passionate. The spark was undeniable. But was that love? It was possible it was lust that had, miraculously, grown into love. She did love Erik. She saw his flaws, his fears, his fantasies, and she loved him.

"You could include that in the book, right?" Sitka said.

There wouldn't be much to write with all the details Angeni would want to exclude, but she said, "Yeah, maybe. Good idea."

"Is it weird for you that all these strangers, like, idolize your relationship?" Sitka asked.

Angeni tried to laugh this off. "I don't know if they *idolize* us."

"Oh, they do," Sitka said.

Her tone implied she found this idolization absurd. Angeni wasn't sure if she was in agreement or offended.

"Well, if that's true, that's just because they don't know everything about us," she said.

"Exactly," Sitka said.

Angeni had spent so much time taming her wild beast, tending to her rage so it didn't control her. But in this moment, she wanted to slap Sitka.

"Is there something about us that you don't approve of?" Angeni asked.

She was trying to keep calm, to not let on that the rage was building inside her.

Sitka looked at her like she was insane.

"What? No," Sitka said. "You two are great."

But was that a hint of sarcasm in her voice? It wasn't clear, and the uncertainty was a special kind of torture.

"Maybe that's enough food for her," Angeni said.

She hated the sound the spoon was making against the little glass jar, the screeching as Sitka attempted to get every last bit of the pâté into Freya's mouth.

"Huh?" Sitka asked.

Was this an act for her, this playing-dumb thing? This *who me* thing?

"The food. I think that's enough," Angeni said.

Freya bounced in her seat, tapping her fingers in her "more" gesture. Sitka made a point of looking from the baby to Angeni and said, "Okay" with a nonchalant shrug that was aggressive in a way Angeni wouldn't be able to explain to anyone else.

"Thanks," Angeni said.

Sitka went to the sink, pulled a paper towel off the roll, and used it to clean Freya's face.

"Is there something you want to say to me?" Angeni asked.

She felt her cheeks flush as the question hung in the air between them. Again, Sitka looked at her as if she was insane, as if whatever tension Angeni was feeling was in her body alone.

Sitka lifted Freya from her high chair and said, coolly, "You're burning the chili."

~

That afternoon was a particularly nonproductive one for Angeni. She sat at her desk, turned on her computer, and then spent an hour just staring out the window. She watched Sitka and Freya on the walking path, meandering with no destination in mind. Every few feet, Sitka would stop and kneel with Freya in her arms, picking up something from the earth to show her. When Angeni did this with Freya, she recited the names of the plants and flowers out loud, hoping to imprint them on her daughter—"This one's called feverfew." Sitka didn't know the names of plants and flowers. She didn't appear that knowledgeable about nature, in general. But it was still nice that she was outside with Freya, exposing her to the sights and smells. Angeni could not shake the feeling that it should have been her out there with her daughter. Maybe her guilt was the root of her writer's block. Or maybe no mother was meant to be creative. Nature knew how all-consuming such a thing could be. Each baby's survival depended on the mother being unable to focus on anything but mothering. Wasn't this what Angeni always told her followers? Somehow, absorbing the lesson herself was alarmingly difficult.

"How's it going?"

Erik peered into the writing room.

"I'm not feeling it today," she told him.

He came to her, bent down to kiss her cheek.

"Tomorrow is another day," he said.

But Angeni knew tomorrow was likely to be similar to today.

The book wasn't due for months, but at which point would she have to give her agent and editor a heads-up that she was not on pace for completing it on time? Was it delusional to hold out hope for a sudden burst of inspiration that would snowball into a three-hundred-page manuscript?

"I'm looking forward to our little date," Erik said.

She continued staring at the blank screen in front of her, the cursor blinking.

"Are you?" he asked her.

"What?"

"Looking forward to our date?"

"Oh," she said. "Yeah."

It sounded like a half-hearted response because it was. He sighed.

"We don't have to force it," he said.

But the defeat in his voice, the sad resignation, was exactly why she had to force it.

"I'm sorry, I've just been preoccupied. I am looking forward to it," she said, making every effort to infuse her words with enthusiasm.

"Okay."

He didn't sound convinced. He kissed her on the cheek and told her he'd see her in a few hours.

~

For their Sunday dinner, Aurora made a giant pot of pasta and unthawed a batch of the marinara sauce they'd put in the freezer weeks ago. Matt made focaccia bread, complete with sprigs of rosemary from the herb garden. It was a feeling of family that Angeni had never experienced as a child. She was doing it—healing the pain of the past with the present-day life she'd created with care. As she lit a candle in the center of the kitchen island, she took in a deep breath, reminding herself that no matter how difficult the book project was, she had this beautiful life, this safe place to fall.

The kitchen island served as their giant family dining table. Sitka sat on one side of Freya's high chair, Angeni on the other. Erik sat across from Angeni, making playful eyes at her throughout the dinner, telling everyone about his "hot date." Their plan was to take a couple of mugs of tea out to the firepit and talk like they used to. It seemed like another lifetime when it had been their daily routine to end each day with each other's attention, luxuriating in each other's company, just staring at the stars or enjoying meandering conversations about nothing and everything. They would go inside at some point and have sex, the fireside conversation meant to be a type of foreplay. Angeni was strangely nervous, as if this was a blind date with a stranger.

Aurora, Matt, and Jer insisted on doing the cleanup so Angeni and Erik could have as much time together as possible.

"I feel bad not helping," Angeni said as they started to clear the table.

"Do not feel bad," Aurora said. "Go! Enjoy each other!"

Angeni still wasn't sure if Aurora could have been the one to call into the Wellest podcast and bring up the question about her "shocking past." She kept looking for any micro-expressions on Aurora's face that would suggest an underlying resentment or bitterness, but found none. Erik had assured her that whoever had called in was just trying to rattle Angeni. "Your past isn't that bad, babe," he'd said. But of course there were parts he didn't know.

"Thank you guys for being so supportive," Angeni said.

Sitka was lifting Freya out of her high chair, unbuttoning the bib from around her neck.

"Maybe I should top her off," Angeni said.

She'd just fed her before dinner. Freya would be fine for a few hours. But something in Angeni felt compelled to tend to her daughter before tending to her husband.

"If you want to," Sitka said with a shrug.

"Babe," Erik said. "Freya's fine. Take my hand and let me escort you outside."

He was right—Freya was fine. If Angeni hesitated any more, the real source of her apprehension would reveal itself. She wasn't in the mood to look deeply into her husband's eyes. That was the truth of it.

"Okay," she said.

Erik grabbed her hand, pulled her gently toward the door.

"Thank you, Sitka, for watching our girl," he said before leading Angeni outside.

~

It was a beautiful evening, the sky an indigo blue as the sun began its descent. It had rained briefly before dinner, but the clouds had already dispersed.

They walked on the dirt path Erik and the guys had made through the dense ground cover of ferns, all their leaves overlapping like they were sewn together in a giant green quilt. Erik wrapped his arms around her. They were such good arms—thick and strong, the sleeves of his flannel shirt tight against his biceps. Why did she feel nothing, not the slightest stirring, in her lower belly?

"You cold?" Erik asked.

"I'm good for now," Angeni said. "Looking forward to the fire."

When they arrived at the firepit, Erik got to work setting the logs and bringing the flames to life. She used to find this so sexy, the way he could command nature in this way.

Angeni chose her favorite tree-stump chair and wrapped her arms around herself to stay warm while the fire got going. She searched her brain for a conversation topic and settled upon one that was more of a selfish choice—nothing to do with the two of them or their relationship, but something she couldn't stop thinking about.

"Does Sitka seem weird to you lately?" she asked.

"Sitka?" he asked.

She was already annoyed. "Yeah. Sitka," she said.

"No, why?"

"I don't know. Sometimes I feel like she hates me," she said.

He sat on the tree stump next to hers.

"Oh, babe," he said.

He put a hand on her thigh, a hand that felt like it pitied her.

"There's some hostility there," she said.

"Hostility? From *Sitka*?"

The exaggerated inflection at the end of his words grated on her. He was saying, without saying it, that she was being ridiculous.

"I don't know how to describe it."

"Ang, she's taking care of our baby. She adores Freya."

"I know that. I'm saying she hates *me*."

He held a stick over the fire, as if roasting marshmallows without the marshmallows.

"Do you think you're having some complicated feelings because she spends so much time with Freya?" he asked.

He was using his gentle voice, the voice he used with her when trying to kindly suggest that she was losing her mind.

"I don't think that's it," she said.

Or was it?

They sat in a moment of silence before she decided to fill it by changing the subject.

"Did you figure out any action we can take against that Nurture Mother account?" she asked him.

"I don't think we're going to be able to shut them down. I did send the account a message," he said. "Do you want me to just block them?"

She shook her head. "That won't look good. Will make me seem petty."

"You think anyone would notice?"

"I don't know anymore. I feel like more people despise me than I realize. They're waiting for me to do the wrong thing."

"That's not true," he said.

She shrugged. She'd already been coming to terms with the fact that it probably was.

"We've been over this," he said. "They're jealous, babe."

"Maybe. Jealousy may be the root of it, but they still despise me."

"Some people are not ready for what you're offering the world."

It was kind of him to do this—always come to her defense. Did he ever doubt her? Did he ever want her to give up all this? She was afraid to ask.

Her thoughts returned to Sitka.

"She asked me today how we met," Angeni said.

"Who?" he asked.

"Sitka."

"Sitka?"

Her skin was hot, from the fire, or from irritation.

"Yes," she said. "Sitka."

"Oh. What did you say?"

"That we met at a retreat," she said. "Not the details, of course. Just that."

"Okay." She could hear his thought: *Is there more?*

"Sometimes I think about that—how we met."

"Love at first sight," he said, a bemused expression on his face.

"Doesn't it bother you, though?"

He looked at her, confusion all over his face. "What?"

"How we met," she said.

She picked up her own stick, threw it in the fire, watched the flames grab at it and consume it.

"Why would it bother me? It was fate that we were both there at the same time. It's a great story."

"Right," she said. "A story."

"Babe, I'm sorry, I'm not following."

"It was just all so . . . rushed. We were supposed to be taking our time."

"Sometimes Spirit surprises you, right?"

"Do you think we would have gotten together if we'd really taken a full year to know each other, no sex to muddy things?"

"*Muddy* things?"

"I mean, sex complicates it. The hormones, the chemicals."

"Babe, are you okay?" he asked.

He twisted in his seat so he was looking at her head-on.

"I'm fine, just talking," she said.

He twisted back around, threw his own stick in the fire.

"I know this is a hard time for you," he said. "You have the book. You're still adjusting to motherhood. I'm trying to be patient."

She flinched at the way he said the last part—*I'm trying to be patient.* There was a fatigue there she hadn't known he felt.

"Oh, I see," she said. "I'm testing your patience."

He put his fingers to his temples like she was giving him a headache.

"Ang, you're trying to pick a fight right now," he said.

"Maybe a fight needs to be picked."

He stood, started pacing. "Don't do this," he said, shaking his head. More exasperation.

"Do what?"

He stopped his pacing, stared at her.

"You're trying to push me away. This is your pattern, remember? You don't think you're worthy of love, so you pick fights so people will leave you and confirm your belief that you'll always be abandoned."

He rattled off the narrative, *her* narrative, like it was old news.

She stood in a futile attempt to be on his level—she was so much shorter than him, and the discrepancy made her feel powerless.

"You resent me," she said, stating it as a fact.

"What?"

"I just realized . . . you resent me."

It was something of a revelation. She'd thought he was different from all the stereotypical new fathers that were fixated on their own unmet needs while their wives turned their attention to the helpless offspring. But no. He wasn't.

"I don't resent you. You're doing your thing, picking a fight."

"Looks like you got me pegged," she said.

"That's not—"

"Are you *bored* of me? Is that it?"

He let his head hang back and stared at the sky above them.

"You're still doing it," he said, speaking to the stars.

"I'm going inside," she said.

She turned on her heel and started walking, waiting for him to come after her. This was the chase they'd played out years ago, in the beginning of their relationship, after the honeymoon phase had ended and their issues reared their ugly heads. She'd thought they had evolved from this. Their entire business was founded on them having evolved from this.

"I'm not following you," he called after her.

He was refusing the chase. She knew that was the right thing to do, rejecting their old dynamic, but she couldn't help but feel it as a rejection of her very self.

Her entire body hummed with heat and anger. She stopped on the path. Her breathing was fast and furious. She raised one arm above her head, her hand clenched in a rebellious fist, then released one finger—*that* finger—toward the sky. It was immature—it was not her higher self—but it felt glorious.

Chapter 19

BRITT

Britt's mother didn't have a will, which came as no shock to Britt. Her mother could barely keep a checking account, could barely manage a grocery list. Without a will, there was no obvious guardian for Britt, and the court had no choice but to turn to foster care. Rainbow promised Britt she would try to obtain guardianship. It was a promise she kept, eventually, after months of effort. In those intervening months, Britt found what her mother never had—rock bottom.

In an effort to keep Britt in the same school district, the court placed Britt with a foster family just a half hour from the mobile home park. The husband and wife, Ron and Ruby, were the type of Catholics who had figurines of saints all around the house, along with a painting of Jesus on the cross in each of the three bedrooms. They could not have children of their own and felt it was their mission in life to take in the children who had been abandoned.

"I wasn't *abandoned*," Britt told them when they gave her their spiel.

Ruby smiled and put her delicate, child-size hand on Britt's shoulder.

"I understand, honey," she said, her voice dripping with pity.

"No, really. My mother died. She didn't *leave* me."

It was a weak defense. Britt's mother had left her long before she died.

~

Britt had told the story of how her mother died so many times that she'd started to believe it. She and Becky had walked in as her mother was holding the gun against her chest. It was an awkward way to commit suicide. *Why not hold the gun to her head?* One of the police officers asked her that question. She was just a kid, so it sufficed to shrug and say, "I have no idea." Self-inflicted gunshot wounds to the chest weren't unheard of. "She was drunk," Britt told them. "I guess she was aiming for the heart."

The bullet had gone straight through the heart, a fact that made it impossible for Britt to sleep most nights. She had shot her mom in the heart. She knew this. Becky knew this. She'd sworn Becky to secrecy, but she was sure Becky had told her mother. This was why Britt didn't believe Rainbow would try to become her guardian. Why would she want a murderer under her roof?

Ron and Ruby housed two other foster children—a fifteen-year-old boy named Carlo who stayed in one of the bedrooms by himself, and a fourteen-year-old girl named Deanna who was less than enthused about sharing a room with Britt.

"We've got a good thing here, so don't go fucking it up," Deanna said as her greeting.

By "a good thing," Deanna meant that she and Carlo did whatever they wanted while their naive foster parents were none the wiser. When Britt was older and looking back on this time in her life, she would conclude that Ron and Ruby knew what was going on. They weren't idiots. They wanted to collect their government money while presenting themselves as morally superior to the world around them. They didn't care about raising upstanding citizens.

Once Deanna and Carlo realized that Britt was not going to disrupt their status quo, they started inviting her to hang out with them. That was when the real trouble started. They met up with other kids, most of them a few years older, at a dilapidated ranger shack in the woods. They passed around joints and beers. Occasionally, a guy named Conrad brought pills he'd gotten ahold of on his shift at a nursing home. Benzos, mostly. Sometimes, oxy.

Oxy was Britt's first experience with love at first sight. One pill, and all the clouds that had been following her around parted, beams of light shining through, illuminating the joy that she'd previously thought impossible. When she was on oxy, she didn't think about her mother. She didn't think about Steve. She didn't think, period. She just floated through space, untethered, free.

It didn't take long for it to go from a solution to a problem. To afford her new habit, she started stealing money from Ron and Ruby's stash in their dresser drawer.

"You're gonna fuck this up," Deanna told her one night in their room. "Ron and Ruby are dumb, but they're not that dumb. You think they're not gonna notice all their money going?"

Britt hadn't thought ahead. She maintained a pleasant distance from consequences.

"I'll cross that bridge when—"

Deanna laughed. "Bitch, every bridge you have's gonna be burned."

~

The inevitable come-to-Jesus (literally, in Ron and Ruby's household) happened over a weeknight dinner. One of the household rules was that they always ate dinner together—Ron, Ruby, Carlo, Deanna, and Britt. They had to go around the table and say one thing they were grateful for from their day, then Ron led them in a prayer thanking God Almighty for the food before them. It was after that prayer that Ron cleared his throat, and Britt knew what was coming.

"I wanted to talk to all of you about something," Ron said.

Deanna eyed Britt. She knew what was coming too. Carlo kept his eyes fixed on his plate, shoveling peas into his mouth.

"We've noticed that some cash of ours is missing," Ruby said.

Britt didn't blink. She looked straight into the eyes of these people taking care of her, doing her very best to project innocence.

"We understand that we all make mistakes. All we ask is that the cash is replaced by the end of the week and that this does not happen again," Ron said.

Ruby folded her hands together and set them on the table in front of her.

"The Lord always forgives," she said.

Deanna and Carlo told Britt that she had to return the money. Britt laughed. It wasn't like she was holding the money in some secret location. It was gone, spent. They knew that. They didn't care. They told her to figure it out.

Britt wasn't even sure how much she'd taken. A couple hundred dollars, at least. She doubted Ron and Ruby knew exactly how much. They just wanted to see that a genuine attempt had been made to return what was theirs.

Britt asked Conrad to loan her the money, but he was wise enough to refuse, reminding her that she still owed him fifty bucks. Britt could think of only one person who would be willing to loan her money—not because she would trust that Britt would pay her back, but because she was a kind person.

~

When Britt knocked on the door that she used to just open as if she lived there, Rainbow answered. She looked the same as always, in one of her flowing dresses, her hair twisted into a bun on top of her head. When she smiled, Britt felt her lower lip tremble and her nose tingle.

"Britt," she said, breathless and shocked.

"Hey."

Britt could have come to visit sooner, but she hadn't. As much as she missed Rainbow and Becky, seeing them would remind her of what she'd done, the secret they all held. Britt had been moved to the high school closer to Ron and Ruby's, so she didn't see Becky at school. These people from her former life were a bus ride away, but felt like they were in another country entirely.

"My god, it's so good to see you," Rainbow said, reaching out, pulling Britt into her. Britt let herself relax into Rainbow, closed her eyes and remembered what it felt like to be loved.

When she opened her eyes, Becky was there, standing behind her mother, her eyes welled up with tears. Rainbow stepped back, and Becky hugged Britt. They both started sobbing, so long and hard that their bodies were shaking against each other. It was only during this release that Britt realized she'd been harboring the expectation that Becky would hate her for what had happened. It was clear now that Becky did not hate her at all.

"We've been so worried about you," Rainbow said.

She took one of Britt's hands in her own, and Becky took the other. They ushered her inside, the three of them collapsing on the L-shaped couch in the living room. Britt took in this place that had been like home. It smelled the same, had the same half-burnt candles, the same tendrils of pothos plants.

"I'm sorry I haven't been in touch," Britt said.

Rainbow sat on one side of her, Becky on the other. They were still holding her hands, their thumbs massaging her palms in unison.

"It's okay. I can't even imagine what it's been like for you," Rainbow said.

"We're going to get you outta there," Becky said with an emphatic nod.

"We are," Rainbow said. "I'll be your guardian. It just takes time for all the approvals and whatnot."

"You still want to do that?" Britt asked. She was dumbfounded. She hadn't been able to let herself believe that Rainbow and Becky still cared.

"Of course," Rainbow said. Her brows were knitted together, as if she found Britt's doubts concerning.

"You've lost weight," Becky said, scanning Britt's body.

"Your eyes," Rainbow said, peering at Britt with an intensity that made her feel naked. She knew Rainbow could see everything.

"You're using," Rainbow said.

"Using what?" Becky asked.

Rainbow didn't respond to Becky, just kept staring at Britt and said, "Aren't you?"

"Just pills," Britt said. "Only sometimes."

She braced herself for sighs of disappointment, words of scolding, but there was none of that. Becky said, "Oh, Britt," and Rainbow squeezed her hand.

"It's okay," she said. "We'll get you off it . . . once we get you here."

They had tea and banana bread and didn't talk any further about the pills. They didn't talk about the shooting, either, not directly. Rainbow asked, gently, if Britt missed her mother, and Britt surprised herself by admitting that she did. Life with her mom had been difficult, but it was a difficult that was familiar. There was stability in the instability. And of course, in between bouts of The Darkness, there were those days of raucous joy, days when her mom's brain chemicals shifted just enough for Britt to sustain her fantasies of things being different. As much as she lived in dread of the down times, she also lived in anticipation of those upswings, those times when she glimpsed her mom's potential, dared to envision a better life for the two of them. There would never be another upswing now. She hadn't realized how much hope she'd harbored until her mother had died, all that hope dying with her.

Britt's palms started to get sweaty as her body informed her that it had been too long since she'd taken one of her pills. She had a few at Ron and Ruby's house. Ron and Ruby! She had almost forgotten about this strange other world she inhabited. She had to be back for dinner. They would already be worried that she hadn't come home directly after school.

Britt told Rainbow and Becky she had to go. She took her teacup to the sink, crumpled up the paper towel that had held her banana bread and threw it in the trash.

"Do you need a ride?" Rainbow asked.

Britt had planned to catch the bus a few blocks away, but she would get back to Ron and Ruby's sooner with a ride.

"Sure, yeah," she said.

Britt rode in the passenger seat as Rainbow drove, Becky sitting in the back. She missed this, the three of them. As they approached Ron and Ruby's neighborhood, Britt felt suddenly ashamed at how she'd ended up here, with foster parents and foster siblings, the court basically affirming that she had nobody else who loved her.

"It's that house right there," Britt said, pointing to the two-story with the beige exterior, paint chipped in several places, plywood in place of a front window that had been broken since Britt arrived.

Britt was thankful nobody was outside to see her pull up with these people who were evidence of her other life. Did Carlo and Deanna have other lives? They must have. Nobody talked about it. Ron and Ruby acted like the three of them had just fallen from the sky.

It was only when Rainbow put the car in park that Britt realized she hadn't even broached the topic of borrowing money. That had been the purpose of her visit, hadn't it? Maybe she'd just told herself that.

"Take care of you, okay?" Rainbow said.

"I will," Britt said, though she wasn't sure if that was true.

"Promise?" Becky said.

Becky stuck out her pinkie finger like they used to do. Britt laughed. Becky kept her pinkie outstretched.

"Come on, now," Becky said.

Britt rolled her eyes and stuck out her own pinkie, interlinking it with Becky's.

"We love you," Rainbow said.

And Britt considered that, just maybe, they did.

~

Britt could not return the cash to Ron and Ruby's dresser drawer by the end of the week. When they had another sit-down talk with Carlo, Deanna, and Britt, Deanna didn't hesitate to identify Britt as the culprit. Britt didn't try to deny it. She wanted to be punished, in a way—for the stealing and so much more. Ron and Ruby said they would have to discuss her punishment. "We're very disappointed in you," Ruby said with a solemn shake of her head. What was there to say to that? Britt was disappointed in everything.

When her case worker, a woman named Nora, came by, Britt assumed Ron and Ruby had asked that she be moved to another home. That was her punishment—complete rejection. It seemed appropriate. But that was not why Nora had come by.

"Your guardianship came through," Nora said.

The three of them—Ron, Ruby, and Britt—were sitting at the kitchen table with Nora when she delivered this news.

"My guardianship?"

"That's great news," Ruby said.

Nora flipped through papers in a manila folder, then looked up and said, "Rainbow Reynolds? The court approved her as your guardian."

"Rainbow? What kind of name is that?" Ron said. He crossed his arms over his chest.

"Is this real?" Britt asked.

She was sure it couldn't be. But Nora said, with a sympathetic smile, "Yes, it's real."

~

Somehow, Britt expected her addiction to oxy to just go away the moment she moved into Rainbow's house. But that wasn't how it worked. She tried going several hours without taking a pill, but then had body aches and heart palpitations so bad she thought she was having a panic attack. Rainbow told her she couldn't stop cold turkey. She had to do it right.

Rainbow had a friend called Harmony who had been through a pill addiction herself. She helped Britt slowly taper off the pills. It took weeks. As Britt started to feel more like herself, she enrolled at her local high school. She and Becky resumed their friendship as if nothing had ever come between them. They didn't talk about the shooting, but clung to each other with a new ferocity that spoke to having experienced something together that nobody else would ever understand.

"I'm so glad you're back," Becky said to her one night as they lay together in bed.

The apartment only had the two bedrooms—Rainbow's and Becky's. Just as they'd done on so many sleepover nights, Britt and Becky slept together in Becky's full-size bed. They often fell asleep holding hands.

"Not just back with us, but back to yourself," Becky clarified.

Becky was rolled on her side, looking away from Britt. Britt rolled over and spooned her.

"I love you like a sister," Britt said.

"I love you like a soulmate," Becky said.

"I'm sorry about what happened," Britt said. It was the most they'd talked about Britt's mother's death since that day.

Britt wasn't sure Becky would know what she was talking about, but without missing a beat, Becky said, "I know you are."

Britt clung tighter to Becky, felt the tears slide down the side of her cheek before landing on Becky's shoulder.

"It was an accident," Becky said. "You didn't mean for it to happen like that."

Britt had been over the event so many times in her mind. It was true that she'd had no conscious intention of hurting her mother, but had her subconscious been in charge? She thought back to that drive with her mother to the motel: *I wish you were dead.*

"Did you tell your mom?" Britt asked.

"I tell her everything," Becky said. "I'm sorry."

"No, it's okay. I figured you had."

"It doesn't change how she feels about you. You know that, right? We both love you."

Britt started to cry more. Becky turned over so they were both facing each other, their knees pulled up toward their chests, bumping against each other.

"I don't know where I'd be without you and your mom," Britt said.

It was true, she really didn't know. In all likelihood, she would have bounced around the foster care system, escaping reality via more pills until she was a full-fledged addict, just like her mother.

"We don't know where we'd be without you either," Becky said.

Britt had never considered that her existence was beneficial to someone else's. She rested her forehead against Becky's forehead until they fell asleep in that position.

~

Rainbow began holding more and more gatherings at her apartment—not just name ceremonies, but also meetings of like-minded seekers, as she called them, looking to further their spiritual growth outside the confines of conventional religion. Every Friday evening, people came—a handful at first, then twenty, then thirty. Eventually, they moved the meetings to a nearby park because the apartment was too small to accommodate so many people.

Rainbow performed short sermons and then welcomed people from the congregation to speak their thoughts on what she'd shared. The sermons were about love—how to cultivate it within oneself and then extend it to others. She spoke of how humans were designed to come together and help each other evolve. "We are all walking each other home," she liked to say.

Britt was enthralled. She took notes in a spiral-bound notebook during every sermon, though Rainbow said that wasn't necessary. "I can just give you my own notebooks. I write down all my sermons before I share them," she'd said. Britt liked the act of note-taking, though. It helped cement the learnings in her brain.

On a rainy Friday evening, the biggest crowd ever was gathered to hear Rainbow, undeterred by the weather. She did a sermon about how world peace starts with our individual actions, specifically having compassion for ourselves and those in our lives. "We are all threads in a beautiful tapestry. The more we ensure we are not frayed internally, the more we can strengthen our bond with our adjoining threads. In this way, humanity is a work of art."

"Your mom is magnetic," Britt said.

"She is," Becky agreed.

They watched as Rainbow finished and people formed a line to come forward and share their own thoughts on the topic. Most of the sharing was praise for Rainbow, gratitude for her wisdom. Britt was in awe, overcome by not only love for her surrogate mother, but also a desire to be something like her one day.

~

Britt stayed with Rainbow and Becky through high school. Both girls graduated with their diplomas. Britt knew she never would have been able to do it without the support of Rainbow and Becky. She would have been a dropout, like her mother had been. When the girls turned eighteen, Rainbow said it was time for their name ceremonies.

They decided it would be intimate, just the three of them. Rainbow wanted it to be special, not a show for the whole congregation, which had grown to more than a hundred regulars at that point.

It was a Saturday evening, a thunderstorm outside, which seemed to add to the feeling of this being a special occasion. They sat in a circle in Rainbow's living room, as they had for the name ceremonies Britt had witnessed in the early years, before Rainbow started holding them at the park.

"Okay, my loves, let's hold hands and take a big inhale," Rainbow said.

They closed their eyes, held hands, and took deep breaths in. They pressed their lips together and hummed. Rainbow said the vibration of the humming awakened something within.

"Thank you, Spirit, for joining us here today," Rainbow said.

Britt could feel it—the attendance of Spirit. There was an electricity in the air around them.

"Dear Becky, what is the name that Spirit is giving you?" Rainbow asked.

Becky arched her neck back, tilting her head toward the sky to receive her new self. She moaned with pleasure.

"The name I'm receiving is . . ." she said. She took one more deep breath in and out. "Aurora."

It was a name she'd never mentioned before. Britt believed it really had just come to her in that moment.

"Aurora," Rainbow repeated.

"Aurora," Rainbow and Britt said in unison.

"Aurora," the three of them said.

They continued breathing and humming.

"Dear Britt, what is the name that Spirit is giving you?" Rainbow asked.

Britt knew that she was supposed to receive a name spontaneously, in that moment. But she'd known for years what her name would be when this time came. She exhaled and inhaled, acting as if she was still receiving the name. She rocked back and forth as she'd seen so many others do. Then she let out one big breath and said:

"Angeni."

If Rainbow or Becky recognized the name from years ago, they didn't let on.

"Angeni," Rainbow repeated.

"Angeni," Rainbow and Becky said in unison.

"Angeni," the three of them said.

Chapter 20

Sasha

Each morning when Sasha woke up to find herself in Angeni Luna's house, she was disoriented. What was she still doing here? She'd take in her surroundings, the baby next to her, the forest outside her window. Each morning, she wondered if this would be the day she would finally talk to Angeni about Daphne. But then the day would begin, and there would be new curiosities, new insights into this woman and her strange world, that would pull Sasha's mind in new directions.

She'd created the Nurture Mother account page on a whim, another way to poke the bear that was Angeni Luna. She figured she could also use this little social experiment in her dissertation, which was taking shape in her head as she immersed herself in Angeni Luna's cult of intensive mothering.

Constantly sacrificing yourself for
your child isn't showing your child
love; it's showing your child that
women's needs don't matter.

That had been her first post, paired with a caption explaining how the goal of this account was to free women from the shackles of the pressures and expectations of intensive mothering.

> The goal of this page is to assure you that your children can thrive without you completely sacrificing yourself to the cause of motherhood. We believe that self-care IS childcare.

She received a flurry of positive responses and understood more about the dopamine hit Angeni Luna felt on a daily basis.

> Here's to women having full lives. Motherhood is one slice of the pie. There are so many other slices

> The fact that there's no such thing as "intensive fatherhood" tells you all you need to know about what's behind this mothering-as-everything BS

> Trying to be the perfect mom is a futile pursuit. Leads to so many mental breakdowns. We need to embrace good enough

She'd been posting daily since that first post. On the day Angeni posted her tone-deaf response to the Cincinnati school shooting—god, this woman was an idiot—Sasha put up two posts:

You are not a bad mother if you
send your children to school.
Children need independence
and space for growth.
So do you.

The answer to gun violence
in schools is not more

homeschooling. The answer is
more gun control.

The comments rolled in. She began accumulating followers at a faster pace. She had more than ten thousand now. She kept thinking about Daphne, how she would have become one of the Angeni Luna mothers. They would have had sisterly debates about it. Sasha would have given anything to squabble with Daphne again.

She thought of Daphne constantly—upon waking and getting her bearings in the morning, at random moments throughout the day, before falling asleep at night. When Angeni had made chili the other day, just the smell had made Sasha have to excuse herself to cry in her room. All those bowls of chili Daphne had made for Sasha over the years. She'd never properly thanked her sister. She could not stop thinking about this—all the things she'd never get to say.

The other day, Angeni Luna had sent Sasha into town to get more cloth diapers from this little twee shop—because of course Angeni Luna insisted that only organic cotton touch her baby's ass. The washing of soiled diapers was a part-time job in itself. It was becoming increasingly apparent that the child-rearing Angeni insisted upon, and advertised on social media, was an all-consuming venture. There was no way Angeni would be able to write a book, or have a single coherent thought, if she did not have Sasha and the others to manage all the requisite tasks.

While getting the cloth diapers in town, Sasha had also picked up a case of formula because she was toying with the idea of giving Freya a bottle at night, coaxing her away from Angeni's beloved boobs. Sasha was so tired of Angeni waxing poetic about breastfeeding. She was so tired of seeing the woman flaunt her bare breasts, offering them to the baby every five minutes, like *See how much she needs me?* There was a haughtiness to her mothering that Sasha couldn't stand. Mothering didn't need to be so precious. Portraying it as Angeni Luna did would send a whole generation of women out of the workforce. Still, the formula idea was mischievous and mean. Sasha wasn't sure about it yet, but she had the formula stashed in her closet, just in case. The mere act of possessing it felt like vengeance.

She was finding that there were all kinds of small opportunities for retribution. Simply being on the land, fooling Angeni Luna on a daily basis, brought a bit of satisfaction. But what brought more satisfaction than anything was Erik coming to her bedroom door.

~

The nighttime routine went like this: Sasha lay in bed, usually scrolling Instagram, perusing the comments on Angeni's page and her own Nurture Mother page. She waited for the telltale sob from Freya down the hall. It started off as a soft cry and began escalating in volume and intensity within just a minute or two.

Sasha would swing her legs over the side of the bed and put on the white silk robe Angeni had gifted her when she'd first arrived. Sasha wasn't sure if it was a thoughtful gesture, or a way for Angeni to request that Sasha please cover herself up when tending to her daughter at night. It couldn't have been a coincidence that Angeni had given her the robe, wrapped in pink tissue paper, after the first night Sasha had helped with the baby, appearing in the doorway of their family bedroom wearing her camisole and pajama shorts.

Sasha would walk down the hallway to the room Freya shared with her parents, the three of them together on their king-size mattress on the floor. All three of them looked up at her when she appeared in the hallway, their eyes telling her different things: Freya's eyes saying *My friend is here*, Angeni's saying *Save me*, and Erik's saying *Save them*.

Sasha would kneel down next to the mattress while Angeni fed Freya, topping her off so that she would be full enough for a few hours. Then Angeni would rest easy, knowing that if Freya cried, it would be for comfort and soothing—not hunger. Sasha's job was to provide that comfort and soothing.

Freya was an efficient eater, done in just a few minutes. Angeni would then place the baby in Sasha's arms with dramatized reluctance. Every night, Sasha would say, "I'll bring her back in a few hours to eat," an automated assurance. And every night, Angeni nodded without saying thank you.

When Sasha brought Freya back to her room, she'd take off her robe, and they'd get settled on a full-size mattress on the floor next to Sasha's regular twin-size bed. Angeni didn't feel comfortable with Freya being in a bed a few feet off the ground—was too worried about her rolling off. It was a fair concern, and Sasha didn't mind the mattress on the floor. It was like their little nest together.

There were times when Freya fussed and cried, but mostly, she just fell asleep on Sasha's chest. Still, Sasha could see why Angeni wanted the break. It was hard to sleep with a baby, even when the baby was clearly peaceful and resting. There was always the anticipation of upset, the anticipation of being suddenly needed. Angeni had transferred the burden of that anticipation to Sasha.

The first night Erik came to her room, Sasha had been awakened by Freya kicking her legs and scrunching her face in obvious discomfort. She was grunting more than crying, but it was clear she was not pleased. Sasha guessed it was painful gas or a stubborn poop. It was amazing how quickly she'd learned the baby's facial expressions. It was an ongoing project of decoding the smallest twitches of muscles, the tiniest shifts in mood. She didn't think she'd ever been this aware of or in sync with another human being before.

Sasha sat up and placed Freya on her back, then moved the baby's legs as if she were riding a bicycle. She'd read online that this helped with tummy issues. Freya's face shifted between unease and giddy excitement over this bicycling motion.

"Do you mind if I come in?"

Sasha looked up, startled. Erik was standing in her doorway. He was wearing the gray sweatpants he often wore, no shirt. Sasha felt herself blush as she looked at his bare chest, the geometric designs tattooed across it.

"Shit, you scared me," she said. Then, "Sorry, no swear words, I know."

It was one of Angeni's rules—no cursing in front of Freya: *I know they're just words, but the inflection of them is so harsh. I don't want her to absorb that.*

Erik smiled. "Sorry to scare you. And you don't have to apologize about the swear word."

The way he said it made it clear he thought the rule was as dumb as Sasha did.

"You wanted to come in?" Sasha asked.

"I was just up. Couldn't sleep. Peeked in. Can I help with her?"

He nodded toward Freya, who was still contorting her face.

"Oh, yeah, sure," Sasha said. "Gas, I think."

He came into the room, and there was a palpable difference in the air when he did. It was a first; he'd never before come into her room with her there. She felt suddenly self-conscious about how much of her body was exposed—her nipples visible through her camisole, arms bare, pajama shorts covering little more than a pair of underwear would. Her robe was across the room, and she didn't want to walk over to retrieve it, so she wrapped a blanket around herself.

Erik sat next to Sasha and took his daughter's tiny feet in his hands, resuming the bicycling motion. Freya seemed to think this was hilarious, her dad helping like this. Sasha couldn't help but stare at his biceps as his arms moved back and forth. He was a beautiful specimen of a man, muscles defined from all the work he did on the land. Sasha hated being drawn to male bodies, found the primal attraction so embarrassing and ridiculous. After all she knew about patriarchy, she should find men abhorrent, and she did, in theory, but then she found herself gazing at their bodies, craving their touch. "Biology's a bitch," Professor Williams had said to Sasha when they'd had one of their more personal chats. Sasha had given in to her impulses several times since losing her virginity at nineteen. She rationalized that sex with men was fine. It gave her pleasure, and for a woman, experiencing pleasure was a true act of resistance. She just refused to enter into a traditional relationship with a man, didn't trust all the ingrained expectations that such a relationship would hold. It was so easy for women to lose themselves when loving men. Society had painted that as romance.

Freya started to giggle loudly, and Sasha wondered if Angeni would hear from the other room. If she did, if she came wandering in, would she find this scene of Sasha and Erik strange? Sasha found it a little strange.

"We really appreciate this," Erik said.

His face was on Freya, so Sasha wasn't sure if the words were for her.

"I think it's hard for Angeni to express gratitude sometimes. She doesn't like to ask for help."

"I get it," Sasha said.

"But we really appreciate it."

"I'm glad I can help."

Freya seemed to suddenly calm, and Erik marveled.

"You fixed her!"

Sasha couldn't help but smile, overcome by a sense of accomplishment she'd only found in academics before.

"I think the gas bubble just passed," she said.

Erik stood. "Well, seemed impressive to me."

He walked toward the door and then turned, as if a thought had just occurred to him.

"Do you two want to join me in the living room? I was going to make some chamomile tea."

Sasha looked at Freya, trying to gauge how quickly she could go back to sleep. Freya looked wide awake, though.

"I don't want to disrupt the routine, of course," Erik said, starting to turn again.

"It might help, actually. She likes the rocking chair out there."

"Okay then."

The blanket still wrapped around her like a cloak, Sasha picked up Freya and followed Erik to the living area. She sat with Freya in the rocking chair next to the fireplace while Erik went to the kitchen and turned on the kettle. They didn't even own a microwave—probably thought of them as another danger of modern life.

Angeni had planted chamomile on the land, along with so many other things that she put into soups and sauces and salves and tinctures and whatever else. Angeni had explained the chamomile process to Sasha—planting the seeds, harvesting the flowers, drying them with a dehydrator. When they brewed tea, they simply placed the dried flowers directly in the cup and poured hot water on top. Sasha had to admit it made for an enjoyable cup of tea, but the time and effort involved seemed excessive. This was part of the lifestyle Angeni was selling her followers, and this was part of the lifestyle that annoyed Sasha. If women spent all their time tending to a garden (when they weren't tending to their husbands and children, of course), they wouldn't have anything more to give to the larger society. How many women in previous generations, when modern conveniences simply weren't available, had set aside ambitions and interests because making a home was a full-time occupation? It didn't have to be a full-time occupation anymore. There were work-arounds, efficiencies, technologies. Angeni seemed to want nothing to do with those.

Erik brought Sasha her cup of tea, and she set it on the little wooden stool next to the rocking chair. Freya was resting against her chest, her little mouth grazing Sasha's neck. Erik sat on the couch across from her and crossed his legs in the yogi position he often assumed.

"You don't usually have trouble sleeping, do you?" Sasha asked.

"Oh, I do," he said. "I usually just stay in bed and hope for the best."

"Counting sheep?"

"I haven't resorted to that yet."

"Angeni sleeps though, right?"

"Out like a light," he said.

"That's good."

"Before you came along, though, she was up all night. I was starting to get a little worried. She said it's like an angel brought you, and I kind of agree."

Sasha rubbed Freya's back with her hand, felt the baby's lips move against her neck, searching for a nipple in her sleep.

"Can I ask what it's like to see your partner go through that?"

It was a question Sasha wouldn't have asked in the daylight. There was something about the night that gave her courage.

"The sleeplessness? I mean, it's stressful. I didn't know how she could continue mothering without sleeping."

"I guess I meant the whole thing—seeing her become a mother, seeing her change like that."

Sasha had been wondering what she'd been like before. Was it motherhood that had made Angeni so insufferable, or was she always that way?

Erik took in a deep breath and leaned back into the couch, pressing his palms to his thighs.

"Oh yeah, that's been . . . a big adjustment."

"I bet."

"I just try to be supportive. I knew that Ang becoming a mother would be a monumental thing for her."

"It's a monumental thing for anyone," Sasha said. Her thoughts went to Daphne, and she had to swallow a few times to keep from crying.

"Yeah, but Ang had a lot of trauma with her own mother, who wasn't very . . . available. That's why this motherhood thing is so important to her."

This motherhood thing. Sasha didn't think she was wrong in sensing his exhaustion.

"She's never mentioned her mother," Sasha said, curious if there was a secret here she could uncover.

"She died a long time ago," Erik said. "Suicide."

"Oh wow, that's awful," Sasha said.

He nodded. "You can see why Ang cares so much about getting motherhood exactly right."

"That makes sense."

It was strange that Angeni had never posted about her mother's death. The drama of a suicide would certainly garner more sympathy among her followers and, ultimately, more followers. In any case, it was sad, Angeni losing her mother in such a horrific way. Sasha wished Angeni would just be real about her story, the big picture of who she was.

"Anyway," he said, abruptly uncrossing his legs and placing his feet on the floor. "It's still so new, you know? Parenthood."

He took a sip of his tea, and the wince on his face told her that it was still too hot.

"It is. I'm sure many new parents feel exactly like you."

"For sure," he said.

"Do you ever think of sharing that stuff? Like, the adjustments and struggles?"

He sat back again, holding his mug with both hands.

"Ang likes to keep it positive. Lots out there these days about how hard it is to be a parent. We want to remind people of the sacredness of it, the beauty."

Sasha paused her rocking and picked up her mug, just to have something to do. She put her lips to the rim, felt the steam rise to them.

He ran a hand through his hair. She found herself staring at his bare chest again.

"I just . . . try to stay grateful. Try not to get too bogged down with the hard stuff."

Sasha nodded. She needed him to trust her, to continue to confide in her.

"That makes sense."

Erik stood then. He stretched his arms overhead, and Sasha watched the extension of his abdominal muscles, the slight dip of the waistband of his pants.

"Sorry the tea is so hot."

"It's okay. I'll drink it when it cools."

"I think I'm going to take mine back to bed, if you don't mind," he said.

"Not at all. She seems happy right now, so we'll just chill here for a bit."

She could tell he felt awkward leaving them there. It was one thing when Sasha and Freya were tucked away in the guest room, hidden from sight. Out here, in the common living space, Sasha's nightly labor was on full display.

"Do you need anything?" he asked.

"We're good, thanks."

"Okay then."

He turned, took a few steps, then turned back.

"Thanks for the chat."

In Sasha's mind, it hadn't been much of a chat, but she told him, "You're welcome."

He disappeared down the hallway, and Sasha kept rocking, her breathing in rhythm with Freya's, until she, too, fell asleep, the chair coming to a halt until daylight.

~

The very next night, he came to the doorway again and said, "Guess who can't sleep again?" The night after that, it was "Me again." After that, just "Hey."

It was possible he had a sudden bout of persistent insomnia, but Sasha liked to think he was coming to enjoy their nightly hangouts. It was all innocent—he made tea, they chatted for a bit in the living room, he went back to bed. But he never mentioned it in the daylight hours. Angeni gave no indication that she knew about it. Maybe he had told her, and she didn't want to give it any attention. That didn't seem like her, though. Sasha could imagine how she would address it: *Sitka, I wanted to thank you for keeping Erik company while he struggles with this sleeplessness.*

I am working on a curative tincture for him. Yes, Angeni would want Sasha to know that she knew. She would want Sasha to see her be very blasé about the whole thing, because Angeni Luna was above petty jealousies.

So it stood to reason that Erik hadn't told Angeni. Given that they were such big proponents of open communication and honesty, there was a significant reason he wasn't telling Angeni. He knew she wouldn't approve, or would have concerns. Sasha liked that it was their secret, even if they hadn't admitted to each other that it was their secret. She liked that they had this nightly rendezvous, even though there was no explicit collaboration or stated intention behind it. And if she was honest with herself, she liked Erik's company. There was a stiffness to her interactions with Angeni and Aurora; she barely talked with Matt and Jer. Aside from Freya, Erik was the only real connection she'd felt on the land.

~

While Angeni and Erik were out by the firepit for their weird little date, Sasha was in the living area with Freya, letting her have tummy time on her floor mat while Sasha was on her phone. She had a new message notification for her Nurture Mother account.

> Hello. I am Angeni Luna's husband and we could not help but notice the similarities in appearance between your page and our @mother.nurture.official page. We ask respectfully that you consider adjusting your aesthetic. Thank you.

So this must be Erik's account, the one he used to monitor Angeni's social media life. It was a private account with the handle @forest_man_83. She typed out a quick response to him.

> Hi, Angeni Luna's husband. Respectfully, I will consider adjusting my aesthetic when your wife

> considers the damage she does with her posts. Thank you.

She knew he wouldn't respond immediately because he was in the middle of their "date." She wondered if he would respond at all. He didn't seem to directly engage with any of the commenters on Angeni's posts. Nobody had ever responded to the first message Sasha had sent in the aftermath of Daphne's death. It appeared it hadn't even been read. With the new back-and-forth, Erik would probably block her from Angeni's page, but Sasha had already decided that was fine. Angeni's page was public. Sasha could continue to view it from her regular Instagram account and then create response posts accordingly.

As she bent down to tickle Freya's belly, she heard the side door open, and Angeni marched inside, clearly upset. It was no more than twenty minutes into her "quality time" with Erik.

"I can take Freya," Angeni said, making a beeline for her daughter and lifting her off the floor.

Freya started to cry. She didn't want to be picked up. She was enjoying playing on the floor. But Angeni was not deterred. With Freya in her arms, she continued her angry march down the hallway and then closed the door to the family bedroom. It wasn't quite a slam shut, but it was forceful and loud.

A few moments later, Erik walked in from outside, looking exhausted, like he'd aged ten years since dinner.

"Everything okay?" Sasha asked.

He opened the fridge, took out a can of sparkling water, cracked the tab, and guzzled it like a frat boy would a beer.

"I don't know," he said.

When she noticed him looking down the hallway, Sasha said, "She took Freya, and they went to the bedroom. She seemed . . . upset."

He came to sit on the couch, on the farthest cushion from Sasha. He let his head fall into his hands, and Sasha took the opportunity to hit the record button on her phone. The first night he'd come to visit her, she'd been too surprised and distracted to record their interaction, but she'd been recording all of them since, continuing her research-gathering mission. So far, he hadn't said anything damning, but just the fact that he was having these meetups with Sasha would be of interest to the Angeni Luna followers who considered him the model partner. Sasha felt a tinge of guilt about the recordings, because she really did like talking to him. She told herself she could always decide not to use them. They were just nice to have, ready to be leveraged should the need arise.

"I don't know what's going on with her," he said.

The words were barely audible, as he spoke them into his palms. He had never said anything like this before, never admitted to anything being wrong with Angeni. In their strange corner of the universe, Angeni Luna was the epitome of perfection.

When he lifted his head, he pressed the heels of his palms into his eyes and rubbed.

"Maybe it's the book that's getting to her," he said, staring ahead, unblinking. He turned to Sasha. "Does she seem stressed about the book?"

"She did mention that she's struggling with it," Sasha said. "Yeah, that was the word she used—*struggling*."

He sighed.

"It's too much to take on. People think she's this strong person, but . . ."

She waited for him to finish his thought, but he didn't.

"It is a lot to take on," Sasha said neutrally. She couldn't help but add, "Especially for someone who's never done a project of that magnitude before."

Especially for someone who has no right to take on a project of that magnitude was what she wanted to say. The fact that the publisher was paying Angeni $200,000 for it was absurd.

"She thinks I resent her," Erik said.

There was an obvious follow-up question to this. Sasha debated whether or not to ask it. What did she have to lose?

"Do you?" she asked.

"I didn't think so. I was trying not to . . ."

There was a "but" he wasn't going to share. As Sasha was trying to think of how to lure out the "but," she was interrupted by the sound of the side door opening.

Erik and Sasha both craned their necks to see Aurora coming inside. Sasha watched Aurora's surprise as she took in the two of them sitting there on the couch.

"Oh," she said. "Hi."

"Hey," Sasha said.

"Where's Angeni?"

Aurora was not hiding her mild panic well.

"Bedroom. With Freya," Erik said.

"What about your date?" Aurora asked.

"Ended earlier than expected," he said.

Aurora glanced down the hallway and then back at them.

"Is everything okay?"

Erik stood from the couch. He put a hand on Aurora's shoulder as he walked by her.

"It's fine," he said. An unconvincing reassurance.

He started down the hallway, shuffling his feet as if he did not want to go where he was going. Aurora watched him for a moment and then turned back to Sasha, her eyes begging Sasha for more information.

"Did he say something happened?" she asked.

"Nope," she said. "Nothing specific."

"Maybe I'll go talk to them. Make sure everything's okay."

Sasha watched Aurora go down the hall, heard her tentative knock on the bedroom door, saw the door open. Aurora slipped inside, and Sasha imagined the mini therapy session that would ensue between the three of them. This place was so strange.

A few minutes later, Erik came out of the bedroom. Sasha tried to be busy on her phone, to appear uninterested in whatever drama was unfolding.

"Ror and Ang are talking," he said. "Think I'm going to sit by the firepit."

He lingered for a moment as he said this, and she wondered if he was considering inviting her.

"Enjoy," she said.

He opened his mouth to say something, then closed it. Then opened it again and muttered, "Thanks."

~

Sasha went to her room shortly after Erik went to the firepit. Freya's before-bedtime feed was due soon, and then Angeni would call for Sasha to take the baby for the first half of the night. Sasha sat against the headboard of her bed, checking the latest activity on her posts. There was a message waiting for her. She tapped to read it. It was a response from Erik.

> My name is Erik, sorry I didn't mention that in the first message. I wanted to say that I read through your posts and I see where you are coming from. I do not think my wife intends any harm, but I understand your perspective. Obviously, it's your right to say what you want to say, and I cannot make you change the appearance of your page either. I wish you the best.

He must have just sent this message, while sitting out by the firepit. She typed a response.

> I have to say I'm pleasantly surprised at how kind your message was. Thank you. I appreciate you saying that you understand my perspective. I know your wife does not intend any harm, but some of what she says IS harmful. Women have died trying to pursue what she preaches. Perhaps you can

> consider speaking with her. She may take it in if it comes from you.

His response was immediate. Here they were, engaging in a real-time conversation.

> Women have died? I'm sorry, I'm not seeing what you mean. I've seen how many people she's affected in a positive way.

Well, this was interesting.

> Women die attempting home births. It happens. She should be more responsible.

She assumed that was going too far, that he would not respond, or would respond with something terse and agitated, but he didn't.

> I'm sorry if this is true. I know she would be horrified to know this. She speaks from her heart and she is very passionate about her beliefs. I will speak with her about this particular issue though. Sending love.

So that was the end of it, at least for now.

~

An hour or so later, Sasha heard Aurora leaving Angeni's room, telling her to sleep well. Once Aurora had gone, Angeni called for Sasha and handed baby Freya to her. Angeni's eyes were red, like she'd been crying.

"Are you okay?" Sasha asked.

"Yes, I will be, after some good sleep."

Sasha whisked the baby away to her room, and they settled on the floor mattress together. Freya was on her chest, her body moving up and down with Sasha's breath. It was in these moments when Sasha thought most of Daphne, of little Theodore and his tiny coffin. She dozed off thinking of her sister, her nephew. The next time her eyes flicked to her phone, it was after two in the morning. She heard a soft knock on her door and realized that was what must have awakened her.

"Yes?" she asked.

The door opened, and Erik was there, in his usual middle-of-the-night attire, which was very little attire at all.

"Sorry, did I wake you?" he asked.

"You did, but it's okay. What's up?"

He looked over her shoulder. "Can I come in?"

She looked over her own shoulder, as if also checking for the presence of someone or something that would make their interaction problematic.

"Um, sure," she said.

Sasha slowly eased herself into a sitting position, Freya still passed out on her chest, her little mouth open, drool creating a small circle of wetness on Sasha's camisole. Ironically, it looked like a circle formed by nipple leak. As she stared at it, she realized how visible her dark nipples were through her thin, white camisole. She felt a flush of embarrassment at how exposed she'd made herself. Had Erik noticed? The room was dark except for a soft glow from the full moon through the window. She was thankful for that.

"I might need another therapy session," he said.

That was how he'd jokingly referred to their last middle-of-the-night meetings, when he'd shared a bit more about his childhood, his parents' divorce, drinking his first beer when he was ten.

"Everything okay?" Sasha asked.

He sat on the floor next to the mattress, close enough that Sasha could reach over and touch him if she wanted. She angled her phone toward her, hit the red record button.

"I don't know if everything's okay," he said. "Angeni is going through something."

"I'm sorry to hear that." She knew if she waited patiently, he would tell her more.

"She seems to think you hate her, by the way," he said. "She has some weird discomfort with you."

Discomfort? Was Angeni onto Sasha?

"Oh," she said. "That is weird."

"I told her it was weird. I told her you love Freya."

"I do love Freya."

After a beat, she said, "Did I do something wrong?"

"Oh, no. No, no, no," he said. "She's got these insecurities. You have to understand . . . Ang had a rough upbringing. Lots of trauma."

That word again—*trauma*. It was everywhere. Everyone and their *trauma*. Everyone and their *childhood wounds*.

"She has some abandonment stuff. She lashes out when she feels threatened. Pushes people away before they can push her away," he said.

Sasha took mental notes, adding this information to her Angeni Anthology.

"It's like all these things are tangled together. Freya, the book project, our marriage . . . You."

Sasha was something for them to discuss, something for them to untangle. She was a potential cause of upheaval.

"I think you can take me off that list," she said. "I'm not trying to cause any trouble."

"You're not. I promise. You've been a friend to me. Really."

She found herself staring at his chest, and he must have noticed, because he said, "The tattoos are kind of weird, right?"

"Oh, um, I don't know. They're tattoos."

"I was totally drunk when I got them, don't even remember getting them. Isn't that awful?"

"Could have been worse. Could have been a tattoo of Donald Duck. Or Betty Boop."

He laughed. "True."

"I like them, actually," she said.

She did. They suited him. They looked like something he would have chosen sober.

"I'm sure the tattoo artist had deep thoughts behind the designs, but I wouldn't know."

"You could assign meanings to them now. Like, retroactive meanings."

He nodded thoughtfully. "I like that. I never thought of that."

She studied the swoosh of ink that traversed his pectoral muscles.

"That," she said, pointing, "could be like an ocean wave."

He glanced down, chin to chest, then up at her.

"Wow, yeah. An ocean wave. That seems . . . right."

He kept his eyes on her for an awkward length of time, so awkward that she had to look down at sleeping Freya on her chest.

"Anyway," Sasha said. "You and Angeni don't have to worry about me. I'm just here minding my own business."

"Yeah," he said.

She could feel the electricity between them, a nearly audible crackle. Was she reading this right? The next words came tumbling out of her mouth:

"I mean, you're not, like, *attracted* to me, right?"

There it was. The elephant in the room, exposed.

When he looked at her, she couldn't make sense of his expression. It was a mixture of surprise and knowing and guilt and confusion and revelation. In just his few seconds of hesitation, she knew the answer to her question.

She did her best to sit still there on the edge of her bed, to not jump in and relieve them of the awkward silence. She watched him struggle with a response.

"I mean, that's sort of irrelevant, isn't it?" he said finally.

He said it with a sheepish grin that made Sasha's cheeks feel hot. He would kiss her if she leaned just a bit closer. She was surprised by how much she wanted that. It wasn't just curiosity about what would happen if they did kiss; it was undeniable chemistry between the two of them.

"Right," she said.

She leaned slightly back, away from any temptation. She didn't trust herself.

"Sitka," he said.

Nothing more. Just her name. His eyes were still on hers. It was like they were playing that childhood game of who could go the longest without blinking. She was determined to win.

She stayed still and silent. She was surprised by his obvious angst. He was admitting, wordlessly, that he was tempted too.

"Sitka," he said, again, "I should go."

She didn't say anything to try to dissuade him. She nodded once to confirm her understanding. He stood and started backing out of the room, still facing her, as if waiting for some shift in her appearance, some utterance of a suggestive word, to change his mind. There was more power in refusing to give him this. She wasn't stupid.

The tension of the moment was broken by a noise coming from the living room. It was the slider door opening. As Erik turned to leave the room, he collided with Aurora.

She yelped, then quickly covered her mouth with her hand.

"Oh my god," she said.

Freya lifted her head from Sasha's chest, but didn't open her eyes. After a moment, she collapsed fully on Sasha again. Aurora and Erik were frozen in place. Sasha waited to hear if Angeni was awakened, waited to hear her footsteps in the hall. There was nothing.

"God, you guys scared me," Aurora said.

"You scared us," Erik said.

Us.

Sasha watched Aurora take in the scene, trying to make sense of Erik there in Sasha's room.

"I couldn't sleep, so I came in for some tea," Aurora said. "Thought I heard voices in here."

"You did hear voices," Erik said. "You're not the only one who couldn't sleep."

Aurora's eyes kept darting between Erik and Sasha, as if her brain was trying to make sense of something. When her eyes landed on Sasha's chest, Sasha knew she was noticing her thin white camisole, the nipples underneath it.

"I've been having some insomnia. Sitka here's been my nightly therapist through it," he said.

"Nightly?" Aurora said.

"Unfortunately," Erik said with a laugh. "I'm going to have to start paying for services."

Services.

Aurora's brow furrowed. Her confusion or disapproval was obvious.

"I'm just about to head back to bed, see if I can catch some z's finally," Erik said.

He glanced back at Sasha one last time, and his eyes locked with hers for a split second. As he turned to leave, Sasha said, "Good luck with that."

He passed by Aurora, who was still standing in the doorway, before disappearing into the hall. Sasha heard the door to the family bedroom open and then close.

"I guess I'll get my tea and head back to bed too," Aurora said, though she didn't make any move to leave. She jutted out her hip against the doorframe and crossed her arms over her chest.

Sasha could have jumped in to assuage her fears, but she decided that wasn't her job. She hadn't done anything wrong. Aurora could spin whatever stories she wanted in her own head; that wasn't Sasha's business.

"I hope you get good rest," Sasha said with a tight smile.

Aurora watched her carefully. Before finally turning to leave, she said, "Yeah, you too."

When Aurora closed the door to her room, Sasha lay flat in her bed, placing one hand on Freya and the other over her own heart. It was beating so hard she could feel the vibrations in her chest.

She sat up, ended the recording on her phone, and texted Jay.

Sasha: this place gets weirder and weirder
Jay: i believe it. get ur ass back here
Sasha: i will. soon.

It was a lie. She couldn't leave soon. Things were just getting interesting.

Chapter 21

Gwen

Gwen ended up in the hospital for four days. Back home, as she neared the end of her course of antibiotics, she was feeling more like herself. The infection was gone, and her body was slowly recovering. Her body, her poor body. It was still reeling from June's birth—or rather, June's eviction. She still didn't relate to the common term *give birth*. She hadn't *given* anything. Everything had been taken from her.

The incision in her right breast was mostly healed. She'd started using the pump on both breasts, resulting in a measly couple of ounces of milk per day. She'd called Mary, the lactation consultant, to come for a home visit. Mary sighed heavily upon hearing Gwen's harrowing story. She said that not pumping the first day in the hospital, coupled with the trauma of the medical event itself, had caused Gwen's supply to plummet. Gwen begged Mary to tell her that it would return, but Mary said she couldn't do that; she just didn't know. Jeff presumed to know and said, "It'll come back soon," as if Gwen's milk supply was an indoor cat that decided to go on a little walkabout before returning home. He told her, again and again, not to worry. As if that were possible. Worry was every mother's vocation.

One early morning, while her body was in between sleep and wakefulness, she had a dream that she was sitting at her kitchen table with Angeni Luna. Angeni was holding Gwen's hands in her own hands. They were so warm, Angeni's hands.

You must have faith in your beautiful body, Angeni said, her voice so soft and soothing. *The female body is so wise. It knows how to care for your dear baby. Please take solace in this. The two of you will find your rhythm once again.*

When Gwen awoke fully, she felt calmer. She turned Angeni's words into a mantra she whispered to June: *The two of us will find our rhythm once again.*

~

Gwen and June had been making the short trip to Leigh's condo every day. At dinner each night, Jeff asked Gwen, "How are Leigh and Belle today?" So quickly, these other human beings had become integrated into their daily lives. Gwen suddenly couldn't imagine Leigh *not* being in her life. She'd become a true friend, a confidant, someone she felt closer to than any of the other female friends she'd had throughout her life.

Gwen had always been baffled, and a little envious, of the bonds some women seemed to have with each other. She was never a "girl's girl." She had female friends, but never anyone who felt like a sister. Most of her friends were from school or sports teams, casual types of relationships in which they talked about the usual things girls talked about. She was never "attached at the hip" with any particular girl. As a teenager, she started to learn that other girls could be your worst enemies. They could smile to your face and then obliterate your reputation behind your back. Her best friend in high school, Cherie, had turned on Gwen after a rumor spread that Gwen had kissed Scott Renner, Cherie's longtime crush. The rumor wasn't true, but it didn't matter. That was the thing with female friendships—they seemed so fragile, so fickle.

Leigh felt solid, though, like someone Gwen could know forever. She could foresee their girls being close too. Gwen had developed a real affection for Belle, and Leigh seemed to adore June. Gwen had never been one to gush over babies. She'd always assumed she'd have to fake excitement around other people's kids, but she really did find Belle delightful. Belle was different from June—more relaxed, less on alert, probably because Leigh was less tightly wound than Gwen. The girls did tummy time together. They cooed and babbled profusely. Leigh was convinced they were having full-on conversations in their own language. When Gwen was at Leigh's condo, she felt like they were in an idyllic haze, like they were doing motherhood the way it was supposed to be done. This, she thought, was the village everyone talked about.

It would have made sense for them to switch off houses, but Gwen loved coming to Leigh's part of town, loved the cozy, well-decorated condo with its amazing views. Leigh said Belle hated the car, so she was more than happy to have Gwen and June come to her.

The four of them sat on the area rug in front of the giant floor-to-ceiling windows. Gwen watched Leigh feed Belle—a quick five minutes per boob before chunky, adorable Belle appeared happy and satiated. Whenever Gwen watched the two of them together, it wasn't so much envy she felt as longing.

"So last dose of antibiotics today. I'm going to put her back on the boob tomorrow," Gwen said.

June had been taking formula without any issues, which still managed to hurt Gwen's feelings. Throughout the whole ordeal, Leigh had taken on the role of cheerleader and therapist.

"I think it will go just fine," Leigh said. "It may take some time for your supply to be fully back, but you'll get there."

"I hope so. Jeff is so sick of me talking about this," Gwen said.

"Sweet Jeff. These men don't get it," Leigh said. "But speaking of Jeff, how did it go last night?"

The previous day, Gwen had told Leigh of her plan to have sex with Jeff. She'd bought the lube and felt it was time to put it to use.

"It was good, actually," Gwen said.

"Lube is magic, right?"

"Game changer," Gwen said.

It was a surprise to both of them, Gwen and Jeff, how enjoyable it was. Gwen's expectations had been low. She was checking something off a list. She didn't expect to come, decided it would be a win if Jeff did. So when she came not once, but twice, she felt a kind of glory that had been missing from her life. She hadn't missed sex, per se, but she had missed the basic pleasure of something going well.

There was this niggling doubt, though, this thought she'd been waiting to share with Leigh.

"I'm a little worried that it didn't hurt because my hormones have changed from not breastfeeding," Gwen said. "Like, my body thinks I'm done with that and is back to reproduction mode."

Leigh appeared to consider it and then shook her head. "Nah," she said. "It's just the lube."

Gwen felt like so many of their conversations were around her strife, her anxieties. She tried to balance it with more questions about Leigh's life.

"How are you and Nathan?" Gwen asked.

Leigh shrugged. "Nothing new there. I feel like when you have a baby, a man becomes so . . . obsolete. Like, they're just in the way."

Gwen laughed. "I think I'm too hard on Jeff. He can't read my mind. I'm always waiting for him to catch up to what I know, but he just hasn't done as much research as me."

"Which is why you *should* be hard on him," Leigh said.

Gwen laughed again. "You sound like someone who doesn't want to be married."

She was joking but also not.

"You're onto me," Leigh said in a playful whisper.

"Oh, come on, you love Nathan," Gwen said.

Though really, Gwen had no idea if Leigh loved Nathan. Gwen had no idea how Leigh defined love. It was so subjective, the ol' trash-versus-treasure thing—one person's good marriage was another person's imprisonment.

"I care for him," Leigh said. "I feel like we're at the end of something, though. I just don't know if it's the end of a chapter or the end of our entire book."

"I think most new parents must feel that way, right?"

"Hard to say. I would assume so, but then I see those couples on the street, taking turns pushing a stroller, kissing each other while waiting at stoplights."

She pretended to gag, sticking out her tongue in mock disgust.

"That's probably a performance," Gwen said.

"For whom?"

"For themselves. For the general public. For their kid."

"I don't know if I'm up for performing all the time," Leigh said.

"So, what? You want to leave Nathan?"

As frustrated as Gwen felt with Jeff at times, she couldn't imagine leaving him. It wasn't that he was super helpful with June, but he was *there*. He was an adult human being who was present—someone to tap in during dire moments. He reminded her of who she used to be—which was both aggravating and essential to her sanity.

"I don't know," Leigh said with a long sigh. "He gave me this delectable baby."

She lifted Belle from the rug and gave her wet, sloppy kisses all over her chubby face. Belle squealed with the absolute glee that only babies and puppies have.

"Maybe give it a year," Gwen said. "There should be, like, a cooling-off period for new mothers."

"Maybe give it a year," Leigh repeated. "That should be the title of my memoir."

"I would read it."

"Nathan is always telling me to wait things out. He says I'm too impulsive. I get discontent, and I want out. He calls it my itchy feet."

"Have you always had the . . . itchy feet?"

"As long as I can remember," she said.

Maybe this was what drew Gwen to Leigh—this sense of mild chaos. Gwen's life had been the opposite of chaos up until they'd cut open her belly. From that moment forward, nothing had felt still or stable. Maybe Leigh had come into her life to show her that life could be lived this way, that it was possible to settle into pandemonium.

"Nathan, like all men I've been with, thinks he can change me. I think men like the challenge, until they get tired."

"Why haven't you just been with a woman, like, from the start?"

"Oh, silly Gwen—that would be way less interesting."

Gwen felt herself flush. She felt naive in Leigh's presence. It brought her back to middle school, when the girls in PE class teased her for not yet wearing a bra.

"Have you ever been with a woman?" Leigh asked her.

"No."

Gwen spat out the response too quickly and immediately worried it gave the impression that she was disapproving.

"Not that I have anything against it," she clarified.

Leigh looked at her with a quizzical expression, eyes squinting.

"You weren't ever curious?" Leigh asked.

Was there something erotic in the way she'd posed the question? Or was Gwen imaging that?

She stared at Leigh's lips, considering. What would it be like to kiss them? They were incredibly plump, the bottom lip more than the top. *Bee-stung*, that was the term. They were the types of lips modern women aspired to, the types of lips people paid money to obtain. Gwen knew Leigh would never inject anything into her face, though. She couldn't even be bothered to wear ChapStick, as evidenced by the vertical lines of her dry lips. Gwen imagined kissing her, transferring some of the gloss on her own lips to Leigh's.

"No, not really curious," Gwen said. "Is that weird?"

Leigh shrugged. "You might be very straight. It happens." Leigh said it like heterosexuality was an unfortunate ailment, like nearsightedness.

"When did you first kiss a woman?"

"A woman? In college. But I kissed a girl in elementary school."

Gwen felt her mouth drop. "Elementary school?"

"Yeah. This girl named Bonnie," Leigh said. She looked pensive. "Nobody is named Bonnie anymore."

"So you knew that young that you were . . ."

Gwen wasn't sure what word to use.

"Curious about girls?" Leigh said, refusing a label.

Gwen nodded.

"Sure," Leigh said. "I mean, when did you know you were curious about boys?"

Gwen remembered back to second grade, when a boy from Calgary transferred to her school midyear. He was placed not only in her class, but in the seat next to hers. His name was Alex, and he had a buzz cut and a dimple on one side when he smiled. She liked how he pronounced *about* like *a boat*. On his second day sitting next to her, she wore her favorite underwear, the pink ones with the lace trim and the Strawberry Shortcake decal. She unfolded the waistband of her skirt just so, hoping he would see the lace trim. It was such a strange thing to do for an eight-year-old. Where had she learned this seduction? She couldn't even remember if he noticed, if he said anything to her. The point was not to get a reaction from him; the point was to see herself in a new way.

"Elementary school," Gwen said.

"Right. See?"

"Some women are . . . late bloomers, though, right? Like, they realize in their forties that they're bi or whatever?"

Leigh shrugged. "Sure. Happens all the time. Though I have to think there were inklings all along and that shit just gets repressed. We all want to be normal, whatever the hell that means."

Gwen had thought she knew what it meant. She'd thought her life was deliciously normal. She had the career she'd planned to have, a husband who was decent by anyone's standards, and now June. She was the American dream personified, and she was more lost than she'd ever been. What could she chalk it up to? Postpartum depression? PTSD from her medical mishaps? A more generalized existential crisis? Just thinking about these possibilities, how it was likely a combination of all of them, she started to cry.

"Oh, honey, what's wrong?" Leigh said, sliding over a few inches on the couch, putting her hand on Gwen's arm.

"I don't know. I just feel so . . ." She started to get choked up and wasn't sure she had the words to finish her thought. She eked out two words: "Not me."

"You've been through a lot," Leigh said.

Had she? Gwen wasn't sure. She kept telling herself she was fine. Didn't other mothers deal with these types of things all the time? C-sections, mastitis—these were par for the course. What was wrong with her? She was used to seeing herself the way her employer saw her. Her annual reviews always included cliché phrases like "rises to the occasion" and "ducks in a row" and "tough as nails" and "doesn't take things lying down." This woman she'd become was an easy crier, a hot mess.

"You have," Leigh said, somehow knowing that Gwen needed this validation, this reassurance. "You've been through a lot."

Leigh took June from Gwen's lap and set her on the floor mat with Belle. Then she inched closer again to Gwen, their thighs touching. Leigh reached a hand around to Gwen's cheek, gently pulled Gwen's head to rest on her shoulder.

"Why am I always crying around you?" Gwen said, embarrassed.

"It's okay," Leigh said. "Let yourself cry."

And Gwen did. She cried there on Leigh's shoulder, her tears dampening Leigh's blouse. Leigh remained very still, not shifting in her seat at all. If Gwen cried on Jeff's shoulder, he wouldn't be able to just sit there. He would have to try to talk her out of her tears. He would shift in his seat, clear his throat, say he had to go to the bathroom. Gwen's discomfort pained him. And the fact of that pained her.

Gwen's breakdown was interrupted by the sound of the front door opening. Before Gwen could lift her head from Leigh's shoulder, Nathan was coming into the room, looking surprised to see them.

"Uh, hi," he said, announcing his presence.

Gwen sat up straight and used the sleeve of her shirt to wipe her eyes. Leigh stood to greet her husband.

"I'm sorry, I'm having a new-mom meltdown," Gwen said by way of explanation, wanting to ease Nathan's mind of any anxieties.

The skepticism was obvious on his face as he looked at Gwen, then back at his wife.

"Meeting got canceled so figured I'd come by, see if you and Belle wanted to head to the sandwich shop."

"Let's all go! We can eat at the park! A little outing!" Leigh said. "What do you think, Gwennie?"

Gwennie. Leigh had never called her that before. The existence of this new nickname felt like a special kind of intimacy.

Gwen, sensing Nathan's uneasiness, said, "Oh, I don't have to—"

"Enough," Leigh said. "We're going."

~

Nathan went to get the sandwiches while Gwen and Leigh took the babies to the park. Neither of them had a picnic blanket, but they had a plethora of swaddling blankets that they laid together to make a patchwork quilt. The babies seemed enthralled with their new surroundings, grabbing at the blades of grass, eyes squinting in the sunlight.

"It's nice to get out," Leigh said, tilting her head up toward the sky.

Gwen had to admit that, yes, it was nice to get out. It was the type of thing Jeff was always suggesting she do.

"I can't wait for Belle to be old enough to use the playground by herself," Leigh said. "Can you even imagine? We could bring a game of fucking Scrabble and drink a bottle of wine while they do the monkey bars."

Gwen let herself think ahead to this future, the two of them still friends when the girls were five, six, seven years old.

"That feels a hundred years away," Gwen said. "But it sounds nice."

"Yeah, time is a bitch right now. Bedtime feels a hundred years away."

Nathan trudged his way up the hill with the plastic bag of sandwiches and sat on one of the swaddling blankets. He looked very stiff and uncomfortable in his work attire, and Gwen felt very stiff and uncomfortable in his presence.

He passed them their sandwiches and then unwrapped his own. After his first bite, there was a smear of avocado on the side of his mouth. It was large and obvious, but Leigh didn't say anything.

"So Leigh says you're a lawyer?" Nathan said, speaking with his mouth full after taking a second too-big bite.

"God, baby, chew and swallow, chew and swallow," Leigh said.

Gwen felt herself blushing, mortified by Leigh's public shaming of her husband. She was talking to him like he was a toddler. Nathan didn't seem fazed, though. He wiped his mouth with a square of paper towel, though he missed the avocado smear, and awaited Gwen's response.

"Yes. A lawyer," she said.

"What kind of law?"

She hadn't talked about this, her career, in ages. It felt like a past life, as believable as her saying she was a seamstress in eighteenth-century France.

"Corporate law. It's really quite dull," she said with a laugh.

She did not want to talk about work. June squealed, as if sensing her mother's shift toward sadness, and Gwen lifted her from the grass, cradled her in the crook of her arm.

"When do you go back?" Nathan asked.

This was why she didn't want to talk about work. She had spoken to human resources, and they had agreed to extend her leave because of the mastitis complication, the additional recovery. Still, she was set to return in two weeks, which felt like no time at all. How would she be recovered from anything in two weeks? She could not imagine zipping up one of her pencil skirts, putting on her heels, leaving June at the day care center they'd picked midpregnancy.

"I'm supposed to go back in a couple weeks," she said.

She picked up her sandwich with her free hand, then set it back down without taking a bite. She felt suddenly nauseated.

"This country is so fucked up," Leigh said.

"Maybe she *wants* to go back to work," Nathan said.

Their relationship seemed rooted in being each other's devil's advocates. Maybe they liked this kind of tension, the constant challenge of it, the push and pull. Maybe this was the excitement Leigh needed to stay.

"She's told me she doesn't," Leigh said.

Gwen wanted to hide in the tube slide while they discussed her life choices.

"Oh my god, did you see Angeni Luna's post after the Cincinnati shooting?" Leigh asked Gwen, turning her entire body away from Nathan to shut him out of the conversation.

"I did," Gwen said.

It was a post that had made Gwen feel even worse about the idea of going back to work. How would she live with herself if the day care she and Jeff had so carefully chosen became the target of some madman with a gun? A truly dedicated mother would stay home during the young years. They were so fleeting, those years. Children needed so much consistency and attention in those years.

"I'm seriously considering homeschooling now," Leigh said.

"You *are*?" Nathan asked, reentering the conversation.

Leigh didn't turn her body to face him but said, "Yes, I am."

"I don't know if I could do that," Gwen said.

She'd never, ever considered homeschooling before. She wasn't cut out for that—lesson planning, teaching her own child, organizing every moment of the day with the goal of ultimate enrichment. Was that the expectation of mothers now?

"I think it's important to consider. Maybe a homeschool pod where the moms take turns with a group of kids. That way the kids still get some socializing," Leigh said.

"Were you going to talk to me about this?" Nathan asked.

"At some point," Leigh said, her back still to him. "Our kid is an infant, so we have time."

"You know, some women want to go back to work," Nathan said.

Leigh whipped around to face him finally. "Is this a commentary on my choice to stay home?"

"Not at all," he said, blithe and calm.

But of course that had to be exactly what it was.

"Nathan wants me to get back to my career," Leigh said to Gwen.

"I just think you would be happier if you had something to focus on besides just Belle," he said.

"What makes you think I'm not happy focusing entirely on Belle?" she asked him. "I just said I want to homeschool her."

He shrugged. "You seem to tell me often that you're not happy."

Gwen distracted herself with June, making silly faces at her to get her to smile. She needed something to look at besides these bickering married people.

"Oh, you misunderstood," Leigh said. "I'm not happy with *you*."

Nathan didn't sound the least bit alarmed. Instead, he seemed inexplicably bored. He pushed his giant body up from the ground and brushed crumbs from his pants.

"I'm going to head back to the office."

He rewrapped the remaining half of his sandwich, tucked it under his arm, and stooped to lift Belle from the grass. He gave her a kiss on her cheek before handing her off to Leigh, who smothered Belle's face with her own kisses.

"I'll pick up Thai for dinner," he said to Leigh. Then, "Bye, Gwen."

Gwen raised her hand in a wave, but he had turned around and stomped off before she managed to say anything.

Leigh turned her attention back to her sandwich, taking rapid-fire bites.

"Is that how you always are with each other?" Gwen asked.

Leigh looked up. "Hmm?"

"That fight," Gwen said.

"Oh, that wasn't a fight. That was just . . . sparring."

"Sparring?"

"It's just what we do."

Gwen wasn't naive. She knew all couples had their things. Some people liked whips and chains. Gwen wouldn't be surprised if Leigh was one of those people.

Gwen watched Leigh consume her sandwich in just a couple of minutes. She was like an animal, wild and unashamed. Gwen's appetite was still gone.

Leigh, ignoring how little Gwen had eaten, said with enthusiasm, "Is this not the best sandwich you've ever had?"

~

They walked back to Leigh's place, and Gwen gathered her things to leave.

"See you tomorrow?" Leigh said.

"Are you sure you don't mind me coming over so much?"

"Oh my god, Gwennie, you are starting to drive me crazy. You ask me that every day. Stop. It's unbecoming."

"Okay," she said, her voice as small and silly as she felt.

"I mean, don't you like spending time together like this?" Leigh asked.

Suddenly she was the one who sounded small and insecure.

"Of course," Gwen said. "I just don't want to overstep or impose or whatever."

Leigh twisted her mouth to the side. "I guess that makes me sad. I thought we were better friends than that."

Gwen was confused.

"Good friends don't worry about overstepping or imposing," Leigh explained. "There's this trust that they are there for each other, that it's never a burden to be there for each other."

Gwen nodded, taking in this definition of friendship. She didn't think she'd ever had a friend like this, wasn't sure she'd ever wanted one.

It seemed too intertwined, too vulnerable, too messy. It seemed like it would ask too much of her.

"I hope we can be friends like that," Leigh said.

Gwen wasn't sure what to say. She felt both honored and intimidated.

"Do you hope that too?" Leigh asked.

This woman had been holding her hand, often literally, through the hardest phase of her life, so there was no other answer besides "Of course."

"I'm so glad," Leigh said.

They stood at the front door of the condo. Leigh wrapped her arms around Gwen and June. As she pulled away, she kissed Gwen's cheek, not long, but longer than a relative would at a family reunion. Gwen had no idea what to make of it. She thought of that word, said in the British accent: *indiscretion*. Instinctively, she put her hand to her cheek, as if looking for a clue left there, something to explain the meaning of such an intimate gesture. There was nothing on Leigh's face to suggest that this little kiss meant anything at all. This was probably how Leigh was—showing affection with a reckless abandon that was unfamiliar to Gwen. What was most bizarre was that Gwen, who had once been described as a "cold fish" by an ex-boyfriend, kind of liked it.

"Okay then," Gwen said. She held June's hand, waved it at Leigh and Belle. "See you ladies tomorrow."

Chapter 22

Angeni Luna

Do not let others shame you
out of being the best possible
mother for your child.

Angeni figured if the @nurture.mother.official account was creating content in direct response to her content, she could create content in direct response to theirs. It wasn't healthy to perpetuate this circular exchange of passive-aggressive energy, but there was also a satisfaction to it, and her soul felt desperate for satisfaction in whatever form she could get it.

She and Erik needed repair. Angeni spoke often of the importance of repair after fights. So often, relationships were destroyed not by fights but by insufficient repair. Repair, when done well, could bring a couple closer. It could make them see, with the benefit of hindsight, that the fight was actually good for their relationship. A quote from one of her webinars: "A relationship without repair will never last."

The thing was, she couldn't bring herself to apologize to Erik. This was their first big fight since having Freya. Before Freya, they were each other's priority. They had the time and space to regulate their nervous systems and approach each other with kindness and compassion. They almost always apologized simultaneously, one approaching the other and the other saying, "I was just going to come talk to you." It was different now. She was busy with Freya. She couldn't help but think he should be the one coming to her. She didn't think she'd done anything wrong, except for sticking her middle finger in the air. That had been childish, but she wasn't even sure he'd seen it. It would be simple enough to broach the subject of their tension, to say, "I know things have been difficult between us lately," and let him take it from there—something they referred to as "the passing of the baton" in their relationship work—but she didn't even want to do that. She was wallowing in feeling bitter and misunderstood, soaking herself in it like it was an Epsom salt bath that had long ago gone cold.

~

When Sitka appeared in the kitchen for her usual breakfast of peanut-butter-and-jam toast, Freya clapped her little hands with joy. Every time Freya saw Sitka, she acted as if she hadn't seen her in days.

"Morning," Sitka said, opening the fridge. "Does Freya need to eat?"

"No, I just fed her," Angeni said.

It was a lie. She had tried to feed Freya. Her boobs were fuller than usual because Freya hadn't cried to eat at her usual early-morning time. They'd all slept—Angeni, Freya, Sitka—right until daybreak, which had never happened before. Sitka had brought the baby to Angeni, elated at what a long stretch of sleep she'd had, but Angeni was worried that Freya had gone so long without eating. She excused Sitka and put Freya on her boobs, but the baby's head just bobbed about, her lips refusing to envelop Angeni's nipples. Angeni had tried to coax her on, pushing gently on the back of her head, but Freya kept thrashing about, turning her head this way and that. Angeni couldn't think of a reason for it. Freya didn't seem sick. Angeni hadn't used a new soap on her body or eaten something unusual that would affect the scent of her milk. Everything was the same as every other day, except for Freya's disinterest.

Her daughter's not-subtle rejection of her body was just one more reason for Angeni's foul mood. Another reason: She had received an email from her editor that morning saying I've been thinking that your book would really do well as more of a memoir. Memoirs are all the rage right now. Thoughts?

She had only one thought: She could not write a memoir.

"I think I'm going to skip my writing time for today," Angeni told Sitka.

Sitka had put her two pieces of sourdough on a plate, going through the motions she went through every morning. She always put the jam on the left slice of bread first, then the peanut butter on the right. She didn't press them together like a sandwich, but ate each piece individually.

"Oh, okay," Sitka said. "So Freya will be with you today?"

"Actually, I was hoping you'd still watch her. I have some things I want to do on The Land."

Sitka shrugged like she couldn't care less and said, "Sure, yeah."

~

After eating her own breakfast of homemade granola and raw milk, Angeni went to the hall closet and pulled the duffel bag from the back of it. It was heavier than she remembered. Behind the duffel bag was the safe. She spun the dial to unlock it and pulled out a box of ammo. It had been so long since she'd gone shooting.

She heaved the bag over her shoulder and made her way outside via the door in their bedroom. She didn't want to have to pass by Sitka and Freya and have them ask what she was doing.

"Ang?"

It was Aurora's voice. Angeni turned to see her coming toward her.

"I was just looking for you," Aurora said. Her eyes went to the duffel bag. "Do you need help with that?"

It must have been obvious that Angeni was straining a bit under the weight.

"No, thank you. I'm good," she said.

"Are you going . . . shooting?" Aurora asked.

Aurora wasn't stupid—she still recognized Angeni's shooting bag after all these years. She'd always thought Angeni's hobby was strange, and the current tone of her voice revealed that that opinion hadn't changed.

"Shooting? No. These are just some gardening tools. Was going to see about pulling some weeds in that back corner of The Land."

The lie came easily. Angeni jutted her chin toward the east end of the property, and Aurora turned to look.

"Oh," Aurora said, her skepticism still obvious. "Do you want help? Company?"

"No, no. I think it'll help me clear my head if I'm alone," Angeni said. "Trying to get in the zone so I can write later."

"Of course," Aurora said.

She stayed standing there, though.

"Did you need something?" Angeni asked.

Aurora looked down, started turning her hands over each other. "I wanted to talk to you about something."

Angeni sighed and set the duffel bag on the ground.

"What is it?"

"I don't want to upset you, with all you have going on," Aurora said. "But I feel like it would be wrong not to tell you."

"Tell me what?"

Angeni felt her heart rate accelerate. This was her body in the hypervigilant state it had been in when she was a child. All her healing . . . was it coming undone?

"Maybe we should sit," Aurora said, looking around helplessly for appropriate seats.

Angeni sat atop the duffel bag, and Aurora, seeing no other alternative, sat on the ground across from her.

"What is it? You're making me nervous," Angeni said.

She still wasn't sure that Aurora wasn't the one who had called into the podcast, making that vague threat by questioning her past. There'd been an awkward distance between them since. She assumed that was what Aurora wanted to discuss.

"I want you to know that I'm not bringing this to your attention as gossip, but out of concern," Aurora said.

Angeni's throat felt suddenly dry. She swallowed.

"I couldn't sleep the other night, and I got up for tea. When I came inside, Erik and Sitka were in her room. Together. I guess Erik was having some insomnia issues, and they, like, *talk*?"

Angeni willed her face to stay soft and calm. Erik and Sitka, talking at night. She knew Erik had insomnia at times. It wasn't unusual for him to get up for tea. She hadn't heard him get out of bed lately because she'd been sleeping so soundly. But it was possible he had. It was possible Sitka was up, too, with Freya.

"He does have bouts of insomnia," Angeni said evenly.

"Yeah, so I guess they're like insomnia buddies or whatever. God, it sounds silly as I'm saying it to you," Aurora said with an uneasy laugh. "I just wanted to make sure you knew."

Angeni hadn't known, and she wanted more information, but she couldn't let Aurora know she had any doubts or worries. Doing so felt like pulling a thread on a delicate tapestry.

"Thank you for letting me know, Ror, but it's nothing to worry about," Angeni said. "Erik does have insomnia, and we all know what a social being he is. He's been wanting to make Sitka feel more included."

Angeni was talking to herself as well as to Aurora. The truth was that the idea of Erik and Sitka hanging out while everyone slept was disquieting, if it was really happening. What if Aurora was lying, trying to turn Angeni against Sitka? Angeni had never known Aurora to have a malicious streak before. Was Sitka that much of a threat to her?

"Right, okay, that makes sense," Aurora said.

"I really value you," Angeni said, looking into Aurora's eyes. "You know that, right?"

Aurora smiled, said, "Yeah, I know. I really value you too. That's why I wanted to make sure you knew about this. But you knew, I can see that now. You and Erik tell each other everything."

They both laughed, but there was still an odd tension between them.

"Well, enjoy your gardening," Aurora said, nodding toward the duffel bag. Did she say it with a hint of sarcasm, or was Angeni imagining that?

"Thank you," Angeni said as Aurora turned and headed back toward the house.

~

The far-east corner of The Land was overgrown, dense with misty forest. On eleven acres of land, there was only so much maintenance that was feasible. She had come to accept that parts of the property would always be wild. Maybe that was what she loved most about this place she called home—the sheer impossibility of taming it.

She made her way through the blanket of ferns, leaves overlapping so that none of the ground beneath was visible. She stopped to inspect the various mushrooms—a grouping of chanterelles, another grouping of boletus. She would teach Freya about mushrooms as she got older—which were magical (for cooking purposes and otherwise), which were dangerous. She couldn't wait to guide her daughter, in so many things. This exuberant joy came with grief. It was only in mothering Freya that Angeni realized just how little mothering she'd received.

My dear, you have mother wounds. That was what a woman named Cheyenne had said to Angeni years ago, at the start of her healing journey. Giving birth to Freya, loving Freya, didn't heal the wounds. Instead, the wounds reopened, fresh blood gushing forth. With precious Freya in her arms, Angeni simply could not understand how her mother could have been so neglectful, so uninterested in the very act of loving her. How did she never hold Angeni on her lap and smother her with kisses? Angeni felt this compulsion with Freya every single day, blowing raspberries on her daughter's belly, smooching up and down her arms.

At the same time, there was this poignant gratitude, this observance that, somehow, Angeni's mother had managed to keep Angeni alive. She must have breastfed her—formula would have been too expensive—and changed her diapers. She must have taken her to the doctor when she needed antibiotics. Angeni had never considered this fundamental caretaking that her mother must have performed. She had been so fixated on all that wasn't done. Having Freya had made her realize all that was.

Angeni had even found gratitude in all that her mother had gotten wrong. By not being a good mother, she had taught Angeni how to be a great one. And now Angeni was helping other mothers be the best mothers they could be. If that wasn't healing, Angeni didn't know what was.

~

Once she was deep in the forest, she sat on a large rock she'd never noticed before. How special it was to discover a little more of your own home. This was how she described the inner healing journey to her followers—ongoing discovery of one's self.

There was an indentation in the rock that invited Angeni to sit. She did. As she unzipped the duffel bag, she wondered what Erik and Sitka talked about, if they were in fact meeting at night. Had Erik told her about their fight at the firepit? Was he venting about their marriage? She couldn't help but think of Sitka wearing her skimpy pajamas, that thin camisole, those short shorts. She was sure Erik found her attractive. It wasn't his fault if he did. He was a man with eyes, and Sitka was a young, beautiful woman. Angeni and Erik prided themselves on openly discussing the inevitability of attractions outside a marriage. They were human. It was natural to find other human beings attractive. That didn't mean they would act on it. They could rise above their own base instincts in honor of the commitment they'd made to each other. It was silly of her to worry. The worry was an insult to what they'd created together.

She had originally planned to shoot the rifle, the Steyr AUG. But now she knew Aurora was suspicious, so she decided to shoot the 1911 with the suppressor to lessen the noise. She could have just told Aurora that yes, she was going shooting, but that would be admitting that she was not in the best frame of mind. Aurora knew, better than anyone, that Angeni only went shooting for therapeutic release.

Angeni hadn't gone shooting since Freya was born. In her years with Erik, she could count on one hand the times she'd taken out the duffel bag. She just hadn't felt the need, and she considered this a sign of her growth and recovery. What did it mean that she felt the urge now, that she could think of nothing else that would make her feel better than shooting? She decided to suspend analysis and just give her soul what it needed.

Erik knew of her hobby, for lack of a better term. He wasn't a gun enthusiast himself, but he seemed to think it gave Angeni an attractive edge. "My lady, the gunslinger," he'd said when she first told him. It was when they were first dating, before anyone knew they were dating. In response, she'd said, "Your pistol is my favorite to sling," and they'd laughed like teenagers in love. He'd watched her shoot a few times, whistled when she hit her targets. That was so long ago now, back when they accompanied each other on outings and took interest in each other's interests.

If he knew she was shooting today, he would probably be concerned, especially considering their recent troubles. So she wouldn't tell him. Whatever went on between her and her guns was her business.

She thought again about her agent's suggestion of writing a memoir. She thought of including the fact that she had been shooting guns since she was a child. This was why she couldn't write a memoir. The type of people who loved her—the hippies, the lovers, the earth mothers—hated guns. They could see some of her, but not all of her.

She loaded the 1911—that satisfying click. She stepped down from her rock and took her position in front of a Douglas fir about ten feet away. She held up the gun, finger on the trigger, squinted, pulled.

Her first shot was a complete miss, the bullet flying past the trunk. Birds squawked overhead, fleeing the trees at the sound of the shot—even with the suppressor, there was a startling bang. She waited to hear if anyone would call for her. Nobody did, though. It was unlikely they'd heard.

Her second shot went right through the trunk of the tree. Exhilarated goose bumps covered her arms. She'd forgotten how good this felt. She took another shot, hitting almost the exact same spot on the tree. She thought of Steve, how he would be proud. She'd never known what became of him. Every so often, she would google his name, but it was too common—Steve Waters—to turn up any meaningful results. He was also the kind of person to go to great lengths to keep himself off the internet.

Steve must have known what became of her mother. Angeni had heard he'd moved shortly after her mother died—just a coincidence, or something more meaningful, Angeni would never know. It wouldn't have been hard for Steve to reach out to Angeni in the wake of her mother's death, before she'd changed her name. She hated that he never did, that he found it so easy to leave her behind forever. With the name change, she'd be harder to find now, even if he wanted to. Sometimes, she told herself he did, he tried, but Britt Taylor no longer existed.

Angeni went through three rapid-fire rounds, thinking about Steve and about her mother, about Erik and the fragile state of their union, about her book that absolutely could not be a memoir, about Freya refusing her breast, about all the haters on Instagram, about the @nurture.mother. official account.

She shot and she shot and she shot, hitting the trunk each time, until she was out of ammunition and her body felt calm and spent, as if she'd just run a marathon or had the best sex of her life.

She resumed her seat on the rock and packed up the duffel bag. Her breasts ached. They were so full. She should have pumped after Freya refused to feed, but she'd never had to pump before. She'd purchased one of those hand pumps when she was pregnant, figuring it might come in handy at some point, but she refused to buy an electric one. She wasn't going to succumb to *machines*.

She made her way out of the forest, feeling like a new woman. She would need to find Sitka and Freya so Freya could feed. Now that she felt more serene, her higher self was present and encouraging her to talk to Sitka, woman to woman. Angeni would thank Sitka for keeping Erik company during his bouts of insomnia. She would watch the expressions on Sitka's face and determine a course of action. Spirit would guide her. Spirit always did.

When she got back to the house, she put the duffel bag back in the closet, behind the winter coats and boots. Then she got in the shower to wash off the faint smell of the gunpowder, a scent that took her back to Steve, to her mother, a scent she had to immediately remove and replace with her homemade vanilla body wash.

She braided her wet hair and put on her favorite dress, a stretchy cotton maxi dress that had accommodated her belly throughout her entire pregnancy. Then she went looking for Sitka and Freya. She hadn't seen them out back, so she headed for the front porch. She watched them through the screen door, the two of them sitting and swaying in the porch swing Matt and Jer had built. Freya was asleep, nuzzled into Sitka's armpit. She pushed open the screen door, and it slammed shut behind her—the hydraulic mechanism that usually made the door close slowly had recently broken. She winced at the sound and mouthed *Sorry* when Sitka looked up at her. Thankfully, Freya didn't stir.

"I need to remind Erik to fix the door," Angeni said in a whisper as she approached the swing. "How long's she been asleep?"

Sitka shrugged. "I kinda lose track of time. A half hour, maybe."

"She hasn't been crying to eat?" Angeni asked.

She felt her boobs leaking, looked down to see the circles of wet forming on her dress.

"She hasn't cried," Sitka said. "Seems pretty content to me."

Angeni wasn't sure what to do. Should she wake Freya to eat? Obviously, Freya wasn't hungry, or she would be awake and crying. Babies were simple in the expression of their needs. But Angeni's breasts were throbbing. If she used her hand pump, she would just dump the milk. She didn't want to use bottles yet—or ever.

Angeni decided that this wasn't the right time to talk to Sitka. That could wait. She didn't want to introduce a possibly stressful conversation when Freya was resting so comfortably.

"Okay, I'll check in a bit later," she said, deciding that she would use the pump. She didn't know why Freya wasn't hungry, but figured it was just an off day. They would be back to normal soon enough.

She pressed her lips to the back of little Freya's head. Her sweet, precious child. She could hardly believe she had created this perfect creature. As she walked back toward the front door, she felt the ache of separation she always felt when stepping away from her daughter. This was why she couldn't fathom sending her daughter to school. It was nearly unbearable to be out of arm's reach on the same property.

She noticed the mail slot by the front door was overfull, junk inserts and envelopes sticking out the top. She would have to bring this up at their next family dinner. They hadn't formally assigned anyone mail duty, had always said that whoever saw the mail should just bring it in, but it seemed a formal assignment was necessary.

She pulled out the stack of mail with a forceful tug, started riffling through it as she went back into the house, this time making sure the door didn't slam behind her. A bright-red envelope caught her attention. It was addressed to her. No return address. She set the stack on the small table by the front door and opened the envelope.

Inside was a single sheet of white paper. Across the center of the page were typed words, all caps, that made her lose her balance.

YOU SHOULD BE CHARGED WITH MURDER.

That was all it said. Just those words.

She stumbled backward.

She turned the paper over, then over again, thinking that more words, an explanation, would magically appear.

There was nothing more, though.

She looked again at the envelope, addressed to her. It was typed, no handwriting to decipher. No return address. She squinted to make out the postmark. Seattle.

You should be charged with murder.

Aurora had taken the ferry to Seattle last week to attend an art show. Would she have sent it from there? Why? Why now?

Unless it wasn't her. But it had to be her. She was the only one who knew what had happened all those years ago. Unless she wasn't.

A wave of nausea rolled through Angeni. She felt like she was at sea, put her hands on the wall next to the door to steady herself. Her vision went blurry as she realized it was happening again. Her body, in all its wisdom, decided that consciousness was too much for her in this moment. Her body, in all its wisdom, fell to the floor.

Chapter 23

Sasha

At the sound of a loud thud near the front door, Sasha rose from the porch swing, Freya still asleep against her chest.

"Angeni?" she said.

As she came through the door, she saw Angeni sprawled out on the wood floor. Sasha held Freya with one hand and used her other hand to shake Angeni's shoulder.

"Angeni?"

When she didn't move, Sasha placed her hand in front of Angeni's mouth, confirmed there was breath coming out of it. She was alive.

Freya roused and, absorbing the tension of the scene, began to wail.

"Aurora? Erik?" Sasha called as she made her way through the house and then to the backyard.

She called for them again as Freya wailed louder. Aurora was the first to come.

"What's wrong?" Aurora asked, panic all over her face as she put her hands on Freya, likely assuming something was the matter with the baby.

"Freya's fine. She just woke up. It's Angeni. I think she passed out again," Sasha said in a rush of words.

Aurora ran inside the house, and Sasha followed behind. Aurora said, "Oh my god" as she knelt next to her friend.

Erik came through the door with Matt and Jer behind him.

"What happened?" Erik asked, joining Aurora on the floor next to Angeni.

"Should I call 911?" Sasha asked.

Before coming to the island, Sasha would have said she wanted Angeni Luna to suffer. But being here, next to her unconscious body on the floor, Sasha was genuinely worried. It wasn't that she had come to regard Angeni as a special human being deserving of care and concern; it was simply that she had come to regard her as human, period.

"I'll call," Matt said, pulling his phone from the back pocket of his jeans.

But just as he did that, Angeni stirred, raising her head from the floor.

"Ang?" Aurora said.

Angeni looked around the room, noticeably disoriented.

"What happened?" she asked.

She put her hand to her head.

"Are you hurt?" Erik asked.

"You passed out," Aurora said.

"My head," Angeni said, rubbing at a spot near her temple. She must have hit her head when she fell.

Angeni pressed up to her knees, and Erik placed his hands on her shoulders.

"Wait, babe. Take it slow, okay?"

Angeni's eyes settled on Freya.

"Is Freya okay?"

"Freya's fine," Aurora assured her.

"It's you we're worried about," Erik said.

"Maybe we need to take her to the hospital, just to make sure her head is okay," Jer suggested.

"The hospital?" Angeni said.

"I think that's a good idea," Erik said. "Sitka, can you be with Freya while I'm gone?"

Sasha nodded. "Of course."

Sasha could feel Aurora's eyes boring into her as she continued to bounce Freya in her arms, lulling the baby to a calm state. Sasha knew Aurora had been suspicious of her since seeing her with Erik. She didn't trust Sasha. She had reason not to.

Erik helped Angeni to her feet. She was unsteady, teetering side to side.

"I'll pull the car around," Matt said, going out the front door ahead of them, keys jangling in his hand.

"Can you walk, babe?" Erik asked Angeni.

She took one shaky step, and that answered his question—she could not walk. He scooped her up into his arms, cradled her like a baby. She looked so small there, helpless.

~

After they left, Aurora announced her plan to do some food prep, on the assumption that Angeni would not be up to her usual tasks when she returned. Aurora loved Angeni. It reminded Sasha of Daphne—that loyalty of sisterhood. Sasha's throat tightened at the thought of Daphne, tears starting to form in her eyes.

Sasha placed Freya in the bouncer and went to collect the mail from the table by the front door. She noticed a paper on the floor that must have fallen from the stack. As she picked it up, she saw that it contained just one line, typed across the middle.

YOU SHOULD BE CHARGED WITH MURDER.

She felt herself get woozy and understood that this was why Angeni had passed out.

Who had sent this?

It was something that Sasha had every right and reason to send, but it hadn't been her.

She rifled through the mail until she found a red envelope that had been opened. There was no return address. The postmark was Seattle.

Her first thought was that someone else had had a similar experience to hers—losing a loved one due to a home birth propagandized by Angeni Luna. She had felt so alone in all this, and, perhaps, she wasn't.

"What is that?" Aurora asked, glancing over from the kitchen.

"What?" Sasha asked.

"You look like you've seen a ghost."

Sasha stood there dumbly, the paper in her hand.

"What is it?" Aurora asked, more concerned. She wiped her hands on a dish towel and then made her way to Sasha.

"I just saw this letter," Sasha said.

Aurora was already taking it from her hands. Sasha watched her face fall as she read.

"Who sent this?" Aurora asked.

Now she was the one who looked like she'd seen a ghost.

"I don't know," Sasha said, showing her the red envelope.

"This is why she passed out," Aurora said.

"Has this happened before?" Sasha asked.

Just how many deaths were there? How many people were sending threatening letters, seeking vengeance?

Aurora shook her head. "No, never."

Aurora folded the paper in half, then in half again, and stuck it in the waistband of her skirt.

"I need to talk to Angeni about this," she said.

Sasha couldn't make out her expression. She looked concerned, but also afraid.

"It must have really upset her," Sasha said.

Aurora was looking out the front window, her eyes still, unblinking.

"I need to talk to her," she said again, "when she's well."

She inhaled deeply through her nose and then turned abruptly and left.

~

In multiple Instagram posts, Angeni had talked about "the wonders of breastfeeding" and her respect for it as a natural, on-demand process—the baby expressed hunger, and the mother's body made exactly the right amount of milk. She explained to her followers that this was why she didn't believe in pumping. Sasha didn't know much of anything about breastfeeding or pumping but became quickly aware, upon perusing Angeni's Instagram page, that this was quite the controversial topic.

> I'm like you. Can't bring myself to pump. Makes me feel like a machine and also like I'm tricking my body into letting down milk. I feed on demand, that's it.

> Ummm, some of us need to pump because we aren't, like, attached to our babies every second of the day and we have shit we have to do . . . ???

> This "I don't even pump" thing is a weird flex. What's wrong with pumping? It's still breast milk.

Angeni tried to explain in follow-up posts that "our ancestors didn't pump" and that she wanted to respect the rhythms of her baby and her body, without disruption from a tool or machine. Some people praised this and said that they were in agreement about keeping the process as "spontaneous and instinctive" as possible. Others acted as if Angeni had declared the earth was flat.

It shocked Sasha, the emotionality of these women. It was a fascinating competition in virtuousness. Sasha couldn't care less what Angeni, or any mother, did with her boobs or the magical milk that came from them. Weren't there more important things to worry about?

All this to say that when Angeni left for the hospital, there was no breast milk on the premises.

"Erik says they want to keep her there overnight," Aurora said.

Freya was getting fussy, and Sasha was walking a figure eight around the living room and kitchen, trying to get her to settle. She knew she wouldn't settle, though. She was hungry.

"Okay, well, Freya needs to eat," Sasha said. "And some bites of chicken liver aren't going to cut it."

She wasn't sure if she should mention that she had a case of formula in her room, hidden in her closet. She knew Aurora would raise an eyebrow at this. To these people, having formula in the house was akin to having narcotic drugs. She couldn't even imagine Angeni's reaction if she knew that Sasha had already given Freya a bottle of formula, which was why Freya hadn't been hungry for her mother's milk. She'd only done it the one time, as a kind of experiment, just to see. She felt surprisingly guilty about the whole thing, had promised herself she wouldn't do it again.

Aurora bit on her thumbnail. "Should I see if we can bring Freya to Angeni?"

Sasha rolled her eyes at the ridiculousness of the situation and decided it was about time to introduce some common sense.

"Can't we just give her formula? For this one day?"

Aurora, still gnawing on her nail, looked up from her phone. Predictably, she looked terror stricken.

"Angeni won't like that," she said.

Her allegiance to Angeni was both admirable and annoying.

"I know she won't," Sasha said. "But I think these are, like, extenuating circumstances."

Aurora started pacing the kitchen.

"I should ask Erik," she said, starting to type.

"Do we need to bother him with that?" Sasha said.

Aurora looked up, seemingly surprised at Sasha's directness.

"I'm not sure you really understand how important Freya's nutrition is to Angeni," Aurora said, carrying the torch of righteousness for her friend.

"Oh, trust me, I know," Sasha said.

Freya wailed and wailed, as if sensing that there was food present and she was being denied access to it. Sasha already knew that Freya took formula just fine. She'd had no hesitation with the bottle.

"Let me ask Erik," Aurora insisted.

She stopped at the island, bent over, texting Erik.

"Okay," Aurora said, looking up with a grave expression on her face. "He said to do the formula, just for today. He's not going to tell Angeni."

Sasha was pleasantly surprised—at both his ability to be logical and his willingness to lie to his soulmate.

"All right, we are one step closer to a happy baby," Sasha said.

"I can run to the store," Aurora said, already reaching for her purse on the island.

"There's formula here," Sasha said, keeping her eyes on Freya's beet-red face.

"There is?"

"I saw some. In the closet in my room," Sasha said. That was all she had to say. Aurora could think whatever she wanted.

"Oh," she said. She dropped her purse on the island.

"And a bottle too."

Aurora appeared perplexed, disbelieving that her beloved Angeni was secretly storing this contraband.

"She must have been thinking ahead to a situation like this one," Aurora said. "That makes me feel better, actually."

Sasha just shrugged.

"But I'm not sure she'll take a bottle," Aurora said. She bit her lip.

"I bet I can make it happen," Sasha said. "Let me try."

Aurora looked on in wonderment as Freya took the bottle, just as Sasha knew she would. Aurora made Sasha swear that they wouldn't tell Angeni about the formula. "We'll just say she gobbled up the whole batch of the pâté, okay?" Aurora said. It was so silly, Sasha half expected a pinkie promise.

By nightfall, Erik was still at the hospital with Angeni, and Freya had guzzled two bottles. Matt and Jer brought pizza from town, something they rarely did because of Angeni's preference for home-cooked meals. They used the same phrase of rationalization as Sasha had—*extenuating circumstances*.

When Aurora, Matt, and Jer retired to their tiny homes at the back of the property, it was just Sasha and Freya in the house alone. Sasha was exhausted from the drama of the day, and judging by how Freya fell asleep in her lap, Freya was exhausted too. Sasha didn't want to get up from the couch and wake Freya, so she closed her eyes right there, figured she'd make her way to her room the next time Freya stirred.

Sasha woke up just after midnight when Erik came through the front door. When he realized Sasha and Freya were there on the couch, he winced, mouthed *I'm sorry*. Freya shifted in Sasha's lap, her face scrunching in discontent. Now was the time to go to her bedroom.

"How is she?" Sasha asked as she stood from the couch, holding Freya against her chest, the baby's mouth rooting into her neck as it sometimes did.

"She's okay," Erik said. "Vomited on the way to the hospital. Concussion. They want to keep her overnight for a couple scans, just to be safe. Has quite a goose egg on her head now."

He looked exhausted, puffy bags under bloodshot eyes.

"Are *you* okay?" Sasha asked.

She started walking down the hallway to her room, curious if he would follow her. He did.

"I'm beat," he said.

She turned into her room, laid Freya on the floor mattress. The baby squirmed for a few seconds and then fell into an instantly deep slumber.

Erik stood in the doorway, lingering, hovering.

"Do you want to talk?" Sasha asked.

She didn't think he would, not after the day's events, but he said, "Yeah. Is that okay?"

She nodded.

"Can I get us tea?" he asked.

She nodded again, and he turned to leave. Sasha sat next to Freya on the mattress, putting her hand on the baby's tummy. She watched it rise and fall with each of Freya's breaths. She hit the record button on her phone and put it face down on the nightstand. A few minutes later, Erik returned with two cups of tea and sat cross-legged on the floor next to the mattress.

"How is she?" he asked, eyes on his sleeping daughter.

"Totally fine," Sasha said.

"Took the formula?"

"Like a champ."

"We won't tell Ang," he said. It was a statement, not a question.

"Okay."

"I don't normally condone lying, but . . ."

"I get it," Sasha said.

They each took sips of their tea, a noticeable awkwardness in the room with them. If Sasha hadn't been sure before, she was sure now that there was an electricity between them.

Erik set his mug on the floor and lowered his head into his hands, fingers massaging his scalp. When he looked up again, his eyes were red and watery.

"You're not okay at all," Sasha said.

She felt more compassion for him than she'd expected to feel. She had come to see him, like she saw Angeni, as human. In other words, flawed and complex.

"I don't know what's going on with Angeni," he said.

Sasha wondered if she should tell him about the ominous letter, the apparent reason for her latest fainting spell. She decided to wait, to see if he'd bring it up. He'd spent the last several hours with Angeni—she would have told him, wouldn't she? Unless she didn't want him to know.

"Like, medically?" Sasha asked.

He shook his head. "More like mentally."

"Mentally," Sasha echoed.

"She feels very . . . far away. She's going through something, and she won't let me in."

"Has this happened before?"

What were the chances that Sasha had placed herself in the middle of this woman's nervous breakdown? What were the chances she'd had a part in causing it?

"No," he said. "I mean, we both had rocky times before we met each other. But I've always known her as so . . . *together*."

"Rocky times?" Sasha inquired, gently.

He lifted his mug, sipped.

"We each had our demons. We each had our way of trying to escape them," he said.

Sasha sipped her own tea, waited for more.

"Angeni's mother . . . she had mental issues. Killed herself—think I already told you that. Angeni and Aurora, they saw it happen."

"Oh my god," Sasha said.

She'd had no idea. It explained a lot—Erik's concern about Angeni's recent episodes, the bond between Angeni and Aurora, Angeni's dedication to being The Best Mother for her own daughter.

"I just feel like I'm losing her," he said.

He started crying again.

Sasha pushed herself up from the floor, went to him, put a hand on his back.

"Taking her to the hospital right now, that was like another trauma for her," he said.

"Trauma?" Sasha asked.

He was looking at the ground in front of him when he said, "Nobody knows this, but she didn't give birth to Freya at home. She had to be rushed to the hospital. The same hospital she's at now."

Sasha suddenly felt like she was on a boat in rough waters. Her vision blurred as the room seemed to spin around her.

"What?" she said.

Sasha tasted the tang of bile in her throat. She removed her hand from his back.

"She lied?" Sasha said.

Erik looked up at her. He appeared confused by her tone, the gravity of it. The Sitka he knew wouldn't have cared so much how Angeni Luna had delivered her baby.

"She didn't *lie*, not outright. She always phrased it as that she labored at home, in the tub. She just didn't mention that Freya was born in the hospital," he said. He would always come to her defense. That was why Angeni had chosen him, wasn't it? "Honestly, I think she's blocked out the hospital . . . but being there now, I don't know what's going to happen to her mentally."

Sasha closed her eyes.

Daphne, are you hearing this? Are you?

When she opened her eyes, the room was no longer spinning around her. She took deep breaths, focused on counting her inhales and exhales. She needed to be alone, to think through this new information. Should she text Jay or wait to tell him in person?

"People think she gave birth in a stupid tub," Sasha said, unable to control the vitriol in her voice.

Erik furrowed his brow, clearly still confused by how much it mattered to her.

"Do you have any idea how many people have decided to have babies in tubs at home because of her?" Sasha was nearly screaming now.

"I'm sorry, I didn't realize this would be so upsetting," Erik said. He seemed genuinely apologetic, clueless as to how this revelation had rocked Sasha's world.

"She's a fake. And she's dangerous," Sasha said, words bursting forth before she had a chance to censor them. "You have to tell people the truth."

He nodded slowly, his eyes locked on hers as if he was trying to assess the extent of this breakdown she was having.

"Isn't that what you two always preach—the power of the truth?"

She thought of the recording in progress on her phone, how she now had the ability to share the truth with the world. She could post it on social media. It was sure to go viral, with Angeni Luna's millions of followers realizing how they had been deceived. People were vicious—they would never let it go. They would call her a fraud, a phony. At first, Sasha would feel a rush of satisfaction. But then what? Sasha knew Angeni Luna well enough to know she would be destroyed by this—emotionally, financially. She had seen the woman *lose consciousness* over less. At some point, whatever satisfaction Sasha felt would turn into remorse. As she realized this, her anger at Erik's revelation dissolved, replaced by despair over all that had happened and couldn't be changed. She started to cry, big heaving sobs that made her whole body shake.

"Sitka, I'm sorry," he said.

She chose to think he was sorry for everything—for going along with Angeni's lies, for Daphne, for little Theodore.

"It's been such a stressful day for everyone," he said.

He reached for her hand, clasped it in his. Then he started to cry again too.

"You are right about the truth," he said, eyes watery. "We all need to be more honest with ourselves."

She squeezed his hand, a gentle consolation, and then released, but he didn't let go. He pushed himself up to his knees and pulled her toward him, wrapped his arms around her body. He held her so tightly. She could feel the fear in him, the desperation for connection. She would be lying if she said it didn't feel good to be held. He was comforting her in the midst of a despair he didn't fully understand.

As he pulled away from her body, their faces remained mere inches apart. His eyes scanned hers, shifting back and forth as if reading her like text. Then he leaned forward and pressed his lips against hers.

She wasn't sure how long they kissed. It felt like hours, but couldn't have been more than a minute. Her mouth was immobile at first, a recipient instead of a participant, but then she let her lips move against his. She couldn't deny the stirring in her lower belly. She desired him—that was just one more difficult truth.

Freya gurgled, and they stopped, separating from each other suddenly. It was like a spell had been broken.

"I'm sorry," Erik said. "I don't know what I was—"

"It's okay," Sasha said. Even though it wasn't. She knew it wasn't.

"It's been such a weird day."

He got to his feet, a frantic scramble. Sasha did the same. As he turned to leave, Sasha turned too. In the same second, they saw her. Aurora. Standing in the doorway, all the color drained from her face.

Chapter 24

Britt

After Britt became Angeni, there was a period of transition when she did not know exactly who she was. Anyone who had known her as Britt continued to call her Britt. Rainbow and Aurora (née Becky) called her Angeni for the most part, but there were slipups. They were bound to happen, Rainbow said. This was part of the process, the caterpillar becoming the butterfly.

Rainbow's congregation continued to grow and, with it, donations from members. The donations didn't amount to much at first. Rainbow relied on her Reiki clinic to pay bills, and she relied on Aurora to help run the clinic. Aurora started painting and hanging her finished works on the walls of the clinic—she got a sale every now and then. Angeni got a job at a natural foods shop so she could contribute to the household. It was there that she began amassing a significant amount of knowledge about herbs and nutrition. She loved that her name tag said ANGENI, that her manager and all the shoppers never knew her as Britt.

When she wasn't working at the store, Angeni helped Rainbow prepare her sermons. Rainbow would share her stream-of-consciousness thoughts with Angeni, usually while smoking a joint, and Angeni would take notes and turn those thoughts into the week's offering. Aurora acted as the administrative assistant, making runs to Kinko's to print off copies for the congregants.

"You have a real gift for this," Rainbow told Angeni one afternoon, after Angeni read back the sermon she'd written.

Angeni could feel her cheeks redden with Rainbow's praise. In this new life with Rainbow, she felt she had purpose. She felt like she mattered.

"You think so?"

"I think you and I are on the same wavelength. You really get what I'm trying to say. You articulate it better than I can," Rainbow went on.

"I don't know if that's true. Your sermons have always been beautiful, long before I started helping."

"Maybe," Rainbow said. "But they're more beautiful now."

"That means a lot to me," Angeni said.

She had to look down because she felt like if she held Rainbow's stare, she would cry.

~

Angeni had Mondays off work and usually spent the day alone in the apartment, lazing about or skimming one of Rainbow's Buddhism books, looking for nuggets of wisdom they could interject into their sermons. On this particular Monday, she was startled by the front door opening, Rainbow coming through saying she wasn't feeling great so she'd left the clinic in Aurora's hands for the day.

Rainbow fell onto the couch in the living room and pulled her knees into her chest.

"Is it your stomach?" Angeni asked.

She knelt down next to the couch, put the underside of her wrist to Rainbow's head.

"It's a splitting headache," Rainbow said.

She was closing her eyes hard, rubbing her temples with her fingers.

"Do you want some medicine?"

Rainbow sat up abruptly. "My god, I can't even think."

Angeni started to panic, with flashbacks to the helplessness she'd felt when her mother was shot. Or rather, when she'd shot her mother. She still couldn't get the language right.

"Should I call someone?" she asked.

Before Rainbow could answer, she opened her eyes with terrifying alarm, looked right at Angeni, and said, "Britt!"

Then she fell forward. Her head would have hit the coffee table if Angeni hadn't caught her.

~

A ruptured brain aneurysm, that was what the doctors said. Half the time, they're fatal. Rainbow was in that half.

Angeni had called Aurora immediately after calling 911. Aurora arrived before the ambulance, and the two women stood there before another dead mother. Rainbow had been complaining of headaches for a few days. Should they have known something this awful could happen? The doctors said they couldn't have known, but they were so accustomed to carrying guilt that they added this to their load.

~

The members of Rainbow's congregation chipped in to pay for a nice memorial service. She'd been cremated, and they spread her ashes at the park where they had done their gatherings. Everyone was so distraught.

After the service, an older woman approached the girls and introduced herself as Cheyenne. She had dark-brown skin, lines etched into her forehead and around her eyes and mouth. Her graying hair was in a thick braid that hung over her shoulder. Angeni remembered Rainbow talking about Cheyenne, referring to her as a wise Sioux elder.

"I know she was your mother, but she also birthed this community," Cheyenne said to Aurora and Angeni. "I've always said *mother* is a verb. She mothered all of us."

A dozen people had stood up to share words at the service, and all of them said something to this effect.

"She loved this community," Aurora said.

"Maybe there is a way to keep it going," Cheyenne said.

But Aurora and Angeni were too grief stricken to even consider what that would mean.

~

There wasn't time to grieve properly. They had to survive. They didn't tell the landlord what had happened, just stayed in the apartment as if nothing had changed. Aurora didn't know enough to fully manage Rainbow's clinic, but she tried, for a while. At first, clients continued coming, accepting whatever amateur massage Aurora provided, sometimes buying a painting too. But then their sympathy ran out, and it no longer made sense to keep the clinic. Without the distraction of running the business, Aurora fell into a depression so severe that she appeared catatonic some days. Angeni picked up as many shifts as she could at the natural foods store—both to offset the lost income from the clinic and to avoid being around Aurora. She loved Aurora, but the darkness of those days reminded Angeni too much of her mother.

Angeni made enough to pay rent and get groceries, thanks to her employee discount from the store and the manager giving her whatever expired items they were going to throw away each day. "I don't know what I'd do without you," Aurora said on several occasions. Angeni didn't know what Aurora would do either. Angeni had learned to survive without her mother because she'd never really had a mother, not in the typical sense. She'd always been on her own in many ways. Aurora had been fused with Rainbow, the two of them closer than any two humans

Angeni had ever seen. Angeni considered it her duty to mother Aurora now. Mother *is a verb.* She owed it to Aurora. She owed it to Rainbow.

In the years since she'd gotten off the pills, Angeni hadn't thought much about them. But in the weeks and months following Rainbow's death, they were there again, in the periphery of her consciousness, whispering to her about how they could take away her pain. Angeni smoked weed instead—too much but not enough to affect her daily functioning. Her manager, a guy with straggly hair and an ever-present hemp necklace, was her supplier. Whenever she was short on cash, he told her she could pay him in other ways, and Angeni knew what he meant. He was a nice guy, not a jerk, never mean. He was easy to please. She would go down on him in the back of the store, in his little closet-sized office next to the walk-in fridge, and he would be so appreciative that she didn't even feel disgusting. She felt pleased, proud.

His name was Ted. He was thirtysomething but had the disposition of a teenager. Angeni lost her virginity to him shortly after her nineteenth birthday. She didn't tell him he was her first and was relieved he didn't ask. She didn't love Ted, she was well aware of that, but she did enjoy sex. It gave her what the pills had—a brief exodus from life, a pleasure that felt almost transcendental. Some nights, they went back to his place, an apartment he shared with two guys who always offered her weed and a pint of the beer they'd brewed in their garage.

For Angeni, Ted was a way out, an excuse not to go home to Aurora and her sadness. She preferred Ted's old, mushy mattress to sleeping next to Aurora in her dead mother's bed. Ted took Angeni to backyard bonfires and bar meetups where she got high and drank and flirted with whatever men were there. Ted was never jealous—"I have no interest in possessing you, baby," he said. It was a type of freedom Angeni thought Rainbow would have approved of. Rainbow had never had a dedicated boyfriend, but it was clear she was loved. The men in her life, labeled as "friends," were doting and kind. They were all sobbing at the memorial service, as if they all believed they'd lost the love of their life.

Aurora never made Angeni feel guilty about the times she was away with Ted or whomever else. She was only thankful, always promising that she would get herself together "one of these days." Angeni didn't know if that was true. All these years, Angeni had wanted a mother like Rainbow. She'd envied Aurora. But now she saw the downside. The loss of a mother like Rainbow was so profound, seemingly insurmountable. Angeni longed for something she'd never had; Aurora longed for something she'd once had. Angeni thought that must be a worse kind of pain.

~

Painting brought Aurora out of her depressive state. It gave her a reason to get out of bed, and getting out of bed gave her a reason to change her clothes and eat a meal. When there was a job opening at the natural foods store, Angeni convinced Ted to hire Aurora. She wasn't sure Aurora would be a great employee, but figured she could cover for her when she had bad days. Aurora was grateful for the job, comforted by the fact that Angeni would work alongside her. The world felt terrifying without her friend there.

Angeni discovered she was pregnant shortly after Aurora started working at the store. Angeni wasn't the type to pay any real attention to her menstrual cycle. She hadn't realized she was late. She discovered she was pregnant in very cinematic fashion—after feeling slightly squeamish all day, she became overcome with nausea while on a shift and had to run to the employee bathroom to vomit. She knew then, but bought a pregnancy test at the drugstore across the street on her lunch break to confirm.

She didn't want to keep the baby. At this point in her life, she hadn't even considered the idea of becoming a mother. It seemed like something far off, if it was going to happen at all. She knew she would never want to be the type of mother her own mother was, and if she had a baby at twenty, that was exactly what she would be.

She told Ted the baby was his, though she had no way of knowing for sure. There had been so many guys—guys she met at the store, guys who came to the store to meet her because they'd heard about her. Ted didn't seem upset or excited. He took the news as if she'd just told him that she'd rearranged the grains aisle—mild surprise, a tinge of interest. He knew she slept around, but he didn't bring up the other possible fathers. He wasn't stupid, just simple.

He asked her if she wanted to keep the baby, and she was shocked by the question. "I'll support you either way," he said. The sentiment was sweet, but Angeni's thoughts weren't muddled by love for him. She could see that he would never be able to support her.

"I can't be a mother," she told him.

"Okay," he said calmly. If he was relieved, as she expected him to be, he didn't show it. It truly seemed like he would have accepted whatever fate she'd dealt him.

"I guess we need to find somewhere to, like, take care of it," she said.

"I know someone who can help."

~

The someone was Cheyenne, the woman who had approached Angeni and Aurora at Rainbow's memorial service. Ted said he'd heard she helped women with "this type of thing," and Angeni had to assume a previous girlfriend of his had needed the same service.

Cheyenne lived in a tiny Craftsman-style house just a few blocks from Angeni and Aurora. The inside was dimly lit and sparsely furnished. Cheyenne led Angeni through the front entryway to the living room, which had just a couch, end table, and lamp, then on to the kitchen, every inch of which was cluttered with various labeled glass bottles and jars.

"Sit, dear," Cheyenne said, motioning to one of the four chairs at the round table, on top of which were stacks of books.

"Thank you, again, for helping me," Angeni said.

"It is a gift I can offer women who need it," Cheyenne said. "I helped Rainbow with this same predicament once."

"Really?" This surprised Angeni. She'd had no idea. Rainbow had never let on.

"Yes, a few years ago. She wouldn't have judged you. I can assure you of that."

Angeni appreciated the assurance, but she didn't need it. She knew Rainbow wouldn't have judged her. Rainbow had always talked to Angeni and Aurora about taking ownership of their bodies, never letting anyone talk them out of their intuition.

"Native American women have been controlling their fertility for centuries," Cheyenne said.

"Really?" Angeni said. "Just with herbs?"

Cheyenne nodded as she moved about her kitchen, opening cabinets, pulling out glass jars as she saw fit.

"Peacock flower, that was a popular one. I like pennyroyal and mugwort," she said.

Angeni watched as she spooned out the herbs and explained what they were. The pennyroyal looked like dried sod with tiny flecks of purple from what were once bright-lavender flowers. The mugwort was clumpy and thick, like couch stuffing or wall insulation. It smelled like dried grass.

"You'll make a tea with these," she said, and proceeded to demonstrate how much to put in a mug before pouring in the hot water.

"It needs to steep a good long while. Twenty minutes or so," she said, glancing at the clock on her wall.

"And that's it? That's all?" Angeni asked, disbelieving.

Cheyenne smiled. "You will need to drink it over the next several days. That's all."

"What do I owe you for this?" Angeni asked. She had brought a hundred dollars with her, money Ted had given her. She hoped that was enough.

When she started fishing in her purse for her wallet, Cheyenne made a tsking sound.

"That's not what I want from you," she said.

Angeni stopped rooting around in her purse and waited for more.

"What I want, after you heal from your current situation, is for you to resume the congregation meetings," Cheyenne said.

It took a moment for Angeni to understand.

"Rainbow's congregation meetings?"

Cheyenne nodded. "Rainbow told me you have the gift."

"The gift? The gift of what?"

"Captivating a community."

Angeni was flattered that Rainbow had thought she possessed any kind of gift, let alone this one. Apparently, she'd even felt compelled to tell Cheyenne about it.

"Oh, well, I don't know about that. But I can try," Angeni said. "Aurora can help me."

Cheyenne nodded. "She can help, yes. But you are the one with the gift."

~

For the next two weeks, Angeni drank the tea daily. It tasted minty and medicinal. On the first day of the third week, her stomach began to cramp. She stayed home from work, told Aurora to take her shift. She sat on the toilet and waited, thinking that losing a pregnancy was nothing more than a heavy period, something that would pass quickly. That was not what it was like, though.

She labored—there was no other way to describe it—for three hours, her body covered in sweat. It was only during this pain that she considered that this would-be baby would not just dissolve within her; this would-be baby would come out. She was giving birth to death.

She felt the baby pass, stared at the huge glob of slimy red on the toilet paper. There were two dark dots—were they eyes? She was overcome with a crushing grief and fell to the bathroom floor, crying harder than she had when her mother died, when Rainbow died. She hadn't wanted the baby—she kept reminding herself of this. But her body didn't know that. Her body only knew that it had lost something it was designed to keep.

She made a silent promise to herself that if she did ever become pregnant again, she would be a better person, a person capable of mothering. She would never again be this person, abandoning her child in a toilet.

~

Angeni's grief over the baby compounded the grief she felt over Rainbow. She took Cheyenne's words to heart. She clung to the idea of having a gift, convinced that gift could also be her salvation.

Aurora loved the idea of resuming the congregation meetings. It was a way to remember her mother, to honor her legacy. Angeni was uncomfortable, suggesting that she be the one to take Rainbow's role, to create and lead the sermons, but Aurora was nothing but supportive.

"I'm too shy. You are made for this. My mom knew it," Aurora said.

So it was decided.

~

They had their first meeting back at the park three weeks after Angeni gave birth to her not-yet baby. Angeni was doubtful that many people would show up. They had spread the word as best as possible, but Angeni couldn't believe anyone would be interested in someone besides Rainbow giving sermons. Much to her surprise, the park was packed with people when Angeni and Aurora pulled up in their car. It was as packed as the day of Rainbow's memorial service.

"I knew it," Aurora said.

Before her death, Rainbow had talked about wanting to do more relationship counseling within the congregation. She'd wanted to teach people how to grow and evolve within their partnerships. "Relationships reveal our greatest triggers, and our triggers are our greatest teachers," Rainbow had said. Angeni made this the topic of her first sermon. She spoke of fostering conscious connection, of being awake and attuned to the full humanity of the people we love. She had been nervous at the start of her talk, but by the end, she had tentatively accepted Rainbow's assessment as true—she had a gift.

~

Within just a few months, congregants were asking Angeni if she would do more intimate relationship counseling sessions for them. Angeni looked to Cheyenne for guidance.

"I think you need to solidify the relationship within yourself before you begin counseling others on theirs," Cheyenne said.

Angeni didn't have to ask what she meant. She knew. She was continuing to fool around with Ted and other random guys. She wasn't smoking much weed or taking any pills, but she still had her ways of escaping.

Cheyenne invited Angeni to attend an ayahuasca journey with other members of the Indigenous healing community. Angeni had never done psychedelics, and this journey proved to be something truly transcendental. She saw herself as a small child. She saw her mother, she forgave her. She saw the faces of all the men she had let into her body. She saw the baby she had lost. After the ceremony, she committed to a year of celibacy.

Shortly after Angeni made that commitment, Cheyenne told her about a retreat on Orcas Island.

"I think it would be good for you. I know the leader. He was familiar with Rainbow's work, and he knows of you. He said he would love to have you as his guest, no cost."

"Wow, that's so kind," Angeni said. "And it would be a good way to meet more people in the healing community."

Cheyenne made her tsk sound.

"I don't want you meeting anyone. I want you to meet yourself. I want you to take this time to be in silent observation of you."

~

The only person who knew the truth of the chemistry between Erik and Angeni on that retreat was Aurora. Angeni had to gush to someone, had to tell someone that she had met the love of her life, The One.

She told Aurora as they sat at the dinner table in their apartment, the same dinner table they used to sit at with Rainbow, eating her homemade macaroni and cheese. It still ached to be in that apartment, to watch the pothos grow and live after Rainbow had died.

"I'm happy for you," Aurora said, though Angeni could tell that was a lie. Their relationship had never before been significantly challenged by a third party. Any men in their lives had been ancillary, and here Angeni was, telling Aurora that she had met someone poised to be her soulmate.

"Oh, Ror. You are forever my soul sister, you know that, right?" Angeni said.

Aurora smiled, but it was a weak smile. "I knew this would happen one day," she said.

"What do you think is happening, exactly?"

"You're going to make a life with him. And you should. I get it. That's what people do. I will have to find my own way."

"It doesn't have to be like that. Since when have I been so unoriginal?"

That made Aurora laugh.

"Maybe we could all live together, the three of us," Angeni said. "I've already talked to Erik about it. We can find a place in Seattle that has room for all of us."

Aurora's face brightened. "Really? I don't want to get in the way."

"You will never be getting in the way, okay?"

Aurora nodded.

"And when you meet your soulmate, the four of us can live together," Angeni said, nudging Aurora in the side.

Aurora rolled her eyes. After a string of disappointing short-term boyfriends, she had sworn off dating for the foreseeable future.

"You're sure Erik is okay with this?" Aurora asked.

"If he wasn't, I wouldn't be with him," Angeni said.

Aurora exhaled a big breath of relief.

"Seattle, though?" Aurora said.

That was where Erik lived and worked. He had a steady gig with a construction company, and all the jobsites were in the Seattle area.

"It'll be exciting, a new beginning," Angeni said.

"What about the congregation?" Aurora asked.

Seattle was a two-and-a-half-hour drive from where they were in Chelan County. It wouldn't be feasible to continue the weekly park gatherings.

"Erik had an idea. We can create a website, social media . . . build an online community. That way we can stay connected with the current congregation and grow beyond that too."

"That's actually smart," Aurora said. "Though I'll miss it here."

"We won't leave anytime soon. I can't tell Cheyenne about Erik yet. I promised her I would take this year of celibacy. Erik and I will keep things quiet until the timing is right. We have time to think it all through, to manifest a life for ourselves."

"*Manifest*," Aurora said. "I like that."

It was a word Erik had used on the retreat, a word he said he was applying to his own life. "I think I manifested you," he'd told Angeni after they first had sex.

"I think this is what I'm meant for, Ror," Angeni said.

Aurora looked less skeptical, more excited. She reached across the table and took both of Angeni's hands into her own. She squeezed them.

"I always knew you were meant for something."

Chapter 25

Gwen

It had been nearly two weeks since Gwen had attempted to resume breastfeeding June, and it was not going well. Whatever amount of milk Gwen's boobs were producing, it wasn't enough. June would fuss on the nipple, pulling it into her mouth, then spitting it out moments later. Before she began to cry in agonized frustration, there was this moment when she would stare up at Gwen, and the look in her eyes was heartbreaking. It was a look of utter bewilderment, like *What the fuck are you giving to me?*

Gwen and June continued to make the trip to Leigh's condo every day during the week, and every day Leigh took the time to assure Gwen that this was just a transition period. "Your body is still recalibrating, figuring out how much milk to make," Leigh said. Gwen tried to believe her. Gwen still thought about that surprising kiss on the cheek. It hadn't happened since, but she kept finding herself staring at Leigh's lips and thinking about kissing them. It was almost like the intensity of their bond demanded some kind of physical expression.

Usually, Gwen attempted to feed June before bringing her over to Leigh's. She didn't want Leigh to witness the embarrassment of their failed feeding relationship. But on this day, Leigh told her to wait to feed June until she got there. "Maybe I can help," Leigh told her, and Gwen felt the irresistible pull of hope.

Gwen had brought pizza from Pagliacci's, Leigh's favorite. Leigh sat on the couch and used her foot to kick open the lid of the pizza box, then leaned forward to lift out a slice. She took a bite as Gwen sat next to her. Gwen half-heartedly pulled her shirt up and over the shelf of her boobs, then unsnapped her bra. Was she imagining it, or were they already deflating, sad little sacks of flesh in comparison to Leigh's round, full *bosom*?

Gwen gently guided June's head toward her right boob and felt the tingly letdown of milk as her ever-wise body anticipated June's mouth. Her poor body; it didn't know her baby wanted nothing to do with her.

June kept trying to crane her head back toward Leigh, as if looking for someone, anyone, to save her from this disappointing situation.

"Your mama loves you, Juney," Leigh said. "Have some of her delicious milk."

Gwen pressed slightly harder on the back of June's head, shoving it into her boob until June's mouth opened with a depressing amount of reluctance and she latched on to the nipple.

"There you go, Juney," Leigh said.

June's eyes remained wide open as she sucked, alert and focused. When she took formula from the bottle, she always closed her eyes, as if the whole experience was peaceful and required minimal effort. After a minute or two, she pulled off Gwen's nipple suddenly, her head whipping back and then flinging forward into Gwen's chest.

"She's headbutting me. That's how pissed she is," Gwen said.

"She can sense your tension," Leigh said. "Try to breathe."

Leigh demonstrated deep breathing, inhaling and exhaling like the Zen mother Gwen would never be.

Gwen coaxed June back onto the breast, despite her squeals of resistance. June sucked again, those eyes wide open, and then again pulled off abruptly. She wailed, opening her mouth so wide that Gwen could see the entire track of her toothless gums on top and bottom.

"Oh my," Leigh said.

Oh my, indeed.

Gwen felt a wave of heat roll through her. She suddenly understood those mothers who lost it and shook their babies. She should have consoled June, whispered to her that it was okay that she didn't want her mother's breasts, but Gwen was not that evolved. She felt rejected, and the only way she knew to respond to this rejection was by holding the baby out to Leigh and saying, "You take her."

Leigh accepted June into her arms but held her at a distance from her body, as if she wasn't sure how to proceed.

"I think you just need to be patient with the process," Leigh said.

She had been saying this for two weeks now. Gwen snapped her bra closed, pulled down her shirt, and stood from the couch.

"I can't," she said. "How about I take Belle for a walk around the block in the stroller while you give June a bottle?"

Gwen rummaged around in her diaper bag and retrieved the bottle of formula, prepped and ready in anticipation of this event. Once June saw the bottle, she fussed in Leigh's arms.

"Okay, yeah, I'm sure Belle would love that, thank you," Leigh said.

Gwen lifted Belle from the floor, silently begging her not to cry. She couldn't handle another infant rejection. Belle was an easygoing baby, though, probably due to her mother's lack of *tension*, and she seemed happy enough to be in Gwen's arms, then in the stroller.

"We'll be back," Gwen said.

~

It was good to get outside, good to be in the presence of a baby who was delighted instead of agitated. At the end of the block, Gwen stopped to text Leigh.

> Sorry. Clearly, I'm not handling this well. We won't be a bother much longer. I have to go back to work on Monday. I really do appreciate everything

Just the night before, Gwen and Jeff had gotten into an argument—"a heated discussion" was Jeff's phrasing—when she'd dared to tell him the secret she'd been keeping from him.

"I don't want to go back to work," she confessed.

She felt immediately lighter with this out in the open instead of festering inside her. The relief, though, was short lived.

"What do you mean? You love work, babe," Jeff said. He was smiling as he said it; he clearly did not understand her despair.

"I just . . . I can't," she said, her eyes filling with tears.

He came to her, put his arms around her in his best attempt to be comforting, but he couldn't manage words that were of any comfort.

"We talked about this, though, before we even got pregnant. We talked about it when we bought this house."

Yes, yes, they had. That was true. He seemed incapable of believing that a woman, upon having a baby, could become a different person.

"I know." She couldn't bring herself to say more. Her throat constricted, and the words piled up, unable to get through.

"We have a house in one of the nicest neighborhoods in Seattle," he said. Then, as if she still didn't get it: "This isn't a one-income neighborhood."

"I know." The same refrain.

He sighed. "I'm sure every new mom feels this way. Then you'll go back to work and remember what you love about it."

Did she once love work? She couldn't even remember. She didn't feel like a person capable of loving much of anything anymore.

"We could move." These three words managed to escape.

He started smiling again, this strange expression incongruent with her turmoil.

"Gwen, we are not moving," he said, adding a little laugh for good measure. "There's no way we could sell the house for more than we bought it for. Besides, you love it here."

Did she love it here? She didn't know, but she nodded anyway.

"Besides, we already paid the deposit at the day care," he added, a twist of the knife.

They had put the deposit on the day care place months before June was born—$2,000 to hold their spot. At the time, Gwen had been thankful to have a spot. She was undeterred by paying more than the monthly rent on their first apartment for the care of their child. She was that committed to returning to work.

Jeff put his hand on the always-tense muscles between her neck and her shoulder, gave them a squeeze. She forced a smile. She wasn't going to get anywhere with him. She'd given him her truth, and he wanted her to take it back to where it had come from.

~

Leigh texted back:

> Oh honey, it's okay, truly. You're being too hard on yourself. I'm sure the work thing is weighing on you. Monday? I didn't realize it was so soon. Let's chat when you're back

By the time Gwen returned, Leigh was done feeding June and had her sitting on Belle's play mat. Belle had fallen asleep in the stroller and was still sleeping as Gwen lifted her out and handed her over to Leigh. Gwen took a deep breath, readying herself for whatever heart-to-heart conversation Leigh wanted to have. Leigh wasn't the type to just let things go.

"Have you seen this?" Leigh asked, holding her phone out to Gwen.

Gwen sat on the floor next to June, who seemed content as ever, and looked at Leigh's phone. It was a Reddit thread titled "Where in the world is Angeni Luna?" Gwen had yet to notice, but apparently Angeni Luna hadn't posted anything in twenty-four hours, and this was highly unusual. Savvy followers said that Erik also had not posted anything.

The rumors were all over the place—their marriage had imploded, Angeni Luna had died, something had happened to baby Freya.

Gwen handed the phone back to Leigh and set June in her lap.

"Don't tell me you're not curious," Leigh said.

Gwen shrugged. "It's, like, a *day*. Maybe she just needed a break."

"No. When these influencers take a break, they make a big to-do about it, like *Oh, I need to take space to protect my mental health*."

Gwen laughed.

"So you think she's dead?"

Leigh's eyes were big with interest. "I don't know. Maybe. Or maybe she had a mental breakdown like the rest of us."

"Now *that* I would like to see."

"Right?"

"I'm sure some crazy person will go over to Bainbridge Island to investigate and report back on Reddit."

"Oh my god, *we* should be that crazy person."

Gwen couldn't tell if she was joking.

"I'm joking!" Leigh said. "You really think I'm insane, don't you?"

"I mean, yes, sometimes."

Leigh threw her head back, cackling. "You and Nathan both."

Gwen debated whether or not to tell Leigh more about her own recent insanity. She decided to do it because Leigh was likely to wave it off as no big deal.

"I've been having these weird, like, dreams about Angeni Luna," Gwen said.

They'd kept happening in the wee morning hours, before her body was fully awake. They were more like visions than dreams. It was always the same scene—Gwen and Angeni Luna sitting at the kitchen table, Angeni holding Gwen's hands and saying reassuring things that Gwen would then carry with her throughout the day.

"Like sex dreams?" Leigh said.

Gwen rolled her eyes. "No, not sex dreams. They're just her talking to me, telling me things I need to hear."

"Aww. That's kind of sweet," Leigh said.

In the latest one, she'd been helping Gwen talk through her feelings about going back to work. *You've established such a wonderful bond with June in the past few months,* she'd said. *Nothing will weaken that.*

"It's weird," Gwen said.

"I don't think so. She's like a fairy godmother or something."

Gwen laughed. It was a bit like that.

"I'm just disappointed it's not sexual. I would like to hear about that," Leigh said.

"Sorry to disappoint." Then, uncomfortable with her admission, Gwen shifted the conversation back to Leigh: "How are you and Nathan doing?"

Leigh shrugged. "We're the same. We kind of hate each other, but in a lazy way that involves taking no meaningful action."

"I think that's called complacency."

"Yeah. That," Leigh said. "How are you and Jeff?"

"Meh."

"Oh, that's my new memoir title. *Meh: A Memoir of Holy Matrimony.*"

"I told him I don't want to go back to work, and he shot me down."

"Really? You've made him seem so nice."

"He *is* nice," she said.

He was. He was just uncompromising in the face of potential financial catastrophe. It wasn't a bad trait.

"He's thinking of the big picture," Gwen clarified. "We can't, like, afford our life if I don't go back to work."

"Then create a different life," Leigh said, as if it were that easy. This was, after all, the vague solution that Angeni Luna offered the world—if you can't be the mother your child needs because of competing responsibilities, you need to abdicate those responsibilities. She'd posted something like that and gotten lots of clapping-hands emojis in the comments.

"But this is the life Jeff wants. This is the life I said I wanted."

Leigh sighed. "That's why I find marriage so stifling. We make these promises to each other, banking on the fact that one person or both people don't change in some fundamental way. Seems wildly unrealistic."

"It's romantic, though. Staying together despite the changes."

"Is it?"

"Ideally," Gwen said, her voice getting small as she started to doubt what she was saying.

Leigh placed Belle on the play mat next to June. The babies seemed to enjoy each other's company more and more, communicating in their own special way with gurgles and grunts.

"Anyway, I'm sorry it's been hard, sweetie," Leigh said.

She patted the couch next to her, beckoning Gwen to sit. Gwen left the babies on the floor and sat next to Leigh, their thighs touching. Leigh clasped Gwen's hand, and there was something about this touch, the simplest of human touches, that made Gwen start to cry. She and Jeff were having sex again, but that didn't make her cry. The entirety of his body pressed against hers wasn't nearly as comforting as Leigh's palm pressed into her palm.

"I want you to have whatever kind of life you want," Leigh said, squeezing Gwen's hand.

Gwen cried harder. Why couldn't Jeff say something like that to her?

"I don't know why I'm always freaking crying around you," she said.

"You need nurturing," Leigh said. "You are depleted. That's why you're crying. That's why you're having dreams about Angeni Luna."

Nurturing. She associated it with what she was doing for June on a day-to-day, minute-to-minute basis. The fact that she needed it for herself came as both a shock and a relief.

"I have an idea," Leigh said. "Let's get out. Do something fun."

Gwen was immediately hesitant. She knew it was doubtful that she and Leigh had the same idea of fun.

"You are seriously looking at me like I'm going to suggest going to a strip club," Leigh said.

"I mean, I *can* see you suggesting that."

"With our babies. Now that would be a scene," she said.

Leigh stood from the couch, looking like a woman on a mission.

"Let's go to the movies. Dark, air-conditioned theater. The girls will nap. We can eat junk food and think about something besides motherhood for a couple hours."

Gwen couldn't remember the last time she'd been to the movies. When they were younger, Gwen and Jeff used to go to the movies a lot. It was an easy date. There was something romantic about cuddling up in the theater, sharing popcorn.

"The matinee price is, like, eight bucks," Leigh said. "They're showing this movie from a few years ago at the indie theater I love. I've been wanting to go, just haven't had the courage to do it alone with Belle."

"What movie?" Gwen asked, still mulling over the idea. Sitting in a theater did sound nice. If Belle or June lost their shit, they could just leave. It was unlikely there'd be many people in the theater to disturb.

"It's called *Portrait of a Lady on Fire*," Leigh said.

Gwen had never heard of it.

"Sounds like another title option for your memoir."

~

The theater was a short walk from Leigh's condo. It wasn't one of those mega-theaters with the heated recliner seats and giant screens. It was tiny. It looked to be an old playhouse that had been converted into a theater. There were only three screens, and they were all showing foreign-language films that Gwen had never heard of. She had assumed her first movie theater experience with June would be a Disney film, a theater packed with raucous children. This was a much more interesting outing.

Leigh paid for their tickets and bought enough candy for several people—Junior Mints, Red Vines, M&M's, Milk Duds. They walked into theater 3 with the girls strapped to their chests. Both babies were quiet, probably too distracted by the newness of this place to raise much of a fuss.

There was nobody else in the theater. They sat in old, creaky seats in the exact middle. Leigh put her Converse-adorned feet up on the seat in front of her and turned Belle to face the screen.

"It's R-rated. Would Angeni Luna approve?" Leigh said.

Gwen put her feet up on the seat in front of her and turned June to face the screen too.

"I'll ask her the next time she appears in my dreams."

The lights dimmed, and Leigh tore open the bag of M&M's. She passed the bag to Gwen, and Gwen shook some of the candy into her palm.

"I cannot remember the last time I had candy," Gwen said.

"Angeni Luna definitely wouldn't approve. So processed. So many chemicals. What happens in the movie theater stays in the movie theater."

The previews started, and the babies looked on, enthralled. When the opening credits of the movie started rolling, Leigh leaned over and said, "This movie is so beautiful. I think you'll love it."

"Wait, you've seen it before?" Gwen said.

Leigh smiled. "It's a fave."

The movie was French, subtitled. Gwen worried she'd fall asleep, but she was pulled into the story immediately. It was set in the late eighteenth century, about a painter named Marianne who is commissioned to paint the portrait of a woman named Héloïse, who is supposed to be married off soon to a wealthy nobleman. She doesn't want to marry him and refuses to sit for a proper portrait, so Marianne must observe her discreetly and paint without Héloïse knowing. As they spend so much time together, they develop a deep connection. It was so beautiful and sensual that Gwen found herself weeping. When she did, Leigh reached over, took Gwen's hand in hers. They sat like that, holding hands, until the end of the movie.

The babies were sleeping when the lights came up. There were tear tracks on Leigh's face—she had cried too.

"I told you it was amazing," Leigh said. She was still holding Gwen's hand. Gwen didn't know what to say. She'd never been moved to tears by a movie before. She was reluctant to stand, unsure her legs would hold her.

One of the theater employees came in with a broom and trash bag. She didn't acknowledge the presence of Gwen, Leigh, and the babies, just went about her business, going up and down the aisles of the theater in search of a mess.

"She does realize there is nobody in here to make a mess, right?" Leigh whispered.

Gwen chuckled. "She's being diligent!"

Leigh stood, finally releasing Gwen's hand to snap Belle into her carrier. A wave of sadness rolled over Gwen at the loss of that hand.

You need nurturing.

~

It was after four o'clock when they got back to Leigh's condo. Gwen kept Leigh company in the kitchen as she pulled things out of the fridge for their dinner. The girls sat in Bumbo seats on the floor, gurgling their version of conversation.

"Did the movie outing help get your mind off things?" Leigh asked.

It had, but just the question brought Gwen back to her sadness about returning to work.

"Yeah, it did, thank you," she said.

"You are such a liar."

Gwen managed a smile. "I don't know. I get flooded with all these feelings. I feel like I've already let June down so much, and now I'm going back to work. I mean, how could she not feel abandoned? It's not like she understands what having a job means."

"Come here," Leigh said. She extended her arms and pulled Gwen into them. They stood there, holding each other for longer than Gwen had ever stood and held someone.

When Leigh released Gwen, she went to the bench seat at the kitchen table and patted the spot next to her. Gwen sat, and Leigh put her arm around Gwen, pulled her against her body, their heads resting against each other.

"It'll all be okay," Leigh said.

After a few moments, Gwen lifted her head, faced Leigh. Leigh was looking at her tenderly, like she truly loved her and cared for her in a way Gwen had never felt cared for before.

Their faces were just a few inches apart, and Gwen found herself drawn toward Leigh, magnetized. She closed her eyes and allowed her lips to find Leigh's lips. Gwen could hear the blood whooshing in her ears. She kept her eyes closed, kept herself contained in this strange world of darkness where kissing her friend felt good for no reason she could explain. It wasn't sexual. Gwen didn't feel any urge or longing for something beyond the kiss. She just wanted to be right here, in this moment.

Leigh didn't pull back. She moved her lips against Gwen's. She took Gwen's top lip in both of her lips; then she did the same with her bottom lip. When Leigh slipped her tongue into Gwen's mouth, it was sensual and kind, not sloppy and greedy like Gwen had experienced with most of the men she'd kissed in her life. They kissed and kissed, not pausing to try to put words to what was happening.

Gwen had no idea how long it had been when Leigh pulled back suddenly and said "Oh shit" before Leigh even opened her eyes.

When Leigh did open her eyes, she realized why Leigh looked panicked.

Nathan was standing in the front entryway, his work bag at his feet, arms crossed over his chest. It was obvious he'd seen enough.

Leigh jumped to her feet, looking nothing like the confident, assured woman who Gwen knew—the woman who wouldn't take shit from anyone.

"Ladies," Nathan said, a punishing monotone.

Gwen knelt down for June, who, picking up on the anxiety in the room, started to cry. Oh, her sensitive baby.

June's car seat was right by the front door, right next to Nathan. Gwen scurried over, careful not to make any eye contact with Nathan. What could she possibly say? She didn't understand what had just happened herself; there was no use trying to explain it to him.

As Gwen buckled June into her seat, she waited for Leigh to come to her—their—defense. She waited for Leigh to say, "Gwen, you don't need to go. We weren't doing anything wrong." Because they weren't, were they?

But Leigh didn't say anything like that. Instead, she said to Nathan, "I know what you're going to say. That was totally wrong, I know. But *she* kissed *me*."

She said this as if Gwen were not right there, in the room. Gwen looked at her friend, craving some eye contact that said *I'm just telling him what he needs to hear; call you later*. But Leigh wouldn't meet her eyes.

There was one more humiliating necessity—grabbing the diaper bag from the living room. She tiptoed out of the kitchen, as if playing along with this ridiculous notion that she wasn't there at all. She got the bag and then tiptoed back to the car seat, lifted June, and left, closing the door behind her. As the door clicked shut, she heard Nathan say, "You've got to be fucking kidding me."

June cried as Gwen took her to the car, and she cried the entire drive home. Not even the motion of the car, the white noise of the roads, could get her to settle.

When Gwen arrived back at her house, the house that was once their dream house and now just seemed like a ball and chain, she parked in the driveway and checked her phone. She expected a text from Leigh, but there was nothing. She decided to send one herself.

> Hey. Sorry about that. I don't know what came over me. You were right—it was all my fault. I think the movie got to me? I hope we can put it behind us

She felt stupid after sending it. Leigh had taken her to that movie. Leigh had participated in the kissing. It was an emotional day. She was vulnerable. She needed *nurturing*.

She waited for Leigh to respond, to tell her not to worry about it, that Nathan had calmed down after she explained things. She stared, willing the three dots to appear. Nothing.

Nothing.

Nothing.

She rested her forehead on the cushioned steering wheel and began to sob. June had finally stopped crying but then ramped up again upon hearing her mother sobbing. Soon, they were both wailing, as if in competition with each other.

"Gwen?"

She lifted her head to see Jeff, sweet Jeff, at her window, his fingers tapping on the glass. She opened her car door.

"What? What's wrong?" he asked.

He looked into the back seat.

"Is June okay?" he asked.

"She's fine," Gwen said.

"Honey, what's wrong?" he asked again.

"I don't know," she said. She did know, but she couldn't possibly tell him. He wouldn't understand.

"Come on," he said, taking her two hands in his.

He helped her out of the front seat, and when he went to get June from the back, Gwen glanced at her phone again.

Nothing.

"Let's get you two inside, okay?" he said.

He walked ahead of her with June, but she stood still. She felt unable to move.

"Babe?" he said. "What is it? What's wrong?"

She shook her head, told him what she knew he wanted to hear: "I'm just having a really hard day."

He set June's car seat on the ground. June had already stopped crying, likely comforted by the presence of Jeff, a sane adult. Jeff put his arms around Gwen, pulled her into him.

"We all have hard days," he said.

Poor Jeff—he had no idea what he was up against.

Chapter 26

Angeni Luna

Angeni hated this hospital. The last time she'd been here had been for Freya's birth. The baby's heart decelerations had everyone so worried, the midwife had insisted on a transfer. Angeni trusted that all would be fine, and it was, but not before so much unnecessary panic and talk of a C-section. She'd delivered Freya vaginally, by sheer will. She'd manifested it. Her body had known what it had to do.

This hospital stay was just as traumatic. When she'd first arrived, she'd been too out of it to protest an overnight stay. She'd had a crushing headache and vomited a handful of times. Erik said she'd been slurring, which was especially alarming because she'd thought she was speaking perfectly fine.

After he left, she fell asleep, only to be awakened for more scans. She fell asleep again, and when she opened her eyes, it was morning, and she felt well enough to panic about having spent the night away from Freya.

It was just past five in the morning when she texted Erik.

Is Freya OK? I have to get out of here. Can you come?

While she waited for him to respond, a nurse came in, and she couldn't resist passing on the same message to him.

"I have to get out of here," she said to him.

He was tapping away at the little computer on wheels. He looked over the top of it, met her eyes.

"Excuse me?"

"I have to get out of here," she repeated. "When are they letting me out?"

"I don't know, ma'am."

Ma'am. This nurse was so baby-faced, couldn't have been more than twenty-five.

"I have a baby at home," she said.

His eyes got big and wide. "Alone?"

She sighed. "She's not *alone*, but she's not with me."

Angeni couldn't help but think about the potential physiological effects of babies being separated from their mothers. There was likely so much cortisol coursing through Freya right now. She hadn't nursed in more than twenty-four hours; she must be howling with hunger, nearing desperation.

"It looks like the doctor will be doing rounds in a couple hours and will go over your scans with you then," the baby-face said.

"A couple *hours*?"

"That's when Dr. Sanger does rounds," he said.

"Did you not hear me? I have a *baby*. At *home*."

He nodded. He didn't understand. It was possible he would never understand, would walk into a future as a father who had no concept of what parenthood required. People like him were the problem—people who did not take nurturing seriously.

A woman in pink scrubs appeared in the doorway.

"Is everything okay in here?"

The woman looked from Angeni to the nurse, concern all over her face. Had Angeni been yelling? It was possible she'd been yelling. She told herself to breathe—in for four, hold, out for four, hold. Repeat. She had to stay composed. She was Angeni Luna. Her persona was reliant upon her being tranquil. A public outburst could destroy her. Cancel culture was alive and well.

"I just wanted to know when I can go home," she said, forcing herself to smile and emit the peaceful calm people expected of her.

"Dr. Sanger will see you on his rounds, and if all's good, we'll discharge," she said.

The male nurse nodded emphatically, like *I told you so*, and then they both left.

~

Erik arrived before Dr. Sanger. He looked exhausted. She doubted he'd slept at all—her poor husband, sick with worry. He insisted Freya was fine. They'd given her enough chicken-liver pâté to hold her over. Angeni didn't believe Freya was fine, though. Even if she'd managed to take in enough calories, which wasn't likely, she would have missed the connection of nursing. She would have missed her mother. Erik wouldn't tell Angeni if Freya wasn't fine, though. He wouldn't want to cause her more distress. The truth was waiting for her at home.

When Dr. Sanger came, he told them that her scans were clear.

"No bleeding or swelling. No structural issues with the brain. All bloodwork is normal too."

"So I can go?" Angeni asked.

"You can go," he said. "Just rest, take it easy for a few days. Then you can gradually resume normal activities."

As if any mother worth anything could take it easy for a few days.

~

Erik was quiet on the drive home, which only made Angeni worry more about Freya. She started to bite her fingernails, something she hadn't done in years.

"You okay?" Erik asked her.

"I'm worried about Freya."

"She's fine. I promise."

"I need to see for myself."

She stuffed her hands underneath her thighs so she would stop gnawing on her nails. She bit her lip instead.

"I'm sure it was hard being at the hospital," Erik said, "but you're out of there now. We'll get you home and back to normal."

Normal. Angeni had forgotten what that was. Nothing had felt normal lately.

"We'll probably have to do a post on Instagram," Erik said. "When you're up for it, I mean."

The regular schedule of her Instagram posts hadn't even crossed Angeni's mind. She had been thinking only about Freya. And despite all attempts not to, she'd been thinking about that letter.

YOU SHOULD BE CHARGED WITH MURDER.

She couldn't mention the letter to Erik because he didn't know why it would be so unsettling. He didn't know what had happened with her mother all those years ago. It had to have been Aurora who'd sent it. But why? What would be the purpose of bringing it up now? Was she tired of carrying their secret? Was she that resentful of Sitka? Angeni thought back to when Erik had come into their lives, how worried Aurora had been about losing importance in Angeni's life.

"People will worry about you," Erik said.

Angeni didn't know what he was referring to, her thoughts elsewhere. "What?"

"People. Online. They're going to wonder where you are, why you haven't posted."

"I can't think about that right now."

"I know. I'm sorry. Just trying to get ahead of it."

"Of what?"

"Gossip. Drama. Anyway, forget it."

When he sighed, it wasn't just exhaustion, but something else. Defeat, despair.

~

Sitka and Freya were standing on the front porch when Erik and Angeni pulled into the driveway. At the sight of her baby, Angeni unbuckled her seat belt and started to rise, not caring that the car was still in motion. Her baby needed her. Her breasts started to swell and tingle, preparing for their duty.

But as she came closer, she saw that Freya was not in any distress at all. She was smiling as Sitka bounced her in her arms. Angeni was overcome with a profound mixture of relief and sorrow at this. Her baby was fine, just as Erik had said. Her baby was seemingly unaffected by the sudden absence of her mother.

Angeni opened the car door and sprinted toward Freya. She still felt woozy and awkward on her feet, but she had to get to her daughter. Freya squealed with reassuring delight as Angeni reached for her and hugged her against her chest.

"Oh, my baby," Angeni said, tears coming in a rush.

She kissed every inch of Freya's face as Freya giggled.

"You must be starving," Angeni said, nuzzling into Freya's neck.

She held Freya against her with one hand and used the other to pull out her left breast, offering it to her daughter.

"I can't believe she's not crying," Angeni said to Sitka.

"She's just so excited to see you," Sitka said. "I'm sure that's distracting her from any discomfort."

Angeni felt buoyed by Sitka's words, but then Freya wouldn't latch, again, and her unease returned.

"Come on, sweetie," Angeni said, shifting Freya a bit to try another angle. She headbutted Angeni's chest, bobbing like a bird, her lips pressed shut.

"Maybe she just needs to be in your arms for a while, to feel your presence, before she's calm enough to eat," Sitka said.

Angeni nodded. She wanted to believe Sitka. But it didn't make sense. Her breasts were supposed to be the ultimate comfort.

"Sitka's probably right," Erik said. "Let's go in, babe."

Angeni watched a look pass between them, and she wasn't sure what to make of it. They were in on something together. It was possible that they were only joined in a mission to get her to relax, but Angeni couldn't help but feel something was amiss.

Erik put his arm around Angeni and guided her inside. Her boob was still out of her shirt. Freya put her hands on it like it was a bouncy ball of mild interest.

Inside, Aurora was in the kitchen, prepping something on the stove. When she saw Angeni, she ran to her.

"Oh my god, I've been so worried," she said.

But Angeni could think only of the letter, the probability of Aurora having sent it. Aurora wrapped her arms around Angeni and Freya, the three of their faces pressed together. Angeni's body, her wise and all-knowing body, went stiff and still. She closed her eyes, tuned in to what her body was telling her. *Do not trust this person.* That was what it was saying.

"I'm making some butternut squash soup. I thought that sounded nourishing," Aurora said.

Angeni tried to muster a smile, but couldn't.

"I used coconut milk. I thought the dairy might be too inflammatory after what your body's been through."

"Thanks," Angeni muttered.

Aurora moved with Angeni and Freya to the couch, Erik and Sitka following behind. They were all hovering over her, their worry palpable.

"Guys, I'm fine," she said.

She sat on the couch, Freya in her lap. Aurora sat next to her, Erik on her other side. Sitka stayed standing.

"Matt and Jer are bringing in some wood for a fire. Hospitals are so cold. I thought you might need to warm up," Aurora said.

Was Aurora overcompensating for what she'd done? Was she regretting the letter, how it had sent Angeni to the hospital?

Matt and Jer came in through the kitchen door, wood in their arms. They placed a few logs in the fireplace, the rest in the rack next to it.

"Good to see you, Ang," Matt said. He lit the fire, and the two of them came to sit next to Aurora on the couch. Their big, questionably happy family.

"Thanks for the fire," Angeni said. She wanted nothing more than to be completely alone with her baby, but couldn't disregard basic politeness.

"No problem, Ang. So happy you're feeling better," Jer said.

"Babe, what do you need?" Erik asked.

Now she saw a look pass between Erik and Aurora, another look she could not decipher completely, though if she wasn't mistaken, Aurora looked irritated with Erik. Sitka paced the length of the couch behind all of them, arms crossed over her chest.

"Do you guys think I could have some privacy with Freya? I want to reassure her that I'm back, that everything is safe," Angeni said.

Aurora nodded effusively, the first to stand from the couch.

"Yes, of course," she said. "Sitka, do you mind stirring the soup? Erik, can I talk to you briefly?"

There was that look again on Aurora's face—that annoyance with Erik.

"Sure," Sitka said. She went to the stove and started to stir the soup lazily, one eye still on Angeni and Freya.

"Briefly, sure," Erik said to Aurora.

Matt and Jer were already heading outside, telling Angeni to let them know if she needed anything at all. Jer said he'd be back to check on the fire in an hour.

Aurora put her hand on Angeni's knee, smiled without showing teeth.

"All is going to be okay," she said to Angeni.

But there was an apprehension in her voice that told Angeni nothing was okay at all.

Chapter 27

Sasha

Sasha didn't know how long she was supposed to stand there at the stove, stirring the butternut squash soup while pretending she didn't hear the frustrated grunts and sighs from Angeni, who was continuing to try—and fail—to get Freya to breastfeed. Did Angeni really think they hadn't taken it upon themselves to feed the baby something besides bites of chicken liver? Was she that delusional? Sasha had thought that Erik or Aurora would cave and tell Angeni about the formula, but everyone had remained tight lipped so far, allowing Angeni to live in her delusion.

Sasha couldn't stop thinking about the home birth lie. Would Daphne still be alive if Angeni had just been honest about her delivery? Sasha could envision the Instagram post detailing the harrowing labor, the dramatic transfer to the hospital. She could imagine Angeni encouraging her followers to listen to their bodies while also listening to medical guidance. This was a fantasy version of Angeni. An honest, humble Angeni. Sasha knew her sister had read every single one of the posts on the @mother.nurture.official page. Would she have thought twice about her birth plan if she'd read about the difficulties Angeni had had? It wasn't crazy to think that, yes, Daphne would still be alive if Angeni had used her platform for authentic connection instead of a false projection of an ideal. Then again, she could also hear Daphne scoff and say *You're giving this woman too much power, Sash. Give ME some credit. I made a bad choice, but it was MY choice.* And that was true. Maybe Angeni wasn't Daphne's demise, just her inspiration.

As she tortured herself thinking about what could have been, she also tortured herself with flashbacks to kissing Erik. He hadn't said a word to Sasha about the kiss, so it was easy to pretend it hadn't happened. It had, though. And Aurora had seen it. She also hadn't said anything to Sasha, though Sasha was sure Aurora was having words with Erik privately. Sasha regretted it, felt ashamed of herself for giving in to base temptation. She should have pushed him away, asserted herself as the morally superior one of the two of them. She could imagine Daphne crossing her arms over her chest and shaking her head at her sister: *You are better than this, Sash.*

Sasha thought it was safe to assume they wouldn't tell Angeni about the kiss. They wouldn't want to upset her, especially given current circumstances. That commitment to truth they claimed—it was just another lie.

It had become exceedingly clear—Sasha had to get out of this place. She no longer felt purposeful. All this evidence she'd obtained of the real Angeni Luna didn't feel satisfying; it felt sad. Sasha wasn't even sure she wanted to expose Angeni anymore. She could. She had the power to do so much damage. But would Daphne want that? She felt in her heart that Daphne would have already forgiven Angeni Luna. Daphne had always been the kinder sister. *You're such a hard-ass, Sash.* She'd said that on more than a few occasions. Sasha thought about what Erik had told her about Angeni's upbringing, about how she'd seen her mother kill herself. Daphne, ever the empath, would have focused on this, would have excused Angeni for so much because of this.

At the very least, she needed space to consider what to do next. She had to leave. She wasn't sure if she should tell Angeni about Daphne before going. Would it make one iota of difference to Daphne, wherever she was? Probably not, and she was quite certain it wouldn't take the grief away. It had been silly of her to think it would.

~

"I just do not understand why she's not hungry," Angeni said, loud enough for Sasha to hear from her post in the kitchen. There was nobody else in the living area, but Sasha wasn't sure if Angeni was inviting conversation.

"Can I get you some soup?" she asked.

"Sure, yes," Angeni said. "Maybe that's it. Maybe Freya can smell the stress hormones on me. I bet that makes the milk taste funny. Or maybe she senses that I'm in a weakened state and has the intuition to let me conserve my energy."

Angeni's belief in her baby's wisdom was baffling, but Sasha just said, "Maybe."

She ladled some of the soup into a bowl for Angeni and brought it to her, setting it on the coffee table in front of the couch.

"Smells delicious," Sasha said.

Freya smiled at Sasha, that big toothless grin that enticed Sasha to smile in return, no matter what her own mental state was. Freya reached out toward Sasha, and Sasha pretended not to notice.

"Mama's here," Angeni said, using her hand to gently turn Freya's head, coax her to look at Angeni. She rocked Freya in her arms, both boobs now out and free, bouncing about.

Angeni tried to transport a spoonful of soup from the bowl to her mouth but spilled mid-transport, the glob of orange landing in her lap, just missing Freya's head.

"Oh jeez, first Mama left you for a night, and now she's dropping hot soup on you," Angeni said with a little laugh.

"Do you want me to hold her while you eat?" Sasha asked.

Angeni considered the offer longer than she usually would. She tightened her grip on Freya, then released slightly as she said, "Okay, just for a few minutes."

Sasha took Freya and seated her in her own lap, facing her.

"Can you actually turn her around so she's looking at me?" Angeni asked.

"Oh, okay," Sasha said, turning Freya around so she was facing Angeni as she took a spoonful of soup.

"It's so yum," Angeni said to Freya in her overly saccharine voice.

Sasha's phone vibrated in her pocket. An incoming text. A few seconds later, another vibration.

"I can take her now," Angeni said after she'd finished about half the bowl.

Sasha handed her the baby and got up from the couch as she pulled her phone out of her pocket.

It was Jay.

Yo.
Did my little note make it there?

Sasha didn't realize she'd audibly gasped until Angeni said, "Everything okay?"

"Um, yeah," Sasha muttered.

She collapsed onto the kitchen island, needing the sturdiness of it to hold up her body as it sagged in disbelief.

Dude. That was you?!

He sent a GIF of a man taking a dramatic bow.

Sasha: Jay. Dude. She, like, passed out when she read it. She went to the hospital and shit
Jay: oh shit. for real? serves her right i guess lol

Jay was still harboring the anger that Sasha had transmitted to him like a virus. She had to get back to him, help him see the pointlessness of it. Sasha looked over at Angeni, still trying to shove her tits in the poor baby's mouth. She couldn't help but feel bad for her.

Freya started to cry, probably annoyed with the tits in her face, and Sasha put down her phone and went to the couch.

"Can I help with anything?" Sasha asked.

Angeni didn't even acknowledge her presence, though. Her tired, red-rimmed eyes were glued to Freya. Sasha could see the muscles of her jaw clenching.

The more Angeni tried to feed Freya, the more Freya cried—and cried, and cried.

"Everything okay?"

Sasha and Angeni turned to see that Aurora had come into the room. Aurora smiled at Angeni but didn't meet Sasha's eyes. Aurora hated her for kissing Erik. She could feel the hostility. Sasha wanted to explain how it was nothing, how Erik was just exhausted, looking for comfort. Men were all dumb creatures, taking too much solace in sexual connection.

"I just don't understand why she's not eating," Angeni said.

"Can I make you some tea?" Aurora asked.

When Angeni didn't respond, Aurora said, "I'm going to make you some chamomile," and went to the kitchen.

"She doesn't seem sick to you, does she?" Angeni asked.

It took a second for Sasha to realize that Angeni was asking her.

"I don't think so," Sasha said, unsure if that was the right answer. "I mean, maybe? I guess that would explain why she wouldn't be hungry."

"The stress of me being away would have compromised her immune system," Angeni said. She was so bereft, Sasha found herself placing a consoling hand on her shoulder.

"She will be okay," Sasha said. Needing something to do in this awkward moment, she stood from the couch and said, "Let me get your tea."

When she turned toward the kitchen, she saw Aurora standing at the island, looking down at her phone, her brows knitted together in concern. It was only when she looked up as Sasha approached that Sasha realized Aurora wasn't looking at her own phone, but at Sasha's—with Jay's text messages on full display.

Chapter 28

GWEN

It was Sunday, the day before Gwen had to return to work. She stood in her walk-in closet. The walk-in closet that had been such a selling point for this house. This house that had been her dream house. Her work clothes had been organized perfectly by a former version of herself, a person who had time and energy to tend so carefully to her wardrobe. There were pants—black, gray, tan. There were pencil skirts. There were blouses, arranged by color. Below, in the shoe rack on the floor, were her pumps and flats. She had once been a person who cared about shoes, who "dressed for success." Since becoming a mother, she'd dressed only for survival.

"How's it going in here?" Jeff asked, coming into the closet with June in his arms. He had sent Gwen in here to pick out an outfit a half hour ago. He must have been wondering what was taking so long.

"I don't know. Nothing seems right," Gwen said.

It was a statement of total truth.

"Hey, I know this is hard," Jeff said, "but I really think this is a rip-the-Band-Aid-off situation. You'll feel much better after tomorrow."

"You're probably right."

She couldn't fathom how he could be right, how anything could feel much better after she handed over her baby (and a hefty sum of money) to relative strangers and then returned to a work environment where she was expected to be on for several hours a day. Jeff didn't want to hear her negativity, though. She had to, for all intents and purposes, suck it up.

~

That night, she lay awake in bed, flat on her back, while Jeff lay flat on his back next to her, the two of them like two cadavers in a morgue. He was sleeping well enough to snore. June was still waking up two or three times a night, and Gwen found herself on alert for her cries, unable to rest.

She sat up against the headboard, tapped her phone awake. It had been two days since the kissing incident with Leigh, and she still hadn't heard from her. She felt mortified by the whole thing, kept replaying it in her head and chastising herself. What had come over her? Beyond the humiliation, she was overcome with grief. She imagined it like an ever-growing multilayered cake, each layer a different source of melancholy—sadness over these first months of new motherhood, sadness over letting June down in so many ways, sadness over going back to work, sadness over her distance from Jeff, sadness over the apparent end of her friendship with Leigh. She longed to hear from her. She fantasized about Leigh forgiving her, absolving her of her shame. They would recommit to their friendship, moving forward with the understanding that what had happened between them had been a one-time blunder not requiring further analysis. Why wasn't Leigh texting her?

Gwen opened Instagram, scrolled mindlessly, looking for something for her brain to grasp on to and mull over so she wouldn't keep ruminating about Leigh. She tapped to Angeni Luna's page. There still hadn't been a post. Under her last post, a slew of commenters was pleading with her to reassure them.

> We miss you, Angeni. Hope all is ok!!!
>
> Starting to worry . . . . . . can u let us know u ok?
>
> Hope rumors aren't true and ur just taking a break

She started to type a message to Leigh:

> Still no word from Angeni Luna. The mystery continues! Miss you, my friend . . .

Then she deleted it. She wasn't the desperate type, and a message like that was desperate.

"You okay?" Jeff said, rolling onto his side and putting a hand on Gwen's thigh. His voice was thick with sleep, his eyes still closed.

"Yeah, sorry, I'm fine."

She put the phone down on the nightstand and slid back to her horizontal position, staring at the ceiling. She channeled Leigh and took several deep breaths. Just as she was finally feeling relaxed enough to sleep, June cried.

~

It was the same as always—Angeni and Gwen sitting at the kitchen table, Angeni holding Gwen's hands with such tender affection.

I know you're uneasy about going back to work, Angeni said. *It doesn't feel right to be away from June. Of course it doesn't. But you have established such a rich connection with June. It will withstand the difficulty of the separation during the days. The bond between the two of you can withstand anything.*

~

"Babe, your alarm's going off," Jeff said.

It took Gwen a minute to realize she was sleeping in June's room. She'd come in to see her in the middle of the night for their new routine—several minutes of attempted breastfeeding, followed by a bottle of formula. Gwen didn't know if June was even getting any milk from her anymore, but they were keeping up the charade. It was possible June just thought the presentation of her mother's boobs was part of the ritual of these feedings. Gwen planned to pump whatever she could at work, even if she managed just a couple of ounces. She owed it to June to keep trying.

Gwen remembered lying down with June on her chest postfeeding. She hadn't intended to fall asleep, but she had. She must have transferred June back to the bassinet at some point, because that was where she was, unbothered by Jeff's appearance in the doorway.

"For work," Jeff said. "Your alarm."

Gwen sat up in bed. She'd set the alarm on her phone for six so she would have plenty of time to get everything ready for the day.

"Sorry," she said, swinging her legs over the side of the bed. June began to stir.

"Want me to start the shower for you?" he asked, rubbing his eyes.

"Sure, yeah," she said.

She checked her mental list:

- Shower
- Dress
- Blow-dry hair
- Makeup
- Breakfast
- Breastfeed/bottle
- Dress June
- Double-check June's day care bag
- Double-check work bag—pump supplies!

When in doubt, she'd always relied on lists, switching into a robotic going-through-the-motions mode that didn't give her time to consider any troublesome feelings. That was the only way she would get through this day and all the days after it—by dismissing her feelings.

By seven thirty, she had accomplished all the items on her list and looked like a woman who was ready for the hours ahead of her. She stood by the front door, June in her car seat on the floor, June's diaper bag and her work bag next to each other.

"You look great, honey," Jeff said.

He seemed pleased. He must have worried that she'd be unable to get out of bed. He must have foreseen a complete breakdown.

"I can go with you to drop off June," he said.

"It's okay. I've got it."

His presence at drop-off wouldn't be a comfort. That was why she didn't want him to come. He'd be far too breezy and chipper, which would only make her feel worse about the avalanche of despair she expected.

"I'm proud of you," he said.

He gave her a kiss on the cheek, then kneeled to give June a kiss on the cheek.

"Look at my girls, going off into the world."

Breezy and chipper.

~

He helped load them into the car, his girls going off into the world. Then he gave Gwen another kiss on the cheek and said he'd call her in an hour to check in. She sat in the driver's seat, seat belt on, and watched him pull out of the driveway in the rearview mirror. When he was down the street, she considered her options. What if they just didn't go? How long could she pretend to go to work while actually staying at home with June? The day care wouldn't call Jeff; they would call the mother. Everyone called the mother. She could say they'd had a change of plans, unenroll, lose the two-grand deposit. She could tell her boss she needed another month, the alternative being a resignation. Jeff would be none the wiser for at least a week or two.

Her phone buzzed with a text, and she hoped it was Leigh checking in because she remembered this was The Day. But it was just Jeff.

You can do this

If he hadn't sent the text, maybe she would have gone forward with her desperate scheme. Those simple words from her oh-so-simple husband were enough to stop the train of her thoughts from barreling down its derelict track. She started the car.

~

They'd selected the Seattle Child Development Center for day care because it was right downtown, near both of their offices. Gwen hadn't been to the facility since they'd selected it, when she was barely pregnant and already touring various places with the hope of getting on a wait list that wasn't too long.

She pulled into the parking lot, and her anxiety spiked immediately. There were so many cars pulling in and out that a woman in an orange vest was there to direct traffic. Gwen was positioned precariously in the driveway, the back half of her car still in the street, making her the target of aggressive honking that kick-started her crying earlier than she'd anticipated.

The woman in the orange vest made eye contact and, upon seeing Gwen's obvious distress, waved her over to a spot near the back of the lot. Gwen was still crying as she pulled in and put the car in park. When she went to open her door, she saw that the woman in the orange vest was standing there, a look of pity on her face that made Gwen want to curl up in a ball on the floor beneath the steering wheel for the rest of the day.

"Oh, honey," the woman said. "First day?"

Gwen muttered, "Yes," but she couldn't look at the woman, couldn't take in her sympathy.

"It gets easier, I promise," the woman said. "Well, not in the parking lot. That's always a bitch. But the whole drop-off thing gets easier."

Gwen was thankful for the comic relief, felt a smile come to her face despite the anguish.

"Can I help you two inside?"

"That's so kind, but I'm okay. I—"

The woman sighed. "I'm going to help you two inside."

The woman in the orange vest was named Sheila, and she insisted on holding June for the walk from the car to the center entrance. Gwen was sure June would start crying in the arms of this stranger, but June appeared too mystified by the overall newness of the situation to register discomfort.

By the time they got inside, Gwen had managed to stop crying. Sheila introduced her to everyone they passed in the lobby and hallway—a flurry of names that Gwen would never remember. Everyone smiled and waved. They were shiny, happy people, the type of people you would want in a childcare environment.

"Ms. Johnson is the teacher in the infant room," Sheila said as they approached the room where June would spend most of the day. Gwen thought the term *teacher* was a little silly, but she just nodded.

Ms. Johnson was young—late twenties, early thirties at the most. She didn't have a wedding ring. It was likely she didn't have children of her own. That was the only reasonable explanation for why she had so much energy available for other people's children.

"This must be June," Ms. Johnson said, her face conveying absolute enthusiasm at the arrival of Gwen's child. Gwen searched for something disingenuous in her huge smile, but couldn't find anything.

"I've been looking forward to you, little one," Ms. Johnson said to June. "You ready, Mom?"

Normally, Gwen hated it when people referred to her as "Mom," invalidating her existence as a human being with a name and referring to her only by her role. But in this instance, she was fine with being "Mom." She didn't care if she was nothing to Ms. Johnson as long as Ms. Johnson treated June like she was everything.

Sheila placed June in Gwen's arms, and Gwen transferred June to Ms. Johnson.

"I have all the instructions you emailed over—thank you for those," Ms. Johnson said. She was addressing Gwen, but her eyes were locked on June's, her face already contorting into all the goofy expressions adults make for babies.

"And you have my number if you need anything at all," Gwen said.

"They send photo updates throughout the day here," Sheila chimed in.

"We sure do," Ms. Johnson said before blubbering her lips at June. June smiled, entranced.

"Okay," Gwen said.

This was the time for her to leave, and yet she felt as if her feet, in her stupid heels, were bolted to the floor.

"I promise she is in great hands and we will have the best day," Ms. Johnson said.

"Thank you," Gwen said.

Gwen reached out to touch the soft hairs on June's head. She thought of that morning's Angeni vision, her mantra for the day: *The bond between the two of us can withstand anything.* She felt her eyes welling up with tears again. June didn't seem upset at all. She didn't understand that she was about to begin a phase of daily separation from the person who loved her most.

"Mama loves you," Gwen said, kissing June on the cheek. "Mama will be back."

The bond between the two of us can withstand anything.

Ms. Johnson lifted June's tiny hand in a wave, and Gwen managed to lift her feet and walk out of the room, Sheila behind her saying, "You did good."

Gwen sat in her car in the parking lot, waiting for Ms. Johnson to come running out to say that she had underestimated June's attachment to her mother and that she did not think June was ready for this type of care. Nobody came out, though. Sheila resumed her parking lot duties, looking over at Gwen every couple of minutes to give her a thumbs-up. Gwen watched the parade of other mothers carrying babies into the center. There were so many of them in their business attire, looking harried and rushed. Gwen knew she was supposed to feel emboldened by them, assured that she wasn't the only mother handing over her baby to people so she could go to work. But she didn't feel emboldened. She just felt remorse. This wasn't how it was supposed to be.

She kept thinking about how supportive Angeni Luna had been in that morning's vision-dream. That wasn't the *real* Angeni Luna, though. That was Gwen's projection of what she wanted to think Angeni Luna would say. The real Angeni Luna always talked about how a mother and her child were not supposed to be separated. It was against nature. That was why Gwen was so emotional. Her tears weren't evidence of something being wrong; they were evidence that she knew what was right. She was sure if she met the real Angeni Luna, she would want Gwen to go back into the day care center and retrieve her child.

Gwen tapped on her phone, checking for an update from Ms. Johnson. There wasn't anything yet, of course. She went to Instagram, checked Angeni Luna's page. No new posts. A text from Jeff appeared at the top of the screen:

You okay? How was drop-off?

She responded:

She's inside. I'm heading to work now

He responded with a thumbs-up emoji just as she looked up to see Sheila giving her another real-life thumbs-up before going inside the center. The arrival rush had ended, and Sheila was done with her parking lot job for the day.

Gwen started her car, but couldn't bring herself to shift into drive. She wasn't ready for this. June wasn't ready for this. Gwen couldn't let down her baby again.

She opened her door, got out, left the car idling in the parking lot while she marched back inside. Ms. Johnson and a couple of her assistants, whose names Gwen had already forgotten, were tending to the babies, eight of them in total. When June saw Gwen come into the room, she started crying, and that was all Gwen needed to know what to do next.

"I'm sorry, I have to take her," Gwen said to Ms. Johnson as they both approached June's crib. Each of the babies had their own small crib.

"Mrs. Fisher, I assure you she'll be just fine," Ms. Johnson said.

One of her assistants, the middle-aged stout one with graying roots, said, "This makes it harder on the babies when the mothers do this."

The mothers. The bothersome mothers.

"I'm sorry—she's my baby, and I'm going to take her with me," Gwen said.

She pushed past the barricade of Ms. Johnson and the stout woman and retrieved crying June from the crib. She grabbed the bag she'd packed for June from a cubby by the door, and then they were gone, ignoring the protests coming from behind them.

Gwen buckled June into her car seat and pulled out of the parking lot quickly. She saw Ms. Johnson and the stout woman and Sheila and the director of the facility, another forgotten name, standing at the entrance with looks of bewilderment on their faces.

Gwen took a left on Union, her brain still thinking she was going to work. But now she had June, and she didn't know what she was going to do. She supposed she could bring June in with her to work, say that she just wanted everyone to meet her baby. They couldn't argue with that, even if they were expecting her to get back to the grind on day one.

She took a left on First. The law firm was on First. She glanced back at June, who had stopped crying and was staring out the window. When she looked back at the road, she realized she'd passed the law office and was coming up to the stoplight at Washington.

"Mommy's brain is not working today," she said to June.

She took a right on Washington, mentally calculating how to get back to First. That was how she ended up on Alaskan Way with all the signs directing drivers to the ferries. There wasn't time to premeditate what came next. She would scrutinize her actions only later. But she got into the left-turn lane and found herself at the tollbooth for the Bainbridge Island ferry, buying a round-trip ticket. She pulled forward into the line of cars waiting to get on the ferry, put her car in park like everyone else. It was only then, when her car was in park in the ferry line, that she wondered what the hell she was doing. But she looked in her rearview mirror and saw several cars lining up behind her. There was no going back now.

She started to text Jeff, then stopped. She wasn't sure what she was doing yet, didn't know what to say. He would be worried. She decided to text Leigh, a Hail Mary.

> Hey. Remember when you said we could be the crazy person to solve the Angeni Luna mystery? I'm getting on the ferry now. I know things have been weird and maybe you never want to talk to me again. But I miss you. Meet me on Bainbridge? Bring Belle. I've got June.

Her hands were shaking as she read it over once, twice. She felt the kind of thrill she imagined fugitives felt when they'd broken free and gone on the run.

The car in front of her started its engine. It was time to board. She started her car, and then she hit send.

Chapter 29

Angeni Luna

Much to Angeni's relief, Freya had resumed breastfeeding several hours after Angeni had returned home from the hospital. Two days later, she was still going strong. It was as if nothing had happened between them, their relationship restored to its previous ease. There was still an odd feeling on The Land. Matt and Jer were acting like themselves, but everyone else seemed to be tiptoeing around her with a peculiar fear. Now that she was feeling better, she decided she needed to talk to Aurora first and foremost. She had to find out if she'd been the one to write the letter.

Angeni, wearing Freya in the carrier against her chest to maximize closeness after the trauma of their separation, found Aurora out front, car keys hanging from a finger. She was going somewhere.

"Where you off to?" Angeni called, standing on the porch, using one hand to shield her eyes from the sun.

Aurora turned around, seemingly startled. The sun appeared to blind her as she squinted in search of Angeni. When her eyes finally settled upon her, she smiled.

"Oh, hi," she said. "I was going to the bay."

It was common for Aurora to go to the bay—Manzanita Bay—whenever she needed to ponder something. Angeni couldn't help but wonder what it was she needed to ponder.

"Mind if we come with?" she asked.

Aurora shrugged, but Angeni caught the slightest hesitation in her voice when she said, "Sure."

~

As they drove down Manzanita Road, Angeni made a mental note to do more outings like this. It was true that The Land provided everything she could possibly need, but there was something liberating about exploring, even if the exploring was nearby.

"We are so lucky to live here," Angeni said. The trees were a blur of green in the periphery of her vision.

"We are," Aurora said.

They turned right on Dock Street and parked where the road ended. This was the not-so-secret access point for Manzanita Bay. Ahead of them, two people were unloading kayaks from their car. They exchanged greetings as they passed, the woman doing a double take at Angeni. Angeni waited for her to say "Aren't you . . ." but thankfully, she didn't. When she was a child, Angeni had said she wanted nothing more than to be famous. But now, upon reflection, she decided the root of it was a desire to be seen. She had become famous, if fame was defined by Instagram follower counts. Her aversion to writing the memoir her editor wanted revealed that she was not yet brave enough to be seen.

The tide in the bay was low, exposing a wide shoreline littered with pebbles, crab legs, and oyster shells. Aurora sat on a piece of driftwood that Mother Nature had provided as the perfect bench. She reached down, collected a handful of pebbles, turned them over in her palm. The kayakers walked past them and placed their kayaks in the water before climbing in and pushing off with a friendly wave.

Angeni sat next to Aurora on the driftwood. She lifted Freya from the carrier and turned her around to face the water.

"So I wanted to talk to you," Angeni said. She bounced Freya in her lap gently.

"I wanted to talk to you too," Aurora said.

They made these proclamations while staring ahead at the water, not at each other.

"I want to ask you something," Angeni said. "And I want you to know that I am at peace with whatever your answer is. I've thought about it a lot. I want us to have a compassionate conversation about it."

Now Aurora looked at her, dread and concern all over her face. "What is it?"

"Did you write that letter that came in the mail?"

Aurora looked confused and then flabbergasted. "*Me?* You think *I* wrote it?"

Angeni had never heard such a defensive tone from her before. It meant that she was either very wrong about her suspicion, or very right.

"Beck, you're the only one who knows what happened," she said.

It was only after she'd said Aurora's birth name that she realized she'd said it. It was a trick of the brain. She was thinking back to that day, remembering the sound of the gunshot, the blood, her mother dying—and it was not Aurora by her side then, but Becky.

"I didn't send it," Aurora said. "I can't believe you think I'd do that. Why would I do that?"

She seemed hurt, so hurt that it made Angeni doubt her accusation. Still, she returned to the indisputable fact: "But you're the only one who knows what happened," she repeated. "Did you tell someone else?"

Aurora shook her head. "Of course not," she said with conviction. "I know who sent it, though."

Angeni's throat tightened. "Who?"

"I saw some text messages on Sitka's phone. Between her and someone named Jay, who said he'd sent the letter."

Freya squirmed in Angeni's lap as Angeni attempted to process this information.

"Jay?"

"Someone Sitka knows," Aurora said. "I think she came into our lives with . . . ill intentions."

Angeni got to her feet abruptly, holding Freya against her chest.

"No," she said. "How in the world would Sitka and this Jay person know about what happened with my mother?"

"I have no idea," Aurora said.

"No, this is a misunderstanding," Angeni said.

She walked toward the water's edge, stared across the bay at Arrow Point. Was Aurora making this up as a way to turn Angeni against Sitka? Was she capable of such manipulation?

"There's something else," Aurora said, still seated on the driftwood behind Angeni. Aurora's voice was small and tentative, and Angeni held Freya tighter in anticipation of what was next.

"I saw Sitka and Erik together," Aurora said.

Angeni continued to stare straight ahead.

"They talk sometimes, at night. Erik has insomnia," Angeni said. She kept her voice calm and even. She would not let Aurora get to her.

"No," Aurora said. "I saw them . . . kissing."

Angeni whipped her head around and stared at Aurora sitting there on the log, looking forlorn.

"You didn't," Angeni said.

"I did," Aurora said. "I didn't know if I should tell you. It worries me, given Erik's . . . history with women. I wanted to wait until you were feeling better and—"

"Why are you doing this?" Angeni asked, instant tears coming to her eyes.

"I can't lie to you," Aurora said.

"You are trying to sabotage things," Angeni said. "You hate Sitka. Is that it?"

Aurora looked stunned. "What? No."

Angeni marched toward her, pebbles and shell fragments crunching beneath her feet.

"Why are you doing this?" Angeni asked, less than a foot of space between them. "After I created this whole life for us."

Aurora stood up so they were eye level. She shook her head vigorously. "Britt, I swear," she said. She was slipping back into their past too. "I'm telling the truth."

Angeni retrieved her phone from her pocket, sent a text to Erik.

Can you come get me? I'm at Manzanita Bay

"Erik's going to pick me up," Angeni said, before Erik had even confirmed. "I need some space. From you."

Angeni walked past Aurora. When she got to the end of Dock Street, she took a left on Manzanita Road and walked up the highway with Freya in her carrier, drivers slowing as they passed her.

Erik texted back:

I'm in the back with Matt and Jer. I'll send Sitka to you

Chapter 30

Sasha

Sasha was in her room, preparing to pack her bags to leave. She didn't have a good feeling about whatever was going to happen next. There was the kiss with Erik, and now Aurora had seen those texts from Jay on her phone. She hadn't said anything to Sasha about them, and there was a chance she didn't know what to make of them, but she had to know Sasha was up to something. Sasha's plan was to disappear the next day without saying goodbye, without having her big talk with Angeni about Daphne. She just wanted to go home.

"Hey," a voice said.

Sasha flinched and turned around to see Erik in her doorway.

"Oh, hey," she said.

He was shirtless, his skin shiny with sweat. He'd been out back with Matt and Jer, working on reinforcing the fence around the property. Nobody seemed to realize the ironic symbolism of this—their collective desire to protect themselves from the outside world when it was obvious that the internal dynamics of their commune were a more threatening problem.

"Can I ask a favor?"

She remembered what he'd said about the formula: *We won't tell Ang*. She expected he would now be requesting her discretion with the kiss situation.

"Sure, yeah," she said.

He had to see her bags on the bed, but he didn't ask her if she was packing, if she was leaving. His eyes were glued to her face.

"Angeni is down by Manzanita Bay with Freya. She needs a ride. Can you pick them up? I'm in the middle of this thing with Matt and Jer."

That was it—a ride?

"Oh, yeah, okay," she said.

"Thank you."

He lingered after this expression of gratitude, and Sasha knew he was also thanking her for her willingness to forget what had happened between them. It was regrettable. It meant nothing. That was what his eyes were telling her.

"No problem," she said.

~

Sasha wondered why Angeni needed a ride. She'd seen her and Freya leave in Aurora's car. Wouldn't they come back in Aurora's car?

As she drove on Manzanita Road, a car that looked like Aurora's approached from the other direction. As it came closer, Sasha saw that it was Aurora's car, with Aurora driving. Aurora's eyes met Sasha's as they passed each other, and Sasha was sure Aurora had been crying. But there wasn't just sadness on her face, but anger too.

Angeni was waiting at the corner of Manzanita Road and Dock Street, Freya strapped to her chest. Sasha pulled up next to them, taking her time so she could study Angeni's face. Had Aurora told her about the kiss, the texts with Jay? Angeni smiled, though. When she opened the passenger door, she said, "Thank you so much for getting us!"

Sasha didn't know whether to ask if something had happened with Aurora. Maybe it was better to take Erik's approach and avoid any potential land mines.

"Did you guys have a nice time at the bay?" Sasha asked.

Upon hearing Sasha's voice, Freya turned her head in Sasha's direction and started squealing and kicking her legs.

"Aw, hi, baby girl," Sasha said.

She really did love this child more than she'd ever expected she would.

Angeni pulled the seat belt around both her and Freya, who was still in the carrier against Angeni's chest, and clicked it into place. Freya's happy babbling turned into frustrated grunts as she realized her mother was not going to unsnap her and let her see Sasha.

"I'll play with you when we get home," Sasha said to Freya.

"She's really quite enamored with you," Angeni said.

The words were kind, but they were said with mild irritation.

"Well, it's mutual."

They drove a few minutes in silence, and Sasha gripped the steering wheel, bracing herself for Angeni's wrath. What did she know? What had Aurora told her?

"I thought you went to the bay with Aurora," Sasha said, nonchalant.

"We did," Angeni said. She audibly exhaled a long breath. "Aurora and I had a heated discussion."

"Oh, I'm sorry," Sasha said. She gripped the steering wheel harder.

"She said some . . . difficult things," Angeni said. "About you, actually."

Out of the corner of her eye, Sasha could feel Angeni looking at her. Sasha kept her eyes on the road when she said, "Oh really?"

"I think it makes her uneasy that you came into our lives and have become so close to us in a short amount of time," Angeni said.

"Right, I can see that," Sasha said, trying to sound as diplomatic and unperturbed as possible.

"Aurora and I . . . we have a complicated history. I'm confident we will resolve this current situation."

"I hope so. You two seem very close," Sasha said.

"We are."

Angeni turned so that she was no longer looking at Sasha but straight ahead.

~

They were almost back to the property, Sasha taking it slow as she turned into their long dirt driveway, when Angeni said: "I know I can trust you, Sitka." Then: "Right?"

Sasha could feel Angeni's eyes on her again as she parked. She turned to Angeni, knowing there was only one acceptable response.

"Of course."

Chapter 31

GWEN

As the ferry began its journey to Bainbridge Island, Gwen started to feel sick to her stomach. June kept looking at her with this intense stare that seemed to be questioning her mother's sanity. Gwen had to look away.

She went out to the deck, hoping the fresh air would help. She was standing at the railing, watching the water rippling beneath her, when an older woman sidled up next to her, eyes fixed on June.

"What a darling baby," the woman said.

Gwen did not feel like engaging with other human beings, but she managed to say, "Thank you."

"Is it your first time on The Boat?" the woman asked.

"Excuse me?"

"The ferry. We call it The Boat. Is it your first time?"

"Oh. Yes, actually," she said. Was this woman not picking up on her *please don't fuck with me* energy?

"You picked a good day. The mountain's out."

The woman jutted her chin toward their left, where Mount Rainier was on full display, something that did not happen every day.

"It gets easier," the woman said.

Had Gwen heard her correctly? Was this really the second stranger of the day to think Gwen looked unmoored enough to need these words?

"Sorry?" Gwen said.

The woman looked at June and then at Gwen. "Motherhood. These early days are so hard. It gets easier."

The woman gave a soft smile and then walked away, her energy as cool and eccentric as a fortune teller's.

~

When the ferry docked at the island, Gwen sat in her car, waiting to drive off, while her phone dinged with messages. She scanned them, looking for Leigh's name, but she hadn't texted. There was a message from the day care asking if everything was okay and if June would be returning later. There was a message from the HR woman at the law firm, saying that maybe there had been a misunderstanding about her return date because they had not seen her in the office. Jeff had texted to see if she was okay.

Even if she'd wanted to respond, she couldn't. The ferry workers in their neon vests were circling their arms, directing the cars to exit.

"Here we go," Gwen said to June.

~

On the ferry ride over, Gwen had thought about her Angeni Luna vision-dreams. Maybe her subconscious had led her to the ferry for a reason. Maybe this was all supposed to happen—she was meant to talk to the real Angeni Luna, to get the validation and support she so craved. Why else would she end up on Bainbridge Island?

After they left the port, Gwen pulled into a strip mall parking lot to try to determine where she was even going. She knew Angeni Luna lived near a Christmas tree farm—she'd mentioned it in one of her holiday-time posts. There was only one Christmas tree farm on the island, as far as she could tell, so that was where she decided to go.

She half expected the female GPS voice to ask her what the hell she was doing, but the voice remained calm and neutral, making it easier for Gwen to think she wasn't *that* crazy. Angeni Luna was a spiritual teacher, a guide. It stood to reason that many people sought out her presence. Gwen would knock on the door, introduce herself, apologize for any intrusion, and express her gratitude for Angeni. If she was lucky, Angeni would invite more conversation, and Gwen would have the opportunity to share some of her turmoil. She was sure Angeni would have the words of wisdom she needed. Maybe they would snap a photo together and she could send it to Leigh. She drafted the text message in her mind:

Look! She's alive. Are you?

If none of that happened, if Angeni Luna was nowhere to be found, as the Reddit threads implied, or if Angeni Luna turned her away, then Gwen and June would get back on the ferry home, their little excursion a secret known only to the two of them.

Chapter 32

ANGENI LUNA

It was early morning, and Freya was sleeping, nestled between Angeni and also-sleeping Erik. Sitka had brought the baby to Angeni sometime around three o'clock, and Angeni had told her it was fine for Freya to stay until morning. Angeni had drifted off after feeding Freya, but she was up again now, alert to a noise from the hallway.

It sounded like someone was in the hallway closet, rummaging. She couldn't imagine who would be up already, and what was in the closet that they could need?

She thought about getting up, but she didn't want to wake Freya. These last hours of sleep were so precious for the three of them. Things had been so hard lately, so depleting. They needed their rest.

The rummaging went on, and she took inventory of the closet. There was an assortment of towels and blankets and winter coats and boots. There were some tools. And there were the guns.

She closed her eyes, focused on deep breathing to try to get herself back to sleep. Finally, the rummaging stopped, and the hallway turned silent again, but Angeni still lay awake, waiting for something—she didn't know what. Eventually, just as dawn broke, she started to drift off.

Chapter 33

SASHA

It was nearly ten in the morning. Sasha had packed her belongings and was ready to go. She'd had one last breakfast with Freya. The energy between Angeni, Aurora, and Erik was still tense and strange, but Sasha just focused on the baby. She was feeling more wistful than she'd anticipated. She would miss Freya. She knew Freya wouldn't remember her as she grew up, but maybe she would remember the feeling Sasha had given her—a feeling of pure love, love without expectations or conditions.

She decided she'd leave during Freya's midmorning nap, when the rest of the group was busy on the land and Angeni was attempting to work on her book. She'd texted Jay:

> vibes here are super weird. coming home today

He'd sent back a GIF of a church choir singing "Hallelujah."

~

After she settled Freya for her nap, Sasha went out to the front porch to take in the views. She understood now why Angeni loved the trees so much. They were like ever-present companions, witnesses, steadfast and strong. It had been a strange time, these weeks as Sitka. It felt like a fever dream. There was no explanation for it besides grief. She missed Daphne so much. Nothing would make that better. Justice for her sister was not taking down a social media influencer. There was no justice for her sister. Justice would be if she was alive again, and she never would be. Somehow, Sasha would have to learn to accept this.

Behind her, she heard the screen on the front door slam shut. Matt and Jer kept talking about fixing it so it wouldn't slam, but they had yet to do so.

As Sasha turned around, she expected to see Angeni there, likely with Freya in her arms because she continued to insist that was how the baby slept best.

But it was not Angeni there.

It was Aurora. And she had a gun.

Instinctively, Sasha put her hands up, as if to show Aurora that she did not have a weapon. Aurora just stood there, a foot beyond the doorway, her arms outstretched, holding the pistol aimed at Sasha.

"What are you doing?" Sasha said.

"You need to tell her the truth. She doesn't believe me."

Aurora didn't sound like herself. Her voice was high pitched and strained. Her eyes looked wild.

"Aurora, please put the gun down."

"About Erik. About the letter. All of it. You need to tell her. You're going to ruin everything. Everything!"

"Okay, yeah, okay," Sasha said. "Just put the gun down, okay?"

Sasha saw Aurora's eyes flick to the cluster of trees separating the house from the main road. Sasha was too afraid to take her eyes off Aurora, but she heard what Aurora must have heard—was it the crunch of footsteps? She could see a slight panic on Aurora's face.

"Who's coming?" Aurora asked Sasha. She took a step toward Sasha, the gun still pointed right at Sasha's face.

"I don't know," Sasha said. "I swear. Maybe just a deer."

Aurora peered at the trees, watching, then turned back to Sasha.

"You need to tell her the truth," she said again.

Chapter 34

GWEN

When Gwen passed the Christmas tree farm, she slowed the car in search of Angeni Luna's property. She pulled to the side of the road at the sight of a signpost with an address on it. She parked with one set of tires on the asphalt, the other on the dirt. She didn't feel right driving down the driveway as if she were an invited guest. She didn't even know if this was the right place.

June was fussy in the back seat, so Gwen took her out of the car seat, held the baby against her as she walked through the trees to get a better look at the front of the house. She recognized it immediately—the rustic wood siding, like a log cabin, and that beautiful wraparound porch, complete with a swing. It was Angeni Luna's house. She reached into her back pocket for her phone, took a photo of the house. Leigh would think she was crazy, but Leigh was also the type to be impressed by crazy.

There were two people on the porch. She recognized the young, darker-skinned woman from a couple of Angeni Luna's posts. She was the newest "auntie" in the commune, or whatever it was. Her eyes went to the other woman, and before she could take in her face, she took in something else—a gun.

She crouched down, desperate to get away from whatever danger she'd walked into. June looked at her with confusion, and Gwen shushed her quietly. If the baby started crying, the women on the porch would see her there, and then what?

She was about halfway between her car and the house. She wondered if she should crawl back to the car or just stay where she was. There were risks either way.

"It's okay, we're okay," she whispered to June, who kept staring at her, waiting for her mother to tell her what to expect in this situation.

Gwen could hear the women talking on the porch. One of them, the one holding the gun, was practically shouting.

"You need to tell her the truth," she said.

What had Gwen gotten herself into? Why had she gotten on that stupid ferry?

"I will, okay? I'll tell her," the other woman said.

"What will you tell her?"

"I'm not Sitka. My name is Sasha Robinson. I came to confront Angeni because of my sister."

"Your sister?"

"My sister. Daphne. She died during a home birth. She loved Angeni. It just got out of hand, this whole thing."

The dark-skinned woman was shouting too. Or shout-sobbing, rather.

"I'm leaving. Today. Okay? Put down the gun, Aurora."

That was her name—Aurora. Angeni Luna's soul sister, best friend. Seeing her with a gun made no sense. It was completely incongruent with what Gwen knew of Angeni Luna's idyllic life.

"Look, I know Angeni didn't even have a home birth, okay? I don't care anymore. Yes, Erik kissed me. It was nothing. It was an impulsive mistake. I just want to go. I'll leave you all alone. I promise."

Angeni didn't have a home birth? This girl had kissed Erik? Gwen's mind raced in attempts to make meaning of what she was hearing. She thought of Leigh, wished she was there with her.

"You need to tell her all this. You can't just run away like a coward. Tell her. She won't believe me," Aurora said.

Gwen didn't like where this was going. She decided to turn around, crawl back to her car, get her child away from these people and their soap opera. But then she heard a new voice on the scene, and she'd watched enough Angeni Luna reels and videos to know it was the woman herself.

Chapter 35

Angeni Luna

Angeni stared at her computer screen. This was her first day trying to get back to working on the book after all the recent drama. She needed to start making some progress. Maybe working on the book would distract her from the friction with Aurora. Since their conversation at the bay, Aurora had been keeping to herself in her tiny house out back, though they had maneuvered around each other in the kitchen this morning. Angeni was waiting for Aurora to come clean, to confess that, yes, she was trying to make trouble because of her discomfort with Sitka. Angeni was prepared to forgive her if she would just confess.

There was a small part of her that wondered if Aurora had been telling the truth—if Erik and Sitka had developed some kind of nighttime relationship that had escalated to a romantic kiss. She had never noticed any chemistry between the two of them, and Angeni was usually quite intuitive about such things. She and Erik had been going through a hard time, and she knew Erik was probably longing for physical affection, but she just couldn't see him kissing Sitka. She was just a girl, a standoffish, difficult-to-read girl. Aurora had to be lying, which was an equally distressing infidelity.

Freya was taking her midmorning nap on the floor mattress in Sitka's room. She was used to sleeping there at night and seemed to prefer it during the day, though Angeni still let her nap on her chest whenever possible. Angeni stood from her chair, convincing herself she needed a break. She went to peek in at Freya. The baby was sleeping soundly, flat on her back with her arms and legs flailed out. Sitka's room looked unusually tidy, the bed made, no toiletries or items of clothing out. In the corner of the room, Angeni saw the two bags Sitka had arrived with. They appeared to be full. Was Sitka leaving?

Angeni closed the door to Sitka's room and went looking for her. She hadn't seen her go out back, so she must be on the front porch. As she came toward the front of the house, she heard shouting. It sounded like Aurora, but she'd never heard Aurora sound like this. She walked faster.

The front door was ajar.

She heard Aurora shout, "You need to tell her all this. You can't just run away like a coward. Tell her. She won't believe me."

Angeni started to push the screen door open, saying, "Ror, what's going on?"

She saw the back of her best friend. Then Aurora turned around. Their eyes quickly met before there was the split-second sound of a gunshot. And then, for the second time in Angeni's week, everything went black.

Chapter 36

Sasha

It all happened so quickly.

Sasha heard the slight squeak of the screen door opening, then Angeni's voice: "Ror, what's going on?"

Aurora was already on edge, her hands shaky, so it was clearly an accident when she turned to Angeni and the gun went off.

Just one shot.

At first, Sasha thought Aurora had fired into the side of the house, into one of the wood logs.

But then she heard Aurora scream.

"Oh my god, Britt!" she said.

Aurora dropped the gun and went to the doorway, where Angeni's body lay slumped. Her eyes were open and alarmed.

"Did you shoot me?" she said, clear as day.

There was a scream from the trees. Someone was there, not a deer after all. Before Sasha could figure out who it was, a car came down the driveway with a man inside that Sasha had never seen before. What was going on?

It was mayhem from there. Erik, having heard the gunshot, came running out front with Freya in his arms. Matt and Jer came running too.

There was so much blood, and Angeni lost consciousness after just a minute or two. Sasha thought she was dead. She could tell everyone else did too.

The man from the car emerged and said, "I've called 911."

Then a woman with a baby came out from the trees and ran to the man, saying, "Jeff?" The man hugged the woman and the baby.

"Is she alive?" Aurora screamed.

Sasha was about to pick up the gun, get it out of the way, but then it occurred to her that she didn't want her fingerprints on it.

Someone was going to be blamed for this, and it wasn't going to be her.

NOW

Chapter 37

GWEN

As Gwen feared, by the time she finishes the story of how she ended up on Angeni Luna's property and witnessed the shooting, Detective Steele is looking at her like she's a total nutcase.

"It's a strange story, I'll give you that," Detective Steele says, eyebrows raised to her hairline.

"Classic case of wrong place, wrong time," Gwen says, trying to be blasé.

"Or wrong place, *right* time," Detective Steele says.

"I don't think someone getting shot qualifies as a 'right time.'"

"What I mean is that having someone unaffiliated with the . . . commune, as you called it . . . witness this event is pretty important for our investigation."

Gwen has told her what she saw, as best she can remember it. She doesn't think the shooting was intentional. It was like the gun went off as Aurora was turning around. A horrific accident.

"I hope I've been helpful," Gwen says.

"You have been."

Detective Steele goes to open the door to their little interrogation room, but Gwen remains seated with June. She is not ready to go yet. She has a question she needs answered.

"Is she okay?"

Detective Steele turns around, her hand lingering on the doorknob as she does.

"Excuse me?"

"Angeni Luna. Is she okay?"

Detective Steele sighs. "I'm really not at liberty to share specifics, but she is alive."

Gwen doesn't realize she's been holding her breath until she exhales.

"That's good," she says, surprised at how relieved she is. She doesn't know Angeni Luna, not personally. But she can't imagine that baby girl, Freya, going through life without her mother. Her eyes start to well up as she looks at June.

"I think your husband is in the waiting room," Detective Steele says, opening the door, giving Gwen another cue to leave.

Gwen stands and goes through the various maneuvers necessary to get June back in her baby wrap while Detective Steele looks on, bewildered at this strange sequence of movements.

At the scene of the shooting, the police and ambulances arrived within minutes, before Gwen and Jeff had a chance to talk. He must have followed her from home to day care drop-off. He was worried about her, and she loved him for that. She can't imagine what he was thinking when she left the day care center with June, went to the ferry terminal, and then drove to Angeni Luna's property. He doesn't even know about Angeni Luna. There is so much she hasn't told him about her inner world. That has been her crucial mistake, hasn't it? She's absorbed the message that mothers are supposed to have it all figured out, and she's been too afraid to admit to him that she doesn't. What she knows now is that no mother has it all figured out, not even Angeni Luna. Gwen has no idea if it's true that Angeni Luna didn't really have a home birth, but she knows from practically memorizing the Instagram video that the actual delivery in the tub was never shown. What else about Angeni Luna isn't real? She can't say she's angry at the woman. If anything, she feels compassion, solidarity. How many new mothers are keeping their shameful secrets, terrified of being anything less than perfect?

~

Jeff is sitting in the waiting room as she approaches. His legs are apart, an elbow resting on each thigh, his head in his hands. It's possible he'll never look at her the same way again. From this point forward, he will see her as someone capable of losing it.

"Hey," she says once she's a few feet away from him.

He lifts his head. The expression on his face is grave, but once he sees her and June, he smiles.

Gwen's eyes, already welled up, spill over with tears at the sight of this smile. His smile says everything she needs to know—he still loves her, he forgives her.

He stands, wraps his arms around Gwen, pulls her and June into his body.

"Babe," he says into her hair, his voice muffled. "I'm so sorry."

"*You're* sorry?"

He leans back so that he can look at her, their faces a few inches apart.

"I didn't know how bad things were," he says. "I just didn't know."

"I didn't want you to know."

"We're going to figure it out, okay? I'm just glad you're both okay."

He kisses Gwen on the cheek, then kisses the top of June's head. Gwen is glad they're okay too.

Gwen's phone buzzes in her pocket. She remembers that she needs to call the day care center and the law firm.

The text is not from either of them, though. It's from Leigh.

> Omg. Have you heard about the shooting? My god. Did you really go to Bainbridge Island? I miss you. I'm sorry about

everything. I'm a real CUNT. Nathan has finally calmed the fuck down so we need to catch up.

Gwen doesn't realize just how happy this silly message makes her until Jeff says, "It's good to see you smiling."

Chapter 38

Angeni Luna

The doctors say she is very lucky. The pathway of the bullet missed the pericardium, the fluid-filled sac surrounding and protecting her heart, by two centimeters. Angeni nearly died the same way her mother had. She doesn't understand the meaning of this yet, but she knows there must be one.

She is on day two in the hospital. The first day was a blur, with the urgency of inserting a chest tube to address her collapsed lung. After they stabilized her, they did surgery to remove any shell fragments and repair the hole in her lung. She is still hooked up to tubes, and the smallest movements hurt, but she is alive. She shouldn't feel anything but gratitude, but she is overcome with a profound sadness.

She has started replaying the scene in her head—Aurora pointing the gun, Angeni's gun, at Sitka before turning around and shooting Angeni. She didn't mean to do it. Angeni is sure of that. It was an accident. Still, she's sure Aurora is still in custody. There is no way of communicating with her. If only she could sit with her, her best friend in the world, they could figure out this mess.

Erik brought her phone to her yesterday, but she has only used it for texting, not for going online. The media knows of what happened. She is not ready for the onslaught of thoughts and prayers for her recovery.

She knows there will be so many questions about Aurora, questions she doesn't want to consider. People will say things like I always thought she seemed a little off, and Angeni will be forced to wonder if she missed something all along.

She has not checked her email, which is how most business-related contacts reach out to her. It's likely her literary agent tried that method first before resorting to the text that now appears on Angeni's screen.

> Angeni, my dear. You poor thing. I am so incredibly sorry. I wanted you to know that my thoughts and prayers are with you. When you are ready to chat, let me know.

Angeni sighs. No doubt, her agent and her publisher are salivating over this recent development. Her potential book sales have skyrocketed. She can't imagine writing the tell-all her editor wants, though. She can't imagine writing anything at all.

She is about to power off her phone when another text comes in. It's from Sitka. She assumes Sitka was brought in for questioning by the police. Maybe she knows what's going on with Aurora. She taps the message, a large block of text.

> Dear Angeni,
> I'm on the ferry back to Seattle. I finished with the police a little while ago. I have been thinking about you and hope you are okay. They wouldn't give me much information. I do not think Aurora had any intent to hurt me. She loves you so much and she saw me as a threat to you. She wanted me to tell you some things, so that's what I'm going to do.
>
> My name is not really Sitka. It's Sasha. I came to Bainbridge with the intention of meeting you so I could tell you about my sister, Daphne. She and her baby died during a home birth inspired by you. She wanted so badly to be the very best mother and I know she thought birthing at home was one way to do

that. I was so angry at you. When you invited me to live with you, I said yes because I wanted to understand you better. I wanted to see what Daphne saw in you. And yes, I wanted some kind of vengeance. I realize now that your suffering doesn't take away my suffering. I'm sorry for thinking it might.

Aurora also wanted you to know that Erik kissed me. It was just once. He was very upset about you being in the hospital. I think he just needed comfort. He regretted it immediately, I could tell. He loves you so much. I trust you two will figure things out.

For what it's worth, I grew to care for you. I adore Freya. If you want to stay in touch, I would like that but I understand if you don't want to. I hope your recovery is quick. I hope life is kind to you.

Sasha

Angeni reads it once, twice, three times. At first, she is shocked, disbelieving. But then it starts to make sense. Angeni knew Sitka was wrestling with something, knew Sitka was aggrieved. Now she knows why. She closes her eyes, remembering the home birth video she'd posted, how arrogant she'd been. Sitka, or Sasha, had a sister. Her sister died. A wave of nausea rolls through Angeni's body.

Erik appears in the doorway with Freya in the carrier on his chest. He's done the straps wrong, and she is seated too high. Angeni does not have the energy to correct him and thinks maybe that's for the best.

"There's Mama," he says in the baby voice he uses with Freya.

Erik kissed Sitka. Aurora wasn't lying—of course she wasn't. This doesn't feel like a jarring revelation. It settles into Angeni's body gently, a feather landing atop a pond of water, causing the smallest ripples. This is how truths settle when we already know them but have resisted their existence.

She stares at Erik as he holds their beautiful child. She is not angry at him, not in this moment, anyway. Maybe the anger will come later, when she has more energy. For now, all she cares about is her baby. Freya smiles so big upon seeing her. Her joy is so pure and simple—the context of the hospital room is lost on her.

Freya squirms against Erik, clenching and unclenching her little fists the way she does when she wants to grab something. It is Angeni she wants to grab.

"Okay, sweetie, we'll sit right next to Mama," Erik says.

It will be a while before Angeni can bear the weight of her own child atop her chest. Angeni can hardly stand thinking about this. She was foolish enough to ask about breastfeeding, and the doctors told her that would not be feasible, considering her injuries and the required recovery. She was despondent for a handful of minutes as she absorbed this reality, then remembered that she'd nearly died. She would force the gratitude until it became natural.

Erik places Freya in the hospital bed next to Angeni, tucked beneath her left arm. Freya puts her tiny hands all over Angeni's body, touching the tubes and the bandages. She is not scared; she is awed. Angeni wants nothing more than to lift her baby high above her head, then bring her down and blow raspberries on her belly. But she can do nothing but stroke the soft skin of her baby's thigh.

"Aw, babe," Erik says. He uses his thumb to wipe a tear from Angeni's cheek. He does love her so much. She has no doubt about that. They are flawed humans, that's all. They will find their way back to each other.

"Have you heard anything about Aurora?" she asks him.

He shakes his head. "They're talking to her, obviously."

"I don't want to press charges, or whatever," Angeni says.

"Okay," he says, but he looks doubtful. Does *he* want to press charges?

"You'll tell the police? No charges. Please," she says.

"I will. But there will have to be some . . . consequences. Babe, that wasn't her gun. She doesn't have a license to have a gun. She was threatening Sitka. You."

When Angeni swallows, it is like a boulder tumbling down her throat.

"She wouldn't hurt me. She was trying to protect me."

"Protect you?"

"It's all a misunderstanding, okay?"

"Okay, babe," he says, his tone placating. "I think you need to focus on getting well."

She nods. What is there to say? Of course she needs to focus on getting well.

"Do you want me to say anything to the community?" he asks.

He means the Instagram community. He must be concerned about her following. He knows people want to hear from her. He knows their curiosity and care will turn to resentment if she is silent too long. That is the way this world is—they do not care for her; they care for what she offers them.

"Not now," she says. "Okay?"

He nods once. "Okay. Whatever you think is best."

Another tear rolls down her cheek. Freya is the one who sees it and instinctively puts her hand on Angeni's face.

"Things are going to get back to normal," Erik says.

In his pleading eyes, she can see that he wants to believe this is true.

"What if I don't want them to get back to normal?"

He cocks his head to the side like a dog trying to decipher a command from its owner. Her poor, loyal husband. She has not let him know her, not completely.

"There are things I need to tell you," she says, "before you decide what kind of 'normal' you want with me."

All these years, they've projected this relationship of depth and transparency, and yet she's never told him the whole truth.

"There are things I need to tell you too," he says.

Her things are worse, though. She is sure of this.

"Let me go first."

"Sure. Yeah. You can tell me anything, babe," he says.

Can she? She figures she may as well try.

She takes as deep a breath as her damaged chest will allow, and then she begins.

"My name wasn't always Angeni."

Chapter 39

Sasha

Sasha is on the ferry to Seattle, watching as Bainbridge Island gets smaller and smaller in the distance. Will she ever come back? She doesn't think so.

She can see that Angeni has read her text, but there are no three dots to indicate an incoming reply. She tells herself that's fine. She didn't write the text with the expectation of a response. She wrote it to share the truth.

As she puts her phone in her pocket, she feels it vibrate with a notification. It's a text, but it's not from Angeni.

Ur ass better be on that ferry

Jay.

When she messaged him from the police station, terrified of what was going to happen, he offered to come to the island. But then Detective Steele let her go. It was late in the evening by then. She went back to Angeni's house to get her things and headed to the ferry this morning.

I'm on! See you soon

Sasha leans against the railing of the ferry, watching the city come into view. It's a beautiful, clear day, the skyscrapers gleaming in the light. She takes out her phone to snap a photo and sends it to Jay. Then she taps over to her collection of saved audio recordings from her time with Angeni Luna. There are thirty-three total. She deletes all of them.

She hasn't decided whether or not to delete the Nurture Mother account. It's not doing any harm—if anything, it's doing good. When she feels ready to return to her dissertation, she may weave it into her analysis of the cultural narrative around mothering.

When the wind picks up, Sasha closes her eyes. Out of the blackness behind her lids, she sees the lights of the ambulance driving up to Angeni Luna's house, the same flashing lights she saw upon learning her sister and her nephew had died.

"I miss you, Daph," she whispers into the wind.

~

After she drives off the ferry, she heads straight for Jay's house. It takes her nearly forty minutes in typical Seattle traffic. When she pulls up, she sees a **FOR RENT** sign in the front. Jay must have been waiting and watching for her from the living room window, because he comes outside before she steps out of the car.

"Sis," he says, pulling her into him, holding her tight.

Her eyes well up at the word—*sis*.

"You're moving?"

Her face is pressed into his shoulder, so the words come out muffled.

"Told the landlord a couple days ago, and he's already got a sign up. I can't stay here," he says.

He doesn't have to say why.

They pull away from each other, and Sasha sees his eyes are welled up too.

"You didn't mention it. I didn't know," Sasha says.

He shrugs. "It was kind of impulsive, I guess. Just made up my mind."

"Where you gonna go?" she asks him.

"I don't know. Probably stay with my buddy from the station until I can find a new spot."

The fact that he doesn't already have something lined up, that he was just that desperate to leave, makes Sasha's throat tighten.

"Actually, I was thinking maybe we could share a place," he says. He is looking at his feet as he proposes this. "We can support each other or whatever."

Sasha can't hold back anymore. The tears cascade down her cheeks.

"The two of us as roomies? Daph would die," she says. "And she'd love it. I would too."

He lifts his chin, and his face breaks into a smile.

"For real?" he says.

"For real," she says, wiping away the tears. "We gotta keep each other from totally losing our shit, right?"

He laughs. It's so good to see him laugh.

"I think you already lost your shit, *Sitka*."

She rolls her eyes. She misses this—the way she and Jay have always teased each other, as if they are true siblings, not just siblings-in-law.

"You hungry?" he asks.

"Starving."

"I've been trying to use Daphne's cookbooks. I swear I'm following the instructions, but nothing tastes right. I've got chili going. Can't promise it's not terrible."

"I'll take my chances."

~

She follows him inside, and it smells just like Daphne's chili. In the kitchen, Daphne's magenta binder of recipes is open on the counter. Sasha goes to it, smiles upon seeing the title at the top of the chili recipe: "Bowl of warmth and love."

She goes to the stove, takes a spoonful of chili, blows on it to cool it, and tastes it.

"It needs more spice," she says.

Daphne's recipes were like scaffolding; the chef added the necessary details.

"Whatever you say," Jay says.

Sasha adds a quarter teaspoon more of the chili powder and cumin, tastes it again.

She can hear Daphne: *That's more like it.*

"Would Daph approve?" Jay asks.

Sasha takes a second bite and says, "I think she would."

She puts the lid back on the pot so it can simmer a few minutes longer. Then she leans back against the counter, arms crossed over her chest, remembering all the times the three of them stood around the kitchen like this, chatting about nothing and everything. Her nose tingles as tears begin to fill her eyes.

"Oh god, don't start crying on me," Jay says.

"They're happy tears, I think."

"Fuck if I know what those are," he says. He lifts the lid on the pot of chili and says, "Maybe we should add them to the chili."

They laugh until they are both crying, both doing impressions of Daphne saying *Why the hell you putting tears in my chili?* When they are done laughing and crying, spent in the best way possible, they sit at the table where the three of them used to sit, dipping their spoons in their bowls of chili.

"It's good," Jay says.

"It is," Sasha agrees.

They let this truth settle over them. For two people convinced that nothing could ever be good again, it is good.

"Not as good as hers," Jay says.

"Duh," Sasha says.

"But yeah, it's good."

Epilogue

Gwen

Two months later

Gwen, Leigh, and the girls are at the same park they visited that day when Nathan brought them sandwiches. Fall is in the air, and the leaves have turned to vibrant reds, oranges, and yellows. It is a new season in more ways than one.

"The last time we were here, Nathan had that awful avocado on his face, remember?" Leigh said.

Gwen laughs. "So you did see it?"

"Of course I did. I wanted to see how long it would take him to notice. Did he go back to work like that? God, I hope so."

When Leigh and Gwen reconnected after the Bainbridge Island drama, there was no torturous rehashing of The Kiss. Leigh kept it simple, said, "You were feeling lonely. I was having my itchy feet. I know you don't want to fuck me. We're friends, as I keep telling Nathan." To which Gwen said, in a mock lawyer voice, "We are in agreement." And that was that.

They have been meeting up on Saturdays, at a park if it's nice out or the mall with the kid play area that will likely be ground zero for the next global pandemic. Nathan and Leigh are still together, doing the dysfunctional dance they seem to enjoy. Gwen and Jeff are doing better. They've started going to couples counseling once a week. Their sitter, Abby, hangs with June while they spend an hour with Therapist Joan and then go to dinner after to discuss the session. It is not a traditional date night, but there are cocktails involved, and it works for them. At the start of therapy, they spent time exploring the impossible standards Gwen had been holding herself to. Jeff was flabbergasted. He said he'd known the "breastfeeding thing" was a big deal, but he didn't know just how much everything was weighing on her. "It's just not like this for dads," he said. That made Gwen laugh: "Duh."

They've talked about improving their communication and accepting each other as different from how they were before they became parents. Gwen harks back to her learnings from the Conscious Couples Instagram account. Even if Angeni Luna was a little bit full of shit, she was also a little bit full of wisdom. Gwen thinks she and Jeff can be one of those couples that evolve and grow together. They want the very best for each other as individual human beings, and that seems like the key to long-lasting love.

Gwen took an extra two weeks off work after the Bainbridge Island event. Jeff told her she didn't have to go back. They could figure it out, financially and otherwise. Once the pressure was off, she decided she'd try going back. She worked out a hybrid schedule with the firm. It allows her to go into the office until noon so she can attend all the meetings, which are typically stacked in the mornings. Then she picks up June from day care, and they go home. Abby helps with June in the afternoons while Gwen works. Gwen doesn't get to play or interact with June much in those hours, but she likes having her close by. It's a compromise that seems to be working.

~

"Look at our babies, sitting up like big girls," Leigh says, as she leans forward and tickles June's belly.

While the first months of motherhood felt like a blur of trauma and torment, this new stage feels more fun. Gwen and June know each other better now—their rhythms, their needs. Gwen no longer lives in fear of failing her daughter. It's like they have a shared understanding that they are both doing their best. What she's learned about Angeni Luna has helped her let go of the ideals she held so close before.

Belle grasps at her mother's arm and whines, which Leigh says means she's hungry. Leigh unbuckles the straps of her denim overalls and lets the front fall forward; then she pulls up the tank top she's wearing underneath and holds Belle to her boob. Leigh will probably be one of those mothers who breastfeeds until her child is three, and Gwen no longer has any strong feelings about this. She stopped breastfeeding June last month, reluctantly at first and then wholeheartedly. The decision came after she returned to the moms' support group and dared to discuss her quandary. It turns out that about half the moms in the group are supplementing with formula now or using formula exclusively. It's not the end of the world. Besides, June's starting on solids, a milestone that reminds Gwen that everything in motherhood, and in life, is temporary.

"Oh my god, I totally forgot to ask you," Leigh says as she switches Belle to her other boob. "Did you see that Angeni Luna reemerged?"

After Bainbridge Island, Gwen made a conscious commitment to stay off social media. It wasn't just because of Angeni Luna, but also because of all the motherhood posts telling her who and how to be. She needed to get back to Gwen. As the weeks have passed, she's been too busy with work and June and Jeff to think much about Instagram at all.

"I didn't see," Gwen says.

Leigh plops Belle back on the grass in front of her, refastens her overalls, and then takes her phone out of her purse. She leans over to show Gwen.

"This is her first post since the whole thing happened," says Leigh.

Gwen looks at the post on the screen.

Sometimes, the best way to nurture your child is to set an example by nurturing yourself. Self-care is childcare.

In the caption, Angeni has written:

> Thank you to everyone who has reached out over the past couple months. I have been recovering physically and emotionally and also thinking about what this community means.
>
> I fear I have become caught up in sharing the character of Angeni Luna with you instead of the real human being. I am not a perfect mother or wife or friend. I have not been entirely truthful in attempts to preserve the image of me I thought you wanted. I have taken down the home birth video because it does not represent how my child really came into the world. She was delivered at the hospital after an emergency transfer there. I labored in my tub at home, but I did not give birth there. I realize now that withholding of truth in ways like this can have repercussions beyond what I previously imagined. I'm sorry.
>
> I have decided to pay back my book advance to my publisher and will no longer be writing a book. I do not think I can share my story in good conscience until I share the most intimate parts of it with my own self and my loved ones. For the foreseeable future, my Instagram accounts will be dormant. I do not plan on engaging with social media anytime soon. For now, I will leave the pages as they are, though I have removed posts that I now find inauthentic.

> I ask that you please reserve any judgments and refrain from gossip at this time. This post will be closed to comments.
>
> I want to end with one more thought, as represented in the graphic here: Self-care is childcare (something I borrowed from the @nurture.mother.official account—check it out!). Over the past several weeks, I have realized that taking care of myself is the best gift I can give my daughter. I want her to understand what it means as a woman to resist the pull to tend to others at all times and instead mother oneself.
>
> I am sending love to all of you. Thank you for being on this journey with me. Until we meet again . . .

When Gwen looks up from Leigh's phone, she's surprised to find herself crying.

"It's beautiful, right?" Leigh says. "Though I'm sort of bummed she's going to do this vanishing act. I want to see the new Angeni Luna. Will she still use cloth diapers? The world wants to know!"

It's a joke, and Gwen should laugh, but she can't bring herself to.

"Aw, Gwennie, you okay?" Leigh says.

"I feel bad for her," Gwen says. That's what it is. This poor woman has had millions of people looking to her for guidance on who and how to be, and all along, she was just like Gwen and so many others, mothering from a place of sole survival, tending to a baby instead of the obvious wounds inside.

"I think she'll be fine on that beautiful property with that hot husband and that gorgeous baby," Leigh says. She puts her phone back in her purse and leans back on her elbows in the grass, squinting her eyes into the fading afternoon sun. Gwen reaches for June, places her in her lap.

"Do you think there's any mother who doesn't worry about being a good mother?" Gwen asks.

"No. I think the worry is ingrained in us. It's evolution. If we were all careless, the human species would die," Leigh says.

"But there must be a way for the babies to live and the mothers to live too," Gwen says.

"I think we're going to crack that code, Gwennie," Leigh says. "Then we can write Angeni Luna's book."

"That's not a bad idea. Two friends, doing motherhood differently, finding personal fulfillment along the way," Gwen says.

Leigh snickers. "*Motherhood Is the Best Hood: A Memoir.*"

"We'll work on the title."

Gwen glances at her phone. It's time for her to head home. Jeff said he'd be home with dinner by five.

"You have to go?" Leigh says, sticking out her bottom lip in a pout.

"Yeah," Gwen says. "But we can talk about our future book next week."

Gwen stands with June in her arms, and Leigh stands with Belle. They hug.

"*Babies Suck: A Memoir,*" Leigh says. "With a kid breastfeeding on the cover."

"No," Gwen says.

"I love you, friend," Leigh says. "But not like that."

This is how they always part ways now.

"I love you, too, but not like that," Gwen says.

~

After Gwen straps June into the car, she sits in the driver's seat and taps onto Instagram. She goes to Angeni's post, reads it again. She decides to send her a direct message, though it's probable she won't see it if she's really going off social media. It's just something she needs to send.

> Hi Angeni. I was the witness at your house that day. I came there because I idolized you, I guess. I was so lost. You might think that people are let down by you now. I just want you to know that I'm not. I'm relieved that you're human. Your truth is all of our truth. We are all just doing our best, aren't we? At some point, I guess we have to realize that's good enough.

She reads it through twice, then hits send.

Acknowledgments

First and foremost, thank you to all the mothers who inspired this book. When I became a mother myself, I found myself absorbed in the stories of so many other mothers. From harrowing to hilarious, those stories found their way into this book. As Gwen says at the end, we are all just doing our best.

Thank you to my wonderful agent, Margaret Riley King, who gave me such perfect notes on the first draft of this novel. It wouldn't be what it is without you. Thank you also to Maddie Grimes, her lovely assistant.

It's been nothing but a pleasure to work with Lake Union. Nancy Holmes, you are a writer's dream—so respectful of the creative process while also being respectful of the all-important deadlines. Jenna Free, you are the editor every writer wants. You just get it. Annie and Brenna, copyeditors extraordinaire, you have saved me from making numerous embarrassing mistakes. Jarrod Taylor, your cover designs are beautiful. I'm so lucky. Thank you to the entire Amazon Publishing team for believing in me and for giving my books such care and attention.

Amy and Peter, thank you for the hospitality (and insider info) while we visited Bainbridge Island. And thank you to Chad, my handsome research assistant.

Last, thank you to my daughter, Mya, the one who made me a mom. You have shown me life through a whole new lens. In reference to the title of this book, being a mother can be challenging, but mothering you is easy.

About the Author

Author Kim Hooper was born in Los Angeles and has worked as an advertising copywriter for twenty years. She holds a bachelor's degree in communications from the University of California San Diego and a master's in professional writing from the University of Southern California. *Mother Is a Verb* is her eighth novel. Hooper's most popular previous titles include *Woman on the Verge*, *No Hiding in Boise*, and *People Who Knew Me*, which is also a podcast series. The *Wall Street Journal* describes her work as "refreshingly raw and honest." Hooper lives in south Orange County with her daughter and a collection of pets—and adores them all. When not writing, the author enjoys running, doing yoga, or reading a good book.